"I was going to kiss you."

Shock froze all her wits.

"Why?" Cressida asked blankly. And then cursed herself. Slapping him; yes. Telling him what a licentious beast he was; quite unexceptionable. But asking him why he'd wanted to kiss her? She ought to be in Bedlam.

His voice became colder. "Gentlemen have these little lapses in taste from time to time. Might I suggest that it is not at all the thing for you to be alone in a bachelor household…?"

* * *

The Chivalrous Rake
Harlequin® Historical #804—June 2006

Praise for Elizabeth Rolls

His Lady Mistress
"Compelling, compassionate and filled with emotional intensity, Rolls' latest is a sexually charged novel that also will tug at your heart."
—*Romantic Times BOOKclub*

The Dutiful Rake
"With poignancy and sensuality, Rolls pens a story of a woman who hides her love for fear of being rejected and a man who is afraid that love and happiness will be taken away from him if he cares too much."
—*Romantic Times BOOKclub*

Elizabeth Rolls

THE Chivalrous Rake

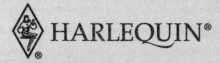

TORONTO • NEW YORK • LONDON
AMSTERDAM • PARIS • SYDNEY • HAMBURG
STOCKHOLM • ATHENS • TOKYO • MILAN • MADRID
PRAGUE • WARSAW • BUDAPEST • AUCKLAND

ISBN 0-373-29404-2

THE CHIVALROUS RAKE

Copyright © 2003 by Elizabeth Rolls

First North American publication 2006

www.eHarlequin.com

Printed in U.S.A.

Available from Harlequin® Historical and
ELIZABETH ROLLS

Please address questions and book requests to:
Harlequin Reader Service
U.S.: 3010 Walden Ave., P.O. Box 1325, Buffalo, NY 14269
Canadian: P.O. Box 609, Fort Erie, Ont. L2A 5X3

Chapter One

Jack Hamilton glared across his bedchamber at the retreating back of his doctor. He'd always considered shooting the messenger to be an irrational and sadly ill-bred response to unwelcome news. Right now he could definitely see the attraction it held for some.

A month! A whole damn month! By that time the hunting season would be nearly over. And what was he supposed to do with himself in the meantime? Play shove ha'penny? When he was situated within easy distance of the Quorn, the Belvoir *and* the Pytchely?

He caught the commiserating look on his valet Fincham's face and uttered a malevolent curse under his breath, directed at his own unforgivable cow-handedness in letting Firebird come down in the first place. Marc would roast him finely when he heard. For a moment he considered not informing Marc of his accident, only to dismiss the idea. The last thing the Earl of Rutherford would want to do would be to come all the way to Leicestershire in the depths of winter to discover that his host couldn't go hunting.

Jack comforted himself with the thought that if he wrote, Marc's ribbing would, perforce, be on paper. He didn't have to read it if he didn't want to.

He reached for his brandy glass without thinking and swore loudly. Wrong arm.

'Er, Mr Hamilton…'

Jack looked up.

The doctor stood by the open door, a rueful smile upon his face. 'It might be an idea to wear a sling until that collarbone knits…'

'A *sling*?' Jack could scarcely believe his ears. 'What the hell do you mean, a sling?'

Wilberforce answered readily, 'Piece of cloth to support your arm—it goes around your neck and ties—'

'I know what a sling is, damn it!' growled Jack. 'What the deuce do you think I need with one? I'm not a child!'

'No, sir. Of course not.'

The doctor's placatory tone failed to convince Jack and he resolutely ignored Fincham's snort of laughter. At least he had the decency to pretend to be coughing.

''Tis just that I have observed that gentlemen such as yourself—er, *active* gentlemen, that is—have a tendency to forget their injury and use the arm. A sling would serve to remind you to rest the arm.'

Jack snorted. 'I'll be reminded of that every time I see my hunters eating their heads off, thanks very much!'

'Very well, sir.' A faint grin crossed the doctor's face. 'Sorry to have been of service, sir.'

'*Sorry to have*…oh!' An unwilling chuckle broke from Jack. 'I take you. Sorry, Wilberforce. It's my own stupid fault. Thank you, and pray give my regards to your wife. I understand you're expecting a happy event.'

The recently married doctor grinned. 'That's right, sir. I'd best be getting back. Alice said she'd wait supper. I wish to God she wouldn't—no saying when I'll get home some nights, but she likes to do it! Good night. And cheer up—at least it wasn't your neck!'

The expression of disbelief on Mr Hamilton's face and

the disgusted snort that accompanied it suggested that, in his opinion, he might as well have broken his neck.

With a friendly wave, and thoroughly unsympathetic smile, the doctor departed.

Jack reached for the brandy, carefully this time, and took a sip. It might serve to sweeten his temper.

It didn't.

His head ached. His shoulder ached and he felt thoroughly dissatisfied with life. With a disgusted mutter at his melancholy mood he got to his feet, cursing as his broken collarbone, and recently relocated shoulder, protested the unwary movement.

'Will you be going to bed now, Mr Jack?' asked Fincham, gathering up Jack's riding coat and discarded shirt.

Jack stared at him. '*Bed?* At this hour? Didn't you hear the doctor? I broke my collarbone, not my blasted neck, Fincham!' He picked up the coat Fincham had laid out for him.

This time Fincham grinned openly. 'No, sir. Be putting you to bed with a shovel if you'd done that. Here, I'll help you with that!' He came over and, ignoring Jack's protest, assisted him into the coat.

It was a good thing, thought Jack, that he disliked tight coats and preferred to be able to shrug himself in without assistance. As it was, he suppressed a curse at the jolt of pain.

'Thanks,' said Jack. 'I'll get out of your way and go down to the library.'

He'd better write that letter to Marc. No doubt he and Meg would be just as happy to remain at Alston Court and dote on their two-month-old son. Probably they'd just accepted his invitation at the christening because they felt sorry for him.

Gathering up his brandy, he left the room. His mood did not improve on the way to the library. *Poor old Jack. All alone up there in Leicestershire.* That sort of thing.

Oh, for God's sake! What the devil was the matter with him? He must have taken more of a bump on the head than he'd realised. Of course Marc and Meg weren't visiting out of pity. They'd accepted because they were friends. He had no closer friend than Marcus Langley, Earl of Rutherford. Not even Marc's marriage had interfered with their friendship.

He sat down at his very untidy desk and reached awkwardly for a pen and paper. He muttered a few imprecations as he realised the quill needed trimming and reached for the pen cutter.

Dear Marc, No doubt you will find this highly amusing but I feel I ought to warn you...

He finished the letter and folded it. Lucky Marc. A wife like Meg and now a son. He couldn't imagine how life could possibly hold more for a man—except, of course, for all the other sons and daughters the pair of them were looking forward to.

He shivered slightly and glanced frowning at the fire. For some peculiar reason his library, which he had always found a companionable sort of room, seemed cold and empty.

He'd noticed that ever since he returned from the christening of Marc's heir—his godson. He'd been conscious of the quiet. Even after the other visitors had left Alston Court, Marc's principal residence, he'd been aware of a sense of life, a hum of purpose, about the place. The way it had been when he'd stayed there as a boy.

It was as though Marc's marriage and the birth of his first child had brought the place back to full life.

Not even a broken collarbone and dislocated shoulder during the hunting season would bother Marc now. Jack grinned. He could only think of one aspect of a broken collarbone that would seriously discompose Marc. And he was fairly sure the inventive Earl of Rutherford would come up with a solution to that as well.

Disgustedly Jack faced the true cause of his recent irritability—he needed a wife. Which was all very well—he had known that for some years. Increasingly his various affairs had left him dissatisfied and restless. He wanted more than a discreet liaison with someone else's neglected and bored wife or a fashionable demi-rep. He wanted someone who was his, and his only. But finding the right female was far easier said than done.

For the last four Seasons he'd been actively, if surreptitiously, looking. He could do without every ambitious mama in Town thrusting darling little nitwits into his arms. He could certainly do without Sally Jersey introducing him to every heiress in sight.

He wanted a love match, not a marriage of convenience for an heir on his side and social advancement on hers. So he'd looked very carefully. So damn carefully that not even the girls he'd considered, nor their mamas for that matter, had realised his interest. And on each occasion the girl in question accepted some other fellow before he'd even got as far as becoming particular in his attentions. Which didn't really worry him—except for the inconvenience of having to select a new target.

All of which suggested that he hadn't cared in the least about any of them, which surprised him. They had, all of them, been nice, quiet, gentle, scholarly girls—bluestockings, even, who wouldn't have bothered him in the least. So why hadn't he felt the least flicker of interest in any of them?

Logically, all of those young ladies should have been perfect. Except for the unavoidable fact that he had thought them all a trifle dull, boring even. And he couldn't, not with the most vigorous stretch of his very fertile imagination, picture himself in bed with any of them.

He sipped at his brandy thoughtfully. Of course, desire and passion were not necessarily the best guides when choosing a bride. They had a tendency to ambush a man at his weakest point, sapping his self-control, rendering common-sense useless. There were safer ways to choose a wife.

It didn't really make sense. None of those girls should have been dull. They were all attractive, charming young ladies. They had all been interested in the same sorts of things he enjoyed. And they had generally agreed with him...

It would be nice to have a wife to come home to. Someone to talk to in the evenings instead of turning to his books. Someone to warm his bed—and his heart. A nice, sweet, companionable girl who would soothe his irritable temper when he broke his collarbone. Someone who wouldn't turn his ordered life upside down. Someone like Meg.

He grimaced. What the devil was he doing, languishing over his best friend's wife? But he had to admit, if Meg had not been well and truly married to Marc before he laid eyes on her, he probably would have courted her. She was just what he liked in a woman. Gentle, charming, unswervingly loyal. Easy to get on with. Elegant loveliness and dignity personified. She was tall, too. Smaller women always seemed to be daunted by his height. Meg didn't always agree with him, of course...in fact, she had even been known to disagree with Marc. Strongly.

He dismissed the thought. Marc *could* be a trifle unreasonable at times. Especially where Meg's safety or health was concerned. He grinned. Marc had been taken thoroughly by surprise in his marriage. *He* was far more rational in his approach to love. You worked out in advance what you liked in a woman and then looked for her. In a rational, logical way.

It hasn't worked yet, has it?

He frowned. The last thing you did was to permit the responses of your body to serve as a guide. Passion and lust were all very well, but he wanted a woman to respect and care for, not just take to bed. Passion and lust could lead a man badly astray in fixing his affections. Capricious guides at best, they were damned deceiving at worst.

He snorted as he picked up a book. He'd learnt that lesson early. Only a fool repeated his own mistakes. Besides, he was older now, more experienced and he was in full control of his responses and desires, as a man should be. So. There it was. He needed a young lady like Meg. Easy. Except the only girl like Meg *was* Meg and she was not only married to, but shatteringly in love with, his best friend.

The right girl must be out there *somewhere*, and this year, when he went to London for the Season, he was going to make an all-out effort to find her. Because it was in the highest degree unlikely that she would come seeking him out up here in the wilds of Leicestershire.

Two mornings later Jack stalked through the wintry wilderness of his garden on his way back from a walk in the woods behind the house. The stark lines of the bare trees, dusted with a light fall of snow, failed to please him. They looked contorted, dead. The whole world appeared unspeakably bleak and dreary.

Even the rambling seventeenth-century house looked uninviting. It even managed to look empty. Which was completely and utterly ridiculous. It had a full complement of staff, all of them hell-bent on cosseting him to death.

He'd had a shocking night, and getting out of bed had been worse. Never before had he realised just how inconvenient a broken collarbone could be, not to mention the residual ache from the dislocated shoulder. Every muscle in his upper body appeared to be connected to his shoulder, reminding him with every step that his hunters were enjoying an unforeseen holiday.

At least he'd managed to escape from the servants, along with their everlasting hot possets, cushions and commiserating looks, to get a breath of air. He hadn't counted on this blasted north wind, which sent spasms of pain through his shoulder and neck every few minutes. He'd have to try and sneak into the library without anyone catching him.

And he was definitely sick of all the callers. His neighbours had developed an appalling lack of tact. He really didn't need to hear all about the capital run the local pack had enjoyed two days ago. And he definitely didn't need to have his incapacitated shoulder treated as a sort of matrimonial godsend. He ground his teeth. If just so much as one more simpering chit was inspired to present him with her own...*special salve for injuries just such as yours, Mr Hamilton*! Well, he wouldn't be responsible for the consequences, that was all.

At least he'd told Evans to deny him to any further callers for a few days. It would be very hard to explain precisely why he'd stuffed a pot of salve down a young lady's bodice. With this in mind, he swung around a garden wall and crashed into the person coming the other way.

A thoroughly blasphemous and graphic exclamation escaped his lips even as his reeling body automatically registered the undoubted femininity of his assailant.

'Blast it, girl!' he went on, toning his language down slightly. 'Don't you ever look where you're going?' He probed cautiously at his shoulder. It *felt* as though everything was still there. Unfortunately. It certainly all ached in the right places. And, as he got a good look at his blushing assailant, a few of the *wrong* places made their presence felt, too. Good Lord! He was an experienced man of six and thirty—not a green youth of twenty to rise to the bait like a trout!

'Just as much as you do through a brick wall, I dare say!'

He blinked and looked down at the girl. He'd never seen

her before as far as he could remember, but something within screamed recognition.

Affronted mint-green eyes glared back as he took in her outmoded and very damp scarlet cloak, muddy boots and untidy hair. Straight and wet, it hung down her back and over her shoulders in dark mahogany strands. He thought it would be auburn when it dried. Dark brows lifted expectantly and he stared back.

What was the world coming to when young ladies assaulted him in his own garden? Who the devil was she anyway? And why did he feel such an overwhelming urge to lift her chin up and wipe the smudge off her tip-tilted, freckled nose? Or kiss it off?

Whoever she was, she had no right to be traipsing about his garden! Even if she did make him feel like a green youth of twenty—*especially* if she made him feel like a green youth of twenty! She had no right to do anything of the sort when his shoulder ached far too much for him to take any pleasure in it.

'Are all the men in Leicestershire as rude as you?' she enquired, pleasantly.

Jack felt his temper straining at its leash. What the devil did she have to be affronted about? He was the one who'd been practically assaulted in his own garden!

She told him, 'Your initial choice of epithet I might forgive, under the circumstances. But you could at least apologise now for using such disgraceful language to a lady!'

Jack glared back. Little vixen! Stung to fury, he allowed his eyes to rove over her, assessing her shapeless, dowdy clothes and general air of untidiness.

'Naturally I would apologise to a lady,' he drawled. 'You must forgive me if I fail to recognise the species when it invades my garden without invitation. I gave quite clear instructions to my servants that I was not at home.

Might I suggest that you return to your carriage? No doubt, if you are a lady, we shall meet at some party or other.'

His gaze lingered on the flare of temper in her eyes, the flush on her cheeks. And he had the distinct impression that her figure, under that appalling excuse for a cloak, would be altogether delightful. There was something about the way she held herself... In fact, she was altogether an attractive little package...and she was shivering in the bitter wind. What on earth were her parents about to be letting her risk her health and reputation in this manner?

He added impersonally, 'I can assure you that the warmth of your carriage will banish your chill far more effectively than my poor self.' Thoughtfully, he continued, 'Damp muslin may have been all the crack twenty years ago, but I can assure you, damp kerseymere doesn't wear well in Leicestershire in the middle of winter!'

The flush flamed to out and out scarlet and the mint-green eyes narrowed. 'Are you Mr Jonathan Hamilton?'

He bowed. 'I have that honour.' Lord! She looked like an angry elf.

She snorted. 'Then Papa must be all about in his head!' With which baffling statement she swung on her heel and headed back towards the house.

Jack followed more slowly, taking time to appreciate the swing of her stride, the lithe grace of her every movement until she disappeared towards the carriage drive. Thoughtfully he headed for a side door. With a bit of luck he could get to the library without any of the staff ever knowing he had escaped. He could make discreet enquiries about his caller later.

Suddenly the winter's day looked brighter. Branches wove an austere tracery against the scudding clouds. It would probably snow again later. He always liked watching it drift down against the windows, liked the blustery howl of the wind...invigorating...got the blood moving. And the house had suddenly sprung to life again, golden stone glowing a mellow welcome. He quickened his stride, no longer noticing the pain of his shoulder.

An apologetic cough caught his attention.

Jack looked up from his book with an irritated frown for his butler. With a bit of luck Evans would think he'd been here in the library all morning. 'I'm not at home, Evans. To anyone. I thought I made that clear.'

'Yes, sir. Quite plain. Indeed, I have denied you, but now that you have returned from your walk—'

'No buts, Evans. I'm not at home…walk? How did…I mean, what walk?' He returned his gaze, if not his attention, to his book. He might have known his escape would not go unnoticed. Perhaps if he ignored Evans, he might go away.

Unfortunately Evans had a tenacity to rival his damned collarbone.

'The walk you took in the woods, sir. If you could just tell me which rooms Mrs Roberts should have made up…'

Jack stared. 'Rooms? What rooms?'

'That's what Mrs Roberts wants to know,' pointed out Evans, with all the confidence of having been butler of Wyckeham Manor before the present master was breeched.

The stare became a glare. 'What guests, Evans? I'm not expecting anyone. Er, am I?'

'Dr Bramley, sir. And—'

'*Bramley?* The Reverend Dr Edward Bramley? My father's cousin?' Relief, it couldn't be disappointment, swept through him. Dr Bramley could have nothing to do with the little hornet in the gardens. Must be coincidence. Putting his book on the wine table, Jack asked, 'What the devil is he doing here? Has he come to stay?'

'Er, yes. The young lady seemed to think—'

'Young *lady*? Evans, in case it has escaped your notice, the Reverend Dr Bramley was, *is*, a gentleman somewhat older than my father would be if he were alive. Unless, of course, the laws of nature have changed…' His voice died away as cold horror washed over him. Perhaps Dr Bramley *could* have something to do with the little hornet in the gardens.

'No, sir,' said Evans in soothing tones. 'The laws of nature are much as they were. Miss Bramley is his daughter.'

Given that piece of information, Jack wondered if the laws of nature had, after all, been suspended. His memories of Dr Bramley, while admittedly sketchy, were of a vague, impractical, unmarried, and certainly celibate, scholar, who had trouble telling a bull from a cow. The only women he'd ever shown the least interest in were firmly ensconced between the pages of Greek tragedy. He couldn't for the life of him imagine Dr Bramley siring anyone, let alone that outspoken little hornet!

'Good God! And they have come to stay?' Mentally he began to rehearse his apology.

'Yes, sir. Shall I show Dr Bramley in, sir?'

'Well, of course you should show him in!' said Jack.

Evans departed swiftly, but not quite swiftly enough to hide the broad grin on his face. Refusing to ponder just what his butler found so amusing about the unexpected visit of an elderly cleric, Jack levered himself out of his chair very carefully.

A few moments later the door opened.

'Dr Bramley,' announced Evans.

Jack's first thought was that his elderly cousin had changed very little. Still the same short, spare frame, his face smiling vaguely. A few more wrinkles and much less hair, but he would have known him anywhere.

'Dr Bramley!' said Jack, coming forward. 'How pleasant to see you, sir. It must be twenty-five years since last you were here.'

The old man stared at him. 'Good gracious! You must

be right. It is Jack, isn't it? You look exactly like your dear father!'

Jack grinned. 'I'm glad to hear it. What brings you here, sir? I thought you were settled in Cornwall. Come and sit by the fire. You must be frozen.'

The old man nodded. 'Yes, I must say that gig was a little cold. Stagecoach wasn't much better, but at least we had our luggage. Ah, that's better!' He held out his hands to the blaze.

'Gig? Stagecoach? What in Hades were you doing in such conveyances? And what's this about your luggage?' If they'd come on the London stage then they must have fetched up at the Bell in Leicester after one in the morning!

Dr Bramley looked up absentmindedly. 'Hmm?' He rubbed his hands. 'Oh, this is nice! Stagecoach? Well, I don't really know, dear boy. Cressida took care of all that. Even managed to persuade the landlady to give me a bed in the smoking room. As for the luggage, she insisted it all had to be left at the inn.'

'Cressida?' was all he said aloud. *A bed in the smoking room? Of the Bell alehouse? Good God!*

'Haven't you met Cressida?' Dr Bramley frowned. 'Hmm…let me see… Twenty-five years, you say…I suppose not, then. She's only about nineteen, or is it twenty? Doesn't matter, she's not twenty-five yet, I'm sure.'

'And she is your daughter?' *Where the devil did she spend the night?*

Dr Bramley blinked. 'Well, yes…I have every reason to believe she's my daughter.'

'You believe…' Even allowing for the old boy's vagueness, it still rocked Jack to his foundations. 'How in heaven's name did that come about?'

Dr Bramley took that quite literally. 'Er…ah…in the usual way, you know.' He gave Jack a surprisingly penetrating look. 'At least, you look as if you'd know.'

Jack felt heat steal along his cheekbones. Lack of sleep

and his aching shoulder had obviously addled his few re-maining wits—of all the atrocious questions to ask a cler-gyman!

His guest went on. 'Yes. Bit of a miscalculation on my part. I can't say I expected…not so quickly…and…er…easily…'

It might have been the heat of the fire turning Dr Bram-ley's bald head crimson, but somehow Jack doubted it. He changed the subject slightly. 'I didn't realise that you'd married, sir.'

The old man nodded. 'No, I didn't intend to. But Ama-bel was in such trouble, losing her post so unfairly as she did…just because that young scoundrel made up to her and got her dismissed… Anyway, I needed a house-keeper…so marriage seemed the best course all round.'

All Jack could glean from this was that his cousin had married as an act of charity.

'Who was Amabel?'

'Who was she?' Dr Bramley stared. 'I thought I ex-plained. She was my wife. Dead now, poor soul.' He shook his head. 'Cressida's mother,' he added, plainly anxious that there should be no further confusion on the issue of his daughter's parentage.

Jack decided to leave it. 'And where is she now?'

Dr Bramley looked quite startled. 'Ah…in her grave, dear boy. Yes, definitely in her grave. I read the service, you know. Cressida dealt with that.'

Dr Bramley, Jack realised, had not changed one jot in twenty-five years. 'Er…I meant, where is Cressida?' He corrected himself. 'Miss Bramley, I should say.'

'Oh.' The old man's relief was palpable. 'Thought you had a touch of the sun for a moment. She's vanished. I dozed off, you know, in the parlour. The fire was so warm. When your man came back for me, she'd taken her cloak back and disappeared.'

'Taken her cloak *back*?' Jack seized on the bit that

didn't make sense. He knew where Cressida—Miss Bramley—had been.

'Yes. She lent it to me in the gig. Practically tied it on me. Makes a man of the cloth look a dashed fool wearing a bright red cape. At my age, too!'

Jack hid his smile. Lord, he'd give a monkey to have seen it. At least the wretched chit had had enough sense to try and keep her poor old father warm. A pity she hadn't had enough *nous* to hire something more suitable than a gig. And as for bringing the poor old boy all the way from Cornwall on the common stage in the dead of winter and leaving their luggage behind—he'd have a bit to say to her on that head! Which reminded him...

'Why on earth didn't you write, sir?' he asked. 'I would have been happy to send a chaise. Even to Cornwall!'

Dr Bramley looked puzzled. Pathetically so. 'But I did write. I remember *that*. Hmm. Maybe it went astray. You'd need to ask Cressida, my boy. She deals with all those sort of things.'

Miss Cressida Bramley crouched by the fire in the parlour into which the terrifyingly austere butler had ushered them and wished she had never thought of leaving it. In fact, she wished that she had never left Cornwall. Why was it that men took one look at her and decided that it was quite unnecessary to treat her with respect? Was it the freckles, the nose, or could it be her red hair?

And why, oh, why, had she been foolish enough to lash back at the tall, dark-haired gentleman in the garden? Who else could he possibly have been except their unsuspecting and now, probably, unwilling host? Obviously he had returned to the house and summoned her father. She could only hope that the Reverend Dr Bramley would make a better impression than his daughter.

Still, he didn't have to be *that* rude. Even if she had startled him, she hadn't bumped him nearly hard enough to have hurt him. Actually she found it hard to imagine anyone would be big enough to harm him. Not even Andrew with his tall elegance of figure had that breadth of shoulder.

Bitterly she jerked her mind away from the memory of Andrew. There was no point remembering…except as an object lesson in how gentlemen viewed girls of her background and circumstances, how little their avowed affection could be trusted. She'd remember that and forget the rest. For now she had better concentrate on her new surroundings.

She looked around the parlour curiously. From all Papa had said, his cousin, Mr Jonathan Hamilton, was shockingly wealthy. Rich enough to buy an abbey. He certainly wasn't spending his money on keeping his home furnished in the latest style of elegance. Even to her inexperienced eye, most of the furnishings and décor were at least seventy to eighty years old. Exactly what the Dowager Lady Fairbridge had stigmatised as '…so dreadfully dowdy…' and encouraged her son to replace the moment their period of mourning had expired.

Yet there was no suggestion of faded fortunes about this room. It might be old-fashioned, but all the furniture was of the finest quality, waxed and polished lovingly, and she could see that the chairs had been reupholstered quite recently. That was why she had crouched near the fire. Sitting on those expensively plump and comfortable chairs in her present damp state was out of the question.

She rather liked this room. It had an air of comfort, as though someone really lived it here and didn't just use the room to impress visitors with how important and wealthy he was. The austerity of the furnishings appealed to her. She had felt terribly uncomfortable in the newly refurbished drawing room at Fairbridge Hall, as though she hardly dared breathe for fear she would sully something.

Perhaps Mr Hamilton was one of those bluff country

squires who couldn't stand change and new-fangled ways. Perhaps he lived here all year round in rural obscurity and wouldn't mind being saddled with a vague, scholarly cleric and his daughter. Certainly the rambling house, nestled against the darkness of the woods, felt welcoming, home-like.

A vision of Mr Hamilton as he had appeared to her in the garden did not lend much credence to this bit of wishful thinking. Granted his heavy cloak had hidden the rest of his attire, but even so she had received the impression of great elegance.

She shivered. If only she hadn't had to leave all their luggage behind at the inn in order to persuade the landlord to loan them that wretched gig! She could have got out of these damp clothes at once.

At least her cloak had kept Papa dry in the gig—if she'd been looking after him properly, he wouldn't have had a chance to give his cloak to that rascally beggar in the first place. So it was all her own fault that she was damp and cold. And going out in the garden in damp clothes, even with the cloak, had been absolutely henwitted.

And now she would have to conciliate a host she felt more like slapping and trust that he possessed enough family feeling to let them stay until she thought of what they were to do next.

'Borrow a dress from the housekeeper, I think,' she said to the dancing flames.

'An excellent idea, Miss Bramley,' came a familiar drawl. Cressida spun around, lost her balance and sat down on the floor with a thump. She stared up at her host, furiously aware of her undignified appearance.

Judging by his expression, Mr Hamilton was equally aware of it. He went on, 'Bringing luggage would have been even better, but I have no doubt that Mrs Roberts will be happy to lend you something.'

He stepped forward and Cressida swallowed. She hadn't

realised that anyone could be so tall. He must be well over six foot, and something about the way he moved suggested leashed power, a very masculine power that his style of dressing did nothing to disguise.

His buckskin breeches—situated on the floor she couldn't help but notice—were moulded to very long, muscular legs. His top boots might be splashed with mud, but she could see that they were beautifully made and well cared for. Dazedly she raised her eyes further. This gentleman did not bother with a skintight coat that nipped him in at the waist, but nevertheless his coat had been made by a master and it fitted comfortably over broad shoulders.

Nervously she lifted her gaze to his face and encountered a slightly amused, and more than slightly cynical, smile. His dark grey eyes set under black brows seemed to take in every detail of her forlorn and damp condition.

Suddenly realising that she was crouching by the fire for all the world like a bedraggled puppy, she began to scramble up and discovered a strong hand under her elbow, lifting her. A knife-thrust of shock went through her at the sensation of his long fingers closing around her arm.

'I can manage…'

His sharply indrawn breath sliced through her protest. Abruptly the hand withdrew. Off balance, she sat down again with an audible and painful thump.

'Bloody hell!' The words were jerked out of her forcibly. She blushed. That was not at all the sort of expression a clergyman's daughter, or any other young lady, ought to use at all, let alone in front of a gentleman. Especially when she had recently raked him down for using similar language.

'Quite, Miss Bramley.' The bland tone made her itch to slap him. Condescending beast!

The other hand was extended to her. Such a strong, capable hand. So safe…comforting.

What happened to condescending beast? How could a

hand look safe? Especially when its partner had just dropped her on the hearth stone on her derrière and made her look an utter fool.

She looked up, ready to tell him exactly what she thought of him. The lines of pain on his whitened face shocked her.

'Sir? Are…are you all right?'

His mouth tightened. 'Perfectly, Miss Bramley. Merely a trifling injury to my shoulder.'

Guilt consumed her. Had she cannoned into him that hard? And if she had, how on earth had she damaged his shoulder? She'd be surprised to learn that her head even reached it. Perhaps he wasn't as strong as he looked.

'Master Jack!' The wail of distress startled Cressida and she blinked as the butler bobbed into view behind his tall master. She hadn't noticed him. Somehow Mr Hamilton had filled, indeed overflowed, her vision.

'Why won't you do as Dr Wilberforce said, and wear a sling? You'll never remember not to use the arm!'

Cressida relaxed slightly. Obviously the injury had preceded their first meeting.

'Oh, shut up, Evans. Go and find Mrs Roberts. Tell her to hunt out one of her dresses for Miss Bramley.'

'I beg your pardon, sir?'

'You heard me… Oh, I see what you mean.' His hand still outstretched, he looked at Cressida assessingly. Up and down and back again.

As if I were a…a filly!

Still, she must have jarred him horribly. Rude as he was, she did not like to think that she had given pain to any fellow creature. Ignoring the outstretched hand, she got up and straightened her skirts.

She opened her mouth to apologise, but her host spoke first.

'Hmm. Yes. Definitely one of Mrs Roberts's smaller

dresses, Evans. And you might find some rope to hold it on.'

'Very good, sir.'

Cressida eyed the butler's retreating back narrowly. She could have sworn he was amused. Whether at her or his master, she couldn't hazard a guess. Drawing a deep breath, she turned back to her host.

He returned her gaze with a faint smile. She fidgeted with the ties of her cloak, and shifted slightly in her damp shoes. Abruptly she became aware of how cold and tired she was. Of how little claim she and her father had on this man. Especially if she could not even do him the courtesy of telling him the truth, not against her father's expressed wishes... And even if she did...would he understand? Or would he turn them out, too? She couldn't risk it. Papa had travelled far enough. Perhaps later she could explain to Mr Hamilton exactly what had happened; that it was her fault Papa had lost his living. Then she could leave once she had found a position. Surely Leicestershire was far enough from Cornwall that rumours would not dog her?

'Miss Bramley?'

'Sir?' She could have sworn he flushed slightly.

'Perhaps you might be able to explain to what I owe the honour of this, er, visit.'

Cressida met his eyes. Dark ice, their expression shuttered—she could read nothing beyond indifference. But his slight hesitation over the word *visit* suggested that he already suspected that it might be a rather long visit.

Duty. Papa is family. She flushed. So was she if it came to that. But she had never felt like family. Had always been conscious that, despite his absent-minded affection, she was an encumbrance her father could well have done without. No doubt Mr Jonathan Hamilton, even if he were prepared to help her father, would feel the same. Without the mitigating affection.

'Circumstances dictated that my father resign his living

in Cornwall.' At least it had the dubious merit of being
the truth and nothing but the truth. The less said about the
whole truth, the better. 'He…he could think of nowhere
else to go.'

'I see.'

He did?

'Naturally I have no objection to your visit,' he drawled.
'It will enliven my dull existence considerably. But I
would have appreciated a letter informing me of your intentions. Your father was under the impression you had
sent one. Had you done so, I could have arranged better
accommodation for you last night and a chaise to meet
you this morning.'

Cressida felt her jaw drop, even as her hackles rose at
the insufferable edge of sarcasm in his voice.

'L…letter?'

'Yes. You know the sort of thing…*Dear Cousin Jack,
we've never met but I would like to inform you that my
father and I are arriving for an extended visit. Please expect us on such and such a date. Sincerely, Cousin…
er…Cressida.*'

'I beg your pardon,' she said quietly. Obviously it hadn't
been enough to stand over Papa while he wrote the letter.
Why on earth hadn't she insisted on posting the wretched
thing herself? She could have dealt with a bit of mud and
a few stones. No doubt her cousin thought she had omitted
to write so that he could have no opportunity to refuse
them.

She could only describe his smile as sardonic. Her temper began to rise.

She was not, absolutely *not*, going to try and exonerate
herself in his eyes by passing the blame straight back to
her father. And she wasn't going to lose her temper with
him. At least, not openly.

His expectantly raised brows suggested that he awaited
some sort of explanation. All sorts of inappropriate re-

sponses jostled on the end of her tongue. Biting them back, she reminded herself firmly that the meek shall inherit the earth. *Possibly…when snow lay in hell. And he'd wait as long for an explanation from her!* She choked that back as well.

'And when do you think your luggage will arrive?'

'When it is sent for.' She didn't trust herself to say more.

'Oh?'

Some of her bubbling anger splashed over. 'Yes,' she snapped. 'I felt that it would be inappropriate of me to give orders to your grooms before we had seen you!'

Shutting her eyes briefly, she reached for control, mentally rehearsing the little prayer Papa had printed out for her use at times when her lamentable temper threatened to slip its leash. *Lord, make me an instrument…*

'Of course…' his tone became pensive '…some might have thought it advisable to hire a closed conveyance, one that could take your luggage. Some might even have chosen to travel post from Cornwall, rather than expose an old man to the rigours of the stage. Not to mention a bed in the smoking room at the Bell.'

Some people had more money than they knew what to do with and ought to mind their own arrogant, misbegotten business!

…of thy peace… 'I dare say.' Cressida felt a glow of pride at the sweetly demure tone she achieved despite the memory of the landlord's pithy dismissal of her insistence that Mr Hamilton was expecting them. *Mr Jack's a real gentleman, he is. His guests don't in general arrive on the stage…* It was only his wife's kindness that had secured the bed in the smoking room. Much to the landlord's disgust, she had allowed Cressida to sleep in the bed of a chambermaid who had gone to spend the night with her family. Nothing, however, could budge him from his refusal to loan the gig without the surety of their luggage.

'If you've quite finished, I should like very much to get out of these damp clothes.'

He inclined his head gravely. 'Of course, Miss Bramley. I am sure Mrs Roberts is waiting.'

He strolled to the door and opened it.

She stared. Then, shaking her wits into place, she hurried towards the door. Obviously he observed at least the outward customs of gentlemanly behaviour.

'Naturally you and your father are welcome to stay for as long as you like,' he said, very politely. 'But you may wish to consider that mine is a bachelor household. You have no chaperon here, which may prove a trifle awkward.'

She stiffened. 'How very kind of you, sir. I hope that it will not be necessary for us to impose upon you for long. I…I have every expectation that a position can be found that will value Papa's scholarship. And in any event, I have formed the intention of seeking a post as a governess, or possibly a companion. So you need not fear that I, at least, will trespass on your generosity for too long or cause you any undue embarrassment.'

His frown returned immediately. 'The devil you will! Neither you nor Dr Bramley have any need to go careering over the countryside looking for employment. You are both entirely welcome to remain here. I meant only—'

She interrupted at once. 'Coming here was a short-term arrangement only. Just until I could think of something else.' Short of the workhouse. She forced that nightmare into the back of her mind. 'At least for myself. Papa may be content to be your pensioner—I am not. Good day, sir.'

She swept out. At least she'd had the last word.

His amused voice followed her. 'Oh, I don't think I'll offer you a pension, Miss Bramley! I'm sure you have many years of active service left in you.'

Temper flared. Eyes narrowed, she turned. 'I dare say. Might I suggest, sir, that you take your butler's advice and put your sling on? It will probably help me to remember to treat your infirmity with consideration.'

Noting his dropped jaw, she knew that this time she'd really had the last word and stalked from the room.

Chapter Two

Jack sat back in his chair by the library fire. He couldn't think of anything else he needed to do right now. The Bramleys' luggage had arrived. Both his guests were partaking of supper in their bedchambers. And he felt as though he'd been hit by a falling tree.

What was it about that chit that tipped him so totally off balance that he couldn't control his temper around her? Damn it all! He hadn't even realised that he had a temper, always excepting his irritation over his shoulder, but Miss Cressida Bramley had discovered it at once. Top-lofty little baggage!

He snorted. She plainly didn't think much of him, either. And he was saddled with her and her father indefinitely. What on earth could have happened to force Dr Bramley to resign his living? Granted he was the world's most absent-minded dreamer, and probably hadn't been a very good minister, but Jack had yet to learn that such drawbacks could deprive a cleric of his parish. Quite the opposite.

Jack hunted through his memories. He hadn't seen Dr Bramley in twenty-five years. All he remembered was a vague, if kindly, gentleman who'd spent most of his visits here in the library and had to be dragged out for meals.

Reclusive, scholarly, bookish—how the devil could a man like that cause a big enough scandal to lose his living?

And how on earth had any female dragged him away from his books for long enough to get through a courtship and marriage ceremony, let alone beget a child? At the very least, finding answers to all these questions would take his mind off his shoulder.

In the meantime, he would have to come up with some way of persuading Dr Bramley and his stiff-necked daughter to stay without trampling on the latter's pride.

In the middle of these cogitations there came a light tap at the door.

'Come in.'

A slightly built, elderly groom came in.

'Evening, Mr Jack.'

'Hello, Clinton.' Jack smiled at his head groom. 'You'd better come over here to the fire. Has the luggage been collected?'

'Aye, sir. Fetched it meself from the Bell and ast a few questions like you wanted.'

Jack nodded. Spying on his guests left a sour taste in his mouth, but he did not wish to upset Dr Bramley, and asking Cressida any more questions was plainly a waste of breath. Besides, the wretched chit unsettled him. The sarcastic edge in his voice when he'd spoken to her had shaken him. It left him feeling completely out of control. Of her. Of himself.

He refused to think about the uncomfortable stirrings of desire in his blood. If he ignored the urging of his baser self, it would doubtless go away like other inconvenient desires he had walked away from over the years.

He gestured to a chair.

'Sit down, man. What did you find out?'

Clinton flushed with pleasure as he lowered his slight frame into the chair and perched respectfully on the extreme edge. 'Thank 'ee, sir. Well, they came off the stage, like the young lady said,' he began. He grinned. 'Seems the driver took quite a fancy to her…'

Jack stiffened, icy fury surging through his veins.

'What!' If she had suffered any insult…any familiarity…

Catching at his self-control, he met Clinton's startled gaze and forced his jaw to relax.

The groom added soothingly, 'In a manner of speaking, as ye might say. One of the hostlers mentioned it. Seems when the road got real bad, they said all the gents had to walk. Well, Miss Cressida wouldn't have none of that. Got out herself, she did, so's her pa could stay inside. Driver's got a lass himself and he looked after her real proper. Wouldn't have none of it. An' he told Sam hostler to make sure she was treated right.'

Good God. Jack throttled his reaction and schooled his features back to an encouraging smile.

'Could you find out why they were on the stage at all?' Even the fact that Cressida had sacrificed her own comfort and safety for her father didn't excuse the initial idiocy of coming by stage. Even the mail would have been better.

'Seemin'ly they ain't got a feather to fly with,' said Clinton with a shrug. 'Sam reckons as how the old gent give his cloak to some rascally beggar and most of their money as well. Landlord was a bit pressed for time an' wouldn't even lend 'em the gig without they left all their luggage. He says to tell you he's real sorry an' there's no charge for the gig. Seems as how his missus felt sorry for Miss Cressida and let her sleep with the maids for the night, while her pa had a bed in the smoking room.' He shook his head in wonderment.

'I…see.' And this time he did. Only too clearly. He'd made a complete and utter fool of himself. Worse—he'd behaved like an arrogant, conceited coxcomb. All because Miss Cressida Bramley's bright eyes had turned him upside down and inside out.

Clinton nodded. 'That's about all, sir.' He hesitated.

Jack raised a brow. 'Just say it, Clinton. I'll guarantee not to sack you.'

'No, sir.' He grinned at his master and then sobered. 'Not wishin' to say nothin' against a kinsman of yours, Mr Jack, but it don't seem that the Reverend did much to help Miss Cressida. Very vague he was, Sam told me. Seems she had to order the whole journey and she was real upset when he give away the last of their money.'

Jack could just imagine. Yet she had silently endured his criticism of her management. He must have gone insane. A chit of that age should not have had to travel on the stage at all, let alone manage the journey and listen to his criticism afterwards.

Why had she let him get away with it?

Too meek? Hardly! The little virago who had raked him down for rudeness in the garden was not the woman to turn the other cheek with becoming meekness. No Patient Griselda there! Far more likely that she would slap back. He recalled her snapping green eyes and short answers. Those blasted freckles had practically quivered with outrage, yet she had held her tongue. Why?

He could think of plenty of women who would have had no hesitation in dumping the blame squarely on the nearest person available, fairly or not. Plainly Cressida was not of that ilk.

'Very well, Clinton.' He nodded dismissal. 'Thank you. I'll come down in the morning to see how Firebird goes on.' Reaching into his pocket, he held out half a crown. 'You'd better have this. That was a cold errand you had.'

Clinton flushed as he took the proffered coin unwillingly. 'Pshaw. That ain't necessary, Mr Jack. I don't mind havin' a jaw with Sam, thankin' you kindly, sir.' He left Jack to some thoroughly unwelcome reflections.

These were once again interrupted by a tap on the door. 'Come in.'

No doubt Clinton had forgotten something… 'Oh, good evening, Dr Bramley.'

The old man, restored to his luggage, looked a far tidier proposition than he had earlier. He advanced into the room, glancing around avidly.

'My, my, my!' His eyes practically glazed over with ecstasy at the sight of all the books. Jack bit back a smile at this evidence of Dr Bramley's abiding passion.

The old man blinked up at the gallery circling the library. 'Is that new?'

Jack nodded. 'Yes. My father had it built just before his death. He worried about Mama going up and down the ladders and she worried about him…and it gave some extra space for all the books he acquired at the Roxburghe sale in 1812.'

Dr Bramley tut-tutted. 'Very sad that His Grace sold the collection. I only heard about the sale later or I should have come up to London.'

Jack breathed a silent prayer of thanks to a merciful deity as he tried to imagine the old boy coming to London and indulging his passions at a book sale which had lasted forty-one days.

'Yes,' mourned Bramley. 'My wife mislaid the information about the sale. To think that *The Decameron* went under the hammer. To have had the chance to buy it!'

'Blandford bought it,' managed Jack, choking inwardly. For something over two thousand pounds. Cressida had more to be grateful for than she knew. *Lord! And people think excessive gambling pernicious!*

'Ah, you mentioned your wife?' He was proud of the subtle, questioning tone he managed to infuse into his voice.

'Amabel?' Dr Bramley sighed. 'She died some years ago. I think. Yes. At least four. It might be five. Cressida would know.'

Jack tried to imagine either of his parents being uncertain of how much time had elapsed since the death of the other. He failed completely.

'I never thought of you as a marrying man,' he observed.

'Hmm?' Dr Bramley examined a volume and replaced it carefully. 'Marrying man, did you say? I wasn't. Never intended to marry. But I can't stand injustice. And I can't abide hypocrisy. What happened to Amabel was both. Her father was a friend of mine and she became a governess after he died. The son of the house where she was employed wouldn't leave her alone. Dare say you know how these things go. Eventually she was turned off without a character. She had nowhere to go, no one else to turn to. So I took her in. Married her myself in the end. Seemed the best thing at the time.' He thought about that. 'Still does, actually. I'm not terribly practical, you know.'

'I had noticed,' said Jack gravely.

'Yes, I thought you would have.' Dr Bramley frowned as he examined a shelf of books. He held up two volumes. 'What are *these* doing together?'

Jack bit back a laugh. At the very least you'd have thought the old chap had caught the books doing something scandalous. 'My father died before he finished sorting and cataloguing…'

'Good gracious! Still not catalogued?' He made it sound like a major sin of omission.

Jack shook his head ruefully. 'Not fully, sir. My father made a start and I've continued, but it's a big job and I have other demands on my time.'

Bramley looked blank, as if quite unable to comprehend how a man could possibly rate anything above his library. 'Well, well. I shall potter in here while we are with you. No doubt Cressida will assist me.'

'Ah, yes,' said Jack. 'What a pity she didn't write to let me know you were coming.'

'She didn't? That's a good specimen.' The old man

frowned absently as he stroked a little jade horse with one thin finger. 'Went to China with your father, you know. Before your time. Oh, no, of course she didn't. I did. That's what brought me down. Here.' He reached into his pocket and brought out a sealed letter. He handed it to Jack with a touch of embarrassment. 'I do apologise. I can't *think* why Cressida would have given it back to me rather than posting it herself, most odd, inconsiderate even. But better late than never. T'ang?' This last was muttered to himself as he picked up the little horse and examined it.

Jack didn't bother to argue with his guest's reasoning. He had better things to do with his breath. 'Quite,' he said, taking the letter. Inwardly he added to the apology he already owed Cressida. At this rate he'd be begging her pardon until Easter. Especially when she found out that she had been volunteered to assist in the library.

He thought about the library after Dr Bramley had retired. Time and more that he did something about it. What he really needed was a librarian of course. Someone to catalogue and keep track of everything. He knew by now that he would never manage to do it all by himself.

A librarian. Where would one find such a man…?

'Catalogue Mr Hamilton's library?' Cressida did not even try to hide her disapproval. 'But, Papa, you said his library is enormous. We aren't going to be here for that long. Just until you can find a living or another suitable post. We don't want to impose on him.' She set down her teacup carefully and marshalled every possible argument. A daunting task over breakfast.

Her father smiled seraphically. 'But it's all different now. If I catalogue the library, I will be doing him a favour. After all, it is one of the finest private collections in the country. No, no. It would be very ill done of me to be

thinking of personal advancement when it is clearly my
duty to remain here.'

'Perhaps he doesn't want his library catalogued,' she
suggested.

'Not want it catalogued?' Dr Bramley appeared shocked
at such heresy.

'If he hasn't had it done already…' She pressed on,
aware she was speaking to a brick wall.

'Of course he wants it catalogued!' spluttered the old
man through a mouthful of ham. 'I should not dream of
leaving until it is done.'

'Very well, Papa. I dare say I can find some mending
to do for him to earn my board.' She could hardly complain if her father had managed to find an eligible situation
for himself without the least thought that it would be impossible for her to remain here for any length of time without giving rise to gossip. He might recognise impropriety
when it walked up and bit him, but only if it had very big,
sharp teeth.

She gazed with sudden distaste at the plate of ham and
eggs to which she had helped herself. The last thing she
wanted was to be the object of someone's charity. Especially a man's. Especially Mr Jonathan Hamilton's!

Her father sneezed. She looked up, concerned. 'Papa,
are you getting a cold?'

He nodded. 'It was rather chilly yesterday. But don't
worry, I'm sure it will prove trifling and I shall be as right
as a trivet in no time. The library will keep my mind off
it.'

'Very well, Papa. We'll stay until it's done.'

Surely the library couldn't be that large. Perhaps Papa
had exaggerated its size. Yes, that was it. They could get
it done in a few weeks and then find some sort of post for
her father. She brightened at the thought. If their host could
be persuaded to furnish Papa with a reference, it would be
even better.

* * *

Blinking up at the ranks of books lining the library walls half an hour later, Cressida rapidly revised her estimate. Weeks? Good lord! It would take years! And she knew who would be scrambling up and down all the ladders, sneezing, while her father drifted from pile to pile in a blissful, dusty daze. Still, she had discovered what Mr Jonathan Hamilton spent his money on. His library.

The books, anyway. While many of the volumes swelling the floor-to-ceiling shelves, and piled haphazardly on the gallery and mezzanine floor, were of obvious antiquity, she could see that many were of much more recent date. A large *bureau plat* piled with more books stood by the fireplace and a very battered and comfortable looking leather chair sat beside it.

It was a strangely old-fashioned room, very plain and austerely functional as though its owners had taken little notice of changing fashions and styles. Rather like the rest of the house that she had seen. Pulling out a book that caught her eye, Cressida wondered if Mr Hamilton were not as wealthy as her father had intimated. In her experience, people of wealth updated their principal residence and furnishings quite regularly.

She put the book back. No, that didn't make sense. There were plenty of servants and no evidence of neglect. The house was beautifully cared for. And their host had all the appearance of a man of wealth. Indeed, she understood that the estate was extensive, and that there were others.

There was one thing she was quite sure of— 'If he really does want this catalogued, we'll certainly earn our keep. We'll be here for years,' she muttered.

'Oh, I do want it catalogued, I assure you.'

She swung around sharply, caught her toe in the edge of the rug and slipped. She felt herself caught and held against a powerful chest with arms that resembled steel bars. At first the thrill of delight that shimmered from her breasts to her toes held her motionless. Her whole body softened against the much harder, masculine one which appeared to have surrounded her. Stunned, she looked up into stormy dark grey eyes. Fire blazed there. She dropped her gaze to his lips. She had the oddest sensation of melting, yielding. Then, shocked at the sensations winging through her, she wriggled furiously. His harshly drawn breath stopped her. The lines around his mouth locked.

She stood still, blinking. Was that pain? Abruptly she remembered his injury. His jaw was set, the lips hard and straight. Goodness, he looked as though he would gladly throttle her. His arms tightened, sending more shockwaves rippling through her and then he released her, setting her away from him with a gentleness at odds with the sudden chill in his face.

Stepping back a little further, she said crossly, 'You really are an idiot, sir! Why don't you put it in a sling?'

His jaw dropped. 'A…a sling, did you say?'

'Well, of course! How else are you to recover if you keep using it?'

She thought for a moment that he might choke. On what she couldn't hazard a guess.

'Oh,' he managed to mutter at last. 'My shoulder.'

It was Cressida's turn to be nonplussed. 'Obviously,' she said. 'Unless you've managed to dislocate anything else since I saw you yesterday.'

He turned purple. 'It is bandaged,' he pointed out in a very strained voice.

She sniffed. 'I dare say. But you need something to remind you not to use that arm.' Seeing his raised brows, she flushed. Drat the man. Why was she wasting her time in trying to make him see sense? No doubt he would only resent it. Especially since she had just called him an idiot.

'I beg your pardon,' she said stiffly. 'I did not mean to interfere in your affairs. I hope I did not jar your arm too badly.'

'Never mind my curst arm,' he snapped. 'That's the least of my problems now! I take it you object to the idea of remaining here.'

'Yes,' said Cressida. 'I do.'

He blinked. 'You're very direct, aren't you?'

She shrugged. 'It saves time. Do you truly want this library catalogued or don't you? I may as well inform you that Papa has decided that it is his duty as a scholar to do so. And I can tell you right now that it will take him years!'

She gestured wildly at the towering shelves. 'Was it your suggestion or his? And who did you think would assist him? He's far too old to be climbing the ladders, even with that gallery.'

'Well, of course, I would be—'

'With that shoulder?' She saw his flush with intense satisfaction. 'I understand it to have been dislocated as well as the broken collarbone, so—'

'For God's sake! Anyone would think that you and my staff expect me to be permanently disabled!' he growled.

She snorted. 'The way you keep using the wretched thing, you probably will be!' She tried to ignore the wry amusement that softened his rather harsh features, the twinkle lurking in his eye. Why did he have to be so attractive? Why couldn't he be old and fat and bald? Then he wouldn't make her feel like a cat having its fur stroked the wrong way.

'Anyway, I'm sure you aren't here all year. And I can tell you that to catalogue this is a massive job!'

Disgustedly, she surveyed the library again. 'If you wanted it done, why not employ a…a librarian?'

'That's exactly what I have done,' he said blandly. 'I'm so glad you approve.'

'Then what is Papa going to—?'

'I've employed your father,' he explained. 'I've pottered

at the library myself but, as you so rightly point out, I need a curator. Now I have one.'

'Now you...' Speech failed her completely. Her jaw dropped open. What did he mean?

'I just saw your father in the breakfast parlour. He has accepted the post of librarian here,' said her outrageous host. 'He was more than happy with the arrangement we came to.'

'Is it...a...a permanent position?' It would be just the thing for Papa, if only it didn't smack of charity. He would be safe.

He won't need you any more. Independence had never looked more depressing.

'I can assure you, Miss Bramley, that my library is not about to disappear,' he responded drily. 'I even add to it on a regular basis. I collect old books and manuscripts, as well as keeping up with whatever interests me in modern trends of literature. Your father will be invaluable.'

'Not with the modern poets, he won't!' said Cressida at once, ignoring the intangible feeling of being suddenly cut adrift.

'And just what does your father class as modern poetry?' he asked.

'Anything later than Spenser,' she answered promptly.

'I see.' He appeared to be trying not to smile. 'Very well, I shall put you in charge of "modern" poetry, and I dare say novels as well.'

She bit off the automatic refusal and nodded vaguely instead. There was no point in arguing with scholars. They rarely heard anything they didn't want to hear. Not that Jack...Mr Hamilton looked like any scholar she had ever met, but looks could be deceptive. Anyway, if Papa had found a position like this, then it was time and more that she got on with her own life. He probably wouldn't even notice that she had gone with all this to keep him busy.

The thought of not being needed, by anyone, swamped

her. She shivered slightly. And then saw Mr Hamilton watching her curiously.

'Is something wrong, Miss Bramley?'

Nothing was wrong. Nothing at all.

She changed the subject. 'I suppose if I don't climb up and down all those ladders, you will,' she said. 'Very well. I will act as my father's assistant for the time being.' In a very few weeks she'd be twenty-one and her own mistress.

'You'll do no such thing,' snapped her host. 'There's nothing the matter with my shoulder, if that's what you mean. And young ladies do not scramble up and down ladders!'

Cressida bristled. 'Certainly not. Young ladies ascend and descend ladders with a modicum of grace and dignity. And they do not put up with wholly unconnected gentlemen telling them what they may or may not do!'

Belatedly she realised that he had again prodded her into losing her temper with him. Just what was it about him that set her all on edge?

'I beg your pardon, Cousin Cressida.'

He spoke gently, humbly even, with not the least trace of sarcasm.

'You…you what?' She could not remember anyone ever, in her whole life, offering her an apology.

'Beg your pardon,' he repeated obligingly. 'That's what a gentleman is supposed to do when he offends a lady.'

He *was* mocking her after all! She turned on him fiercely.

'Let me tell you something, Mr Hamilton. I want nothing from you, nothing! Not even your spurious apologies! Do you hear me? And I would infinitely prefer that you did not call me Cousin. I have no claim on you. Our connection is of the remotest nature. Since I am to act as my father's assistant I am, in some regards, in your employ. I should vastly prefer that our relationship remain quite formal.'

He exploded with satisfying force. 'Let me tell you something, my girl; any employee who spoke to me as you do would be dismissed instantly!' Dark grey eyes blazed into hers. His lips were white with fury. 'I'll make one thing quite clear; yes, I do want my library catalogued and I will certainly pay Dr Bramley for his expertise, but at no time will I consider you and your father to be anything but my guests! And members of my family. And I'll call you what I damned well please, *Cousin Cressida!*'

Cressida knew when she'd lost a battle, but that didn't have to prevent her having the parting shot. 'Spoken like a true gentleman. Good morning, Mr Hamilton. I shall ask Papa when he wishes to make a start. In the meantime I shall offer to assist your housekeeper with the mending!'

Jack stared at the door, which had shut in his face with something perilously close to a bang. He couldn't remember the last time anyone had raked him down like that. Always excepting the trimming she'd given him yesterday. And he hadn't even managed to apologise for that. What the devil was it about her that put him all on end? Apart from that annoying talent of hers for getting the last word. That would drive a saint to blasphemy.

And he was definitely no saint. The nagging ache in his groin assured him of that. Not that he would have described the sensation as *dislocated…*

Obviously it didn't help that every time he saw her, he wanted to take her in his arms and kiss her senseless. Not to mention the other things he'd like to do with her. None of which were at all eligible for a young lady to all intents and purposes under his protection. Or in his employ, as the top-lofty little peagoose had put it. As though she were a chambermaid! He'd tripped over a chambermaid before, but the only reaction he'd had had been to pick up the linen she'd dropped and apologise.

With Cressida he'd ended up instantly and painfully aroused the moment he felt her breasts crushed against his chest. And that little wriggle—he'd felt her thighs shift against him. He groaned at the memory. God, she'd be sweet. When she'd looked up, her lips slightly parted, it had required all his self-control not to take her mouth. Her lips had looked so soft, so pink. All warm and moist, like raspberries. Thinking about it left his body aching with desire.

Only the realisation that she had not the least idea of the effect she had on him had stopped him. *Or did she? Was he about to repeat one of his own mistakes? With his eyes wide open?*

Grimly he remembered Selina. Lord, it must be fifteen or more years ago. Just after he came on the town. Selina Pilkington had tied him in knots. The number of times he had conveniently found her alone…the times she turned her ankle, lost a shoe, stumbled during a dance. She hadn't tried to get herself compromised, not really.

She had been far more subtle than that. All those times her breasts accidentally brushed his arm, the times she stumbled during a dance and he had found those same soft breasts crushed against his chest. Looking back on it, she hadn't been subtle at all, but subtlety would have been wasted on a cub of twenty…especially a chivalrous, young fool like Jack Hamilton.

By the end of that long-ago Season he had wanted her so badly he had been prepared to offer for her and to hell with his parents' unspoken misgivings. It had taken Marc, cynical, observant Marc, to make him think.

Going to offer for her, are you? Hmm. Prefer a filly that doesn't go lame all the time myself…

They had an invigorating bout of fisticuffs and afterwards, as they mopped up, Jack remembered to ask Marc precisely what he meant. Marc pointed out brutally that Miss Pilkington was perfectly surefooted, and never lost her slipper unless Jack was by.

She's leading you around like a puppy, old chap. Every-

*one else knows that Lady Pilkington has the chit ear-
marked for the highest bidder. You always seem to forget
that, for a mere commoner, you're quite a prize.*

So why the devil wasn't Lady Pilkington coursing the
even-more-eligible Viscount Brandon, heir to the Earl of
Rutherford?

Marc grinned. *What? After I greeted them in the park
while I had Harriette Wilson on my arm? Thanks. My
sense of self-preservation is a bit more highly developed
than yours!*

Jack laughed at the memory. He'd nearly called Marc
out over that incident. Greeting two delicately bred and
virtuous females while squiring the most notorious demi-
rep of the day had caused an uproar. Of course Marc apologised profusely—and claimed he hadn't remembered it
was Harriette with him…that he'd thought Lady Pilkington
had nodded to him…

In the end, that bout of fisticuffs with Marc saved him.
With a black eye and a swollen lip, he went into the country for a few days until he could present a more creditable
appearance. A few days became three weeks. Marc had
brought a couple of very lively little fillies along…and
Jack discovered that he was not really in love with Selina
Pilkington at all. He just had a surfeit of wild oats of which
to dispose.

By the time he got back to town, Miss Pilkington was
casting her lures to Viscount Ripley. The engagement was
announced a few weeks later. At which Jack breathed a
hearty sigh of relief.

Looking back on it, he couldn't really blame Selina for
her tactics. All was fair in love and war. Girls had to
marry. Society dictated that it should be so. And then pro-
ceeded heartily to condemn any enterprising female who
went beyond the very faintly drawn line in her matrimonial
campaign.

But he loathed a tease…and if Miss Cressida Bramley

thought she could bamboozle him with a few well-placed wriggles, then she could think again.

Oh, for heaven's sake! Of course she wasn't like Selina. She'd been reared in the depths of Cornwall by a vicar and a bluestocking mother... He frowned slightly, remembering Dr Bramley's explanation for his marriage. Had Cressida's mother simply overplayed her hand in the age-old game of hunt-the-husband? Had she played her trump card and lost it? And was Cressida going to try a similar ploy?

Good lord! What maggot had got into him to be feeling so suspicious and hunted? Cressida could know very little of the desires of men and the teasing games that marriage-minded, up-to-snuff young ladies could play. And as far as he could tell, she didn't like him above half.

Since when did a female intent on seducing a man into marriage abuse him like a Billingsgate fishwife, just because he had teased her a little?

Of course, it would help if she liked him before *he* seduced *her*...

Seduced her? Where in Hades had that come from? He had absolutely no intention of seducing any girl of good character, let alone his cousin! He'd end up having to marry her and he was damned if he'd marry any girl just because he couldn't keep his hands off her.

What he *was* going to do was put her over his knee and spank her if he caught her so much as touching a needle and thread in connection with mending! After all, he was a mature and responsible man of thirty-six, in full control of his actions and reactions.

Cressida didn't stop until she had reached her own room. Moodily she stared at the snow whirling down outside the window. She couldn't even go for a ramble to work off some of her fury. No, she was trapped. And she was making the same mistake she had made before; allowing her attraction to a man to blind her judgement.

Jack Hamilton might behave like a gentleman at the moment, but it would be rank insanity to depend on his continued good behaviour if he thought she was attracted to him. No doubt he felt that her position as his guest and his cousin's daughter put her off limits. Until he knew the truth about her.

Andrew certainly hadn't hesitated—why should Jack? Granted, he didn't seem to be the sort to wrap it up in pretty lies about love, but that wouldn't change the truth. He'd offer her exactly what Andrew had. Apparently in a gentleman's eyes that was all she was worth. And Andrew had only offered that because nothing better was on offer. He'd made it quite plain that she had little to recommend her to a man of discrimination.

And surely her mother's warnings were sufficient to keep her safe this time? That and her own experience.

The best thing she could do would be to stay out of Jack's...*Mr Hamilton's*...way until she could leave and find respectable employment of her own. Papa would be safe here. There would be nothing to upset him. He would be taken care of far better than she could ever do it. With that library to catalogue and care for, he'd never notice she was gone.

Shivering slightly, she went over to look out at the snow. It was heavier now, hiding the woods and gardens. Cold, so cold. She'd never realised the world was such a chilly place. Perhaps she ought to be grateful to Andrew for teaching her that.

Chapter Three

The following morning was Sunday. Jack stood up as Cressida entered the breakfast parlour. He saw at once that she had dressed for church. She carried her scarlet cloak over her arm and held a bible and prayerbook. All in all she was much tidier this morning, her hair tightly braided and coiled, not a stray wisp or tangle to be seen.

'Good morning, cousin.' She must have got over her annoyance by now. And he, of course, was fully in control. Of himself and everything else. Calm, reserved, the soul of dignity. He smiled determinedly. 'You won't mind if I go on with my breakfast?' He sat down again.

His smile bounced off a cool wall of propriety. 'Of course not. Good morning, sir. Is my father down yet? I assumed that he would wish to attend church this morning.'

Jack took a sip of coffee. 'Dr Bramley finds himself unwell this morning. He—'

'Is his cold worse?' The coolness had dropped from her voice and Jack glanced up. He could not doubt the concern in her voice, her eyes. The outspoken, impertinent chit obviously had a considerable affection for her father.

'It's nothing to worry yourself about,' he said soothingly. 'But he should not be going out until he feels better. I assured him that I would escort you to church myself.'

'Oh.'

Miss Cressida Bramley neither looked, nor sounded, as though this arrangement met with her approval.

'I…I'm not quite sure that I will be going to church this morning,' she said.

Jack's mask slipped a trifle and he glared at her. What the devil had he done now? And what had happened to his resolve?

'Really?' He managed to infuse his voice with boredom. 'Then why have you brought down your bible and prayer-book?'

She glared in her turn. 'I can read the service for myself, sir. There is no need—'

'In a cloak?' He let his amusement show. 'There are fires laid in most rooms, cousin. Obviously you intended to go to church. You will be perfectly safe with me. The village of Ratby is quite close. The closed carriage and a couple of hot bricks will keep you warm this time.'

Heightened colour washed over her cheeks. 'You needn't rub it in, sir. I am quite aware that I ought to have left Papa in the warmth at the inn with our luggage while I drove out here in the gig, but at the time—'

'You should have done *what*?' Jack nearly choked on a mouthful of beef.

'Left Papa at the inn.' She looked at him as though she thought him a bit simple. 'He wouldn't have caught this horrid cold if I'd—'

'Driven an open carriage with an unknown horse, by yourself, over unfamiliar roads, in the depths of winter!' he finished for her. 'For God's sake, sit down and have some breakfast before I spank you!'

Belatedly he realised that as invitations went, this had little to recommend it.

Plainly Cressida thought so, too. Green eyes narrowed

into chips of ice. 'Naturally I am all eagerness to avail myself of such a gracious offer!'

She stalked over to the table and sat down.

'Coffee?' asked Jack, feeling slightly dazed. Where had that surge of protective outrage come from? After all, she had managed the gig, found her way here, and, from all he knew of Dr Bramley, it was highly unlikely that he had been of the least help with either horse or route. If ever a female was capable of looking after herself, it was Cressida Bramley.

She was family, though, and as such he really ought to look after her. Delightful and erudite as Dr Bramley was, he obviously depended on Cressida rather than the other way round. For some reason that bothered him considerably. Almost as much as the knowledge that sitting in the intimacy of a closed carriage with Miss Cressida Bramley for any length of time would be pure torture. A handful of snow would be far more to the point than a hot brick.

'Is there any tea?'

He raised his brows. 'Of course.' Rising to his feet again, he made a fresh pot at the urn and brought it to her. The gentle summery scent of rosewater drifted from her braided hair. It wreathed and beckoned, entwining itself around his senses. Abruptly he put the pot down and moved away. So much for being in control of himself.

'Now, church—' he began, daring to breathe again.

She interrupted. 'There is not the least need for you to put yourself out, sir. I will remain here this morning in case Papa requires anything. And if I wished to attend church I am quite capable of walking there. I drove through Ratby on the way out here. As you say, it is not far.'

Jack took a grip on his temper. 'Cousin, I am not exactly a heathen. I have every intention of going to church myself. And since my head groom will probably refuse to let me use the curricle, we will take the closed carriage anyway.' He shut off every mental and physical reaction to the thought. 'And your father is probably asleep again. The staff will look after him.'

To his chagrin she frowned, nibbling at her lower lip as she mulled it over. He gritted his teeth. No doubt she was looking for a polite way of refusing.

'Oh. Well, in that case, I suppose it's all right.'

Obviously she hadn't found one.

Sitting next to his cousin in church, Jack reflected that he had never had such an unflattering response to an invitation in his life. Usually people liked him, didn't they? *You don't usually tell girls to sit down and eat their breakfast on pain of being spanked.*

That had been a whisker. He very much doubted that his shoulder would permit such a thing. And besides, he'd never raised a hand to a woman in his life. But the hollowness of the threat didn't excuse the impropriety of making it. He concentrated on the lessons, read in the Rector's quiet, assured voice. Something had to give his thoughts a more proper direction than imagining his hand on any of Cressida's curves, let alone her... A rustling of pages and the rumble of feet on wooden boards recalled him with a thump.

Belatedly he realised that the congregation had risen to its collective feet. Blast. It was time for the hymn and he didn't have his book ready.

He was still hunting for the right page when the hymn began and his fingers faltered helplessly in their task. He stood, caught in delight as the knowledge dawned on him that he'd brought a lark to church. Dazed, he listened as Cressida's achingly sweet voice soared effortlessly against the ragged singing of the congregation. It pierced him in its loveliness, haunting, alluring. And she stood, apparently quite unaware of the shock she had dealt him, simply singing, looking straight ahead, not bothering even to glance at her book.

Pulling himself together, he sought hurriedly in his own book for the right page. His suddenly nerveless fingers fumbled and he dropped the book with a thud.

Cressida's book suddenly appeared before him. Flushed with embarrassment at his clumsiness, he muttered a swift thanks and began to sing. He enjoyed the opera when he was in town, but he'd never understood why Ulysses had risked his life to hear the Sirens. Now he knew. Never before had he realised that a girl's voice could entwine itself in a man's senses like perfume.

An accomplishment. That's all it was. One of the skills a young lady ought to have. Nothing else. And he was not about to be snared by a young lady's *accomplishments*.

As they left the church at the conclusion of the service he said politely, 'I don't know when I've enjoyed the hymns quite so much, cousin. Thank you.'

Green eyes, wide with puzzlement, blinked up at him. 'They were lovely tunes, weren't they? But I don't know why you should thank me. I assume the Rector chose them.'

'I meant your voice, cousin. It's quite lovely.'

He snorted to himself. Typical of a female to angle for the more obvious compliment!

'My *voice*?' She looked up at him blankly. 'There's nothing special about it.'

It was Jack's turn to stare. She meant it. She really meant it. She truly didn't think that her voice was at all special.

Dazed, he pulled himself together in time to greet the Rector at the door and present Cressida. In doing so he became fully aware that practically the entire parish was either hovering around the porch or treading on his heels in an effort to discover who Cressida might be. He had absolutely no doubt at all that the Bramleys' arrival in the neighbourhood had been duly noted and commented upon.

'My cousin, Miss Bramley, Rector. She and her father are my guests. Dr Bramley finds himself unwell this morning. A most tiring journey from Cornwall.'

Cressida, he saw, blushed scarlet at his unthinking words. An absurd sense of guilt swamped him. Damn! He hadn't meant to imply that she hadn't looked after her father. Much against his will, he was forced to acknowledge that, given her youth and inexperience, she had done remarkably well. Especially when hampered with a travelling companion who could be counted upon to disburse every penny they possessed to the poor.

The local Squire and his lady came up with their daughter.

Jack groaned silently. Miss Stanhope was the front-running local candidate for the position of Mrs Jack Hamilton. It had all been decided by her very decisive mama. She was an heiress, well bred, well brought up. Her lands would round out his own estates very nicely and, since he had taken no other bride in the last few years, it could only be surmised that he was waiting for Miss Stanhope to grow up.

Jack was only too happy to wait. Until hell froze over. As far as he could see, Miss Stanhope had bearen hell to it by several lengths.

'Morning, Jack. How's that shoulder, m' boy? Glad to see you up and about,' boomed the Squire. 'And who's this? Cousin, did I hear you say?'

Jack felt his hackles rise at the expression of avid interest on Sir William Stanhope's rubicund face as he made the introductions. His wife was eyeing Cressida's worn cloak and morning gown in a way which suggested she already had the chit firmly labelled—*poor relation*—and no danger to her matrimonial plans for himself.

His teeth gritted, Jack presented Cressida.

'Miss Bramley.'

The faint tone of condescension and the way the Squire's lady held out two begrudging fingers sent a flare of anger through Jack. Lady Stanhope's habit of looking down her very long nose at those she considered her social inferiors would have sent most women cross-eyed.

He shot a sideways glance at Cressida, half-expecting her to give Lady Stanhope a set down.

'Lady Stanhope, I'm honoured to meet you.'

Jack blinked at the low, deferential voice. Was this the same little termagant who'd raked him down in the garden when they met, and practically every other time she'd seen him, including over the breakfast cups this morning? He thrust aside the acidic little voice that suggested his own behaviour over the last two days would not have given Cressida a favourable view of *his* manners.

Vaguely he realised that Sir William was repeating himself and responded. 'That's right, sir. No more hunting this season, and if my staff had their way I'd be laid up in bed with a hot brick!'

Sir William chuckled in very masculine way. 'Better ways to warm your bed than that, lad!' Then he cast a rather conscious glance at the ladies. 'Not with your cousin in the house of course, but you know what I mean!'

Smiling determinedly, Jack changed the subject at once by asking after Sir William's hunters. That should get the old boy safely off the dangerous subject of beds and how to warm them.

Nodding occasionally as Sir William thrashed out the benefits of applying fomentations to the leg of an injured horse, he kept track of Cressida's conversation with Lady Stanhope and her daughter.

'*Where* did you say you were from, Miss Bramley? Cornwall? Ah, near St Austell. I have a cousin there. She married *very* well, of course.'

To his absolute horror he heard the words '...position

as a governess, or companion' uttered in unnaturally polite
accents.

Sharply he swung around in time to see Lady Stanhope's nose elevate itself by a few more degrees.

'Well, as to that, I should need to be quite assured of
your credentials, Miss, er, Bramley.'

And even worse, Miss Stanhope's contribution: 'Oh, I
don't think I know *anyone* who has to do that! How lowering it would be!'

His eyes narrowed. 'My cousin is funning you, Lady
Stanhope,' he cut in smoothly. 'She has absolutely no need
to seek employment. Dr Bramley will be remaining with
me to assist with my library and Miss Bramley will naturally remain as well.'

Lady Stanhope appeared to have bitten into a lemon.
'Unchaperoned, Mr Hamilton? I venture to—'

Sir William interrupted. 'Pshaw! Fiddle faddle, my lady.
Jack's a man of honour! No one in their right mind would
think anything of it! Girl's got a father. Clergyman, ain't
he? Used to visit years ago when Jack was a lad. Family!
Nothing in it.'

Jack had the distinct impression that, had a table been
handy, the Squire would have administered a substantial
kick under it to his wife.

Lady Stanhope looked thoroughly unconvinced and said
with grudging insincerity, 'Well, of course, one would not
like to suggest anything in the least improper, but society
does view these things…'

'I'm sure, Lady Stanhope, that your understanding
would count for a great deal,' said Jack basely. The words
nearly choked him, but he had the satisfaction of seeing
Lady Stanhope rolled up. Any appeal to her social influence and standing was a certain winner. The part of his
mind he reserved for cynical comment on social double
standards and out-and-out hypocrisy suggested another,
even more ignoble, reason.

He dealt the death blow without hesitation. 'I should be sorry to think that in having family members to stay, I would in any way be jeopardising either Miss Bramley's reputation or my own.' The effort involved in maintaining a straight face nearly killed him. Especially as he saw all the possible ramifications of the situation occur belatedly to Lady Stanhope.

Before anything else could be said, he made his farewells and hustled Cressida towards the carriage, bestowing polite, if hasty, greetings upon the rest of the congregation.

Cressida kept her mouth firmly shut until the carriage door closed behind them and the horses were set in motion. Then her much-tried control deserted her.

'Just what did you mean by telling Lady Stanhope that I don't need a job?' She had spent the entire walk to the carriage reminding herself not to curse at him and was justifiably pleased at her restraint. There! She could rein in her temper if she really tried. All it took was strength of mind.

'Exactly what I said,' he replied.

Her eyes narrowed at his cool, dismissive tones, but she began the usual litany, *Lord, make me an instrument of thy peace...*

'I consider you to be under my protection...'

'You *what*?'

The Lord's Instrument of Peace exploded in impious fury.

'Not like that!' he snapped. 'You are my cousin—'

'A distant connection!'

'Cousin!' he repeated. 'Your father intends to remain within my household. I can hardly permit his daughter to go out and make her way in the world! You have not the least idea of the dangers you would be exposed to, nor the least idea of how to protect yourself!'

'I'm perfectly capable of looking after myself!'

'Well, you shouldn't be,' he growled.

'And how do you propose to stop Lady Stanhope's gossip?' she asked.

His grin would have incited a saint to violence. Cressida had to lace her fingers together tightly within her battered old velvet muff.

'I already did.' He looked as smug as a fox in a henrun. 'Lady Stanhope is hardly likely to gossip when the end result would be that the neighbourhood's most eligible bachelor would find himself obliged to offer the protection of his name to a poor relation instead of offering for her daughter.'

Cressida took a very deep, careful breath. And another. Then she counted to ten. Satisfied that she had expurgated all the more unladylike elements from what she wished to say, she took another breath and began.

'Might I ask what gives you the idea I'd accept your *obliging* offer,' she asked. Her dulcet tones surprised even her.

'Oh, I've no doubt you'd refuse. At first.'

Her ladylike mask slipped a trifle and she glared. 'I'd refuse—utterly.'

His raised brows made her long to hit him.

'Really? Then it's just as well Lady Stanhope hasn't had time to realise that your intellect is disordered, or your reputation would have been in tatters before we reached the carriage.'

It had been shredded before she left Cornwall, but he didn't need to know that. Instead she managed to ask, with only a hint of sarcasm, 'And might one be informed why not wishing to marry you is evidence of a disordered intellect?'

He shrugged. 'Apparently I am considered to be an eligible match.'

'You're a conceited coxcomb!' The words burst from her. How dare he insinuate that she would leap at the first man to offer like a cock at a blackberry! She swept on in fury. 'Not every woman considers wealth as her primary motivation for marriage. Some consider being able to respect their husband to be more important than a respect for his purse!'

'Are you saying you don't respect me?'

She glared at him suspiciously. Was he daring to laugh at her?

'Let me put it this way,' she said dangerously. 'I always find it difficult to respect a man who offers me a spanking before breakfast! So I'll wish Miss Stanhope joy of you, sir. No doubt you will deal extremely together! Far be it from me to prevent a match so obviously made in heaven!'

This time there was absolutely no doubt. Jack Hamilton stared at her in apparent disbelief for a split second and then fell back against the squabs, laughing uproariously.

'Will that be all, sir?'

'Hmm? Oh, yes. Thank you, Fincham. I won't need you again tonight.'

'Goodnight then, sir.'

'Goodnight.'

The door clicked shut behind Fincham, and Jack eased himself into bed. Being helped out of his clothes was bad enough. Being assisted into bed was unthinkable.

He wriggled his shoulders carefully against the soft feathers in an unavailing attempt to find a comfortable position for his shoulder. And the hot brick wrapped in flannel at his feet was driving him demented. Sir William's words taunted him ceaselessly—*Better ways than that to warm your bed…*

As if he needed the reminder! His body was making no bones about suggesting all sorts of ineligible ways to warm his bed. And all of them were utterly impossible. Never before in his life had he found himself fantasising over the seduction of an innocent. That he could have been doing so in church actually shocked him. He couldn't remember when he'd last been shocked by his own desires. He was used to them by now. Come to think of it, he couldn't remember ever having wanted a woman so much in his entire life.

The whole thing was impossible. He could not, under any circumstances seduce a gently bred girl living in his house who was also his cousin. Not unless he was planning to marry her. And Miss Cressida Bramley was not at all the sort of girl he planned to marry.

She'd drive him mad. Pert, outspoken, far too independent and damnably hot at hand—she was the last woman on earth a man desiring a peaceful life of domestic harmony should marry. Even if he did want her like hell burning. He gritted his teeth. Burning passion was not, in his opinion, a valid reason for matrimony.

She did make him laugh, though. That crack of hers about finding it difficult to respect a man who offered to spank her before breakfast... He smiled at the memory. Most females would have had the vapours after what he'd implied. Not Cressida. She'd ripped back at him and given as good as she got. And then thrown it up at him when he'd had the hide to ask if she respected him.

Still, she wasn't the sort of girl he wanted to marry, so he'd better keep his thoughts safely occupied and his hands off her. He frowned into the darkness. He could keep his hands off her easily enough. Especially if he avoided speaking to her or looking at her. His thoughts were another matter entirely. In fact they were being thoroughly uncooperative—they kept on reminding him that he was lying in bed. Alone.

Over the next three days Cressida came to the conclusion that she'd been quite wrong about Mr Jack Hamilton. Far from showing the least inclination to flirt with her, let alone seduce her, he ignored her presence as much as he could. He greeted her politely at breakfast and thereafter barely spoke to her except in connection with the library, and even then he scarcely glanced at her.

Cressida relaxed. Men intent on seduction were all sweetness and light, flattering. They didn't ensconce themselves at one end of the library and grunt when one brought them a pile of musty old tomes. They didn't brusquely point out a smudge of dirt on one's face and then retire into one of the aforesaid musty old tomes. And they certainly didn't hand one to a seat at the dinner table and then remove their hand as though it had been stung. It mightn't be flattering that he disliked her, but at least it was safe.

She liked him, though. Too much for her own comfort. She liked the consideration with which he treated his staff. Even the lowliest maid would greet him with respectful pleasure. The upper servants were even more respectful— in front of their underlings. But Cressida shook with laughter as she remembered Evans catching his master sneaking back into the house after a walk. The scolding the master of the house had received for not wearing a muffler had been all the funnier for being couched in such polite terms.

And the memory of Jack's—Mr Hamilton's—face as he bore with it, and promised to remember next time, never failed to make her smile. He'd been as meek and mild as a lamb. Which puzzled Cressida. Because generally, she didn't think he was a very meek sort of man. He exploded like gunpowder every time *she* mentioned the word *sling*.

After three days Cressida came to the conclusion that Jack Hamilton considered her too far beneath his touch even to converse with. Yet she couldn't bring herself to dislike him. He treated her father with affection and respect. That was all that mattered. Her birthday was not far off. After that she'd have to leave. If she could find a position. First she had to find someone willing to give her a reference.

* * *

Jack drew a deep breath and opened the library door. It was doubtless the last breath he'd take free of dust until he came out again. And he'd need all his self-control not to watch surreptitiously as Cressida scrambled up and down the ladders. No matter how many times he told himself that he was concerned she'd slip, that he was ready to leap to the rescue, he knew it for a lie. He was completely and utterly fascinated by the tantalising glimpses of shapely ankles, not to mention slender, rounded calves.

He routinely thanked a merciful God for the presence of Dr Bramley at the other end of the library. Not that the old chap would notice anything less disturbing than the rape of all the Sabine women at once, but his presence did somehow help Jack keep a rein on his desires. That, and the rising suspicion that he'd met a female who left Selina and her parlour tricks for dead.

He stepped in and found a scene of charming domesticity, without the soothing presence of Dr Bramley.

Cressida sat in a chair by the fire, her legs curled up under her, not an ankle in sight, sewing. The warmth of the fire had brought a flush of colour to her normally pale cheeks and its flames were mirrored in the deep auburn of her hair. For once she did not have it scraped back into its braids or an equally unflattering bun. It hung loose over one shoulder, half-hiding her delicate profile.

So thick, so silky. A man could slide his hands into it and burn...

Memory froze him. All those times he had unexpectedly found Selina unchaperoned... Then he saw what Cressida was sewing. And forgot everything.

'Just what the bloody hell do you think you're doing?' he roared, slamming the door behind him.

Cressida gave a shriek of surprise, cursed vigorously and sucked her finger. The shirt she was mending fell to the floor, along with the work basket she had knocked off the wine table in her fright. Buttons, thread and pins tumbled everywhere.

Jack viewed the scene with satisfaction. Total confusion; just like himself.

He stalked over and bent to pick up the shirt. It was snatched from his grasp.

'How dare you!' blazed Cressida.

'This is my home,' he informed her, noting a smudge of dust on her nose. 'I'll dare anything I like. And I have maids to do my mending!'

Her eyes widened. 'How very nice for you, sir. I congratulate you.'

Jack throttled the urge to shake her. Or to kiss away the dust. 'The next time I find you doing my mending...' He left the sentence hanging and held out his hand for the shirt.

To his smug satisfaction, she gave it to him without further argument. Hah! Maybe she was learning that he was not to be baited like this. How dare she insinuate herself into his household in this way. Mending his shirts, indeed!

'Nothing to say, Cressida?' He couldn't resist teasing her a little.

'Have I your permission?' she asked sweetly.

'Don't be henwitted,' he growled. Perhaps he had been a little overbearing.

She smiled, and every nerve in his body sat up and screamed a warning. 'You might find it a little tight over the shoulders, but I dare say one of the maids could let it out for you. And lengthen the arms, of course. And I'm not quite sure that it will do up around your neck.'

Green ice glittered in her eyes as she warmed to her theme.

'Of course...' her voice dripped honey '...it's entirely possible that it won't even get over your thick head!'

A horrible suspicion formed itself in Jack's mind. Oh, hell and the devil! Surely not?

He shook out the shirt and bit off a curse. The damn thing was far too small for him. He seriously doubted that he would even get it over his shoulders.

'And perhaps you would be so good as to lend Papa one of your shirts while I make him another, since you have taken such an unaccountable liking to this one, sir.'

Heat washed over Jack's cheekbones in a crimson wave. He couldn't remember ever feeling so foolish in all his thirty-six years. And he certainly couldn't remember the last time he had blushed. If he ever had.

'I…I beg your pardon, Cressida.' The words came stiffly. 'It…it was just that I thought it was my shirt…that you were…' He hesitated.

'Going to ruin it?' she suggested. 'Rip it to pieces? Or sew up the sleeves, perhaps?'

He smiled wryly. His younger sister, Nan, had done just that on several occasions. Sneaked into his room and sewn up all his shirts when he had annoyed her. She had a quick tongue, too.

'Would you?' he asked.

She flushed in her turn. 'I'd be more likely to sew up your mouth,' she shot back at him. 'And you needn't bother apologising. You swear at me all the time and I've had quite enough insincerity to last me a lifetime! At least your language is preferable to that. Now, if you wouldn't mind giving Papa's shirt back to me, I can finish mending it!'

He handed the shirt to her and knelt down beside her chair. Damn it, she was right. He *did* swear at her. And he could hardly explain why.

I beg your pardon, cousin, but I keep swearing at you because I can't take you to bed. As an apology it lacked a certain something.

'What on earth are you doing?'

'Picking up your things.' He suppressed a curse as he pricked his finger on a pin. 'Good lord! How many of these damn—er, dashed pins do you have?' They were everywhere.

'Absolutely no idea,' returned Cressida. 'Why don't you count them while you're down there and tell me? They go in that box.' She indicated a little wooden box and reached down for it. Just as Jack did.

Their heads nearly collided. Their eyes did.

Jack found himself gazing into stormy green eyes, inches from his face. He froze. Such long lashes. She was staring back, her gaze startled. He was close enough to feel her sweet breath on his lips. Shaken, he made the mistake of looking down. Softly curved pink lips parted slightly...would they really taste of raspberries? He leaned closer and raised his hand to her jawline, feathering gentle fingertips over it. They strayed to her throat. Soft, silken. He hadn't known a woman's skin could be quite that delicate. The need to taste her lips throbbed in time to the rhythm of his blood, luring him on. He leaned forward. Just one taste, just one...

Her eyes widened in shock and he heard the sharp intake of breath as she jerked back out of reach and scrambled to her feet, bumping him as she did so.

Taken by surprise, Jack lost his balance and crashed to the floor.

White-hot talons of pain raked his shoulder.

'Bloody hell!' He shut his eyes and set his jaw against all the other curses that rose to his lips and breathed deeply until the nausea subsided. To be replaced by suspicion. *Damn. She hooked you again.*

'Sir?'

He opened his eyes unwillingly to find Cressida leaning over him, the shock in her eyes replaced by worry. Equally fraudulent, no doubt.

'Are you all right? Is your shoulder paining you?'

'Not at all,' he lied.

Her mouth flattened. 'Here, let me help you.'

Before he could protest she was kneeling beside him, her right arm under his left shoulder, trying to lift him to a sitting position. A different sort of pain shot through him as her soft breast brushed against his body. Heat flooded his loins as he sat up.

'What the devil did you do that for?' he asked savagely. Damn the chit and damn his response to her. She didn't even like him, yet she was baiting him just the way Selina had. And even knowing what she was up to didn't help. He rose to the bait every time. Literally.

Cressida felt the heat steal into her cheeks again. What on earth was wrong with her? He'd made a mistake and he'd been trying to atone for it. Of course he hadn't been going to kiss her. What would a man like Jack Hamilton want to kiss her for? He made it quite plain that he disliked her.

She must have imagined that softer glow in his eyes, the dawning smile that had turned her heart over. He was glaring at her now. As for his caress—perhaps she had a smudge of dirt on her face…or, or something. He looked like he'd rather strangle her.

'I…I didn't mean to knock you over,' she said. 'You… you startled me.'

He snorted.

'I'm terribly sorry,' she said. 'I…was mistaken.'

'Mistaken?' He looked puzzled. 'Mistaken about what?'

Too late Cressida realised the trap she had set for herself. She floundered.

'I…er…ah…nothing,' she said shortly.

'Nothing?' He appeared to have recovered all his usual self-command, even sitting on the hearthstone unconsciously rubbing his shoulder.

'Don't do that,' she said, reaching for his hand. 'You'll jar it again.'

She found that her hand was held in a gentle steel vice. A vice that made her hand tremble, sent tingling shocks right through her.

She tugged. 'Let me go!'

'When you tell me what you were mistaken about.'

The steel vice shifted slightly, a large thumb rubbing over the back of her hand.

Cressida trembled. If she tugged hard enough she could free herself. But she might tip him over again, hurt his shoulder.

'Will you promise to let me go and not to laugh if I tell you?' She felt like a complete idiot, and if she didn't end this scene quickly Papa would come back from his rest and find them on the floor together. She shuddered to think of his likely reaction.

'You have my word of honour as a gentleman,' said Jack.

She swallowed. She really hadn't needed the reminder that he was a gentleman.

'I...I...well...I thought you were...goingtokissme.' She finished the sentence at a flat gallop and charged on. 'I realise that it was silly of me and that you don't even like me, but I just thought you were and I didn't want you to, so...I really didn't mean to knock you over.'

'You thought I was about to kiss you?' His voice was even.

'Yes.'

'May I ask what gave you that impression?' Very even. Quite mild.

'I...I don't know...you just looked...as if...as if you were...' She trailed off, hot with shame and embarrassment. Of course he hadn't been.

'Going to kiss you,' he finished. 'And you think I don't like you and that I'll believe you didn't want me to kiss you.'

He levered himself off the ground carefully. Instinctively Cressida reached to help him.

'No!' he snapped. She ignored him and slipped his arm over her shoulder, supporting him as he rose.

He removed his arm and stepped away immediately.

'Do not do that again, Miss Bramley,' he said. 'I am fully awake on all suits. You will find me a difficult mark.'

What was he talking about? And *Miss Bramley*? He'd been calling her Cressida, much to her fury, for days. She was shocked to discover how much it hurt to become Miss Bramley again.

'Not…not help you? Why not? It was my fault you landed on the floor. You mustn't think I will hurt myself. I'm quite used to helping Papa when he has the gout.'

For a moment she thought he might explode. His face reddened and he seemed to swell with affront. Was it somehow dreadfully improper to help him up?

His eventual answer was not at all what she expected.

'Because you were perfectly right.'

Right? About what? Kissing me? Then she knew. He disliked her so much he couldn't bear to have her help him or touch him. *Stupid little fool that you are! Of course he didn't want to kiss you! Andrew wouldn't have either if anything better had offered. He told you so. Freckles, red hair and that nose…*

'I was going to kiss you.'

Shock froze all her wits.

'Why?' she asked blankly. And then cursed herself. Slapping him: yes. Telling him what a licentious beast he was: quite unexceptionable. But asking him why he'd wanted to kiss her? She ought to be in Bedlam.

His voice became colder. 'Gentlemen have these little lapses of taste from time to time. Might I suggest that it is not at all the thing for you to be alone in a bachelor household—'

Pain slashed through her.

'No, you may not!' she interrupted. 'Next time you have one of your *little lapses of taste*, I suggest you go out and bury yourself in a snowdrift for a few hours! In the meantime, I shall give thanks to God that I am not, in the general way, up to your exacting standards!'

Flaming with fury, she swept up the shirt and headed for the door.

'Cressida!'

She swung around.

'Go to the devil! And I much prefer *Miss Bramley*! Good afternoon, sir.'

Jack blinked at the slam of the door and then groaned. Someone ought to have smothered him in his cradle. And if his mother and sister ever discovered just what a nodcock he was making of himself they'd rectify the omission. How on earth was he to explain his confusion to Cressida when he didn't understand it himself?

And in the meantime, how was he to apologise since every time he got near her they had another fight? He swore. She might have a point in recommending a snowdrift. Something had to cool him down! Maybe he had imagined that she was teasing him on purpose. Oh, lord. No doubt she'd gone up to her room. It would be cold up there. Guilt lashed at him. She'd been sitting comfortably by the fire, mending her father's shirt…her *father's* shirt, he reminded himself mercilessly. And he had barged in and practically accused her of trying to trap him into marriage.

He found that he was pacing around the room, restless, unable to settle to the work he had intended to do.

He had a sneaking suspicion that she hadn't had the least idea what he was talking about. For which he ought to be devoutly grateful. Her freckles had been close to dancing in fury anyway.

Her room would be cold, though. The bedchamber fires would not be lit until closer to dinnertime. *Oh, for good-*

ness sake! She can light the fire, can't she? She's not stupid!

His pacing took him past the window seat where Cressida often sat. Especially when he was in the library. He winced. Well away from the fire. She either sat here or was scrambling up and down ladders for her father.

A couple of books lay on the seat. He glanced at the one on top. Hmm. Not his taste. Mrs Radcliffe and…he picked it up to see the other… Good Lord! Southey's *Life of Nelson*. Eclectic, if not downright catholic. A reluctant grin tugged at his lips. Predictability was not one of Cressida's leading traits.

Why didn't she take the books up to her bedchamber to read?

The answer came like a body blow. She felt unwelcome in his home. He kept noticing little things that told him how deeply she felt her poor-relation status. How determined she was not to be thought encroaching. Like these books. She was obviously reading them. Yet they remained there. She never took them up to her room. And she would never ring and ask for the fire to be lit or light it herself.

If he wanted her to have a fire in her room, he would have to light it himself. Or at least arrange for someone else to light it. Cressida wasn't *that* unpredictable. If he tried to walk into her room right now she'd throw something at him. He felt like throwing things at himself.

He crossed to the fireplace and tugged the bellpull. His gaze drifted to the familiar items on the chimneypiece and caught, puzzled. Something was missing. What was it? Then he knew. Where the devil had that little T'ang horse got to? It had been here last night in its place. Where could it be now?

Chapter Four

Cressida stormed up to her room and slammed that door as well. Then she sat down on her bed and clenched her fists. She wasn't going to cry. She *wasn't*. She had nothing to cry about. Just that he thought wanting to kiss her was a lapse of taste.

Scowling ferociously, she went over to the dressing table and stared into the mirror. Her hair wasn't nearly as carrotish as it had once been. It was more auburn now. And since it was winter, the freckles on her nose were mere ghosts of their usual summer splendour. Hardly noticeable, really. But how she hated her nose! It turned up slightly, and there wasn't much she could do about that or her green eyes. She had filled out a bit, though. Actually, she'd filled out a bit too much in places. Her velvet evening gown had been made for a skinny sixteen-year-old. The more ample charms of twenty were nearly bursting out of it. Some lace, perhaps…

She glared at her reflection. There! See? She wasn't attractive at all. Maybe it was a lapse of taste. In which case she ought to be duly grateful.

She sat there for some time, trying to convince herself, only to be interrupted by a discreet tap on the door.

'Who…who is it?' If it was Jack… She looked around for a missile.

'It's Nell, miss. Come to light your fire.'

The door opened and a rosy-cheeked maid came in. She smiled at Cressida and said, 'Master thought as how you might be cold and asked me to light your fire, miss.'

Cressida felt her jaw drop.

The maid, taking silence for assent, dealt quickly with the fire and straightened up. 'There y'are, miss. Master said to ask you if you wanted tea on a tray.'

Tea. On a tray. She couldn't remember anyone, since her mother's death, making a fuss of her. Except Andrew. And that definitely didn't count. Did this?

'I…I don't think…'

The maid smiled. 'Why don't you have a nice rest, miss? I'll bring the tea up later. Just ring when you're ready.'

She bobbed a curtsy and left. Cressida stared at the door, trying to imagine the response of Andrew's mother, Lady Fairbridge, if a maidservant had addressed her with that degree of familiarity. It was even harder to imagine the maidservant addressing Lady Fairbridge with such open-hearted friendliness. Yet she kept on noticing the way Jack's staff looked after him. Fussed over him and his shoulder. Where had they learnt such things?

She could see it drove him to distraction at times, yet he never snapped at them. Just tried to dodge their ministrations without hurting any feelings. She had never seen servants behave like that before. Nor the affection Jack plainly felt for the senior members of his staff.

And now he had sent a maid to light her fire and offer her tea. Why?

To wheedle his way into your good graces, suggested a very nasty, suspicious little voice.

No, that's not like him. Especially if he doesn't like me. He wouldn't bother.

Kicking off her slippers, she curled up on the bed and drew the counterpane over herself. Still pondering the question, she fell asleep.

When she woke up, the deepening shadows told her that the afternoon light was nearly spent. Yawning, she sat up and looked around. Much to her surprise the fire still blazed brightly. How very odd. Surely it would have died down. She must have been asleep for a couple of hours. Had the maid come back? A warmth that had nothing to do with the fire stole through her at the thought that some-one had cared enough to come and build up the fire while she slept. Even a maid.

Stretching deliciously, she swung her legs off the bed— and saw her workbasket sitting on a chair. She frowned. In the dim light it looked odd. What was that on top of it?

She went over and stared. Snowdrops, and the books she had been reading. A bunch of snowdrops tied with a silver ribbon lay on top of the books with a sealed piece of paper tucked under them.

With trembling fingers she reached for the note. Care-fully she broke it and read.

My dear Cressida,

You have every right to be angry with me. I be-haved disgracefully. That was what I meant about a lapse of taste—that I was going to kiss you. Wanting to kiss you is not a lapse of taste.

I hope I found all the pins, but I forgot to count them.

Please accept my apologies.

Jack.

There was no mention of the snowdrops. It was unnec-essary. She lifted them to her face and breathed their fresh-ness. No one had ever given her flowers before… She caught herself up. Andrew had given her flowers. An expensive posy he had bought, probably on a whim, in Truro.

Jack, on the other hand, had gone out on a chilly winter's day with an aching shoulder and found what flowers he could. Simply because he knew he had hurt her feelings. And he had sent up the books, which she would never have dreamed of taking from the library. Was he trying to tell her she was welcome?

She had been right the first time. No one had ever given her flowers before—only a calculated lure.

How is it different? Except that the lure touches your heart this time and not merely your vanity. How can you tell? You were wrong last time and just look at the consequences. Will you risk your father losing this post?

She trembled. Surely this was different.

The differences screamed at her. Andrew's attempted seduction had been carried out in a situation of the utmost inconvenience, from his point of view, in front of an entire community. Jack, on the other hand, had the distinct advantage of having her in his own house. He had every opportunity to seduce her…

Oh, don't be such a confirmed ninnyhammer! Why on earth would he do such a thing? He doesn't even like you, let alone find you attractive. Just because he said he wanted to kiss you…men have these indiscriminate urges. Mama said so. He asked the maid to bring your things up because he felt guilty. Nothing more.

A light tap on the door distracted her.

'Come in.'

The maid put her head in. 'Oh, you're awake. I'll bring up the tea, shall I?'

'That would be lovely. And thank you for building up the fire again. Did you bring my sewing up?' She indicated the workbox.

'Me, miss? Oh, no. I've been in the stillroom helping Mrs Roberts. We all have.' She smiled and left.

He had been into her room. The impropriety of his behaviour crashed into her. He had actually entered her room.
While she was sleeping. And there was no one else on this
corridor. Her father's room was in the same corridor as
Jack's. Well out of earshot, even if he didn't take laudanum as a sleeping draught.

*And I couldn't scream for help anyway. Just look what
happened last time Papa decided to ask a man's intentions.*

She couldn't quite believe that she was thinking this
way about Jack Hamilton. Suspicious, hostile. Just because
a handsome man had admitted that he wanted to kiss her
and had given her a bunch of snowdrops to apologise for
his tactlessness. He was a gentleman to the tips of his
fingers. How could she possibly believe that he would behave so shabbily?

She *didn't* believe it. Just because he had entered her
room? It was his house after all and, even if entering a
woman's room while she slept was the height of impropriety, there was a big jump from impropriety to dishon-
our. She didn't believe it was a jump Jack Hamilton would
make.

But it would be much safer to behave as though she did.
At all costs she must keep her distance. And make sure he
kept his.

By a stroke of Providence, Papa had fallen feet first into
a post that would suit him perfectly. Especially since he
would no longer have any practical need for her own presence. He would be looked after far better than she could
ever manage.

She would take no more risks that might ruin her father's peace. And she would definitely ignore the little
voice that suggested she was even more worried about disturbing her own peace. Because she was as far beneath
Jack Hamilton's touch as a daisy to the sun that warms it.

Jack shifted uncomfortably in his seat and tried to concentrate on what Dr Bramley had to say on the subject of

mediaeval manuscripts. It completely failed to hold his attention. He ached too much.

His shoulder was fine. It hardly twinged at all now, except when he forgot not to use the arm. His problem sat at the opposite end of the table, picking at her dinner. He must have been out of his mind to leave those flowers. Just because the little baggage had somehow managed to convince him that, under her fury at being caught out, she was genuinely hurt.

Of course she hadn't been hurt. If she had, she wouldn't be sitting there in that green velvet gown she always wore to dinner. If ever a gown was built to make the most of a lady's assets, that one was. She was practically popping out of the damn…dashed…thing. She would be if it wasn't for that inadequate scrap of lace pinned in the neckline. All that did was veil her charms, while doing nothing to disguise them.

He couldn't even tell the maid who waited on her to lay out something else. Even *his* servants would gossip if he did that. He grimaced inwardly—dash it all, even he'd gossip!

He had to hand it to her. She was up to all the rigs.

She had scarcely glanced his way all evening since he had handed her to her chair. She had made it plain that she had read his note and accepted his apology. And then she had retreated behind a wall of silence, responding politely when he spoke to her, but offering nothing of her own.

Hah! Probably miffed because you bubbled her.

Her father didn't seem to notice the arctic atmosphere.

'You know, dear boy, that manuscript is far too ornate to be…'

With an effort Jack dragged his mind back to the subject at hand and listened attentively. Dr Bramley was probably right, but…

'What does Cressida think?' he asked. Now she'd have to respond with something more than a *yes* or *no*.

She glanced up from folding her napkin.

'What do I think?' She placed the napkin precisely by her plate. 'I think it is time I relieved you gentlemen of my company and left you to your port.'

Oh, curse it! He stood up, swearing silently.

She rose and went to her father. 'Goodnight, Papa.'

He looked up vaguely. 'Goodnight, my dear. Did you leave the laudanum by my bed?'

Jack caught the faint frown on her brow. Even if she did drive him to distraction, he couldn't deny her protective affection for her father. He had the oddest notion that there was very little she wouldn't do for the old man. It was part of her charm and Jack was very far from denying Cressida's charms. Merely his own reaction to them.

'I did, but, Papa, don't you think—?'

'Thank you, my dear. My stomach, you know.'

She bent to kiss him, providing Jack with a distracting insight into her charms. 'Well, don't take more than a few drops. Goodnight.'

Jack watched her leave the room, his gaze rivetted on the supple line of her back, the graceful, tempting curves of her waist and hips. He would have to do something about this. The more he thought about it, spending a few hours in a nice cold snowdrift had a great deal to recommend it and would be more to the point than a hot brick.

It might serve to remind him that passion could distract a man from all the other ingredients of a suitable marriage—such as interests in common and a comfortable friendship with each other. He shouldn't be thinking of how vulnerable she had looked, sleeping with her cheek cradled in her hand and the quilt slipping off her shoulders. And he shouldn't be thinking of the grateful little wriggle she had given when he tucked the quilt more securely around her.

Damn...*dash* it all, he shouldn't even have been there! He'd make quite sure he never did anything so corkbrained again.

'What the deuce have you got there?'

Jack's voice broke Cressida's concentration.

She looked up from the papers and frowned. How utterly typical of him to change his routine just as she was feeling comfortable with it. She had spent three days carefully avoiding the dratted man and she certainly hadn't expected to see him at this hour. He usually went for a walk after lunch.

No doubt he would think she was encroaching. Maybe she shouldn't have started rummaging through the box, but it was all so interesting, before she'd known it she'd been curled up in the window seat in the pale, wintry sun with dusty old papers strewn everywhere. Papa had slept badly the night before and was a trifle feverish, so she had persuaded him to remain in bed.

'You did say you wanted the library catalogued and everything sorted, didn't you?' she asked.

'Well, yes.' He looked amused. 'But that looks like my great-grandmother's box of papers. There won't be anything interesting in there.'

She snorted. How typical of a man. They always assumed that women had nothing interesting to say or pass on.

'Does it ever occur to you that, without women, you men would starve?' she asked. 'After all, I have noticed that you do like jam. There are several recipes for preserves in here. Plum jam, medlar jelly, even one for quince paste. Although I can't believe quinces would do very well here. Too cold. And you do like your furniture polished. Probably by this, judging by the scent of lavender in the house.' She waved a recipe for beeswax polish laced with lavender at him.

Jack stared at her.

She went on. 'Think about it. Her household-accounts books are here. You can read about all her expenses, how the house was run and who came to stay, even what she wore when they entertained the Duke of Rutland. It's fascinating. You...you know how they *lived*, what they enjoyed, what they had for breakfast. You can *see* it. That's just as interesting as Thucydides and his everlasting Peloponnesian War.'

His entire world tilted. And he found himself wondering what Thucydides had liked for breakfast. He could remember his great-grandmother living in the Dower House. She had died when he was about ten. She liked ham and eggs for breakfast without fail. One morning she asked her maid for a cup of tea instead and died five minutes later without any further warning.

He looked at the papers strewn around the window seat. Some were covered in his great-grandmother's spidery hand. Some looked even older. All her papers had been brought up to the house after her death and placed in this old deed box. Then it had been forgotten. He hadn't thought about the old lady in years. He did now.

He and Nan had liked nothing better than to run down to the Dower House and visit her. She'd always grumbled about how much they ate, even as she filled their plates with cake and biscuits. And they grinned and ignored everything except the twinkle in her eye. Lord, he could almost smell her special spice biscuits now, warm from the oven.

As a child he had wondered how she managed to know they were coming and order the biscuits so that they had just come out of the oven as they arrived. Years later he noticed that the side door he and Nan always used to sneak out of the house was visible from the Dower House drawing room half a mile away. He could just imagine the old lady bustling off to the kitchen and giving orders to the cook. And then going back to await her visitors and grumble that if their noses were any sharper, they'd cut themselves off their owners' faces.

Before he knew it he was picking up bits of paper and scanning them. He looked up to see Cressida watching him oddly.

'Are you looking for something in particular?'

He flushed, feeling remarkably foolish. 'She…she had a recipe for spice biscuits,' he began. And stopped. Impossible to put into words how the memory of those biscuits affected him. It wasn't merely that he wanted to taste them again; somehow they reminded him of his childhood, long days fishing with Nan, learning to ride and visiting the Dower House.

Cressida frowned and picked up a small pile, flipping through it. She set it down again. 'No, that's not it. I was sorting them into categories, you know, herbal remedies…' She looked up with a perfectly straight face. 'There's one here for comfrey salve. You could rub it on your shoulder. When you don't take your sling off.'

'My valet got some from Mrs Roberts,' admitted Jack with a smile. Somehow her teasing felt comfortable. 'He supervises me putting it on nightly!'

Cressida's returning smile warmed him. 'Oh, well,' she said, 'I shan't worry, then. Now, where was I…household cleaners and…ah! here we are…special spice biscuits. Hmm. Cinnamon, ginger, nutmeg.' She looked up with a faint twinkle. 'Does that sound about right?'

Jack's mouth started to water. 'Er…yes. Yes, it does.'

She cast him a mischievous glance. 'Just listen to this!' Her voice took on the reedy accents of old age: 'Tell Cook double batch. Jack and Nan impossibly greedy!'

Still giggling, she scrambled off the window seat and headed for the door.

Jack felt suddenly bereft. 'Where are you going?'

She turned back with a smile. 'To my room, of course.

Your great-grandmama's writing is a little hard to make out. I'll copy this out and give it to Cook. You can have your spice biscuits for afternoon tea.' The smile turned wistful. 'Things like that are important, you know. Every time I wear a piece of Mama's jewellery, I think of her. I dare say these biscuits are just the same. Maybe *your* great-grandchildren will remember them one day.'

With that she was gone, leaving Jack staring after her. How in Hades did she understand what he felt when he hadn't even been able to put it into words? And how the *devil* could she make a biscuit recipe seem as important a part of his family's traditions as the coat of arms over the fireplace? He shook his head and went back to the box of papers.

Then he paused. This was something Cressida was doing. She obviously found it interesting. Perhaps she wouldn't like it if he interfered. Reluctantly he put the papers down. He should let her get on with it in her own way.

But not in the blasted window seat. She needed a desk. Then she'd have space to sort the piles out and somewhere to write.

He looked around the library. His father's *bureau plat* that he used now stood near the fireplace, absolutely littered with books and papers. And there was another desk that he had cleared for Dr Bramley, similarly festooned with papers, manuscripts and books. Oddly enough, Dr Bramley's desk was somewhat more organised than his own. Probably because Cressida helped him.

There was nothing in here; but what about that writing table in his mother's private sitting room? Perfect. It had one drop side so it didn't take up much room when not actually in use. And if it were placed here, at right angles to the window, Cressida could use the desk when she needed it, or read on the window seat if she wished. He had a funny feeling that she liked the window seat. Perhaps because he had always liked it.

She had looked so comfortable, sitting there with the sun on her hair. In that light there had been just the suspicion of a scattering of freckles on her nose, oddly childish and endearing. And when she'd first glanced up at him, her eyes had that oddly focused, yet abstracted, look her father had when he was interrupted. As though she had been dragged back from another world. He liked seeing her there. She looked…right. Of course, when it was too cold over here, he could insist she came to the fire…

Something else occurred to him. She hadn't choked him off, found an irreproachable excuse to be elsewhere as she had without fail since he'd been addlebrained enough to enter her bedchamber. He hadn't realised quite how much he looked forward to seeing her. To having her tell him he ought to be wearing a sling.

Determinedly he got up and went to the bell pull. He'd have the table brought in before she got back. And he needed to make quite sure she knew it was for her own use. He began to consider exactly what she would require and a queer sense of satisfaction warmed him. Complete. That was it. He felt complete.

Cressida stared at the elegant mahogany writing table. It stood at right angles to the window seat and all her papers had been placed neatly upon it. Where on earth had it come from?

A discreet cough interrupted her wonderment.

'Is it in the right place, Miss Cressida?'

She turned and found Evans smiling at her in a most avuncular way.

'Oh, oh, yes! But…'

'The master assured us that was the right spot, but if you'd like it moved…'

How had Jack known how much she loved the light in

the window seat? This way she could read there and move to the desk when she needed to write…

'Oh, no, it's perfect,' she assured Evans. 'But who moved my papers?' Her fingers flickered over them. Yes, they were all in their piles, just as she had sorted them.

Evans chuckled. 'Mr Jack did that. Wouldn't let us touch them. He said as how you'd found old Lady Kate's biscuit recipe and were taking it to Cook.' His smile became reminiscent. 'I remember those biscuits. Cook wouldn't. She only came twenty years ago. Quite a newcomer, but I dare say she'll manage.'

A giggle escaped Cressida. Twenty years, and he could still describe the cook as a *newcomer*! Then she saw the twinkle.

'How long have you been here, Evans?'

The twinkle deepened. 'Me, Miss Cressida? I was born here. My old dad was butler to Mr Jack's granddad. When I was a lad Lady Kate was already down at the Dower House. She made those biscuits for his dad before Mr Jack and Miss Nan.' He blinked slightly. 'Now, if that table's right, I should be getting back to my pantry.'

Cressida sat down at the table and stared blindly at the neatly arranged papers. He'd done it himself. He'd made quite sure her papers weren't disturbed and he'd given her a space to work. With shaking fingers she reached out to touch the little brass standish. He had thought of everything. Sand in the pounce-box, ink, quills, everything. Even a steel pen-trimmer so the ink wouldn't sputter. A lamp.

Why? Why had he bothered?

Then she remembered the way he had sat with her on the window seat, his delight when she had found the recipe for him. She had always been aware of his attraction for her, but she had ignored it, telling herself he disliked her, that he was overbearing, bossy.

There was nothing overbearing about the man who had

sat there as excited as a little boy at the prospect of a treat, for all he'd tried to hide it. And the man who had found her a desk and then gone to the trouble of equipping it? She shuddered to think of what her foolish heart could do with that sort of encouragement.

He was just being kind.

She groaned. That sort of observation was useless. There was nothing wrong with him being kind. It was an endearing trait, especially when free of any hint of condescension. Except that to fall in love with Mr Jack Hamilton would be about the most henwitted thing she could possibly do.

Just the thought that he might be coming to like her a little warmed her. Literally. Even her feet felt warm. She frowned. How very odd. So far from the fireplace, this corner of the room was usually rather chilly, yet her feet did feel warm.

Puzzled, she bent down and looked under the desk and stared in disbelief at the brass box with its pierced sides and lid. An old-fashioned foot warmer. Her heart shook within her. He'd even filled it with embers.

She sat up slowly and stared unseeingly at the standish. She would have to be careful. It would be so easy to kick that box over and embers could very quickly become a dangerous all-consuming blaze.

Jack was heading back to the library when Evans caught him. He'd left Cressida to discover the desk for herself, but now he wanted to see her. See if she liked it. Had he remembered everything?

'Ah, Mr Jack. There you are.'

At the butler's triumphant tones, Jack turned warily.

'Yes, Evans? Is there something…?'

Then he groaned. Evans had his *visitors* face on. 'Not now, man! Who is it?' Evans could deny him, say he'd gone out for a walk. He would if that would make the old chap feel better. Then he saw the admonishing frown.

'The Stanhopes, sir.'

Blast! Evans only called him *sir* when he wished to remind him of his obligations.

'Oh, very well!' he grumbled. The Stanhopes! No doubt with Miss Stanhope's everlasting eyelashes raising a breeze calculated to send his shoulder into spasms.

'Where did you billet them?'

Evans's outraged expression put him right at once. 'The drawing room. Of course. Sorry, Evans. I'll go at once. Have some tea sent up.'

A thought struck him. 'Oh, Evans—you might mention to Miss Bramley that I have visitors. Tell her that tea will be served in the drawing room.'

A visit of ceremony from the Stanhopes would be far more entertaining if Cressida were there. Besides, it would serve to demonstrate to Lady Stanhope that he regarded Miss Bramley as family. *Not* a poor relation.

The first thing to go wrong was that her ladyship had decided to push the pace a little on his pursuit of Miss Stanhope.

'I understand it is *all the crack*, as you younger people say, for ladies to drive themselves. I thought perhaps we, Sir William and myself, might presume upon our long friendship and ask if you would mind very much showing dear Alison how to handle *the ribbons*.' She gave a tinkle of laughter. 'Dear me! The expressions one must use! I believe one must handle them *in form*.'

Jack thought his own expression must be quite something, but he choked back the instinctive response that, yes, he would mind very much. He'd seen dear Alison's hands on a horse's mouth when she rode and the thought of entrusting his horses' delicate mouths to her was enough to make him blench. The confounded wench didn't even *like* horses. He'd never seen her pet her mount at all, let alone speak to it, or encourage it. Miss Stanhope only communicated with a horse via her whip and spur.

He was in the middle of denying himself the honour of attending to Miss Stanhope's education when he discovered that Evans had sent in the spice biscuits, along with the usual sandwiches and scones. Sir William, he knew, adored biscuits. Dash it all, he'd once seen the man demolish a whole plate of shortbread! Where on earth was Cressida? If she didn't show her front soon, all the biscuits would be gone. Even as he watched, Sir William started on his third.

Still fending off disaster... 'Do but consider, Lady Stanhope, the dangers attending a young lady driving herself!' He racked his brains for some way of distracting Sir William from the biscuits.

'Have you tried the scones, Sir William? The blackberry jam was particularly good this year.' Good God! He sounded like his own mother.

Sir William waved his efforts at hospitality aside. 'Don't you fret yourself about me, m' boy. I'll do very nicely with these biscuits!'

Jack watched with barely concealed hostility as several more biscuits met their end. How many more could the man eat in the time remaining? A visit such as this should not last more than half an hour. Stealing a surreptitious look at the gilt clock on the chimneypiece, Jack calculated that there were at least fifteen minutes to go and that there wouldn't be a single biscuit left. No doubt Cressida had decided to abandon him to his fate and remain safely in the library.

On cue, Lady Stanhope asked, 'And where is your little cousin, Miss...Miss Brambly, is it not?'

'Miss *Bramley*,' said Jack, with icy emphasis, 'is in the library, I believe.'

Lucky wench! Except that she was missing out on the biscuits.

'Ah, I see,' said Lady Stanhope. 'Very wise. And I dare say she is more comfortable taking her tea there. I had a cousin who had to be *told* it would be more agreeable if she took her meals in the library. So unpleasant. She actually came to the drawing room! Such airs as she gave herself!'

The inference that Miss Bramley was being kept in her place nearly choked him.

Hanging on to the tenets of hospitality, he said politely, 'Naturally, since I usually take my tea in the library, it is very much more comfortable if my *guests* do so as well.'

Changing the subject, he asked when the Stanhopes were planning on removing to town for the Season.

'Oh, well, as to that. I am not quite decided when we shall go up,' confided Lady Stanhope. 'To be sure, it was most enjoyable last year, and dear Alison did very well, very well indeed—so kind of you to dance with her—but it was so tiring for her. We might go a little later this year.'

Jack's shoulder went into spasms at the mere thought of dancing with Miss Stanhope again. He made immediate plans to spend the Season buried in Leicestershire. The countryside was prettier than London in spring anyway.

'And you, sir? Will you be going up to town early?' Miss Stanhope cast a languishing glance at him, lashes aflutter.

Jack ruthlessly trampled his innate honesty. 'Oh, at the earliest opportunity, Miss Stanhope.' He could almost hear their plans undergoing rapid revision at this thoroughly misleading reply. Excellent. He'd make all the arrangements to go up, he'd even remove to his lodgings in town if necessary. Then, the moment the Stanhopes were safely ensconced in whatever house they had hired, he could come back. Now all he had to do was persuade Sir William to leave the biscuits alone.

He barely stifled a groan as Miss Stanhope reached for a biscuit. Lord! If she started in on them! Somehow he had to get rid of his unwanted guests.

Inspiration struck as her hand hovered greedily over the plate.

'Good God! There's that dashed mouse again! Cheeky little beggar.'

Feminine squawks of outrage rent the air and Jack, to whom such noises were usually anathema, viewed the success of his admittedly shabby stratagem with ill-concealed triumph. Jerking back in horror, Miss Stanhope had knocked the wine table. Even as he watched, it tottered and fell, scattering biscuits and Sir William's tea across the carpet.

The visit came to a swift end. Miss Stanhope and her mama evinced such an ardent desire to remove themselves from the vicinity of a mouse that Jack wondered about the advisability of actually importing a few rodents. There must be some in the stables, and if they actually saw one next time…

He saw them out with an apology whose graciousness was only rivalled by its insincerity.

Then he turned back to survey the casualties. The top of the wine table had hit the fender, adding a new dent to the piecrust edge. Nothing to worry about there. It was a shame about the broken tea bowl and saucer, but the plate hadn't broken and who cared about a few broken biscuits? They'd be better than no biscuits.

He piled the wounded on to the plate and headed for the library again, still weighing the advantages and disadvantages of mice.

Chapter Five

Cressida looked up from her desk as Jack entered the library. She stiffened, half-expecting to see the Stanhopes troop in behind him. Then she frowned, refocusing on Jack.

Why on earth was he carrying a plate of...he came closer...biscuits? Worse—why was he smiling in just that particular way that made her heart turn upside down? Despite the foot warmer, she felt a chill ripple through her.

She mustn't fall in love with him. She mustn't.

'Have...have your visitors left?' Curse her voice! Did it have to wobble like a jelly just because he had walked into the room? Apparently it did. And she was tolerably certain that had she been standing, her knees would have wobbled with it. Because he was still smiling at her as he lowered his big frame on to the window seat and had put the biscuits beside him with an inviting gesture.

'They have, thank God,' he said, stretching out his long legs. 'Coward! You might have come in. I barely saved the biscuits for you!'

For her? He'd saved them for her?

'I...thought I should get on with shelving the books Papa had finished.' It had the merit of being partly true. She had shelved them. It had taken, oh, all of ten minutes.

She hurried on. 'I must thank you for the desk, sir. I am very much obliged to you.'

'Are you?' His deep voice stroked her senses.

'Well, yes. Yes, of course I am,' she said, trying to ignore the shivers of pleasure in her heart. 'It…it was very kind of you. You thought of everything.'

He smiled and she nearly fled. It was worse than the last one. Warm and inviting. Tempting beyond all belief.

'Then come and sit beside me and have a biscuit.' The smile deepened, enough for a foolish girl to drown in. 'Tell me what else you found in Lady Kate's box.'

She swallowed hard. After all, he had sat with her on the window seat earlier and the ceiling had remained in place. It wasn't Jack that was dangerous, merely her own silly fancies. As long as she remembered that he was simply being kind, she would be safe.

'I found a recipe for apricot ratafia,' she offered.

'You surprise me,' he said drily. 'She loathed the stuff. Always drank her brandy unadulterated. Would you like a biscuit?'

'Yes, please.' She took one from the plate and the faint, but unmistakable, aroma of nutmeg teased her. 'Oh! Are these…?' She bit into it and smiled. Lady Kate's biscuits. No wonder Jack had remembered them all these years.

She finished the biscuit and turned to him unguardedly, smiling up at him. Then she saw his eyes. They were all she could see. Heated and intent. On her. She knew what he was about to do. Every nerve, every muscle sang with the knowledge. Her brain screamed a warning. *Run!* Her heart, useless organ, had melted and taken her body along with it. She stayed.

He leaned forward and took her lips in the gentlest, sweetest caress imaginable. She stilled in shock, her lips parting on a soft gasp of surprise. A large hand framed her jaw with exquisite care and she found her head tilted back even as an arm like steel encircled her and drew her closer.

Dazed wonder held her motionless. Not frozen—spreading heat surged in her blood. Her breath jerked in as his tongue traced the shape of her lips in a silky caress.

And then her body responded instinctively. She pressed closer yet and opened her mouth a little more, innocently pleading.

Her response was more than Jack's very rocky self-control could take. Lord, but she was sweet. And the sensation of that trembling mouth opening beneath his was a temptation to make strong men weak. Even her shock, and he could practically taste that, felt sweet. With a groan of pleasure he took what she offered, deepening the kiss and sliding his tongue over hers, gently plundering.

His mind reeled. She tasted of biscuit, of summer, of Cressida. And of desire.

Need ripped through him in a wave of heat that shocked him. He barely retained enough control to pull back before it swamped him, but he did it. He forced his arms back to his sides and dragged his mouth from the soft surrender of hers with every muscle screaming in protest. Hard as iron, his body rebelled savagely against the dictates of honour. Breathing hard, he stared down at her as her eyes slowly fluttered open.

What on earth was he to say? He hadn't meant to kiss her, but that smile…it was more than flesh and blood could resist. How could he apologise? He couldn't read the expression in her eyes. They were shuttered, but her mouth, soft and pink, quivered slightly.

'Excuse me, sir.'

Excuse me, sir?

He watched in stunned disbelief as Cressida stood up and walked from the library without another word.

Excuse me, sir? What the hell sort of a response was that?

* * *

In the quiet chill of her room Cressida made her decision.

She had to avoid him. Totally. She must never be alone with him again. Not because she feared him, but because she feared her own response. Wonderingly she touched her lips and felt an echo of pleasure. She had thought kisses to be something a man took and a woman endured. With Jack she had been invited to share.

Her fingers fiddled aimlessly with the fringe on her shawl. She had to face the truth: with Andrew, her danger had come from him, from the fact that he had attempted to force her acceptance of his demands. With Jack, the danger came from within, from her own desire to accept whatever he might be prepared to offer.

Worse, it was not just a physical desire she felt. She enjoyed being with him, teasing him, laughing with him and stopping him using his arm. In short, she cared about him. From caring it would be a very short step to love.

A step that would lead straight over a cliff. A small, frightened corner of her mind whispered that she was already poised to make that step, that her weight had already shifted. Somehow she had to pull herself back. It was one thing to be pushed to the brink of disaster, quite another to leap over oneself. Surely she wasn't that foolish. Was she?

Jack glared at the empty corner near the window seat. As far as he could tell Cressida had not used her desk at all. She no longer sat in the window seat. She no longer browsed on her own account, but came to the library only with her father and she confined herself strictly to helping him.

She had even taken to breakfasting in her room. On tea and toast he had ascertained. Dash it all, she'd starve to death! She was always hungry in the mornings, but now she never came down.

He knew why: Dr Bramley often came down late and Cressida had no intention of finding herself alone with her host.

Excuse me, sir.

He shouldn't have kissed her. She'd responded, though. Hadn't she? His body ached with longing as the memory of her softly surrendering lips coursed through his blood. And her shock.

Memory took him back further. To the day he'd found her mending her father's shirt and nearly kissed her. She hadn't wanted him to kiss her then. She'd said as much. Maybe she hadn't wanted him to kiss her at all. Maybe she was avoiding him to make quite sure it didn't happen again.

Didn't she know she only had to *tell* him?

An infuriated growl escaped him. Hell! *He* didn't know it. How should she? He ought to be grateful to her for removing temptation from his path, but damn it all—he missed her!

He missed her flitting up and down the ladders, missed her constant queries and arguments about the most logical places to shelve books. He missed her laughter and, above all, he missed *her*. The sheer fact of her being there.

It didn't help that he wanted to kiss her again. Resolutely he closed his mind to all the other things he wanted to do with her.

He couldn't understand it. The whole situation defied all logic. He had never been the sort of person to be ruled by his desires. If a desire was inconvenient, or its fulfilment would be dishonourable, one stepped away from it. Without hesitation. Certainly one did not wander about snapping at all and sundry as if one had a permanent headache. Which one did, of course, owing to unrelieved tension and a build up of sleepless nights.

Perhaps she'd told her father where she could be found?

Startled at the carefully phrased question, Dr Bramley gazed around the library.

'Dear me. Isn't she here? Hmm…no… Wait a moment, she did say something about going out…for a walk or some such nonsense. But she brought me enough books to keep me going for the time being. She can put them back on the shelves later, I dare say, so don't worry that we'll get behind, dear boy.'

Jack suppressed a curse. Cressida knew perfectly well that he spent a couple of hours on estate business in the mornings before coming to the library. So she came down early, did as much as she possibly could, left her father supplied with a mountain of books and fled. Before the owner of the books showed his front.

Tactically he had to applaud her. After he had wrung her neck. But to do that he'd have to find her. So far he had not had the least success in tracking her down. She had to be in the house somewhere. She couldn't possibly have been serious about going out. It was far too cold for her to be outside. She'd catch her death!

He frowned. Headstrong little peagoose! He'd better make sure. One of the servants would know if she had gone out…

Jack shook his head as he remembered this, striding towards the stables. Cressida ought not to be wandering about alone beyond the house and gardens. And God alone knew where she had gone to. Certainly neither her father nor the servants knew where she was. Jack took scant comfort from Evans's assurance that *Miss Cressida was well wrapped up, sir.*

He'd have to find her and see for himself, make quite sure she didn't do this again. It was his duty as her cousin, her host, the head of her family… Oh, devil take it! He just wanted to see her.

His mind froze, recalling another girl who had tantalised, held out glimmering lures and then retreated in maidenly coyness. Was Cressida playing that game after all? He couldn't quite believe it, yet all the outward signs were there. And, by God, it was working! Here he was, running after her like a puppy with a ball!

His steps slowed. Perhaps he should return to the house and ignore her ploy, if ploy it was. Then he shook his head. No. Even if she was a scheming little hussy, she was, in a manner of speaking, under his protection. She ought not to be out on such a cold day. And, no matter what Clinton had to say on the matter, he was going to have a horse saddled so that he could go after her.

He set his jaw. Cressida was avoiding him again. She had been for two days. Ever since he'd had the table brought in for her, she had adopted an air of cool propriety. She agreed politely with whatever he said, offered no opinion of her own and when he had accidentally knocked his shoulder in her presence, had not so much as muttered the word *sling*.

He shouldn't have kissed her, of course. That had only added to his confusion.

Jack swung into the stable yard, swearing under his breath.

He'd never known anything like that kiss. Lord, he'd always expected kissing an untutored innocent to be rather boring. The jolt of desire that shot through him at the sweet hesitation as she accepted his lips had shocked him witless. He'd thought he knew what it was to want a woman. He hadn't had the least idea. Never before had he wanted, damn it, *needed* a woman to the edge of insanity. His body hardened in a rush just thinking about it.

If he'd been thinking clearly, or rather, thinking at all, he'd never have kissed her. As it was, now she probably expected an offer from him! He muttered a few more curses. That would be insanity: allowing his unruly passions to choose his bride for him.

Where the devil was Clinton? Might as well get the

argument over and done with. It would serve to take his mind off the increasingly permanent pain in his breeches. Not to mention the cynical voice suggesting that young ladies in expectation of an honourable proposal from a wealthy man did not commonly avoid him as though he had sprouted horns and a tail. Unless, of course, she thought that by so doing she could fret him into offering faster… He ground his teeth and changed direction. He'd check on Firebird first, *then* yell for Clinton.

'Just keep his nose out of my book, Danny. I'm nearly done. Next time I'll leave the sugar outside!'

The unexpected voice coming from his injured hunter's stall stopped Jack dead in his tracks. What the devil was Cressida doing in there?

'Aye, Miss Cress'da. Got a long nose 'as Firebird.'

Good God! That was Daniel, Clinton's youngest boy. What were the pair of them up to?

A soft chuckle set his heart pounding. 'He certainly has! A long whiskery nose. I couldn't have done this without you. And I've got a surprise here for you as well.'

An embarrassed and wholly unintelligible mutter followed.

'I wouldn't dream of offering you money, Danny. Hold still…'

A long pause, followed by, 'There. All done.'

The sound of tearing paper.

'I did two. Do you think your parents would like this?'

There was a gasp. 'Cripes, Miss Cress'da! It looks jus' like me! I didn' know you was doing that! Thought you was jus' doin' old Firebird. You shoulda tol' me.'

Cressida's warm laugh greeted this. 'No. You'd have gone all stiff. Give it to your parents.'

'Aye, miss. Can I let Firebird go now?'

'Just let me put my book away safely…there. All right you big, slobbering idiot, here it is.'

Jack looked over the half-door to discover Danny Clinton, clutching a piece of paper, perched on the edge of the manger and Cressida seated on an upturned bucket as she fed sugar to his favourite hunter.

Something inside him turned over at the sight. The big chestnut towered over her, yet she sat with his long aristocratic nose in her lap, rubbing his ears with her free hand and crooning nonsense to him as he crunched up the sugar.

'Morning, Mister Jack,' piped Danny.

Something resembling a squeak escaped Cressida's lips and she jerked around. Firebird just crunched faster and shoved his face against her, imperiously demanding more sugar.

'Hullo, Danny,' said Jack, smiling as he entered the loose box.

He turned his attention to Cressida. 'There you are, my dear. Your father was wondering where you were.'

Her eyebrows nearly disappeared into her hairline as he uttered this lie.

'Really? Was that before or after you drew his attention to my absence?'

'Look at this, Mister Jack,' enthused Danny. 'Miss Cress'da did it for me mam and da'.' He held the sketch out proudly.

Biting down hard on all the things he would have liked to say to Cressida, Jack took the proffered sketch. And stared.

'Good God!'

Anyone who looked at this sketch and couldn't see that the lad was bubbling over with mischief would have to be blind. Anyone who had ever seen Danny would recognise him instantly from this. It was uncanny. Somehow, in a few strokes, Cressida had conveyed all the boy's energy and his love of horses. The grubby hand stroking a satin nose was somehow reverent. And the horse; Cressida had seen straight past the powerful, raking hunter to the gentle giant whiffling at an urchin's pockets.

He looked down at Cressida as he handed the drawing back to Danny, but she was busying herself putting all her sketching equipment away. From what he could see the back of her neck was absolutely scarlet. Unfortunately for his peace of mind she was bent over nearly double finding everything.

He swallowed hard. At least she was well wrapped up instead of wearing summer muslins. He hated to think of what the sight of that sweetly rounded bottom would do to him under those circumstances.

'Tell your mother I'll get that framed for her if she would like, Danny,' said Jack, sending a heartfelt prayer of thanks to God for the lad's restraining presence as well as Cressida's voluminous skirts.

Danny swelled. 'Coo. A picksher of me on the wall! Not but what it's really of Firebird. I was jus' holding him acos he wouldn't keep his nose out of Miss Cress'da's face. Bye, Mister Jack! Bye, miss. An' thank you!'

Jack forced himself to think about that as he watched Cressida pack up. Absently he scratched Firebird's ears. Some artists might have seen it like that. Many would probably not have bothered even to include the boy, let alone make him such an integral part of the sketch. They would have just concentrated their efforts on the magnificent hunter. Cressida had elected to show the affectionate bond between the two, the intangible link that was symbolised by a grubby hand on an aristocratic nose.

And she had sent the boy away with a sketch for his mother. Jack did not doubt for one moment that Bess Clinton would have the treasure framed to hang in pride of place in the parlour. Did Cressida have the least idea what a priceless gift she had bestowed?

He watched as Cressida straightened up and turned to face him. It didn't help much. She was slightly flushed from bending down. All he could think of was how much more flushed she'd be if he kissed her the way he wanted to. Gently at first, of course—but after she'd got over the surprise and responded to him… His whole body shook with longing. Madness. He'd be in over his head the moment his lips touched hers.

'Were you looking for me? Did Papa want some more books fetched?'

The quiet question dragged him back from his discreditable imaginings. He was damned if he'd admit to her that he had been looking for her. That he'd been worried.

'Your father has plenty of books,' said Jack. 'And although I did wonder where you were, I came to the stables to see Firebird, since it is my fault he has that bandage on his leg.' God in heaven keep him from saying, or worse, doing, the wrong thing. Stick to horses. They were always a safe subject. No one could get into trouble talking about horses.

The flush on Cressida's cheeks flared anew. How could she have possibly thought that he would look for her. No doubt he hadn't really wondered where she was. That was just a polite fiction.

'I'll get out of your way then.' She headed for the door, carefully giving Jack a wide berth.

Not wide enough. Shock tingled through her body as she felt her wrist caught in a gentle, inescapable grip. She stiffened, her immediate instinct to tug herself free. Then she realised; he had used his right hand. If she pulled hard enough to free herself, she would hurt him. Again.

She stood still. 'You are cheating, sir.' With a massive effort she kept her voice polite.

'Cheating, Cress? In what way?'

Ignoring the assault on her name as a red herring, she answered. 'You are holding me with your right hand. You must know perfectly well that if I try to free myself I'll hurt you.'

Damn his eyes! How dare he smile like that!

'I did, of course, but I can't say I was sure that you did.

Call it a gamble, my dear. Once in a while they pay off. Tell me—do you do much sketching.'

'Not enough,' she said shortly. 'I'm very out of practice.' Would he never release her wrist?

'My mother used to sketch a great deal,' said Jack. 'Come to think of it, she still does.'

The affection in his voice struck at Cressida. 'Your… your mother is still alive?' She had never thought of Jack as having a mother. She knew his father was dead.

He looked surprised. 'Oh, yes. She lives in London most of the year now.'

'Oh, not here?'

Jack shook his head and said with a grin, 'No. Mama says if I want a woman to manage the house I can marry one. But I keep the Dower House prepared for her. She was here for Christmas with my sister, Lady Barraclough, and her husband and all their family. They left just before I broke my collarbone, thank God.'

'Pardon?'

'They fuss,' explained Jack. 'Worse than you and the staff.'

'I don't fuss.' This came out between gritted teeth.

'No? Then why haven't you thumped me on the shoulder and jerked your hand free? Or wouldn't that suit your plans?'

What plans?

Recovering quickly, she riposted, 'Good manners and common decency! Don't you recognise them?'

He grinned. '*Touché*. My mother and sister would be proud of you.'

She ignored that. The female relatives of eligible gentlemen were not wont to approve the daughters of impoverished clergymen.

'Was there something you needed to know, or would you be so kind as to release my wrist? Stop that, Firebird!'

The big chestnut, despairing of any more sugar, had started tugging at his bandage with his teeth.

Jack swore. Releasing Cressida, he stepped forward, caught the horse's halter and brought his head up.

'Idiot horse. You have to leave that on a bit longer, old son. It's there to help you!'

She should have bolted, but temptation shimmered.

'My, my,' said Cressida. 'Just like a certain gentleman who won't wear a sling, perhaps?'

Jack glared at her as he petted Firebird.

'Not at all. I fail to see any resemblance.'

'Really,' asked Cressida. 'I can see several. Stubborn, quite incapable of taking advice. Nosy, of course. Shall I go on?'

Jack shook his head. A dangerous light glinted in his eye. 'Before you do, I ought to point out one salient difference.'

'Oh? Intelligence?' asked Cressida in dulcet tones, ignoring the warning in his voice. If she was impertinent enough she'd put him off her completely. Gentlemen, she had noted, hated backchat.

'Apart from that, of course,' said Jack with a slow smile. 'Firebird is a gelding.'

Cressida felt her cheeks burn as she took in his meaning and saw the devilish glint in his eye.

'Oh…ah…is…does that make a big difference?' Somehow she'd managed to blush even more deeply.

Jack appeared to be choking, but he straightened his features almost at once. 'Quite a big difference,' he said gravely.

She hardly knew where to look. On consideration, his face seemed the safest option, but the bland expression, so wickedly at odds with the twinkle in his eyes, was hardly reassuring. Apparently she had said something monumentally stupid.

'Quite a number of Mama's sketches are still here,' he

added conversationally. 'Indeed, she did quite a few of my father's favourite hunters. Perhaps you might like to see them?'

Shock and then anger flared. Her own mother's well-loved voice echoed from the vaults of memory,

Above all, my love, be very suspicious of any gentleman offering to show you his…etchings, indeed any artworks, or his family jewels for that matter…

Mama had never explained precisely what these terms alluded to, but she had made quite sure Cressida knew how a virtuous young lady should respond.

She spoke as coldly as she possibly could.

'How very kind of you, but if that is tantamount to offering to show me your…*etchings*, then I must beg to be excused. I fear that I do not deserve such an honour.'

His dropped jaw afforded her considerable satisfaction. No doubt he had not expected her to understand. Well, now he would know that she did, that she was no ignorant miss for his plucking, but knew precisely what she was about. Even if she didn't know why etchings and family jewels were so dangerous.

He took one swift step towards her and stopped, hard control in every line of his powerful frame. Her breath came in on a gasp as she registered the clenched fists, his eyes like shards of steel. She *wouldn't* step back. How dare he intimidate her like this?

'If you weren't your father's daughter and my guest…' He paused for breath. And then continued, each word clipped and furious. 'I'd put you over my knee and spank you for that piece of vulgarity!'

'Why, you—'

He cut her off ruthlessly. 'And if you were a man I'd call you out. Instead—' Abruptly his hands gripped her shoulders and he jerked her forward, bringing his mouth down on hers in a hard, brief kiss. As suddenly he released her and stepped back. 'And that was definitely a lapse of judgement, not taste!' his voice grated. With that he turned on his heel and strode out, slamming the stable door behind him.

Cressida leaned against the side of the stall and wondered if her insides would ever stop shaking.

Jack stalked out of the stable yard, barely acknowledging Clinton's startled greeting beyond a grunt. Plainly, horses were not a safe subject after all. And if he didn't get himself under control soon, he was going to murder someone—probably Cressida. If he didn't seduce her first, that was.

Good grief! There he was, thinking about seduction again. When had he last seduced a gently born damsel of good, if decided, character and virtue?

Never.

Good character? A damned tease, more like.

Here he was, worrying that she intended to tease him into marriage and she had the gall, the unmitigated *gall*, to imply that he'd offer her a slip on the shoulder! That he'd actually seduce her. What the devil had he done to warrant that piece of missishness?

Naturally, having opened the floodgates on that line of thought, answers came in a veritable deluge.

You threatened to spank her. You told her you wanted to kiss her. You went into her room, while she was asleep, no less! To leave snowdrops. Then you did kiss her. Twice. And threatened to spank her again.

Put like that, he could see that Cressida had every excuse for a bout of missishness.

Even the desk, he realised with a stab of hurt, could be construed as buttering her up. And as for his efforts just now…he groaned. Why had he ever thought horses a safe topic of conversation?

He picked up the pace as he headed back to the house along a path edged with lavender. Usually, he walked through here slowly, enjoying the fragrant fronds brushing against him. Not today. The soothing scent of lavender always hung round Cressida's clothes. Now it infuriated him.

He'd never seduced a virgin in his life and he'd certainly never tampered with the affections of gently born girls who might reasonably expect an offer of marriage. Not even the girls he'd thought of offering for. He hadn't got that far. Certainly he'd never got as far as making dubious comparisons between stallions and geldings!

And what in Hades had he been about to kiss her again? Let alone like that. As though he meant it as an insult. When in truth he had been longing to reassure himself that her lips really were as sensuously yielding as he remembered. Never had he known a kiss to be so sweet with innocence and the promise of pleasure.

Most of his carnal dealings had been restricted to the Fashionable Impure, the demi-reps—women who made their living as courtesans. He'd also had a few discreet affairs with women of his own class; widows and married ladies blessed, or cursed depending on one's point of view, with husbands who couldn't care less, as long as the paternity of their heirs wasn't called into question. Nothing that could have prepared him for Cressida. Certainly the couple of kisses he'd stolen from Selina hadn't done so.

It wasn't that he objected to causing scandal—a nice juicy scandal kept society's wheels turning—it was just that he had always considered that the purpose of an affair ought to be mutual pleasure. Leaving a woman facing an enraged spouse did not fit into his definition of mutual pleasure.

He swung around a corner, which brought the main drive into view, and came to a dead halt. Damn. There was a chaise approaching the house. Well, with a bit of luck the occupants hadn't seen him. Evans could deny him in good faith if he stayed out of sight.

He stood partially behind a rose arbour and watched the chaise. Funny. Neighbours wouldn't use a post chaise just to pay him a visit. They must have the wrong place. But those bays—a bang-up set-out of blood and bone—looked rather familiar. Part of his mind toyed with that while he went back to the more pressing problem.

What on earth was wrong with him that he was thinking of seducing Cressida? He had nothing but loathing for hardened rakes who seduced, or worse, forced innocent girls and left them to their ruin. Even if the girl was a tease, a gentleman should have enough control for both of them. So if he intended to seduce Cressida…that meant he had suddenly become the greatest scoundrel unhung…or that he was intending to marry her.

Marry her? Marry that hot-tempered, outrageous little baggage, who twisted him in knots and had him saying things he'd never said to a gently bred female in his life? Not to mention the things he wanted to do.

Those bays really did look very familiar…

Marry her? He'd be lucky to finish proposing before she tore strips off him! Besides, he was damned if he'd let the little minx tease him into it. Marriage to Cressida Bramley was the last thing he wanted. She'd turn his ordered life upside down. So he couldn't possibly *intend* to seduce Cressida Bramley. He just wanted to. There was a difference, he hoped. Her ability to tip him off balance shortened the odds considerably. But, since she was nothing in the least like the sort of female he planned to fall in love with and marry, he'd better start working on his self-control.

Oh, hell and the devil. No use thinking about it. Concentrate on those Welsh bays! They were just as good as Marc's team… He looked again. God in heaven! They *were* Marc's bays!

Dazed, he watched as one of his footmen rushed out to let down the steps of the chaise. He couldn't quite believe

it until he saw the tall, athletic form of the Earl of Rutherford leap down and hold out his arms to someone in the
chaise. A tiny shawl-wrapped bundle was handed down to
him. Jack watched with suddenly envious eyes as his
friend cradled the precious burden in one arm and held the
other hand up to his wife. They had both come. With little
Jon, Jack's godson.

'Marc! Meg!' He strode towards them. 'What the devil
are you doing here?'

Marc swung around and grinned. 'Visiting. Aren't we
welcome?'

'I can probably find a garret for you,' Jack assured him.
'Hello, Meg, sweetheart.' He enveloped the Countess in
an overwhelming hug, lifting her quite off her feet.

'Jack! Put me down, you great bear! You'll hurt your
shoulder.'

Jack groaned. 'Heaven help me. Another female fussing
about my blasted shoulder.'

He set her down anyway and cast a wicked grin at Marc.
'Nothing to say about my manhandling your wife, old
chap?'

Marc shook his head. 'Not yet. We all know Meg has
ways of dealing with idiots! If you're lucky she'll just
thump you in the shoulder.'

'Oh, never mind that,' said Meg. 'Jack, what did you
mean by sending Marc that idiotish letter telling us not to
come, because you couldn't hunt? Of all the stupid no-
tions! How you could possibly think we wouldn't come is
beyond me!'

'Come in out of the cold,' urged Jack. 'My godson
won't like it at all. How is he?'

'Asleep,' Marc informed him. 'And long may he remain
that way. He becomes very grumpy when he doesn't have
enough sleep.'

'Like his papa?' suggested Jack.

Marc grinned wickedly. 'I've discovered certain compensations for losing sleep. However, let's get him inside and see what sort of nursery your housekeeper has arranged. We'd have been here days ago, but we travelled in short stages to make sure he didn't get too tired or cold.'

Jack smiled. 'I'll ring for her at once...' Then the oddness of Marc's comment hit him. 'Hold hard there. Did you say *has* arranged? Are you expected?'

'Of course we are,' smiled Meg. 'I wrote to Mrs Roberts telling her to expect us by today!'

'My God!' said Jack deeply. 'They never said a word! Piracy! Piracy and mutiny—one of these days I'll turn the lot of 'em off without a character between them!'

'Well, when you do,' said Meg cheerfully, 'just let me know. We'll have them all happily!'

Chapter Six

Cressida stared at the door of her bedchamber, devoutly wishing that she didn't have to go beyond it. An Earl and a Countess. Jack's intimate friends. Here. She flushed at the memory of the last time she had come under the eye of a Viscountess. No doubt a Countess would be even more dismissive. Especially if she had heard anything about the scheming Miss Bramley.

Perhaps she should send a message down that she had the headache. If she sat here fretting for very much longer it would be the literal truth. How on earth she was going to face Jack at dinner, after that conversation in the stable, with a Countess at the end of the table, defeated her.

And that was another thing—how ever was Jack going to arrange the seating? They had been dining at a circular table in a small parlour. With such exalted guests, would Jack use the main dining room?

She sighed. Cowering up here was out of the question. If the maid who waited on her was to be believed, Lord Rutherford's estates were nowhere near Cornwall. They couldn't possibly have heard what amounted to village tattle—she was being ridiculous, oversensitive.

She stood up swiftly and smoothed down her gown. It might be old fashioned, and have been remodelled from a cloak of her mother's, but it was the only one she had and at least it was velvet. The soft, rich green still glowed in the firelight and the ivory lace she had pinned into the rather low neckline gave it a more modish air.

No doubt the Countess would be festooned with diamonds, like Andrew's mother, Lady Fairbridge. Well, she had nothing, save her mama's cut-steel necklace of flowers. She lifted it out of its box and smiled sadly. No matter that she wouldn't exchange it for a thousand diamond necklaces, she did just wish that the rest of the world didn't judge so much on what one could afford.

Love didn't seem to work that way.

Cressida slipped into the drawing room, wishing that there were more people, furious with herself for being nervous.

What do an Earl and Countess matter to you? Why should you care?

She couldn't see the Countess at first. Jack's large body hid her as he laughed at something she had said.

Cressida stiffened. No doubt he found her far more entertaining than his gauche, not to mention rude, little cousin. He hadn't even noticed her come in.

Oh, for goodness sake! How could he? He has his back to you.

It was the Earl, tall, tawny haired, with eyes of a much lighter grey than Jack's, who came forward.

'Good evening. You, I take it, must be Miss Bramley. Jack is far too busy flirting with my wife to introduce us, so I'll presume on your relationship with him and save him the trouble. How do you do, Miss Bramley? I'm Rutherford.'

He held out his hand with a friendly smile.

Cressida swallowed. What on earth was she meant to do when a whole, live Earl held out his hand and appeared to invite her to address him simply as *Rutherford*? Remember her place, that's what.

'G…good evening, my lord.'

She placed her hand in his and wondered what he would do with it. And why, although he was quite as handsome as Jack, she didn't suffer a single palpitation as he bowed over her hand.

A faint smile as he straightened drew a hesitant answering smile from her. Then, 'I don't bite, you know.'

'D…don't you?' *Oh, help! Can't you do better than that?*

But his shoulders were shaking and his rather cool grey eyes had warmed with laughter.

'No, Miss Bramley. Whatever whiskers Jack has told you about me, I don't bite!'

She felt heat stealing into her cheeks. And felt it drain away as she realised Jack's eyes were upon her. Cold, aloof. Oh, bother him! Why did she always have to feel as though the world tilted every time they were in the same room? And why didn't she feel absolutely disgusted and outraged at his behaviour this afternoon? Surely any self-respecting clergyman's daughter would have been shocked!

Then, as Jack moved, she saw the Countess of Rutherford, standing with an expectant smile on her face, eagerness in her smoky blue eyes.

Why, she looks as though she wants to meet me! And, *Good heavens! She's no older than I am.*

Jack was bringing the lady forward.

'Meg, may I present my second cousin, Miss Cressida Bramley? Miss Bramley, this is Lady Rutherford.'

Lady Rutherford stared at him, opened her mouth and shut it again.

'How do you do, Miss Bramley,' she said, and held out her hand.

Cressida took it shyly. Lady Fairbridge had never offered more than two languid fingers to anyone she considered her social inferior. Did Lady Rutherford imagine that her relationship to Jack somehow elevated her?

The Earl turned back to Cressida. 'You know, I thought I was acquainted with all Jack's relations, including your father, I might add. I'm on Christian name terms with all those of my generation. There's no reason to make you an exception.'

Cressida could think of one perfectly valid reason. And the reason's dark grey eyes were boring into her all of a sudden. She couldn't—wouldn't—call him *Jack*. After this afternoon she doubted that he even wanted her to. Indeed, his manner of presenting her to Lady Rutherford suggested it.

His very next words confirmed it. 'How very kind of you, Marc. But I'm afraid Miss Bramley prefers to observe all the niceties governing social conduct. She frowns upon any hint of familiarity.'

The chill in his voice cut at her. Desperately seeking to change the subject, she looked about. 'Is my father not down yet? Perhaps I should go and find him.' And send a message back down that she had developed a sudden headache and retired for the night. If she cried enough, it would be true.

'Dr Bramley has retired for the night,' Jack informed her. 'He is feeling unwell. His stomach, I believe.'

'Oh, then pray excuse me…I should go up to—'

Jack cut her off ruthlessly. 'He has everything he needs. I saw to it myself. He has no need of you, Miss Bramley.'

Shocked, Cressida stared up at him. No, her father had very little need of her in this house. At least in Cornwall she had been useful to him, running the house and helping with his parishioners. Here everything was done by one of the staff.

'One of the maids has instructions to go to him should he ring for anything.'

'Thank you,' she said bleakly. 'But if Papa is not down, there is no need for me to—'

'Nonsense,' said Lady Rutherford. 'Jack's shoulder must be aching for him to be such a curmudgeon. You can't possibly leave me with only these two for company. Come, Miss Bramley...Jack's a grouchy old bear this evening and he and Marc will talk forever about some horrid mill or Jack's last curricle race!'

Her lovely smile beckoned, easing Cressida's hurt. *Has no need of you...has no need...no need...* The words echoed mercilessly. She would have to leave, find a position. But how was she to do that without a reference?

Two hours later Cressida followed Lady Rutherford from the dining room in a daze. This was not the sort of aristocrat she was used to. Why on earth would a Countess make the least effort to include Miss Cressida Bramley in the conversation, let alone rake her host down for being *a grouchy old bear*?

And why would such an exalted being as an Earl chat to her at all? Let alone about parish duties and the way they fitted in with the duties of a landlord! If she didn't know better, she'd think they actually liked her. *Maybe they do.*

She shied away from the thought as if it had stung her. *They wouldn't like you if they knew the truth. Lady Rutherford would be shocked and Lord Rutherford would refuse to have you anywhere near his wife.*

Out in the hall Lady Rutherford turned to her and said with a smile, 'Will you excuse me, Miss Bramley? I must go upstairs.'

There. Why would she wish to spend her evening with a dowdy nobody? But perhaps she might be prepared to write you that reference... 'Of course, my lady. I quite understand,' said Cressida very politely. She found to her discomfort that Lady Rutherford's smoky blue eyes were looking at her with disconcerting penetration.

'I don't think you do,' said her ladyship. 'I need to go upstairs to give Jon his feed. He's not weaned yet, you see.'

Cressida blinked. 'You feed him yourself?' Lady Fairbridge had expressed very strong views on how disgusting such a procedure was and that no female of consideration would so demean herself. Then she flushed. Who was she to question a Countess?

Lady Rutherford only smiled. 'Of course. I know it's not fashionable, but it's so lovely. At home I have him brought down to the library after dinner and Marc sits with me, but I suspect poor Jack would find that a little hard to cope with!' Her giggle was infectious. 'Just imagine his face!'

'You're very fond of Ja— Mr Hamilton, aren't you?' asked Cressida, shivering at an unbidden vision of herself nursing Jack's child while he sat by.

Lady Rutherford nodded. 'After Marc, there is no one dearer. He is such a kind, *chivalrous* soul. Now, I must be off. I shall see you in the morning. Perhaps your papa may be better. Goodnight, Miss Bramley. I dare say I shan't come down again. Feeding Jon always makes me so terribly sleepy!'

'Goodnight,' responded Cressida.

She walked slowly towards the library. What would it be like to feed a baby? She had never understood why Lady Fairbridge had found the whole idea so disgusting. Cuddling a baby was wonderful, and just think how content Rosie the house cow had been when she had a calf. Surely it wasn't all that different for a woman? Why else would God have given women breasts?

A fire was lit in the library and the curtains were all drawn. She looked longingly at her desk, but knew she mustn't stay. With Lady Rutherford upstairs, it would be most improper.

No, she would take a book and go to bed after checking on Papa. She yawned. Was the sky still clear? She might go for a walk tomorrow if the weather held.

She went over to the long window and tweaked the curtain back to peer out. A full moon was rising over the woods and she sighed with pleasure. Unhesitatingly she slipped behind the curtain and sat down on the window seat, drawing the curtain closed to banish the light of the room.

Silver light glimmered over the woods and snowy gardens. Trees stood frosted with silver against a sky that pulsed with stars. She smiled up at them, recognising Orion and his dogs, the Big Dipper and other friends her mother had shown her. As a child she had been convinced that the stars were windows in heaven that God and the angels could peep through.

Gazing up as she leant against the window, she wondered if her mother could peep through. What would she think of her foolish daughter? Would she be disappointed if she could see what a muddle Cressida had made of everything?

Look after Papa, darling. He's very kind, but so vague. And he was so good to me that I have always tried to repay that.

She hadn't looked after Papa properly. Instead she had put him in the position where he had tried to protect her with disastrous results. She had cost him his living. But at least he could be happy and safe here. Mr Hamilton...Jack...would look after him. Cressida smiled to herself sleepily. Even if he was a grouchy old bear, he liked Papa. It would be nice if he liked her, too... But she would have to warn him, explain what sometimes happened if Papa was upset. Surely if she warned him about this little idiosyncrasy before she left, he would understand... After all, Papa meant no harm.

The stars blazed down and the moon gleamed through the window as she dozed.

She awakened, cold and shivering, to hear voices.

'Thought you'd be upstairs with Jon, but Lucy said he went straight off to sleep and you'd come down for a book.'

She stretched sleepily. Good heavens, that sounded like Lord Rutherford.

'Yes. I thought you'd be talking to Jack for a while. Where is he?'

That was Lady Rutherford.

'Gone up. Come here, sweetheart.'

Cressida blinked at the husky growl. The Earl had spoken affectionately enough to his Countess at dinner—but this! Perhaps she ought to let them know she was there... She hesitated for a moment, embarrassed to be caught hiding in the curtains like a child. Silence ensued. Had they gone?

A sob mingled with a deep groan. 'Meg...God, I want you. Kiss me again...'

Stunned, Cressida peeped out between the curtains and nearly sprained her jaw.

Lord Rutherford sat in one of the chairs by the fire with his Countess in his lap...what on earth was he doing, kissing her like that? It looked as though he was biting her lower lip, devouring her. Was she enjoying it?

Logic and memory told Cressida that no woman could possibly enjoy being mauled by a man. Observation told her that the Countess was not being mauled and that she was enjoying it very much. She was pressing herself against the Earl, threading her hands through his hair to draw him even closer. And surely those were whimpers of pleasure... Good lord, his hand was on her breast! A shaft of pure fire shot through her own breasts, merely watching the Earl's fingers shift and tease…and release his wife's breast from her bodice…heat, yearning, a melting ache…just like she had felt when Jack kissed her. It hadn't been at all like that with Andrew. He had grabbed and demanded, terrifying her…intent on nothing but his own pleasure. *Just as well. If you hadn't fought him in the end, you'd be in a worse mess now…Papa would have been too late.*

Eyes wide, she watched as the Earl traced kisses down his wife's throat…and lower. *What would that feel like with Jack?* Now the little sobs she had heard, became intelligible.

'Marc?'

He lifted his mouth from her breast. 'More?'

'Yes…oh, yes.'

'Little wanton.'

He teased affectionately before returning to her breast while his hand caressed its way over her waist to her hip and lower until it slipped under the heavy velvet skirts… the aching heat in Cressida's breasts rippled lower. It was obvious from the way the velvet bunched over his elbow just where the Earl's hand was… Her breath jerked inwards at the thought of Jack touching her so intimately.

Shocked, she felt her own thighs melt in longing as the Countess shifted slightly in her husband's arms…allowing him greater access. Cressida heard his murmur.

'So soft…Meg, dearest Meg…'

Shaken, Cressida drew back silently into the silver-lit window embrasure. She should not be here. No wonder girls were told little or nothing of the marriage bed. Her body ached and burned just watching. And listening. Desperately she pressed her hands over her ears to shut out the sweet sounds and stared out into the silver night…so lovely…so peaceful… Would they stay there for very long? It was bitterly cold behind the curtain, cut off from the warmth and light of the room.

Blushing, she took her hands away from her ears. Just for a moment, just to find out if they were still there…

'…should go up, dearest. If we stay any longer…'

Cressida's cheeks scorched to flame and her knees wobbled as Lord Rutherford seduced his wife with hot, loving words, describing exactly what he wanted. Words that spoke of her pleasure as much as his…

She sank on to the window seat, trembling. If they ever found out she had overheard this… Could she open the window and slip out? Would they hear? She might freeze to death, but at least she would no longer be intruding on their privacy…their intimacy… Ashamed of her accidental intrusion, she looked closely at the latch. It would open easily enough, but would the window creak? Would the draught catch the curtains and alert them to her presence? Perhaps if she only opened it a crack, enough to slip out. Her hand went to the latch. Cold moonlight mocked her, the snowy garden no longer looked inviting.

'Marc?'

She barely recognised the Countess's voice. So husky, so…aching. She should go at once.

'We must go up. This isn't *our* library… What if Jack walked in?'

A masculine chuckle Cressida could only describe as wicked answered this, even as she stilled her hand on the latch.

'Almost, my love, you tempt me. But poor old Evans would have a seizure. Come along, little tease. Time for bed.'

Somehow Cressida doubted that the Earl intended sleep in the near future. She breathed a silent sigh of relief as she heard them getting up.

'Here. Let me settle your skirts. No need to shock Evans too much.'

'What about your cravat?'

'Have you ruined my cravat *again*, woman?'

'While you were strewing my hairpins around the floor.'

'Baggage. Find them in the morning. It'll give Jack something to occupy his mind if he spots them.'

'Speaking of Jack…'

'Yes, sweetheart…is that your earring?'

'Oh, yes. Whatever do you think is bothering Jack?'

'Nettle rash.'

'Pardon?'

'Nettle rash. In his breeches. Now, stop worrying about Jack's problems and come to bed and worry about mine.'

Nettle rash? Startled, Cressida peeped out through the gap again. What on earth did Rutherford mean?

'Oh?' The Countess reached up and twined her arms around his neck. 'I wasn't aware you had any problems in bed.' Her voice was outrageously provocative as she shifted her hips sinuously against her husband.

'I don't,' growled the Earl, lowering his mouth to hers briefly. 'I have you instead.'

He led her from the room, shutting the door firmly behind them.

After waiting a few minutes to make sure they had really gone, Cressida emerged. The chair they had occupied looked no different. She had sat in it herself earlier in the day. Much sat in, saggy. It was wickedly comfortable, but required a massive effort to pull oneself out. Jack always gravitated to it when he didn't want to use his desk. And winced every time he dragged himself out of it.

Firebird is a gelding…

Colour scorched into Cressida's cheeks as she recalled her longing to feel those long fingers on her throat and jaw again. Had *he* ever sat there with a woman in his lap, seducing her? Loving her? Cressida shook her head. Such a thing had never occurred to her. Certainly not between the married couples she had known. Between her parents there had been gentle affection and, on her mother's part, gratitude. Lady Fairbridge and her late spouse? She nearly giggled at the thought of that august lady being seduced by anyone, let alone the gross and frequently inebriated peer.

Andrew? The fourth Viscount Fairbridge. A shudder tore through her. He had terrified her. The more since she had trusted him, had thought he loved her. Even afterwards she had blamed herself. Until she found out what he really wanted of her. Love had nothing to do with what Andrew had wanted from her.

What did Jack want from her? His kisses had been so different from Andrew's demands. Were his feelings different, too? Had he just been teasing her when he made that outrageous remark? He had certainly been furious at the interpretation she had put on his words. Insulted.

And why did she keep looking at that wretched chair and imagining Jack in it instead of the Earl of Rutherford? Of course, Jack sat in that chair all the time. It was his. But did she have to imagine what it would be like to be nestled in his lap?

Abruptly she turned to the ladder. She'd shelve all those books Papa had put on the finished pile and then choose something to read in bed. Tucking a pile of books under her arm, she scrambled up the ladder. She trod on the skirt almost immediately and cursed as she grabbed frantically for the ladder. Books cascaded merrily to the floor.

'Drat!' She picked up her skirts and got down carefully. This skirt was quite a bit longer than her morning gowns. It nearly touched the ground. Cressida looked around guiltily, half-expecting the books to indict her on grounds of impropriety as she tucked her skirts up into the sash at her waist.

No one would come in at this hour.

She picked up the books again and re-ascended the ladder. Happily she glanced at the books as she began to shelve them. Latin poetry…hmm…she'd read most of these…Virgil, Horace, Catullus, she shelved them without a second glance. Ovid? She knew her father had copies of Ovid, but he had never permitted her to read any. Why not? All she really knew about him was that he had offended the Emperor and got himself banished.

Curiously, she opened one of them…what was it called? *Ars Amatoria*… Mentally she translated…*The Art of Love*? Good heavens! She hesitated…perhaps she ought not to read it. Papa always said many of the classics were quite unsuitable for a female. He'd only taught her Latin and Greek because he loved to share his knowledge and there was no one else to teach.

Oh, bother it. It was only a book, after all. What harm could a book do? She thrust away the knowledge that many would consider it quite improper for a female to read anything more inflammatory than a sermon to improve her mind, an etiquette manual, or a household list, that some considered even the mildest novel to be corrupting. Anything called *The Art of Love* would certainly not qualify as *improving*.

Defiantly, she opened the volume and began to flick through the pages. Very quickly she could see why her father had put Ovid on the proscribed list. Scandalous…no wonder that moralist Augustus had exiled the poet to the Black Sea…she read on, entranced at the outrageous advice the long-dead poet offered to men intent on the pursuit and seduction of women… Goodness! it was a sort of etiquette manual for lovers and a great deal more to the point than the one she had telling young ladies how to go on. She noted with interest that the poet agreed with Lord Rutherford and felt women should enjoy the procedure as much as men, although the phrases he used didn't make much sense… And then she found the poet's advice to women intent on being seduced.

Her eyes widened as she scanned the dancing couplets. A couple of choked giggles escaped as she read the advice for accomplishments and bodily care to attract a lover. Not so unlike her own etiquette manual after all…until she came to some extremely graphic and explicit advice near the end.

Her cheeks flamed. She had lived in the country all her life and had seen enough horses, cattle, dogs and sheep to have grasped the mechanics of the act of procreation. But, goodness gracious! She had certainly never realised just how much *variation* was possible. *The Mirror of Graces* didn't mention anything like this!

'What in Hades do you think you're doing up there at this hour?'

The furious voice came from just beneath her. Forgetting her precarious perch on the ladder, she spun around and slipped.

Swearing, Jack leapt forward. She landed heavily in his arms in a tumble of green velvet.

'Oof!' he grunted as he staggered under the impact.

Having temporarily given up on sleep, Jack had come down for a book. Something dull and turgid preferably. The last thing he had expected, or wanted, to find was the object of his fantasies perched above eye level with her skirts hiked above her knees. It didn't help when he'd been fantasising about her legs, to discover that the limbs in question were every bit as graceful and silken as his heated imagination had surmised.

That was bad enough. Realising that she was shelving his books, at midnight for God's sake, put the finishing touches of guilt to his response. But he hadn't meant to startle her into falling off the ladder. He ought to put her down immediately. Anything to halt the inevitable effect her soft, feminine weight had on his very shaky self-control. Anything to get those startled, indignant eyes further away from him. Before he added to their surprise by covering her soft pink lips with his mouth and kissing her, and himself, senseless.

Any man of resolution, not to mention honour, would

have set her on her feet by now. Plainly he possessed neither honour, nor resolution, because she still lay in his arms, staring worriedly into his eyes as though she thought he might bite her.

He wouldn't have cared to bet any sum that he wasn't about to do just that. Her pulse, beating wildly in her throat, cried out for his lips…

'J…Jack? Do you think you should put me down now? Your…your shoulder…'

Shock rippled through him. She had called him Jack, at last. And she lay so sweetly, so trustingly in his arms.

You blithering ass! She's worried about hurting your shoulder. And then, insidiously: *Or did she wait for you? Did she intend something like this?*

Abruptly, he set her down, but found he could not release her. He shifted his grip to her shoulders, his hands sliding sensuously over the old, worn velvet. Only the fine trembling of her body told him of her tension. Her eyes met his steadily, wide, puzzled. *Does she understand? Is this a clever trick?*

Then the tip of her tongue slipped out to sheen the soft invitation of her lips. He fought a brief, hard battle for his self-control and lost. The longing to kiss her throbbed in his blood, surged to a blazing need to feel her mouth helpless under his. Maybe that would answer his questions. Common sense suggested he retreat immediately. He ignored it. *How far would she go?*

'I shouldn't do this,' he whispered hoarsely.

Cressida trembled at the heat in his eyes. 'Do what?'

'This.' Slowly, hungrily, he lowered his mouth to hers.

She had plenty of warning. She knew what he intended, and had every chance to escape. She chose to stay.

At first his kisses were gentle, teasing, a feathering of firm, warm lips over hers. One large hand cupped her chin, tilting her face up. The other arm cradled her against his body, pressed her against the hard wall of his chest along with that wretched copy of Ovid.

He kissed her as he had kissed her in here once before. Tender and ravishing all at once, shot through with fierce restraint. A gasp shuddered through her as she felt his teeth close lightly on her lower lip, felt his tongue stroke the captive flesh in a hot, silky caress. The book fell unheeded, all theory forgotten as her hands slid instinctively to his shoulders, clinging for support as her knees shook.

Heat poured from him, into her. Inviting, imploring her response. Not forcing her abject surrender. Willingly, she parted her lips for him and sighed her pleasure as his tongue found and laved the sweet inner surfaces. Never had she known that a man's arms could be so gently inescapable. That long fingers could brush over suddenly sensitised skin with the delicacy of a butterfly, leaving tingling fire in their wake. Her last vestige of fainting reason noted that Jack, if not familiar with the letter of the text she had just been reading, was thoroughly versed in its spirit.

One hand curved over her nape, caressed the soft skin there. Instinctively she tilted her head back further to increase the sensuous pressure of his teasing fingers. His fingers speared into her hair, loosening the pins which pattered to the hearth as her hair cascaded around her shoulders. And she felt his lips trail fire down her exposed neck, felt the hot probing of his tongue in the hollow at the base of her throat.

His other hand curved around the softness of her waist and hip, holding her against him. Never had she been so conscious of a man's power as she was now; when it was held in check. She knew, none better, that if he wanted to, he could overpower her in a trice. That knowledge should have terrified her. It didn't. Instead she pressed herself closer to his heat and hardness, sliding her hands over his shoulders and shivering as his hand flexed on her hip.

Slowly, tenderly that hand shifted over the curve of her waist, burned over her ribs until it rested just below one soft breast. A languorous, seductive thumb brushed her nipple which flamed to aching life. Her cry of shock was muffled by his mouth, which came back to hers in swift need, taking all he had previously claimed and asking for more. His tongue traced her lower lip, probed gently. With a sob, she obeyed the unspoken command and opened her mouth.

His groan shuddered through her as slowly, inexorably he stroked his tongue into her mouth, taking it in a surge of silken penetration. Heat took her body in slow pulsing rhythms that throbbed with fiery pleasure. His hand at her breast stroked and caressed through the heavy velvet, dragging the material across the burning peak. She heard a tearing sound, felt the fragile, old lace give where she had pinned it to her bodice…a warning bell rang. Then his loins shifted against her in the same compelling rhythm as his tongue, deep in her mouth. Need melted her, her thighs trembled with want… This was so different…surely it was different…

How can it be different, you little fool? Because he uses tenderness rather than force? Seduces rather than attempts to force you? The end result is still the same. She should stop him. Should have already stopped him. She should not even have let him kiss her again.

She didn't want to stop him. Then: *What if he doesn't want to stop? What if you can't stop him?* And hard on its heels: fear. Streaking through her, freezing her blood, just as one long finger slipped beneath the torn lace to trace the swell of her breasts above the bodice, gently stroking silken skin. Desperately she tore her mouth free and gasped, 'No! Please, let me go!' She pushed at his chest and realised just how helpless she was against his strength.

Jack felt the frantic change, the desperate attempt to escape. The temptation to hold her a little longer, take her a little further along the path that beckoned in shimmering delight, tugged at him. He mustn't. Didn't dare. He couldn't trust himself to pull back if this went any further. At some point his intention to teach her a lesson in the dangers of teasing had burned to ashes in the consuming need to teach her the delights of passion. He had his answer. She would go far enough to drive him insane. He released her, stepping back, dragging air into his lungs.

Forcing his voice to glacial boredom, he began, 'Perhaps that may show you…' Then he saw her face. 'Cressida?'

She didn't reply. Simply stared at him, through him, her face accusingly white and strained, as though she looked on a nightmare. For a moment he wondered if she would faint. Unconsciously his hand reached out to her. Her gaze snapped into focus and she jerked back out of reach.

'No!' The harsh fear in her voice stabbed into him. Then she whirled and fled.

Shame, mingled with frustration, lashed him. Even if she had teased, he should have had more self-control than to terrify her. He was supposed to be a gentleman, supposed to have enough control and discretion for both of them.

But did she tease on purpose? Experience hooted derisively that he could even question it. Lord! She could give Selina Pilkington tips. She was bolder, too. Selina had never permitted more that one or two chaste kisses.

Bolder? Or more innocent? Did she really know what she was doing? Some deeper instinct told him that she'd had no idea. And even if she had, he should not have behaved as he had. There were other ways to explain to a girl that her ploys were unacceptable. Far less risky ways. He'd deal with it in the morning. For now he'd go up to bed. With a book.

Savagely he thrust away the knowledge that he'd rather go to bed with Cressida. If only this were London. At least he could have gone out and found a woman to ease his frustration. On the heels of the thought came a shattering realisation; it wouldn't work. He didn't want some anonymous woman for a quick tumble in a strange bed. He wanted to make love. To Cressida. In *his* bed. He had never wanted that before. A man's bed should be reserved for his…wife. Wildly his mind sheered away from the implications of *that* thought.

A book. He needed a book.

His gaze lit on the one she had dropped. She'd been perched on the top of the ladder reading. A reluctant grin curved his lips. He did the same thing himself. That was partially why the library was taking so long. Neither he, nor his father, had ever been able to resist the temptation to browse.

The book looked familiar… He frowned. No, it couldn't be. Surely not. The book lay there, silently assuring him that it could be. Dumbfounded, he picked it up and read the title. It was. He thrust it into a space as though it had burned his hand. Not quite what he'd had in mind for bedtime reading. He couldn't see that it would advance the cause of peaceful sleep one iota.

As he turned to leave his foot scrunched on something. Glancing down, he saw the scatter of hairpins his unrestrained embrace had shaken from Cressida's auburn tresses. They had wound about his hand, a burning silken snare. The memory tore at him.

Grimly he set his jaw against it and bent down to pick up the pins. He would return them in the morning. If Cressida had started taking tips from Ovid, the sooner he made his opinions known, the better. Ovid's ideas could be unsettling enough in writing; he shuddered to think what their effect might be made flesh, so to speak.

And there was something else. *He* would not take advantage of Cressida's ploys and use them to his own ends. He hoped. But another, less scrupulous, fellow might. Had she fully realised the danger she courted? Had her sudden panic just now been genuine, or was it all part of the tease?

His eyes narrowed as another plan wreathed in his brain. With a bit of luck he'd teach Miss Cressida Bramley a lesson she wouldn't forget in a hurry. And he'd make damned sure that *he* was well and truly chaperoned this time.

Chapter Seven

'I beg your pardon, Papa?'

Cressida pushed a lock of hair out of her face and turned to look at her father. He was frowning up at her from his desk.

'I said that volume should not go there. It was on the other pile, my dear. It should go over *there*.' He pointed to a section of shelves further along.

She sighed and rubbed her eyes again. They felt unpleasantly scratchy from lack of sleep. And her hair kept collapsing into her face since she had not enough hairpins to keep it up this morning. Normally such a thing would not have bothered her one whit. This morning she felt thoroughly annoyed about it since, in addition to tickling her face, it reminded her of how disgracefully she had behaved the previous night.

'Sorry, Papa,' she said aloud, even as she cursed silently and twisted her hair up into yet another inadequate knot. She had come down early to find her hairpins but they were nowhere to be seen. Which puzzled her exceedingly. If a maid had found *her* pins, then why were Lady Rutherford's pins still scattered around the hearth where they had fallen? And why was she so irritable this morning?

Could it be the lack of sleep? Or could she be sickening for something? Certainly she ached in some odd places...

Dispiritedly she returned to her shelving, placing the books automatically, not even remotely interested in browsing. A glance down at her father found him doing just that. His faint frown and pursed lips spoke of total absorption. A reluctant smile curved her lips. An earthquake might shift him, but not much less.

What on earth should she say to Jack this morning? She bit her lip. She had behaved like the veriest wanton last night. If Jack were not a man of honour... She trembled at what would have happened. She had thought about it all night.

He would have forced you... He wouldn't have needed to use force. If he hadn't released you, you would have surrendered.

The thought sent more tremors feathering down her spine. Especially since those odd aches intensified. Fear. It had to be fear. Anything else was impossible. She dared not contemplate anything else as she had in the chilly darkness. It would be madness to believe...to hope again.

But why had he kissed her so? No one but a fool would doubt Jack Hamilton's sense of honour. And no honourable man kissed a girl as he had without... No. Impossible. She had to stop this stupid dreaming. Now. Before she gave herself away. Besides, she could not accept an offer without telling him why they had left Cornwall. And even if he gallantly renewed his offer afterwards she would not accept. She could not offer Jack a tarnished name as a marriage portion.

She stared unseeingly out at the gloomy day. The sparkling magic of the previous night had been replaced by grimly lowering clouds. More snow. She shivered despite the heat of the fire, wishing she had a warmer gown.

Or that she could become colder. Once you were cold enough you no longer noticed it, she had heard tell. You drifted off into a false sense of warmth and security. Once you were colder than the snow…

The sound of a throat being loudly cleared dragged her back.

'Hmm?' She looked around vaguely. And grabbed for the ladder. Blast it all! Why did he keep sneaking up on her?

'Perhaps I might have a moment of your time, cousin?'

It sounded as if he had asked several times from the note of languid boredom in his voice.

'My…my time?' Cressida could not control the wobble in her own voice.

'Yes,' he said. 'Privately.'

Privately?

'No,' she said baldly. And added belatedly, 'Thank you.' Somehow it sounded thoroughly inappropriate. Hurriedly she went on. 'I do not think it…it would be at all saf—a good idea,' she amended, 'for us to be alone, after…after…' Her voice failed. *After you kissed me? After we kissed each other? After you nearly seduced me? After I nearly ruined myself?* Nothing seemed quite right. Prudently she remained at the top of the ladder and left the sentence to finish itself in Jack's mind.

'My dear cousin, while I laud your prudence, the other end of the library will suffice. Your father's presence is surety enough while I return your property.'

He held up a single hairpin, no more.

One was quite enough. Cressida could feel the blush extend much lower than her cheeks and throat. That only increased the heat of the blush. Surely it was only embarrassment at the memory and not the memory itself. Numbly she came down from the ladder, praying that he wouldn't try to assist her.

'Cressida?' Her father's voice brought them both up short.

'Y…yes, Papa?'

'Jack taking you for a walk, m'dear?' He smiled fondly. 'Better fetch your cloak, then. It looks cold out.'

'I…er…I don't think…'

'Just to the end of the library, sir,' answered Jack. 'With your permission.'

She noted the change in his tone at once. To her father, he spoke…kindly…with not a hint of the cold hauteur he had used with her.

Coolly he possessed himself of her hand and placed it on his arm to conduct her to the far end of the library. Fury seethed in her breast. She had no choice. If she objected and Papa heard, then he would take her part instantly. She knew that now.

The sun had broken through briefly and light poured through the north windows, gilding the worn Persian rugs with frosty brilliance. So cold, so bright. Her hand on his arm felt cold, too. As though it had frozen there. Yet she could feel the heat pouring out of him. Why couldn't it warm her hand?

He halted her right by the windows near her desk, in full light, although, as she looked up at him in unspoken question, the sun cravenly retreated behind the overriding gloom of the day. She did not have that option and would not take it anyway.

He dropped the formality at once, holding her hand between his and rubbing his thumb over her palm in a way that sent tremors of pleasure through her. Shocked she tried to jerk her hand away. How could such a simple caress send heat flooding through her?

His fingers tightened slightly. 'Cressida, you were perfectly right to call a halt to last night's…er…proceedings,' he began.

Proceedings?

'It was most inopportune of me to leap so far ahead without discussing the situation with you.'

What situation?

'Yes, indeed. I should have spoken earlier, but my passions ran away with me.'

Oh, dear God. Surely he doesn't mean to make an offer…? If he thinks that he compromised me…

'It was most inconsiderate of me to push matters so far. Naturally you will wish to know my terms and assess the matter in a rational light. Your father, of course, may disapprove…'

'*Why would Papa disapprove?*' She heard herself ask the question as if from a great distance.

He smiled. 'My dear Cressida! Most clergyman would disapprove of their daughters taking such a step. Indeed, most men. I should not be making such an offer had you not clearly signalled that it would be welcome.' His smile flayed her. 'I quite understand that I am probably your first. If that is indeed the case, of course I will be only too happy to compensate accordingly.'

'What…what exactly are you suggesting, sir?' Her lips felt stiff, chilled. The answer already battered at her mercilessly, but her heart refused to accept the appalling blow that loomed.

'That you should be my mistress, of course,' he said calmly. 'I'm only human, my dear. After the lures you cast out, I should have to be dead not to notice your charms…'

'Cressida?' Dr Bramley's puzzled voice broke in on them.

'Y…yes, Papa?'

'There was a copy of Ovid here yesterday. Do you know where it is?' Suspiciously, 'I do hope you haven't been reading it.'

'I…er…ah…' She floundered. 'It must be…'

'Oh, yes. I see it now. However did it get *there*? Thank you.'

Scarlet, she turned back to Jack.

'I'm sure you found it instructive,' he said pensively.

'And, of course, putting theories into practice is even more instructive.'

'You…you think I wish to be your…your mistress?'

The world had shattered around her into shards of ice, shining, deadly. Andrew had shamed her, dented her pride. The knowledge that Jack thought of her in such terms left her chilled to the bone. Knowing deep in her soul that if not for the bitter ice, she would feel her heart tearing apart.

He shrugged. 'But of course. In a girl better connected, or less intelligent, I would have assumed she wanted to tease me into marriage…but in your circumstances…'

She knew the litany by heart. *No connections, your mother's reputation dubious, no dowry, not even beauty to tempt a man… This is what comes of allowing your heart to override your judgement. Another man who thinks you will become his mistress.*

Something must have shown on her face.

'Cressida?' Faintly surprised. 'Is that it? You thought I might offer marriage?' He laughed gently. 'No, no, my dear. That is impossible. I do sympathise with your circumstances, indeed, I am very sorry for you, but marriage! You will do very nicely as my mistress…'

He went on, outlining exactly what she could expect of him. What he would expect of her. Every word sliced into her as he reduced her to a filly at auction. And he had offered pity.

'No.' Her shaken voice cut across his summary of the financial agreement.

'Not enough? There is, of course, room for negotiation.'

He didn't sound even remotely concerned as he raised his offer. The indifference in his voice shook her wits back into order. Later there would be time to weep with disillusionment. She realised that, despite her caution, her mistrust, some deep unacknowledged corner of her heart had hoped, had believed, he loved her. Now, if it killed her, she would give the arrogant beast a setdown he would never forget. Pride, after all, had its uses.

''Tis not that, sir.' She forced herself to sound as uninterested as he, not to betray by so much as a tremor the pain that ripped her apart. 'I gave the matter considerable thought last night, and have come to the conclusion that I was vastly mistaken in thinking I should like to become your mistress. On reflection, I believe that it will not amuse me at all. I am sure your offer is more than generous, but I believe it will suit me better after all to look elsewhere.'

Her voice she could control. Just. She could do nothing about the fiery blush that scorched her cheeks and throat. To disguise it, she bent to fiddle with her slipper. To her horror, she could feel the heat behind her eyes become blinding. In a moment it would spill over. Retreat. She had to escape.

Abruptly she stood up. 'Perhaps, sir, you would be so good as to give me my hairpins? I should like to put my hair up properly.' She risked a glance at him. Only to regret it instantly.

Steely grey eyes bored into her. 'Miss Bramley, if I find you casting lures at my good friend, Lord Rutherford, you may rest assured that you will be ejected from this house by the following morning.'

Cressida lost her temper. Completely. How dare he suggest that she would do such a vile thing! Well, if that was what he thought of her, then she was only too happy to assist him.

'Oh?' she said sweetly. 'Do you think he might be interested? I had the impression that Lord Rutherford was so enamoured of his Countess that he would scarce notice another female, but if you think—'

'Good morning, Jack. Good morning, Miss Bramley.'

As one they turned and Cressida felt all the blood drain from her face. Indeed, from her body. Nausea swept her as she faced the Countess of Rutherford, who hadn't even bothered to attempt putting her hair up; it hung nearly to her waist.

'Just looking for my hairpins,' she said. And flushed delicately pink.

Cressida began to breathe again. *She couldn't have heard.*

Then, coming closer, 'Oh.' The Countess went even pinker. 'You've found them, Jack.'

Jack's face had gone brick red. 'They're not...I mean... they belong...'

'They're mine,' said Cressida. She reached out to take them from his hand and dropped the lot as her fingers touched him.

For his part, Jack felt as though her soft touch had scorched him. He wanted more than anything in the world to drag her into his arms and kiss her until she knew she belonged to him.

She had thought of becoming his mistress. His offer hadn't shocked her in the least. Somewhere, deep down, that hurt. And she had changed her mind. That hurt even more. She had said she didn't want him. Rage consumed him, fraying the edges of his self-control.

'Here, let me help you.' Meg had bent down to pick up the scattered pins with Cressida. 'Miss Bramley? Are you all right?'

Meg's concerned tones sliced at Jack. Lord! If she only knew what the little hussy had said.

'It's...it's nothing. Some dust in my eye. Thank you. I...I think your pins are still by the fireplace. I mean... there are some there.'

She had risen to her feet, and was hurrying from the room, but not quickly enough. Something glinted on the ends of her lashes and slid down her cheek. Guilt and shame lashed at Jack. Along with the horrible suspicion that he had just made a dreadful mistake.

'Cress!' He started after her instinctively, but a small hand caught his wrist.

'You've probably said quite enough for one morning.'

Turning, he found Meg's normally gentle eyes had hardened to blue steel.

'Miss Bramley can put her hair *up* without your assistance, Jack,' she pointed out. 'And, since you were obviously in the middle of a fight when I walked in, she would probably prefer to cry without your further assistance.'

'Damn it, Meg! You don't know what—'

'No,' she said. 'And I don't want to.' She paused. 'Yet. Right now I need to find my hairpins.'

'Cressida, my dear...'

Jack turned towards Dr Bramley, who was peering at them in obvious puzzlement.

'Oh. That's not Cressida.' Dr Bramley made this pronouncement with an air of discovery, as Meg turned. 'Has she left the room?'

Speech failed Jack. He nodded feebly.

'I thought she might know where that little jade horse and the ivory Buddha have disappeared to,' explained Dr Bramley.

Jack frowned and looked to the place where the Buddha had always sat. It was gone. Anger shot through him. If one of the servants... No. Impossible. They had all been here for years. Yet the T'ang horse was missing and now the Buddha... Could they have been broken accidentally and a maid was too scared to confess?

Meg had found her pins and was engaged in putting her hair up in front of a mirror.

'Is it the T'ang horse, Jack?' she enquired through a mouthful of pins.

'Yes,' he said shortly. His father had given it to him for his twenty-first birthday. An accidental breakage was one thing, but if someone had stolen it... He set his jaw. Whoever it was would find themselves the recipient of a dubious honour—namely, being the first servant he had ever dismissed without a character.

And he still had to decide what to do about Cressida. More and more the memory of those tears convinced him that he had made a complete and utter codshead of himself. Had he really asked a gently bred, virtuous girl to be his mistress? Chills of horror slithered up and down his spine.

What the hell would you have done if she'd accepted?

Cressida stared at the very solid drawing room door and gathered up all of her courage. It was only a door after all. And the woman on the other side of it was just that—a woman. Even a Countess could only say no and after Jack's offer this morning, she would have to take the risk. She had no choice now.

Taking a deep breath, Cressida opened the door and went in. 'Lady Rutherford?'

At first Lady Rutherford did not respond. Then her head came up from her book with a jerk. Cressida noted that her rich brown curls were very elegantly braided and anchored with what was no doubt an army of hairpins.

'Oh, heavens! I'm so sorry, Miss Bramley. Half the time when people address me by my title I don't realise who they mean.'

Cressida blinked. How could a Countess possibly forget her rank and title?

'Is there something I can do for you, Miss Bramley? Do sit down.'

Nervously, Cressida approached. She hardly ever came in here. Jack only used it for receiving visitors, but Lady Rutherford had said that if she were to use the library, Dr Bramley would be driven demented by little Jonathan. So she had taken over the drawing room. A large wicker basket sat by her chair, containing, Cressida surmised, Viscount Brandon, heir to the earldom of Rutherford.

Cressida perched on the edge of a chair near the fire and

twisted her fingers together. She had rehearsed her speech for an hour. It ought not to be so difficult. If only she didn't keep on thinking about hairpins.

Dragging in a deep breath, she plunged in, reminding herself to whisper. 'Lady Rutherford, could you write me a reference as a governess? If I were to speak to you in French and Italian, demonstrate to you my proficiency in sketching and music—and I can use the globes, of course, and all the other things that a governess is supposed to be able to do—could you please write me a reference?'

Lady Rutherford's lovely smile dawned. 'If you were to speak to me in rapid and fluent French or Italian, I should probably have to apply to my husband for a translation!' she said in a normal tone of voice. 'And as for music and sketching! I've not the least doubt that your skill far out-shines mine. Oh, and don't worry too much about Jon,' she added. 'He's nearly due to wake up anyway and nothing less than a musket blast would wake him.'

'But...but surely...a...a Countess?' Cressida could not keep the note of amazement out of her voice. 'I thought... that all...'

'That all elegant young ladies of birth and fortune were educated?' Lady Rutherford's voice held amusement and a faint hint of embarrassment. 'You see, I wasn't reared like most future countesses. I was taught none of the things you take for granted. After I married I spent quite a lot of my allowance paying for tutors and the like. Until Marc found out and told all of my teachers to submit their bills to him!'

She grinned. 'So while I'll write you that reference gladly, you should consider the fact that some people might consider my opinion a trifle suspect! Shall I ring for tea?'

'P...pardon?' She was going to write the reference. And despite Lady Rutherford's disclaimer, Cressida knew that most people would take a Countess's word on anything. Absolutely anything.

'Tea. Or should I say, *thé*?' Lady Rutherford laughed. 'I've been sharing the governess my sister-in-law's daughters have. For French and Italian conversation. If you and I speak French to one another, then my reference will be even better!' She rang the bell.

'Just French conversation, or would you like Italian as well, Lady Rutherford?' Cressida found herself asking.

Lady Rutherford swung around. '*Would* you?' A faint frown creased her brow. 'I'll write that reference anyway, if you really want me to. I didn't mean to *blackmail* you. And I do mean to pay you, after all…'

'No!' gasped Cressida. 'I can't possibly take money from *you*, Lady Rutherford.'

'Do you think you could just call me Meg?' asked Lady Rutherford plaintively. 'It seems so silly when you are Jack's cousin and he and Marc and I are all on Christian name terms. I've never known Jack to be so idiotish before.'

'I…I don't think Mr Hamilton wishes to be on such terms with me,' said Cressida. And at once realised that she had uttered the biggest whisker of her life. Having offered her a *carte blanche*, Jack was no doubt prepared to be on far more informal, not to say intimate, terms with her.

'That,' said Lady Rutherford, viewing her flaming cheeks with evident interest, 'is very definitely his problem, not ours. If you call me Lady Rutherford again I won't write my best reference.'

An indignant squall from the basket interrupted them.

Cressida watched entranced as Lady Rutherford knelt down and picked up her son, crooning to him softly. Longing flooded her. This could never be hers. Never. You could miss what you'd never had. Seeing another woman nurse a baby in her arms as she unbuttoned her bodice with deft fingers, seeing the baby settle contentedly to his feed, brought an almost physical pang of need.

'Do you really want to be a governess?' asked Lady Rutherford.

'Not much,' admitted Cressida, shutting her heart to what she really wanted. 'But now Papa is safely settled here, there isn't much choice. I...I couldn't possibly stay here permanently.'

'Hmm. I suppose not. People can have such dreadfully commonplace minds about that sort of thing.' Lady Rutherford wriggled her shoulders a little.

'Do you need a cushion?' asked Cressida.

'Oh, yes, please.'

Careful not to disturb the baby, Cressida slipped a cushion behind Lady Rutherford. 'Is that all right, Lady—'

Blue steel flashed up at her. *'Meg.'* She really meant it. She wanted to be friends.

'M...Meg.'

'Lovely. That's much more comfortable,' said Meg happily. 'When Jon's finished, why don't we give him to my maid to look after and go for a walk before it snows again? It's a little cold to take him out.' She smiled. 'You can tell me exactly what to put in this reference. In French, of course!'

'Or Italian,' suggested Cressida, with a perfectly straight face.

Meg grinned. 'Indeed. Now, if you wouldn't mind tying that ribbon to the door knob in the hall, Jack and the male servants will know not to come in just now.'

Jack looked at the list in his hand and swore again. While helping Dr Bramley, he had surreptitiously checked the entire library and discovered a number of other small, but very valuable, items missing. He didn't care so much about the monetary value, but some of them were of great sentimental value, heirlooms, gifts, things which spoke to him of his father and grandfather. And even that paled into insignificance beside the hurt he felt at the betrayal of trust implicit in these thefts.

Someone he trusted, someone he knew, had sneaked in here and stolen these things. Under ordinary circumstances he would have expected the maid who dusted in here to notice, but with the library in such a muddle, she might well have thought they had been put away.

Unless she took them, thinking they wouldn't be noticed.

He ground his teeth. Loathsome to be so suspicious, but someone had taken them. He'd better make enquiries. Perhaps Evans or Mrs Roberts had put them away for safe-keeping.

Without telling you? And why not move all the jades and ivories?

'Something wrong, old chap?'

He turned. So preoccupied had he been, that Marc had come right up to him.

'Hello, back from your ride?' said Jack. 'Where's Meg?'

Marc grinned. 'Met her in the gardens.' He dropped into a chair and stretched out his long legs, crossing one muddy, booted ankle over the other. 'Walking with your cousin. Chatting in French, actually. She's very fluent, I must say.'

Jack nodded. 'Yes, she said that she was making progress.'

Marc flicked him an amused glance. 'Miss Bramley, I meant. Not Meg.'

Dr Bramley looked up from his desk. 'Fluent? Cressida? I should think so. My wife, poor Amabel, was most particular about her French. And Italian. She sings very nicely, too. Having been a governess herself, Amabel was very well qualified to educate her.'

'Did she also teach her Latin?' asked Jack feelingly.

'Er, no.' Dr Bramley looked rather conscious. 'I'm afraid I did that. And Greek. I do like teaching, you know.

She has such a quick mind. And I must say, her way of looking at things often gives my own thinking a jolt. Salutary, most salutary. But I did warn her that people would think it most improper if they found out. And I never let her read the more *explicit* texts, of course.'

'Of course not,' said Jack in a slightly strangled voice. Since when did a chit like Cressida wait for permission? She had certainly given his own thinking a jolt. And not just his thinking.

Dr Bramley returned to his catalogue and drifted back into the past.

'I believe,' said Marc, with a provocative grin, 'that Meg and Miss Bramley intend to concentrate on French in the afternoons and Italian in the evenings while we linger over our port. I wonder when they mean to fit in Latin?'

Jack snorted. 'You'd better hope they don't,' he muttered. 'Or you'll find Meg up a ladder reading Ovid!'

'Really?' purred Marc in a soft voice that reached only Jack. 'Is that how Miss Bramley lost her hairpins? How simply fascinating. Yes, I dare say Ovid would come under the heading of *more explicit*.'

Jack controlled himself with a violent effort, reminding himself that not only was his shoulder not up to planting Marc a facer, but that it would not be at all consistent with the role of host. And the last thing he wanted was for Dr Bramley to know anything about those confounded hairpins.

'Have I moved any of the ivories or jade, Mr Hamilton, sir?'

Betsy's eyes widened in shock and Jack could see the sudden tension stiffening the maid's body as she realised that she had been caught in a servant's worst nightmare.

'Oh, no, sir. I thought you must of moved them. Being as how all them books is being shifted and sorted. Or I'd of said something to you as w…well as Mrs Roberts.' Her voice shook. 'P…please, sir, I…I wouldn't never…'

'You mentioned something to Mrs Roberts?' asked Jack intently. Thank God! That practically cleared her. Betsy was hardly the sort to try a bluff like that!

Mrs Roberts spoke up. 'Betsy did mention the little horse, Mr Jack. Several days back. She said as how you must have put it away. I didn't think anything of it. She's a good lass, sir.'

'Indeed she is, Mr Jack,' said Evans firmly.

Jack smiled reassuringly. 'I can see that. Very well. Thank you, Robby. Evans. And you, Betsy. Can you by any chance recall how often you noticed things missing?'

'Oh, yessir!' she said eagerly, the tension ebbing from her visibly. 'Most every morning. I noticed cos I'm allus so careful to dust them gentle like. Like friends they are. Makes you think. Someone all those years ago carvin' them. Like they're still alive an' talkin' to you.' She flushed. 'Bit silly, I suppose.'

Jack shook his head. 'Not at all, Betsy. That's one of the reasons I like them. Off you go. And don't worry. You're not suspected and none of the other servants are going to know that we asked you anything. So don't mention this to anyone.'

'No, sir. Thank you, sir,' she gasped and removed herself.

Jack looked at his housekeeper and butler. 'It's not her. Can't be. But if she thinks things are missing most mornings, then all I have to do is slip down to the library one evening after you snuff the lights, Evans.'

Evans nodded slowly. 'Aye, Mr Jack.' He sighed. 'I just can't think who'd be daft enough to do such a thing. Even if one of the servants was in trouble of some sort, I'd have thought they'd come to me. Or Mary, here.' He indicated Mrs Roberts. 'And asked us to approach you.' He shook his head. 'But night after night... It has to be someone inside the house.'

Mrs Roberts bristled. 'And when I find out who it is, I'll give 'em what for. The very idea! Stealing! In *this* house!'

Chapter Eight

Jack glared at the drawing-room door. Never had he felt so unwelcome in his own house. Yet he hesitated to open that door. And open it he must. An apology spoken through two inches of solid oak was no apology at all. He knew she was in there. For the last two days Cressida had eschewed the library entirely, leaving it to himself and Marc to assist her father.

He saw her at meals, or with Meg, who had become the most over-conscientious chaperon he'd ever been cursed with. No doubt Meg would be in there now. He double-checked the door handle. No ribbon this time. Never before had he realised just how much nursing a baby could do.

He walked in to find Cressida with his godson asleep in her arms. Meg was curled up on the sofa, stitching industriously at what appeared to be a dress.

'Oh, hello, Jack. I found this in the attic,' she said cheerfully, indicating the brown velvet in her arms. 'Yards of it, in an old gown. No wonder our grandmothers never had more than two or three. This must have cost a fortune! You don't mind, do you?' She looked back to her task.

He shook his head, dazed. Of all wives, Meg was the last to need to make her own gowns out of someone else's cast offs. He looked closely at the velvet.

'Is that shade of brown going to suit you, Meg?'

The flashing needle stilled, but she didn't glance up. 'For goodness' sake, Jack! It's amber and it will look ravishing on *Cressida*. That green gown is all very well in colour, but a girl changes between sixteen and twenty, in case you hadn't noticed. More than can be accommodated by letting out seams. It's time she had a new one and this is my *thank you* for all the French and Italian conversation, since Cressida won't let me pay her.'

Understanding flayed him. He'd thought that Cressida wore a skin-tight gown to display her charms. It had never occurred to him that she might not have another. And she had refused Meg's money. What a damned fool he had made of himself.

Reluctantly he turned to his quarry. His heart lurched. Cressida had his godson nestled in her arms. Her head was bent over him, and Jack could see her lips moving as she whispered tenderly to the child.

He didn't fully understand the body blow of savage longing that pierced him like a two-edged sword, but it left him breathless and shaken. He wanted that little scrap of humanity to be *his*. *His* baby, *his* son and heir snuggled in Cressida's arms. His and Cressida's. Clutching at logic, he reminded himself of all the reasons that Cressida would not make him a suitable wife. Outspoken, outrageous, hottempered...

He still had an apology to make. 'Er, Cress...' She looked up. Slowly. He blinked. Lord. If looks could kill, he'd be lying dead on the carpet. Hastily he corrected himself. 'Ah, Miss Bramley, would you care to come for a walk?'

He received the distinct impression that she would have liked to tell him to go to hell, but she smiled sweetly and said, 'No, thank you. Sir.'

He gritted his teeth and tried to ignore Meg's amused gaze. Cressida had been like this for days. So polite he couldn't fault her. A shining example of feminine virtue and propriety. He could have cheerfully throttled her. How the hell was he meant to apologise for his insulting offer if he could never get her alone?

'There is something I wish to speak to you about privately,' he said. Perhaps Meg would take the hint and remove herself.

She certainly heard the hint. 'Oh, don't mind me, Jack.' She had bent virtuously over her sewing.

He couldn't throttle Meg. Marc would object. And he was rather fond of her himself. Most of the time.

'Miss Bramley,' he tried once more.

She looked up from the baby again and this time Jack found himself gazing into shuttered green. Not even anger showed. Her voice was very quiet. 'My opinion has not altered. You can have nothing to say to me, sir, that cannot be said in front of Lady Rutherford.' She lowered her gaze back to the baby.

His jaw dropped. And then he pulled himself together. If the little devil thought that he would offer her a grovelling apology publicly, then she could... *She isn't expecting an apology. She probably thinks you mean to press your offer.*

He hesitated. Long fingers clenched into fists as he looked down at her shining auburn hair, neatly confined in a chignon. The urge to stroke the gleaming fire burnt into him. Damn it all, she wouldn't even look at him.

Why should she? You made her a shameful offer with her father at the far end of the room. And you cavil at making an apology with someone else present?

He'd have to do it. 'Miss Bramley...Cressida...' he began. What the devil had happened to his neckcloth to make it so tight? He tugged at it irritably. 'I...I made a complete fool of myself the other morning. What I said...suggested...was shameful. My...my assumptions, all of them, were insulting and I apologise unreservedly.'

He dared say no more. He very much doubted, since Meg was still speaking to him, that Cressida had told her the full story. Shifting nervously, he waited.

She looked up. His head lurched and he had to harden every muscle in his body against the urge to bend down and take her in his arms to kiss away the sadness in her eyes.

'Another lapse of judgement, sir?'

He nodded.

Her lips tightened. 'Very well. I dare say it was not altogether your fault. I...I am well aware that my own judgement is sadly lacking in...in such matters. If my—'

Suddenly he realised want she was about to do. Namely apologise because *he* had asked *her* to be his mistress.

'*No!*' Furiously he glared at her. And spoke very softly. 'Cressida, you will not attempt to shoulder any of the blame for my behaviour. I won't have it. Do you understand me?'

Speechless for once, she nodded, but Jack took little satisfaction in having reduced her to silence.

Quickly he turned on his heel and stalked out. If anything, his apology seemed to have caused her more hurt. Before, when she had looked at him, he had seen only cool indifference. Now he had seen the hurt he had caused her, quivering like a wounded creature hiding in the green depths of her eyes. A wary, suspicious creature, expecting nothing but pain.

The little clock on the chimneypiece reminded her sweetly that it was five o'clock in the morning. The sort of time on a winter's morning that any sane young lady should be tucked up in bed. Not sitting in a draughty library before the fire had even been laid. On her birthday.

Cressida shifted the lamp closer, edged her feet nearer the footwarmer and wrapped her shawl tightly about her shoulders against the chill of the room. She read the advertisement again. If she got the position it would be the closest thing to a birthday present she could expect.

A thorough knowledge of French, Italian, music and watercolour sketching. She should have a mind improved by proper reading...impeccable references...

She'd just ignore that bit about proper reading. After all, she had at least *read* the requisite sermons and moral treatises considered necessary to improve the frippery female mind. If hers wasn't improved by the experience, that was her business, not her employer's. In every other particular, she was qualified for the job. She certainly had impeccable references. Meg's glowing testimonial to her capabilities sat on the desk before her. And Lord Rutherford would frank it for her. Meg had said so.

Yawning, she pulled a sheet of paper towards her and began to draft a reply. Her eyes felt unpleasantly scratchy. Perhaps she should go up to bed again. She might be able to sleep now. No, she might as well reply to this and get it off today... She had been unable to sleep all night, surely she could stay awake long enough to finish this... Resolutely she dipped her pen in the standish...

'*Lawkes!*'

The startled shriek jolted her awake. Dazedly she shook her head. Where was she?

'Oh, it's you, miss! Lor', I thought as how you was the thief for a minute there!'

She turned around to find a housemaid, fully armed with dusters, bucket and brushes standing just inside the door. 'Thief? What on earth are you talking about? Betsy, isn't it?'

Betsy nodded delightedly. 'That's right, miss. I do feel a silly. But I didn't see 'twas you just at first, hunched over like you was. An' with all Mr Jack's things missin'...well, I was about to run out into the corridor an' yell!'

'Oh,' said Cressida, cold dread flooding her. She felt her way carefully. 'Nothing has turned up yet, I take it.'

'Nothin', miss.' Betsy shook her head. 'All them nice little bits of jade an' ivory. Real pretty they was. Mr Jack's real upset, I reckon. Mrs Roberts reckons as how the little horse was given him by his pa, for his birthday…'

She prattled on, but Cressida took very little in. She remembered the jade horse. T'ang, Papa had said, pointing it out to her. Jack had said nothing about any thefts. Why not?

'…think at first that Mr Jack might of thought I'd taken stuff, but Mr Evans and Mrs Roberts spoke up for me. Mr Jack's a real gentleman, he is, and he took their word…'

A real gentleman… Yes, he was. And thank God for it. Many another so-called gentleman would have accused the nearest servant and had her charged. Even if not proved guilty, that would be enough to condemn her to either the workhouse or prostitution.

Nausea swept her and left her shaking. Dear God, what should she do now? She could not stand by and take the risk that some innocent servant might be blamed. Even gossip could destroy a character overnight. She would not wish that fate on another soul.

Betsy looked around indulgently at the piles of books and folios. 'Reckon I'll just be clearing out the fireplace, miss. Shall I light it for you when I'm done?'

'Hmm?' Cressida blinked. 'Light the fire? Oh…n…no, thank you, Betsy. I…I won't be here much longer.'

Please God, she would be away from here entirely in a matter of weeks. Then—could she leave? And she had still to decide what to do about the missing items.

Betsy finished her work and left, and Cressida sat on, her letter forgotten in front of her. Vaguely she knew that she must finish it, send it off, but suddenly it had lost its importance. She turned around to stare blindly across the room at the fireplace, as if hoping to find answers in the dancing firelight.

Firelight? Her mind focused abruptly. The fire had been lit. Betsy had ignored her instructions and lit the fire anyway. They were all so kind. That no longer surprised her. Lady Fairbridge had always maintained that servants took their tone from their mistress. Or, in this case, from their master.

Bitterly she faced the truth. She had fallen in love with Jack Hamilton. A man who, even if he had cared for her enough, ought not to marry her. She knew, none better, that, at his level of society, love was not enough to justify a union. A bride must bring a dowry, increase a family's wealth and power. She had nothing and no one, except her father. Above all, a bride must bring an untarnished name. As far as the world was concerned, she was ruined. Damaged goods.

He might not know that her reputation had been ruined, but he knew well enough that he could not possibly marry her. So he had offered her what he could. What he thought she expected. Then, somehow, he had realised his mistake. He had apologised.

And he had spent the last two days trying to make amends for his error. At least, she assumed that was the reasoning behind all the odd little attentions he had been paying her. He had been trying to assure her of his regard. His respect. He couldn't possibly know that the mere touch of his hand, tucking hers into the crook of his arm sent heat waves pouring through her. That every time he spoke to her gently her heart leapt and danced. That his eyes on her as she sang to her own accompaniment after dinner in the evenings felt like the sweetest caress…a featherlight brush of tenderness possible only in dreams…

'Good God! What the devil are you about now?'

Jack's stunned accents tore into her dream. She must have dozed off again. Blinking her eyes to clear her head, she found Jack standing at her elbow with the reference in his hand, staring at it as though he had been personally insulted.

'What in Hades is *this* for?' he growled, flinging her precious reference down in front of her.

She snatched it up and glared back, but spoke in tones of sweet reason, guaranteed to annoy him. 'It's a reference. *Most* employers require one. For respectable positions, anyway.'

'For *respect*—' He appeared to be choking. 'You don't need a position as a governess!'

'Yes, I do,' she contradicted him flatly. Much easier on her heart if they had a good fight. As long as she didn't permit herself to dwell on how handsome he looked with his storm-dark eyes.

'What do you want to be a governess for anyway?' he snarled.

She didn't, not particularly, but she met his fulminating eye squarely. 'Because, apart from your own generous offer of employment, of course, it is the only occupation for which I have any qualification. And while it may not be as well paid as the position you offered, it is infinitely more to my liking.'

For a moment she thought he might strangle her. 'I apologised for that,' he growled at last. 'You can forget this tomfoolery. I forbid it!'

There was no pleasing some people. He didn't really like her, for all his kindness. Made it quite plain that she could not remain in his home unchaperoned, and then, when she made plans to leave, he complained about it.

'And just how do you propose to stop me?'

His eyes glittered with triumph. 'By having your father stop you, that's how. You have to obey him. By law.'

Anger shot through her. 'Not since midnight, I don't,' she flashed at him. 'I might *choose* to follow his advice out of respect and affection, but I certainly don't have to obey *your* vicarious orders!'

Oh, damn! She bit her lip. The last thing she had meant to do was draw attention to her birthday. Perhaps he hadn't noticed.

'What do you mean, *since midnight*?'

Of course he had noticed. The wretched man noticed everything.

'That is none of your business!' she snapped.

She could practically see his mind working, adding it together. And getting four.

Abruptly the anger drained from his face. 'It's your birthday,' he said, in tones that wrenched at her heart. 'Your twenty-first birthday. And instead of waking up excited, wondering what presents you will receive, you're down here, writing bloody job applications, knowing full well that your father probably won't even remember to wish you a happy birthday.'

Words struggled in her throat. 'It's…it's not that,' she managed. 'I…I don't m…mind…' Her voice wobbled helplessly as she fought back tears. His anger she could deflect. Tenderness slipped past her guard.

Dragging in a deep breath, she set her jaw and forced her voice to a semblance of normality. 'I came down early to write this letter privately. I had no intention of disturbing you. Indeed, I had no idea that you ever came down this early.'

His jaw looked as though it had turned to solid, chilly granite. But she knew it wasn't. That it was quite warm and deliciously scratchy…

'I came down to check something,' he said quietly. 'Cressida, you cannot become a governess. You must realise that.'

He had come down to check something… What? To see if anything else had disappeared? Oh, God. What was she to do?

'Cressida?' She flinched back as he moved towards her. If he touched her again… He stopped instantly. 'I'm sorry. I didn't mean to startle you.'

She shuddered at the note of concern.

'Are you all right?'

'Yes,' she lied. 'I had better go.'

He looked as if she had struck him. 'Damn it, Cress! You must know by now you've nothing to fear from me!'

Tears pricked hotly. 'I don't fear you.' Her voice sounded queer, unfocused. 'I…I know that you will force nothing on me.' Gathering up her unfinished letter and the reference, she left the library.

Jack stared at the shut door. *I know that you will force nothing on me.* Her words could have but one meaning. She thought that he might still seduce her, so she was intending to remove herself from his home, his life, as fast as she possibly could.

A governess! God in heaven! He could just imagine what the outcome of that would be. Most ladies were reluctant to employ young and attractive governesses. There was always the danger that older sons, or husbands, could become entangled. Most of them worried more about the sons—who could find themselves obliged to marry the girl they had ruined. Always assuming she had connections with enough power to force the issue. And so many governesses were used as drudges by the mistress of the house.

He shuddered to think of what could happen to Cressida. *I know that you will force nothing on me.* There were plenty of men who would be only too happy to force whatever they liked on her. Good God! Hadn't her mother's experience taught her that?

He stalked over to his desk, swearing in frustration. What the devil had Meg been about to write her that blasted reference? Cressida didn't need a job—she needed someone to look after her. A pleasant, kindly…husband. That was it. He firmly ignored the outraged response from his baser self at the thought of another man possessing Cressida. Curse it all! He couldn't offer for her himself. She wasn't at all the sort of girl he'd imagined as his wife. He just had a bad case of lust. So logically he ought not to mind her marrying someone else. Someone who could make her happy. He wanted that above all things.

A…a curate or some such thing. Someone meek and mild, who wouldn't mind that she was a bit of a bluestocking. The only problem was that she had no dowry. Very few curates could afford to marry a girl who could bring nothing to her marriage.

He frowned as he sat down. There was a very simple answer, of course. He could provide her with a dowry. If she'd accept it, which he took leave to doubt. Cressida, among all her other faults, had the devil's own pride. His fingers drummed on the desk as he thought it through. Somehow there had to be a way of furnishing Cressida with a dowry without wounding her pride.

In the meantime, it was her birthday. Since Dr Bramley had said nothing he probably wasn't aware of the date. Blast it all, he wasn't even sure of her age! With a violent effort of imagination, Jack tried to envision what it would be like to wake up on your birthday and know that not a single present, nor birthday greeting, would come your way. That no one would make a fuss, or care in the least.

Well, he cared. And she'd have at least one present. Now, what the devil could he give her? He was her cousin, after all. A small token would be quite unexceptionable. He frowned, thinking. What would she like? Most women liked jewellery, of course. And the only jewellery he had ever seen her wearing was that cut-steel necklace of flowers.

Of course, a gentleman ought only to give a girl the most trifling of gifts and *never* jewellery, but he was her cousin… What about those carved ivory beads he had picked up on his travels years ago? The ones he had intended for Nan, but she had been married to Barraclough by the time he returned and had more jewels than she knew what to do with.

They'd be in his bedchamber somewhere. Just as well—if they had been down here, the thief might have taken them.

'Ah hah! Here she is at last!'

Cressida stopped dead just inside the drawing room as the Earl of Rutherford announced her entrance. She wasn't late, was she? She had taken rather longer dressing than usual. Her new gown looked so nice, she had experimented for quite a while with her hair, trying to achieve a new style.

His lordship came forward and offered her his arm. 'Happy birthday, my dear. And congratulations. Jack tells me you attained your majority today.'

She felt her jaw drop and her eyes flew to Jack's face. No one had said anything all day. She had assumed he had not said anything.

He was watching her with an odd smile as Rutherford led her into the room.

Meg came forward and tilted her head as she examined the gown. 'Hmm. Just right for you. And this will add the finishing touch. Stand still.' She slipped a lace fichu around Cressida's shoulders and twitched it into place. 'There. Perfect. Happy birthday, Cressida.'

She ought to say something. Something gracious, like *thank you*, but the words stuck in her throat, lost in the choking lump there. She saw Meg's smile through a haze of tears.

Her father came to her with a self-deprecating smile. 'I'm sorry, my love, I forgot the date until Jack reminded me. But I do have a present for you. I always meant you to have it on this day. Happy birthday.'

He put his hand into his pocket and drew out a small, oval-shaped object.

Recognition robbed her of speech even before he kissed her and handed her his present. Her fingers trembling, she took the miniature of her mother and gazed at it. Tiny, on ivory, it showed her mother as a young girl, smiling gently out at the world she had left.

'And Jack has something for you,' went on the old man. 'He asked my permission to give it to you, so you need feel no impropriety in accepting it, my dear.'

Jack had something for her? Biting her lip, she turned to him.

He approached her hesitantly. 'It's nothing much,' he muttered. 'Mere trumpery. But I thought they'd look pretty with that gown...' Flushing deeply, he handed her a small wooden box.

Carefully she put the precious miniature down on a side table and opened the little box. A necklace of carved ivory roses met her gaze in accusing innocence. Ivory. And Jack had given it to her.

Horror struck, she stared at it. She mustn't accept it, she couldn't. Papa didn't understand...and she could never tell him.

Even as she fought for the words to decline the gift, she became aware of Jack gently taking the box from her numb fingers.

'Here. Let me.' His deep voice caressed her senses even as deft fingers unclipped her mother's necklace and laid it down carefully. Then the ivory necklace was placed around her neck. She trembled uncontrollably as she felt his fingertips brush her sensitive nape as he did up the clasp.

'There. All done.' His voice was suddenly harsh, tight. Wildly at odds with the gentle, lingering touch on her throat. Then it was removed abruptly as he stepped back.

'Jack...I can't accept...'

He interrupted. 'Yes, you can. Your father and I discussed it. There is no impropriety attached.'

The sudden intensity in his voice told her he had misunderstood. That he still felt guilty over his disgraceful offer and thought her reluctance stemmed from that. She fell silent. She would have to explain, but not here, not now.

Rutherford came forward and said, 'Not being your cousin, there would be every impropriety attached to me offering you a gift. London is full of people, Meg among them, who will tell you that my reputation is disgraceful, but I would like to extend an invitation: Meg and I would consider ourselves honoured if you would come to London and visit us for the Season.'

Six months ago such an invitation would have sent her into the boughs with delight. Now all she could do was try not to cry as she mumbled something non-committal. She would have to explain herself to Jack in the morning. After she had put things right.

Jack shifted restlessly in his chair, stifling a yawn. After three and he still couldn't get to sleep. This chair had always seemed extremely comfortable, but that was before he tried to sleep in it. Under those circumstances a man discovered every single lump and sag a chair had to offer.

He knew perfectly well that his inability to sleep could not be blamed entirely on the chair. He doubted that he'd sleep properly in his own very large and comfortable bed after finding Cressida writing a job application on her birthday. His eyes felt as scratchy as his temper, but every time he closed his eyes visions of Cressida arose to haunt him. Cressida making her way in the world as a governess, ordered about by an unfeeling mistress, her quick wits and sharp tongue curbed by polite necessity. Her green eyes lowered and shadowed. Her birthday forever forgotten.

They were the more cheerful efforts of his imagination.

The ones that really bothered him involved men. Those ones had him pacing back and forth in a fury of frustration as he plotted ways and means to stop Cressida's insane scheme. In his more rational moments he knew there was little he could do to prevent her doing precisely what she wished.

He ran his hands through his already untidy hair and frowned. Riding roughshod over Cressida just didn't work. She didn't appreciate it any more than he would. Guile? He rejected it out of hand. He'd tried it once and she had called his bluff. He still shuddered to think what would have happened if she had taken him up on his offer. Lord, he'd have had to offer for her.

Would that be such a bad thing?

What!

You do like her, you know. And you'd never be dull with her around.

He'd never have any peace either. She had turned his peaceful existence inside out. But the disquieting thought persisted. Maybe he didn't want that old, peace any more. Maybe he wanted a new sort of peace.

He wriggled his shoulders again. Maybe he should just take himself up to bed and forget about the thief for to-night. If he could think of a way to persuade Cressida to accept a dowry...or him. The idea was shattering. That irritating voice had understated things a trifle. He didn't merely *like* Cressida. Whatever he felt, liking was too pale a word for it. He shied away from the idea. Bed. Much the best place. As long as he didn't dream—

The click of a latch effectively banished all thoughts of retiring to his warm, comfortable bed and its distracting dreams.

A light glimmered as the door opened and a small, slender figure came in. He knew instantly who it was, despite the dark. Something about the walk as she crossed to her desk. And...roses...he could smell roses.

What on earth did she want at this hour? Surely not another job application! He couldn't quite see what she was doing...the candle flickered so much... Why didn't she light a branch, or the lamp on the desk?

He shifted slightly in preparation to stand up and let her know that he was there... And saw it. An ivory in her hands, a pale glimmer in the candlelight.

Shock held him and then vanished in a surge of blinding rage. Bloody hell. Here he'd been sitting worrying about her, trying to think of a way to furnish her with a dowry so that she might make a creditable marriage and all the time the little baggage had been providing herself with one. His mind lurched away from the thought that he'd been within a whisker of admitting something to himself. Something he hadn't quite believed...

Thank heavens he hadn't. She'd been robbing him blind. But he had her now and, by God, he'd make her pay for betraying his trust.

He spoke as he stood up. 'You'll find it easier to see what you're doing if you light the lamp, my dear.'

Chapter Nine

She nearly dropped the satchel as the icy voice came out of the darkness. Fright choked her, only to ebb as she realised who stood near the fireplace. And flared again as she remembered just what she was doing.

'J…Jack?' She cursed the shake in her voice and fumbled with the satchel, trying to slip the tiger back in. She hadn't wanted him to know…not like this.

'The same.' His tall figure coalesced out of the shadows into the uncertain light. 'Allow me to help you.'

'N…no. That's quite all right,' she stammered. To her horror she realised that he held a branch of unlit candles. Fear froze the blood in her veins as he took one and reached out, lighting it from her single taper.

The flickering light as he lit his branch threw queer shadows on his face. Surely it was a trick of the light that made his mouth look so hard, so flat, and gave that savage blaze to his eyes. Surely he didn't—*couldn't*—believe that she would…

He spoke again as he set the branch down on her desk. 'Much better. Now we can see what we're doing.' He reached out for the satchel and removed it from her nerveless fingers. He did believe it. She could see his eyes properly now. Hard as tempered steel, they narrowed as he delved into the bag and drew out the ivory tiger.

'How very odd.' His sarcasm sliced at her. 'It was a necklace earlier this evening.'

'I…I can explain…' she began. Explain what? He'd never believe her…

'Of course you can,' he agreed coldly. 'It remains to be seen though, to whom you make your explanation. To me. Or to a magistrate.'

A magistrate!

'No!' The cry wrenched itself from her without warning and frantically she forced back the ones which would have followed. Dear God, no! Anything but that! It would mean hanging, transportation at the very least. Bile rose in her throat at the thought, a strangling terror.

'Jack, please, no! You must list—' She caught back the cry. The truth was impossible. His fury scorched her. She didn't dare tell him the truth. Not while he was still so angry. Perhaps when he calmed down… Shaking, she faced his coruscating rage.

His words bit into her. 'Listen? To you? After you have insinuated yourself into my household and then robbed me? A pity you outfoxed yourself. You might else have snared a richer prize.'

Dazed, she could only wonder vaguely what he meant. 'Prize?'

His lip curled. 'Oh, yes. All your teasing. Followed by that sudden and uncharacteristic bout of modesty. For Lady Rutherford's benefit, no doubt. It might have worked. I might have been prepared to offer more than a *carte blanche* and a trumpery necklace.'

She stared and swallowed as he held her wide gaze trapped. Deliberately he placed the satchel on the table and came swiftly towards her. She retreated sharply, flinging up a hand to ward him off. Too late. He caught her wrist in a crushing grip and brought her up close.

His face set in hard planes as he said coldly, 'As it is, you have attempted to rob me. What can you give me in return to settle the debt and convince me not to call a magistrate?'

She could tell him the truth… Terror shot through her at the thought of his likely reaction. She bit her lip. That would be worse than useless. It might ensure her own safety, but at what cost? If she paid his price, it would give her a breathing space, time to find a way out… Nausea rose. That he could believe her capable of such a betrayal…it stabbed to the depths of her soul.

What else can he believe?

Shuddering, she met his eyes and forced the words from her throat. 'There is only one thing I possess that you could have the slightest use for.'

A sardonic smile played about his lips. 'Assuming, of course, that you haven't already traded it to buy off an earlier outraged victim.' His gaze narrowed. 'Is that it? Is that why your father had to resign his living?'

The accusation took her by surprise. Rage flared. 'You bastard!' Her free hand swung up and caught him across the cheek with a ringing crack.

With a startled curse he caught that hand and imprisoned it as well. 'A little late for outraged virtue, Cressida,' he noted. 'You've offered yourself to me in exchange for my forbearance. After all, the stakes are high. Transportation or the gallows. Or…'

He left the sentence hanging and she shuddered as the room blurred around her, blackness swirling in. Frantically she shook her head to clear it…she couldn't afford to faint. No matter what he said to her. Or did.

Abruptly that cruel grip on her wrists disappeared. Bereft of its support, she staggered, clutching at the desk to steady herself. But her limbs felt stiff, leaden and an icy void had opened inside her, cold leaching out of its black depths, numbing her from within, sealing off pain and fear.

His voice ripped at her again. 'Are you refusing me? Are you daring to risk your life against your…*honour*?'

She shut her eyes against the roiling nausea, against the scorn in his voice that made the word *honour* an insult.

'Did it ever occur to you, I wonder, what might happen if some other poor soul, one of the servants perhaps, was accused of your crimes? Or what your father's shame and despair might be if you were found out?'

Tears scorched behind her eyelids, threatening to spill over. She could not bear any more. 'Please…stop. I am not…refusing you…' She clenched her fists so hard the nails bit into her palms. 'If you want your…your recompense…' She shut her eyes, attempting to hold back the flood. Anything would be better than hearing him flay her character any further and imagining what his reaction might be if he knew the truth. No doubt he would kick them out. He would never know the truth…

'Just let me go—I will find a job, somewhere for my father… The…the truth would kill him. Let us settle this now.' She shut her eyes, fully expecting to feel his hands drag her back against him.

Silence. A fraught, seething silence which lengthened until her nerves screamed for something, anything to relieve the tension.

'Get out.'

Her eyes opened to meet steely, grey daggers.

'I'll take no woman under any sort of coercion. Get out,' he repeated, 'before I change my mind. But rid yourself of the notion that your father should suffer for your sins, or that you will be leaving. Now that I know what you are, you will behave here. But I won't send you out with Meg's reference, knowing the truth. If you attempt it, I'll make sure your employer is apprised of the truth.' His lip curled. 'If you wish for *employment*, I'm sure I can find an occupation for you, complete with a discreet cottage on my land.'

'No,' she whispered, but even as she spoke, feeling began to return, and with it, terror. If they didn't leave…

'Out,' he said, very softly. 'Before my anger at what a damned fool I am gets the better of my judgement.'

She whirled and fled, the door banging behind her.

Jack sank into a chair with a harsh groan and dropped his head on his hands. He felt as though he had been ripped apart. She was a liar, a thief, a conniving little tease. And she was also the finest actress he had ever met. All he wanted was to go after her and comfort the pain and despair he had seen in her face.

Yet he knew what she had said about sparing her father was just to save herself. She knew him well enough to know that he would not willingly destroy her father. Just as she must have known that he would never coerce any woman into submission, no matter what she had done. In short, his sweet little cousin had played him for a fool. And he had had his eyes wide open while she did it.

He swore. There was nothing more to be done now. He had caught his thief. He might as well go up to bed and get what sleep he could. Later this morning he would have to make a decision about Cressida. If he allowed her to leave and take up a position elsewhere, it could only be a matter of time before someone else caught her. Someone who would have no hesitation in hauling her before a magistrate… He shuddered. Better for her to face the gallows than transportation.

Or be forced to become your mistress?

She's a thief, for God's sake! Damn it to hell, most men would have just dragged her to the nearest magistrate.

She's your cousin. And destitute. Saddled with a father who gives his last penny to a beggar, along with his cloak. Can you blame her?

So why the devil didn't she come to me for assistance, advice?

He'd never sleep. Not now. Not with this churning inside him. It was going to take him quite a while for his emotions to catch up with his intellect and realise that he couldn't possibly be in love with a thieving little jade…

He might as well put back her evening's haul. Obviously she had been to a few other rooms before coming in here. Sadly he picked up the tiger he had taken out of the bag and looked at it. And frowned.

He must be imagining things…no, he wasn't. That damned tiger had been here in the library after dinner. On Dr Bramley's desk. He remembered seeing it when he came in, wondering how the thief decided what to take. The tiger had been up on a high shelf…until Marc had brought it down that morning.

Cressida hadn't come to the library after dinner.

Doubt seeped through him in icy waves of merciless horror. If it had been here in the library earlier, how the hell could it have found its way into Cressida's bag?

With shaking fingers he opened the bag and looked in. Bundles. Little packages, carefully wrapped in handkerchiefs and scraps of amber velvet and tied with string.

He opened one at random and stared, dumbfounded as the T'ang horse fell glimmering into his hands. What on earth? Why would a thief bring all the spoils of previous raids along with her? It didn't make sense. Unless she got cold feet. Unless she was putting them back.

He swore softly. Had she realised the danger? His gaze fell on the tiger again. How had that got into the bag? *Had* it been on Dr Bramley's desk?

They had all come in here after dinner. Except for Cressida. She had gone straight up to bed. Meg had been alone with little Jonathan when the gentlemen came in. She had said Cressida had a headache. That she had gone straight from the dining room… He knew the headache was a lie. She had been upset about something. And the tiger had been here. He was sure of it. So how…?

All at once the scene rose before him… Marc, standing

where he was now, glancing down at Meg, laughing at something she had said...and Dr Bramley, seated at his desk, fidgeting aimlessly with his papers...he'd seemed even more absent-minded than ever... The tiger had been there. He distinctly recalled the old man knocking it over and picking it up again; he'd gone up to bed shortly afterwards...

Cressida couldn't possibly have taken it. His whole body sagged with relief. Thank God, thank God... Thank God for what? That he had accused her of being a thief? That he had threatened to...to force her to become his mistress? Honesty compelled him to abandon that euphemism. Savagely he confronted what he had done—he had, in effect, threatened to rape her.

He shuddered, sickened at his own lack of control, his brutality... *She must have known you wouldn't do such a thing, that it was an empty threat...that you would never force yourself on a woman...*

He shut his eyes in pain, remembering the fear and despair in her face. She hadn't known. Why should she? And he had finished up by telling her that he would take her as his mistress.

She couldn't possibly have taken that tiger. Only one person could have done that. Which meant Cressida had been trying to right the wrong. She had been putting the things back. And she hadn't trusted him enough to tell him the truth. Instead she'd risked her life and honour to keep the truth from him.

Slowly, with shaking fingers, he unwrapped each of the small bundles and placed them one by one on the desk. Scraps of amber velvet fluttered to the floor. Material left over from the gown Meg had made for Cressida.

He groaned. He knew now why Cressida had gone straight upstairs after dinner. Why she had been so upset when he gave her the necklace. She had painstakingly wrapped every single one of his treasures to protect them.

After which she had waited until the dead of night to put them back where they belonged.

Leaving the jades and ivories on the desk, he went slowly upstairs. He'd never felt so exhausted in his life. He had to pass Cressida's door on the way to his room. Unconsciously his stride slowed until he found himself standing outside her bedchamber in the dark corridor.

Should he knock? Tell her he knew she hadn't stolen anything and apologise now. His hand lifted, hesitated. And then he heard it—a queer, muffled sound, the sound of a girl weeping. As though her face was buried in a pillow. As though her heart would break, knowing that there was no one to trust, no one to confide in.

Silence. He waited, hardly breathing. Another sob came. Barely audible, it felt like a shell exploding in his stomach. His hand went to the latch, and stilled.

He dropped his hand and leaned against the panelled wall. His shoulders sagged. What would she think if he walked in, after what he'd said to her in the library? His stomach clenched. She'd probably think he'd changed his mind about not settling the 'debt' here and now. Even if he knocked…she'd be terrified…as she had been in the library.

Only until you explain… Explain what? You don't understand yet yourself.

Grimly he faced the real reason why he should not open that door. He didn't trust his own reactions. He wanted to hold her, comfort her, yes. But beneath his horror at what he'd done, and said, desire lay in wait. He'd never been in control of himself where Cressida was concerned. And tonight, when he'd accused her of theft, and told her she could become his mistress or face a magistrate… despairingly he acknowledged that he'd be the last person she would want anywhere near her now.

Let us settle this now…

Her broken words tore at him as another muffled sob

came from behind the door. He shut his eyes, trying to banish the image of Cressida weeping, her face buried in the pillow, choking back tears.

Bitterly he remembered his thoughts before she came into the library. The realisation that he cared for her. That turning his life upside down might not be such a bad thing. Oh, hell! He might as well admit it: he loved her. At last he understood Cressida's ability to drive him demented. Why he always felt so totally out of control with her. Why everything always felt so out of place with her.

His body had worked it out before his brain had even woken up to what his heart was saying. This was the girl. The one above all others that he wanted to cherish, protect and possess. At last. The knowledge stunned him. It didn't feel in the least as he'd expected—a sort of polite, gentle affection. The sort of affection a logical, sensible man ought to feel. This was a wild burning in his soul, an urgent need to possess and protect. And all the other feelings were there as well: tenderness, friendship.

Love. People said it all the time until the meaning faded. The word had seemed so bland, so colourless to him. Yet what he felt was like a rainbow burning, shot with life and passion. He couldn't begin to imagine a word that would come close to expressing it. He'd have to make do with *love*.

And in the space of half an hour he had given her cause never to want to see, let alone speak to, him again. Somehow he thought that Cressida might find a declaration of love a trifle hard to accept after what had passed between them. He shuddered. There was always the chance that she might find it utterly repugnant.

Dr Bramley looked up at Jack, plainly dazed and with the beginnings of horror in his lined, old face.

'You…you say *Cressida* had all these? That you caught

her with them? But…she wouldn't… Jack, I do assure you—'

Jack interrupted gently. 'I think she was putting them back, sir. And I know she couldn't possibly have taken that tiger. It was on your desk last night. Do you recall?'

The old man shook his head, whether in denial or confusion, Jack couldn't tell. 'Then, are you saying…?'

'I'm asking,' said Jack softly. 'Can you think of any reason for Cressida to have had them and to put them back without telling me she had found them?'

'Yes,' said Dr Bramley. 'I suppose I must have taken them.'

For all he'd realised the truth, this mode of confession still floored Jack. 'You…you suppose?'

Dr Bramley seemed to have aged ten years. His face looked grey and pinched. 'It's the confounded laudanum. I take it for the stomach cramps. To help the pain and it lets me sleep at nights.' He groaned.

Jack blinked. He'd known the old man took laudanum, but plenty of people took laudanum without ill effects…although, come to think of it, he knew his mother refused to take it. She had always said it gave her nightmares and affected her memory…

'I'm sorry, my boy, but you know, I do tend to forget things anyway. The laudanum makes that even worse and when I stop taking it after a bout of stomach cramps, it's worse still. And that confounded habit of mine of picking things up and fiddling, I just slip things in my pockets without noticing.'

'But wouldn't you notice them after a while, sir?'

Miserably the old man shook his head. 'Probably not. My wife used to find all manner of missing household items in my bedchamber. Usually put in my valise, for some reason. It never seemed to matter very much…at home, you know. I…I never thought it could happen somewhere else.'

His scared old eyes met Jack's. 'It's been much worse since Amabel died. She looked after me, you know. As Cressida does. But it's not quite the same. I…I became very fond of her, you know. Despite the circumstances of our marriage. And one day Cressida will have to leave. She will have to find a position of some sort… I…I have nothing to leave her, you know, and there is no one else to look after her.'

So the old man had lashed himself into a frenzy of worry, which probably made the stomach cramps worse—and he took laudanum for the pain. Jack swore mentally as he untangled the whole sorry mess. What to do now? First he had to deal with the frightened old man before him.

'Stop worrying, sir,' he said gently. 'As you said yourself, these things don't matter much at home, and this is your home now. I will explain it to the staff and tell them that it is just a case of absent-mindedness. And if anything else goes missing, we know who to ask.'

He took a close look at the shaken old man and strode across to a side table. 'Here.' He poured a generous measure of brandy. 'Drink this.' Placing it in Dr Bramley's hand, he forced a smile. 'There's nothing to worry about.'

After taking a careful sip, Dr Bramley asked the question Jack had been dreading. 'What did you say to Cressida?'

'I…I thought at first that she…that she had…' He gritted his teeth. 'I threatened to haul her before a magistrate.' *Or into my bed.*

Bramley nodded, wincing. 'And then I suppose she told you the truth.'

All the breath left Jack's lungs in a rush as though he had been dealt a body blow. Did the man know so little of his daughter?

'No,' he said quietly. 'Dr Bramley, I think you have not understood how furious I was. I will not distress you with the things that I said to your daughter, but rather than expose you to my anger, she told me nothing. She allowed me to think that she was the thief, despite my…threats.' He could not bring himself to tell the old man the whole. Not yet.

'She…she did that?' Dr Bramley dropped his face into his hands and shuddered. 'Dear God…' his voice came muffled '…what have I done? What have I done?'

'Sir—' Jack felt desperate '—it wasn't your fault…'

'There is something else you need to know, Jack,' said Dr Bramley. 'The reason I had to resign my living and leave Cornwall. You…you see, this is not the first time I have accidentally appropriated things in this way…'

Jack emerged from the library, his face white, fury surging through every vein in scalding torrents. If he ever got his hands on that *bastard*, Andrew Fairbridge, he'd make the elegant Viscount rue the day he was born. He'd horsewhip him! And then he'd thrash him to within an inch of his life!

What sort of a man made up to a gently bred girl, leading her to expect an honourable offer, and then tried to give her a slip on the shoulder? What sort of man waited until he knew the girl to be alone on a wintry evening with her father out administering the last rites to a dying parishioner and then came around to offer her a *carte blanche*?

His fists clenched. Andrew Fairbridge was damned lucky that several hundred miles of bad roads lay between Cornwall and Leicestershire, because otherwise he'd be dead in short order.

He strode through the front hall, seeing it through a red mist of rage, scarcely hearing Evans speak to him, and mounted the stairs. Nightmare visions of what Dr Bramley had found when he arrived home made his stomach clench.

Thank God that his parishioner had not spent the whole night dying. That Bramley had got home in time.

Jack swore savagely as he thought of Cressida, struggling with Fairbridge, despairing. His booted feet hit the floor with unwonted fury as he imagined Fairbridge's insolent disavowal of any honourable intent towards Cressida.

He could well imagine Lady Fairbridge's fury at her son's indiscretion. Especially when the Rector of the parish arrived on the doorstep, hot on the Viscount's heels, to demand he do the honourable thing and marry Cressida. Marriage to a dowerless girl without connections would not have been part of Lady Fairbridge's plans for her son.

Bramley's voice echoed in his head…*I only wanted to protect her. She begged me not to go. Said she would rather die than marry any man under such circumstances, but I ignored her. And then it snowed and I had to spend the night up at the Hall…and the butler found the snuff box in my pocket the next morning. He'd seen me pick it up…* Jack felt sick as he remembered the old man's tears. *They told me if I tried to force Fairbridge to marry Cressida, that they would have me taken up for theft…*

And then they'd taken away his living and made quite sure that Cressida's name was ruined anyway, put it about that she was loose, available to the highest bidder, just in case anyone questioned Fairbridge's conduct.

His jaw hardened. Someone was going to question Fairbridge's conduct all right. He was going to call the villain out over this. With swords, so that he could carve Fairbridge's apology out of his sorry hide, one slice at a time.

He pulled up short. Damn. If he challenged Fairbridge, then the cur would have his choice of weapons. And Fairbridge preferred pistols, as did most gentlemen these days. Not that Jack had the least objection to pistols, but he wanted to kill Fairbridge slowly. Very slowly.

He strode around a corner and cannoned into someone.

A soft, female someone who bounced off his body with a very unladylike exclamation.

'Damn it...I mean, dash it, Jack!' said Meg. 'What are you doing, charging around like a mad bull?' She eyed him thoughtfully. 'Are you feeling quite the thing? You look terrible. And have you seen Cressida? Evans says she went out ages ago.'

Jack felt all the blood drain from his face. She had gone out? That must be what Evans had been saying to him. Where? And why? Surely she hadn't left?

'Was she...carrying anything?'

Meg stared. 'For a walk? I shouldn't think so. Evans didn't say. He just thought she ought to be back by now.'

Of course she wouldn't have left. Jack lashed himself for even thinking it. She'd never leave her father. Not now. Not when she believed he had to be protected from... He shuddered.

'Jack?' Meg's puzzled voice dragged him back. 'Are you sure that you're all right? Is your shoulder hurting?'

His shoulder was fine. But his self-respect and heart had taken just about as much battery as they could deal with. He'd just been raging at Fairbridge's treatment of Cressida and her father. What he had done last night was just as bad, if not worse.

He met Meg's eyes reluctantly. 'I'll go and find her, Meg. Don't worry. It's my fault. We...we had a disagreement.'

Her nod lacerated him. She didn't seem surprised at all. 'I see. That explains why Evans thought she was upset.'

Jack headed towards the stables. Clinton might break a blood vessel, but it couldn't be helped. He'd have to ride. Wilberforce had only told him not to hunt. He hadn't actually said not to ride and Clinton could do as he was damn well told for a change.

'Ride? Damn it all, Mr Jack, sir. Doctor said as how you weren't to ride this month!'

Jack glared. 'He only told me not to hunt, man! Just saddle Pericles and be done with it.'

His headgroom glared right back and snorted. 'Told me not to saddle a horse for ye this side of Lent is what he said! Hunting, my—' his eye fell on his youngest son, listening avidly to this sterling example of how to conduct yourself with your betters '—foot,' he concluded lamely.

'You take yourself off, young Danny.' He turned from the boy and rounded on Jack. 'Now, see here, Mr Jack, you shouldn't be riding until—'

Jack swore. 'Damn it, Clinton! Miss Bramley went out some hours ago. I need to ride after her. She should be back by now—God only knows which way she went!' He cast a worried glance at the sky. The clouds were getting heavier by the minute. If it snowed, or rained… He had to find her.

Clinton wavered visibly. 'Miss Cressida? Well now, ye should have said. I'll saddle up and go after her, and you—'

'No.' Somehow Jack managed to speak quietly, but Clinton paused and took a very careful look at his master.

'Pericles, you said.' He sighed. 'Yessir. But I'd take it kindly if'n ye make quite sure the Doctor knows this was your idea!'

'Mr Jack, sir…'

'Yes, Danny?' Jack tried not to sound too quelling, but, judging by the look on Danny's face, he'd failed conspicuously.

Danny gulped. 'Ah…um…Miss Cress'da…she went up through the woods.'

Jack blinked. 'She did?' That was something. At least she'd be sheltered from the worst of any weather.

Danny nodded vigorously. 'Yessir. Saw her when I was

walkin' Firebird out a couple of hours back. You know that clearing where all the snowdrops is? She was there.'

Relief poured through him. At least he had the general direction now. And it had rained last night. He should be able to follow her easily enough.

Riding out five minutes later on the big grey, Pericles, he acknowledged to himself that finding Cressida was one thing. Persuading her to remain within his household in any capacity would be quite another. Especially the capacity he had in mind for her.

Chapter Ten

Cressida set her shoulders against the bitter north wind and trudged on a little faster. Her heavy list boots squelched depressingly through the mud of last night's rain. She shouldn't have come so far, but she needed to think without having to worry about interruption. The only problem was that she felt so horribly tired. And her brain had frozen along with her heart, and her body wasn't far behind. She should have turned for home an hour earlier than she had.

She couldn't get past the knowledge that Jack had thought she was a tease and out to snare him... A tear slid down her cheek at the thought. If only he knew, she'd never accept an offer from someone like him, let alone someone she cared for that much. She had nothing to offer but a ruined name...

You won't have to refuse him! He thinks you are a thief, remember? He'd rather take you as his mistress!

She stepped over a fallen branch. She couldn't blame Jack for jumping to conclusions. After all, he had caught her with all the jades and ivories. What else was he to think?

That you found them? That you were putting them back? In the middle of the night? Without bothering to light a lamp or a few more candles? You couldn't have looked more guilty if you'd tried!

But he'd sounded as though he hated her. As though he had always despised her. Grimly she ploughed on. It would be easier if she could dislike him, or at the very least feel indifferent. But she couldn't. She cared for him as she had never cared for Andrew. How she could ever have confused a schoolgirl's admiration for a handsome face for love she didn't know. But she had. Now her childish infatuation paled against the reality of what she felt for Jack.

He threatened to take you before a magistrate... What will happen if Papa keeps on getting muddled and moving things? What if Jack finds out?

Now she was trapped. She couldn't leave alone. And she couldn't persuade her father to leave. Not without telling him what had happened. And she couldn't do that. The chill bit into her and she shivered, walking a little faster.

She would have to tell Jack the truth. She would have to trust him. There was no other choice and she had meant to tell him this morning anyway. All last night had done was make it more difficult. It did not absolve her of the obligation. She picked up the pace a little more. Better to get it over with sooner rather than later.

Another fallen branch loomed. Hurrying, she stepped over it, catching the hem of her cloak on it. The jerk as the snag brought her up short threw her off balance and her foot slipped in the treacherous mud. With a startled shriek Cressida flailed wildly, trying to save herself. The muddy ground and branch leaped up to meet her and she felt a shock of pain shoot through her ankle as she fell.

Jack looked up at the lowering sky. Damn those clouds! And damn that leaden smell of snow threatening on the wind. It probably wouldn't be too serious this late in the season, but he couldn't bear the thought of Cressida out in it, perhaps lost, cold and abandoned.

She isn't abandoned, you idiot! She went for a walk and you're looking for her.

But Cressida didn't know he was looking for her. She didn't even know that he had found out the truth. Desperately, he pushed Pericles into a hard canter, ignoring the jabbing pains in his shoulder. The big grey gelding's hooves thudded on the muddy path, flinging up gouts of mud. He was already mired to the belly and Jack wasn't much better. His heavy frieze cloak kept out the cold and damp but it was liberally spattered with mud.

He rode with fierce concentration. The slipperiness of the path demanded his attention, but he searched the way ahead constantly for a glimpse of Cressida through the trees. He could see her tracks, clear in the path. At least he hoped they were hers. He'd left the snowdrops a mile back, following the bootprints on. Surely she wouldn't have gone much further, not with that sky.

Something cold and soft landed on his face. Several more fluttered past his face and drifted to rest in Pericles's mane.

'Hell!' The exclamation burst from him and the horse's ears flickered back curiously even as he snorted his disapproval of the snow landing on his nose.

'Sorry, old man,' said Jack. 'You'll have to pick up the pace a bit more.' He sent Pericles into a gallop, praying that he wouldn't bring the horse down and setting his jaw against the pain pounding in his shoulder to the beat of flying hooves.

And then he saw it—the flash of scarlet through the grey tree trunks. Was it? His heart stood still as he reined Pericles in hard, peering ahead—it was! His heart leapt and the breath he'd been unconsciously holding rushed out of him. She was safe—in a manner of speaking.

There was something odd about the way she moved, something jerky, quite unlike her usual light step. Pericles shifted restlessly under him in the cold wind and Jack gave him the office to move.

What had Cressida done to herself? He cursed as he saw the stick she was leaning on, saw that she was limping. Oh, God! Well, at least if she was walking on it, she hadn't broken her ankle, but still…if he hadn't savaged her last night, she wouldn't be out here. Guilt flayed him and he nudged Pericles into a trot.

Her glance flashed up and he saw the exact moment she realised who was riding towards her, the moment she froze in her tracks and stumbled as she dropped the stick, falling headlong on the muddy path.

'Cress!' Flinging himself off Pericles, he was beside her in a moment, reaching for her. Her tired, numb voice checked him.

'There was no need to worry yourself, sir. I wasn't running away from…our…agreement.' She struggled to a sitting position and he saw her face. Set, and pinched blue with cold and pain.

Sick horror churned as he realised what she meant. Why she thought he had come after her.

Shaking, he lifted his hand to her cheek and froze as she flinched away, refusing to look at him.

'Cress, for God's sake! I didn't come out because I thought you had run away from me. You *can't* think I came out to drag you back to…' His voice cracked. What else was she to think after the things he had said to her? 'I came out because I was worried about you, because I had to find you…and tell you…I saw your father this morning. He told me what happened in Cornwall, why he lost his living, how Fairbridge duped you.'

'He…he told you?' She couldn't hold her voice steady. Just the cold, she told herself.

'Everything,' he assured her. 'Except that you hadn't stolen anything. I mean, he did tell me, but I already knew that.'

How? She couldn't think clearly. Her ankle throbbed and she was so horridly cold. All she wanted was to curl up and go to sleep. In her dreams Jack would miraculously know all the things she had omitted to tell him. He would have forgiven her and he would ask to marry her…

The sensation of strong hands lifting her heavy, muddy skirts and rolling her stocking down jerked her back to grim reality. Frantically she grabbed at her skirts and pushed them back down, shoving his hands away.

'Cress, I'm trying to see how badly your ankle is hurt. That's all.'

Meeting his gaze, she was slightly reassured. 'That's all?'

'That's all.' He flipped her skirts out of the way again and unlaced her boot. 'It's a little cold for tumbling maidens in the woods.'

She jerked her foot away and stifled a cry of pain.

'Did I hurt you?' He caught her ankle in long, gentle fingers and probed carefully around the swelling.

Biting down hard on her lower lip, she eventually managed to lie without her voice shaking. 'My ankle is perfectly stout, thank you.'

'Um-hmm.' He sounded as though he'd barely registered her words and kept turning the joint this way and that.

Cressida went back to biting her lip.

'Perfectly stout, is it?' He slipped her boot back on. 'Well, that explains why you were using the stick, of course. And limping. But even if you weren't lying through your teeth, we need to get home a trifle faster than you can go on foot.' He laced her boot lightly. 'I'll tie that up for you at home. Your father will be having a fit if he realises that you are out.'

She cried out in shock as he gathered her into his arms and lifted her. 'Come along. We need to get home, before this blasted snow gets heavier.' Flakes swirled around them in a drifting dance.

'You…you aren't angry with Papa?' Relief breathed through her. He had always been kind to her father. And now that he knew the truth, her father would be safe. She could count on Jack to protect him.

'No. I'm not angry with him.'

She fought the urge to rest her head on his broad shoulder. Forever.

'Only with you.' His voice sounded clipped as he swung her up onto his horse and settled her safely in the saddle before vaulting up behind her. She shuddered uncontrollably as his arms came around her to take up the reins.

'Sir, I…I can walk.' She couldn't sit, *lie* there, cradled safely against his large body, knowing that he disliked her, that he was angry with her. Especially not when her entire body wanted to sing aloud with joy.

'The devil you can.' His terse response sounded as though it had been bitten off. 'I'd rather get home before dark, thank you.'

She held herself stiffly, trying not to watch as he transferred the reins to one big, capable hand. Then she realised that he had unbuttoned his cloak, was putting it around her and easing her against his chest.

'What are you doing?' She gasped as she felt one arm settle around her waist, anchoring her to him.

'Making sure you don't fall off and keeping both of us warm.' He buttoned the heavy cloak up around the pair of them. 'Cress, why the devil didn't you tell me the truth last night?' The arm tightened.

'Why do you think?' she whispered.

'Because you thought I'd drag your father off to the nearest magistrate! Is that it?' Every word came clipped and savage. 'Damn it, Cressida! The risk you took!'

Anger flared. 'I risked what was mine to risk!' A horrible thought speared her. 'You…you did not tell Papa what you…suggested, did you?'

'No, I did not!' A savage pause. 'And the word is *threatened*. My confession stopped short of admitting to your father that I'd threatened to take you as my mistress. Willing or otherwise.'

Relief rushed through Cressida. If Papa didn't know, then he wouldn't try to force Jack to marry her.

'That's all right, then,' she said, wishing that his arms weren't cradling her so tenderly and that her wretched heart would calm down. *He wants to get home quickly. If it wasn't snowing, you'd be perched up here alone while he led the horse.*

'No, it's not all right. Cressida, I have to know—did you care very much for Fairbridge?'

A knife turned in her heart. She shut her eyes and repressed a shudder. 'At the time…I…thought I did.' She couldn't go on, couldn't explain how youthful admiration for the dashing Viscount had bubbled over into infatuation when he finally noticed her. Andrew was charming, he was wealthy. And he had noticed her.

'And you believed that he intended marriage?'

'Yes.' *Wretched little fool that I was, I believed his lies.*

'It was never very likely, my dear.' His voice was very gentle.

'You don't have to rub it in,' she replied savagely. 'Do you think I believed it easily? That a girl with no beauty…' she felt him tense, '…no connections and less dowry could possibly have caught a man of wealth and position? At first I ignored his attentions, but eventually he told me that he loved me, that he wished to court me…'

'He told you *that*? He used those words?'

'Yes,' she whispered. 'He told me that his mother would not approve, but that he wanted me anyway. That his mother would come around to the match in the end…'

'Did he actually ask you to marry him?'

She nodded against his chest. It felt so powerful beneath her cheek. So very reassuring. She ought not to be telling him all this, he would think her a wanton and a fool, but she had to tell someone. It had all been bottled up for so long.

'Then what?'

'He…he said that since we were betrothed, we should meet more often. Privately. I…I was coming to the house daily to tutor his younger sisters in French conversation, so it wasn't hard. He would meet me afterwards and escort me home…' She trembled.

'Cress, did he…?'

'He kissed me.' She shuddered, remembering. 'I didn't like it very much. He said that I was a little prude, that he would school me better after we were married… That was when I began to wonder if I really wanted to be married. I began to avoid him. I thought he would forget about me soon enough.'

'He referred to marriage between you, actually used the word?'

'Yes.'

'And the night he came to the Rectory?'

She tried to ignore the churning nausea. Chills that had nothing to do with the drifting snow coursed through her. 'He said that his mother had refused to countenance the match. That she would need some extra persuading to give her consent. That he wanted me, and if I was carrying a potential heir, his mother would come around—'

'*What?*' The explosion rocked her. Arms which had cradled turned to steel.

'I was furious. I realised then how he'd duped me and I refused, so he…he…' Shaking, she fell silent, unable to go on.

'He tried to force you?'

She couldn't tell from the icy softness of his voice what he felt, only that he felt it intensely. Anger? Scorn? Disgust? Desperately she fought the tears which threatened to spill over her cold cheeks. 'He didn't believe that I meant it when I refused him.'

The choked whisper froze Jack's blood. Hearing what Dr Bramley knew of the story had enraged him. But this! Andrew Fairbridge was a dead man. The effort of reining in his fury kept him silent for a moment. He breathed deeply, trying to ignore the heady scent of rosewater that hung about her hair. Light and teasing, it stroked his senses, urging him to rest his cheek on the snow-starred silk of her hair. He dropped a featherlight kiss on the top of her head and heard the suppressed sob.

She had cared for that bastard, had trusted him. And he had taken her trust and dreams and trampled on them with about as much thought as he would have given to robbing her of her virtue. Less, in fact. He'd wanted her virtue.

She was speaking again. 'After Papa realised that, and that…Lord Fairbridge had mentioned marriage to me, he went straight up to the hall to demand that Lord Fairbridge marry me—' She broke off. The tremors that coursed through her shook Jack to his soul. 'I begged him not to go. By then…I…I didn't want to marry…anyone… I felt sickened…by what had happened…by what he wanted of me, but Papa wasn't listening. He…he has a…a tendency to be chivalrous and—'

'I know the rest,' said Jack, desperate to spare her part of this painful recital. 'He was taking laudanum for his stomach cramps and what with that and his upset over what had happened, he pocketed Fairbridge's snuffbox and the butler saw him do it.' He ground his teeth in rage. 'So Lady Fairbridge offered him the choice between prosecution and dropping his threat of a suit for breach of promise.'

Silence, cold and muffled by the falling snow.

'Yes,' said Cressida eventually.

He realised at once. There was more, something her father had no inkling of, something Cressida would prefer not to say.

'What else?'

'N…nothing.'

He pulled Pericles up and transferred the reins to one hand. With his free one he caught her chin. Gently he forced it up, willing his long fingers to remain still on the silken skin, ruthlessly suppressing the urge to cover the trembling lips with his own and kiss her until the whole world whirled into oblivion.

'What else? Tell me, sweetheart.' He could not help the endearment, it slipped from him before he knew it was there.

And she shuddered. 'Andrew never really wanted me,' she said quietly. 'All he wanted was to ruin me so that he could force Papa to resign the living.'

'*What?*'

She nodded wearily. 'He…he came to see me again. Two days later on the Sunday afternoon. By then everyone in the village knew what had happened. I…I couldn't even leave the house without being insulted, let alone go to church. That…that was why the letter Papa wrote to you never got posted. I couldn't go and he must have forgotten.' She drew a deep breath. 'Papa was resting when Fairbridge arrived…'

Sheer terror at what might have happened held Jack in an icy grip.

'Yes?' He scarcely recognised his own voice.

'He told me to tell Papa that it would be necessary to leave the living…that my behaviour…and his act of theft—' She broke off on a sob. 'That was when I realised. His younger brother had just taken orders. They wanted the living for him. I had played right into his hands.'

Every drop of blood congealed to solid ice in his veins as he understood her determination to protect her father this time and heard the self-loathing in her voice.

Shivering, she went on. 'He told me that I could still be his mistress. I…I was so angry I picked up the poker and…'

'Clubbed him with it,' suggested Jack, when she paused. It was the least of what he'd do to Fairbridge when he caught up with him.

'N…not exactly,' said Cressida. 'I did swing at him, but he grabbed it. Only it was still hot from me stirring up the fire a moment before. So he screamed and left me alone.'

Despite his mingled fury and horror over what had happened to her, Jack choked slightly. 'I can just imagine,' he said unsteadily. There was, after all, a certain rough justice in Cressida having fought the brute off with a red-hot poker. A certain irony that he doubted Cressida appreciated.

But if she had flatly refused to consider becoming Fairbridge's mistress, then why…? 'Last night,' he said, very carefully, 'When I…asked…demanded…that you… Damn it all, Cressida! You didn't refuse! You let me think that you were a thief and that you were prepared to…to…' He couldn't even say it. The very thought shamed him.

'It was Papa's life this time…you were so angry… and…'

He couldn't let her go on. 'Don't, Cressida,' he said harshly. 'Don't remind me. I behaved as badly as Fairbridge, but I swear to you, I would never have acted on any of those threats. It was just that—'

He broke off. This was neither the time nor the place for this particular conversation. She needed warmth, food and sleep. He needed time to sort out his tangled thoughts. One thing seared itself into him with blinding clarity: he was going to protect Cressida one way or another, whether she liked it or not.

'Never mind,' he said quietly. 'All that matters is that you're safe. We'll sort it out tomorrow. For now we'll get home, bind up your ankle and you can have a sleep.'

She didn't answer beyond nodding her head, the movement caressing his chest.

Silence enveloped them apart from the squelch of Pericles's hooves and an occasional disgusted snort as snowflakes settled on his nose. Jack tightened his hold as Cressida relaxed, grew heavier until he knew she was asleep. Warm and trusting, she slept in his arms.

The wood, which he had scarcely noticed on the way out, suddenly leapt into life despite the gently falling snow. In sheltered places violets glowed purple and the elm blossom defied the cold, its tender green veil banishing winter. Spring was here and Cressida was exactly where she belonged. And the first thing he was going to do when he got home was burn that curst reference Meg had written for her. The future Mrs Jonathan Hamilton had absolutely no need to hire out as a governess.

Chapter Eleven

'No.'

'Damn it, Cressida! I want you to marry me, not be my mistress!' Her unhesitating, not to say uncompromising, response flayed his conscience raw.

She faced him unflinchingly, her chin set at a stubborn angle, her mouth a flat line.

'No. I won't marry you.'

Jack cursed inwardly. Not even he could misconstrue that refusal. She wouldn't accept his proposal. He bit his lip. How the devil was he meant to protect her and see that she was kept safe and happy if she wouldn't marry him? Now that he knew the whole story, governessing was doubly impossible. Fairbridge had ruined her reputation beyond all repair save by a creditable marriage. The savage hypocrisy of society ensured that, even though she had saved herself, she was considered fallen. Soiled. If she married him, then she was safe beyond the tongues of all save the most hidebound. And even they would not dare cut her. They might murmur, but, by God, they had better do it damn quietly!

Frustrated, he frowned at the girl facing him quietly over his desk. She still looked as though she hadn't slept enough, but at least that haunted look had gone from her eyes. Small comfort when the tension in her frame was almost palpable.

He ran his hand through his hair. 'Cress, it's the only way to protect you from this mess. Don't you see…?'

'Why do you wish to protect me?'

'Why do I… *Why?*' Sheer disbelief robbed him of coherent speech for a moment. Then he said, carefully, 'I should have thought that was obvious.' He got the impression that she was choosing her words.

'I'm afraid not, sir.'

He clenched his fists. *Sir.* She held him at a distance with that cool formality.

'You see,' she continued, 'I have no idea why you think I need protecting, or why you should be the one to do it.'

One thing at a time. Jack took a very deep breath. 'Sweetheart, Fairbridge may not have ruined *you*, but he has certainly ruined your reputation. For most people that is enough. And Fairbridge made quite sure your credit was destroyed from what you said. He is not the only member of society with estates in Cornwall. Others who move in society will have heard the tale by now. If you try to find employment as a governess, it will only be a matter of time before word gets back to your employer.'

He watched contritely as she whitened. No need to add the obvious. She'd be turned off at once without a character, if she were lucky and it was her mistress who found out. The master of the household might well decide to hold his knowledge over her head and sample the wares before hurling her to the wolves.

'I see.' The tight control of her voice told Jack that she did, indeed, see. 'And why do you think that you ought to protect me?'

This was the tricky one.

'My behaviour towards you has been appalling. I've insulted you, asked you on two separate occasions to be my mistress…' He gritted his teeth. Now was not the moment to try and explain his earlier confusion, his overwhelming desire for her. He could well understand that she might be more than a little suspicious of male passion. As for his love…he didn't even know how to say it convincingly, but he'd have to try.

'Cressida, you are a member of my family. Our fathers were the closest of friends. And you were staying in my house where you ought to have been safe from insult. My own honour demands that I offer for you. And you must know that I…that I care for you. We…we would get on well together.' There! He'd said it!

Sort of.

A racking shudder nearly tore her apart. Despair and acceptance combined. His honour. No more. And certainly no less. Honour, chivalry, kindness. Everything any sane woman could desire in her husband. He was even a little fond of her. But they wouldn't make him return her love. And without that… She had no choice. Loving him as she did, she could not permit him to make such a sacrifice.

Swallowing tears, she answered. 'Very well, sir. You have satisfied the demands of your honour. And I must satisfy mine, which demands that I refuse you. Since my reputation was in tatters before we met and the circumstances had nothing to do with you, then—'

The expletive Jack uttered was no less shocking for being so softly uttered.

She felt her eyes widen in disbelief.

He flushed. 'I beg your pardon, Cress. But that is the most complete and utter—' He caught himself. 'It's arrant nonsense.'

'No, it's not.'

'Sweetheart…'

'No! I won't! I…I can't!'

I mustn't.

Frantically she fought for control, her fists clenching so hard the nails dug into her palms. She could resist anything but his tenderness. She loved him for his kindness and his chivalry, but she could withstand them. Against his tenderness she had no defence. It would shred her resolve in minutes and she'd be sobbing in his arms, confessing that she loved him. He'd never let her go then. He'd feel doubly responsible. She couldn't, simply couldn't, trap him like that in a web of his own decency.

'Please, don't ask me again, Jack. I can't bear it.'

'Damn!' Something inside Jack ripped apart at the broken whisper, and he strode around the desk and lifted her to her feet. He wanted to kiss her like he wanted to keep breathing. He shut his eyes and fought the urge. She needed comfort. So instead he enfolded her in his arms and held her gently, his cheek resting on her hair, one large hand caressing it, long fingers tugging it free of the ribbon.

He realised what he had done as he felt the cool, silken tresses spill over his hand, slide between his fingers as they wove their own soft spell of enchantment. He should release her, step away. Before he ruined everything again.

He could feel her resistance, then it was gone and she yielded, softening against him with a shuddering sob. He would let her go in a minute. As soon as he could. When he stopped breathing. She felt so utterly right in his arms. Sweet and relaxed. Warm soft breasts were pressed against him as she wound her arms about his waist, leaning against him trustingly. This time he would get it right. He had to take this slowly. Give her time to realise that he wasn't going to ravish her. At least not before he had managed to ask her father's permission to marry her. Hopefully not before her father had actually tied the knot. Tightly. He wasn't going to make any promises he couldn't keep, but he certainly wasn't going to kiss her now. He had to give her time to come to know him.

Her cheek shifted against his chest. Through his riding coat, waistcoat and a linen shirt, Jack felt the unintentional caress scorch into him. Every muscle in his body hardened as his hand came up helplessly to trace the line of her exposed cheek. So soft, so delicate. His blood took flight as the image came to him of that soft skin rubbing over his bare chest. His fingers shook as he stroked, found the corner of her mouth. Dear God. Nothing had ever been softer. Nothing had ever yielded quite so sweetly.

What was a man to do against that sort of temptation? His hand had found its way beneath her chin, urging it up gently. Need shuddered through him as he realised that a single teasing finger was all the encouragement she required. That she was responding—to his need and her own. That all she had ever done had been to respond honestly.

Shame lanced through Cressida.

'No.' She turned her head away from him. 'No. Please let me go.' This time she did not struggle. She knew he would release her. Even if he truly wanted her, his sense of honour would not permit him to force anything from her.

His arms dropped from her.

'Cressida…'

She had turned away from him.

He watched her go, his heart aching as he saw her straighten her shoulders and lift her head. The quiet thud of the door closing echoed in his soul.

She was going to leave. Nothing he could say would have the least effect on her decision.

How the devil was he supposed to go back to life without her?

The question stopped him cold. *Life without Cressida?*

He couldn't imagine it. He didn't even want to imagine it. *Without Cressida.* It sounded unspeakably dreary and empty. Chilly, too. Like his bed. And his heart wouldn't be any better.

He had to stop her leaving. He groaned. Why shouldn't she leave? He'd done everything to convince her that he held her in the lowest possible regard and, to crown his follies, he'd just proposed a marriage of convenience dictated by his conscience. His declaration of love had been tacked on the end like an afterthought. She had every reason to dislike him.

He couldn't force her into marriage. But only in marriage would she be safe. His own and the Rutherfords' sponsorship would go a fair way, but she needed a husband. The violent surge of irrational rage caught him by surprise. The thought of Cressida married to any but himself had him pacing back and forth. *It's unthinkable.*

Well, it has to be thought of. If she won't have me...

He came to a halt by the window out onto the terrace and stared out into the bleak, bare garden. He found it hard to believe that it would ever bloom again. How could he possibly have been so stupid, so caught up in his theorising about the ideal wife, not to see the truth when it had literally hurled itself into his arms?

His fist clenched unconsciously. He'd been a blind fool, but Lord! He'd never expected love to be such a damnably confusing complaint. Never in all his life had he been knocked endways by a woman. He hadn't expected to feel so...so bewildered by the whole thing. He'd always thought that love, when it finally came, would be a gentle, warm sort of thing. Naturally he had expected to feel desire for his wife, but not this fierce urge to possess at all costs.

No. Not at all costs. Not at the cost of Cressida's peace and happiness. That seemed to be the other queer thing about love. Her needs, her desires, ranked far above his in the order of things. He would give his right hand to spare her any further pain. Or even his life. And that was exactly what it felt like. His life. It wouldn't be worth living without Cressida.

If she couldn't bear the thought of marriage to him, then he would have to let her go. Protecting her was more important than possessing her. Or at least it damned well ought to be. His entire being howled in protest at the idea of her belonging to another man.

Savagely he forced himself to consider practicalities in a detached, rational manner. If Cressida were to marry— he ground his teeth—she needed to meet eligible men. Unfortunately, except for himself, eligible men were not exactly thick on the ground up here in Leicestershire. At least they were of course, but they were hunting foxes, not brides. And the end of the foxhunting season was nearly upon them anyway.

London. They'd have to take her to London. Introduce her into society. As his cousin and the friend of Lady Rutherford, she would be accepted. No doubt the Fairbridges would be in town. His mouth set in a hard line. Fairbridge would keep his mouth shut if he knew what was good for him. Reluctantly he abandoned any idea of calling the bastard to account for what he had done. It would cause gossip that might damage Cressida's chances.

Then he faced the biggest hurdle. Money. They would need money to buy her a suitable wardrobe to figure in fashionable society. And, above all, she needed a dowry. Very few eligible men were prepared to offer for a girl who was literally penniless. Not even those with more money than was good for them. A girl needed a dowry.

So he'd have to furnish her with one. A respectable amount. Enough to make her an eligible match, but not enough to interest the fortune hunters. It wouldn't make more than a small dent in his yearly income. He sighed as he faced the real problem. He'd thought before about a dowry for Cressida. God knew he had more money than he knew what to do with, but she'd never accept it. Not from him. Probably not from anyone but her father. He'd have to hoax her…

A calm, sympathetic voice broke in on his thoughts. 'I take it your proposal didn't go too well.'

Reluctantly, he turned to face Marc. 'You could put it like that. How the devil did you know?'

'What? That you were going to offer for Cressida? Or that she refused you?'

'Both,' responded Jack. He might have known that Marc would know what was afoot. After all, he'd told him the whole sorry story last night over a bottle of brandy.

Marc shrugged. 'Anyone who knows you could have worked out that you would feel obliged to offer for her under these circumstances. What remained to be seen was if she would accept you.' He strolled over to a side table and poured two glasses of brandy.

'Bit early for that, isn't it?' asked Jack irritably, perfectly aware that he was behaving badly.

With a faint smile, Marc shook his head. 'Not in the circumstances. Actually, in my humble opinion, you should have had one before you proposed.' He came over and shoved a cut glass tumbler into Jack's hand.

'I did,' growled Jack, with a brief nod of thanks. 'How did you know she refused me?'

Marc hesitated for a moment and then said unemotionally, 'Just that girls don't usually cry their eyes out after accepting an offer of marriage from one of the wealthiest men in the country. Even if he is a mere Mister. I knew you'd asked to see her this morning, so the rest was easy.'

Pain stabbed Jack. 'She was crying?' His voice came out hoarsely. Oh, hell! Could he do nothing but hurt her?

Marc nodded. 'Anything I can do, old chap?' He sipped his brandy.

Jack took a mouthful of brandy. It burned its way down, warming him very slightly. Almost as much as Marc's quiet presence.

'I'll need help getting her married off.'

Marc choked and spluttered over his drink. Obligingly Jack thumped him on the back.

'I…I beg your pardon?'

'You heard me.' Jack didn't feel up to actually repeating what he'd said. Just the thought of it was enough to rip him apart. Saying it made it seem real, as though it had already happened.

'Mmm. I *heard* you,' agreed Marc. 'But I'm damned if I understood you.'

Goaded to the end of his patience, Jack snapped, 'I should have thought the reasons were absolutely bloody obvious!' Then he groaned. 'Oh, lord. I'm sorry, Marc. Just ignore me. It's all such a confounded mess!'

'Love is a bit like that,' commented Marc. 'But I can guarantee one thing: watching her marry someone else won't help matters in the least!'

Silently Jack agreed. But that didn't alter the facts. Cressida had refused even to consider marriage to him. He couldn't force her to marry him. She had said she couldn't bear it. So he would have to bear it instead. If he couldn't possess her and protect her himself, then he would have to see that someone else did it. And pretend that he didn't care.

In the meantime Cressida needed a dowry.

It was only after he and Marc had thrashed out all the details, and Marc had gone to find Meg, that Jack recalled his words. *Love is a bit like that.* No surprise, nothing. Just a calm acceptance of the fact. Now he thought about it, he had never actually told Marc that he had fallen in love with Cressida.

But Marc had seen it all along. Probably before he had seen it for himself. No doubt Marc's perspicacity sprang from personal experience and long friendship. He bethought himself of Marc's final suggestion.

You know, old chap, there's no need to be quite so self-sacrificing. Once you've given her the opportunity to meet other eligible fellows, you can always court her yourself. If she can see that you are courting her because you want her, that there is no obligation on your part...take my

*word for it, no woman appreciates knowing that a man
has offered for her from the promptings of honour.*

Hope gleamed dully.

'Good heavens!' The uncharacteristic exclamation from
her father broke through Cressida's fog of tiredness. She
really hadn't slept well in the last two weeks. Not even
knowing that her father was safe, that Jack understood his
odd lapses and was perfectly happy to ask him to check
his chamber from time to time if things went missing, had
the power to raise her depressed spirits.

'How can this be?' Dr Bramley had a letter in his hand,
an odd circumstance in itself.

'Who is it from, Papa?' asked Cressida, helping herself
to a scone. They had so few acquaintances apart from those
in Cornwall. She could think of no one who knew they
were here.

'A firm of solicitors, Chadwick and Simms.' He looked
up at Jack. 'Mr Simms describes himself as your man of
business.'

It seemed to Cressida that Jack looked up from his
breakfast with a complete lack of interest.

'That's correct, sir. He is. I mentioned your residence
here in a letter a couple of weeks ago.'

'Well, that explains how he knew where to find me. But
good heavens! What an amazing thing.'

'What is, Papa?' Cressida asked patiently.

'This letter, of course. I didn't even know he had died!
Sad. All getting old now. But Morwell!'

'Papa! Who was Morwell?'

'If you mean Thurston Morwell, he was a distant family
connection,' interjected Jack. 'He died last year.' He
turned to Dr Bramley. 'My father often spoke of the tour
the three of you made on the continent.'

Dr Bramley nodded. 'Very close we all were, but I

didn't expect this! Goodness me! Why, I shan't know what to do with such a sum of money!'

Cressida nearly dropped her scone. 'Money?'

Dr Bramley waved the letter at her. 'Apparently he left me ten thousand pounds! Dear me, just think what I can do with that. There must be so many poor, deserving souls I can help now!'

She bit back a groan of despair. Would Papa never, just for one moment, give some thought to his own security and well-being? Perhaps at the very least she could persuade him to invest the money safely in the Funds and subscribe to charity out of the income.

'Papa, do you think—?'

'Yes, indeed, I shall have to talk to the Vicar about how best to lay out this little windfall,' continued Dr Bramley enthusiastically.

'Papa—'

'With respect, sir, I have a suggestion for you.'

Jack's deep voice cut across Cressida effortlessly. 'You might find a worthy cause somewhat closer to home, if you think about it.'

'I might?'

The scone slipped from Cressida's suddenly nerveless fingers, landing on the floor at the Earl of Rutherford's feet. Just what the devil did Jack mean by that? He *knew* how little money they had. Where was Papa to go if the wretch's next accident out hunting resulted in a broken neck rather than a broken collarbone?

Jack's next words crashed into her just as Lord Rutherford handed her another scone.

'Settle the money on Cressida, if you feel that you have no need for it. She wouldn't need to become a governess, then. And the Rutherfords and I can take her up to London and introduce her to society. She would marry well with a respectable dowry.'

The floor tilted in a most disconcerting way as her

breath slammed out of her and the scone disintegrated in her suddenly trembling fingers. Had he taken leave of his senses? London society? If the Fairbridges once got wind of her in London, they'd destroy her. And Papa needed the money!

Dr Bramley, however, had welcomed the idea with enthusiasm. 'Of course! I never thought of that. It *would* provide a dowry for her. What an excellent idea! Well, that's settled then.' He smiled happily at Cressida. 'I'm sure you will be very happy, m'dear.' He turned to Jack. 'I dare say you could give instructions to Simms, could you? You'll know how these things are done.'

Lord Rutherford handed her yet another scone.

Breathing deeply, Cressida reached for self-control. Just to be on the safe side, she took a large bite of the scone. If she had a mouthful, she couldn't say all the blistering things that she wanted to say to the pair of them. Saying them to Papa would be a waste of breath. And saying them to Jack would have to wait until she caught him alone.

She cornered Jack in the estate office. He'd been there all morning with his agent. Now he was finally alone.

'Come in.'

His deep voice answering her firm tap sent shivers up and down her spine. Stiffening her spine and quelling the shivers, she went in. All she had to do was say exactly what she had spent the last three hours thinking about. All he had to do was listen. It ought to be simple.

He looked up and smiled as he saw her. Simple suddenly developed problems. How on earth was she supposed to concentrate when he looked at her like that? Determinedly she started.

'Papa needs the money, I don't.' Oh, bother. That was several sentences into her prepared speech. And those dark grey eyes had crinkled up at the corners distracting her even further.

'You're always direct, Cressida,' he observed.

She flushed to the roots of her hair. 'What I meant to say was—'

He interrupted smoothly. 'That you are concerned about your father's well-being if he gives away all his legacy. That you don't want a dowry because you have no intention of marrying and that you don't want to go to London because you will doubtless meet Fairbridge and his mother there. Does that about sum it up?'

Now his smile brought tears pricking hotly behind her eyelids. Unable to speak, she nodded. That covered nearly all her objections. The only one missing was the one about needing to escape before she succumbed to the temptation of telling him that she regretted refusing his offer. Or rather that she regretted having to refuse it. *He doesn't love you. His offer sprang from motives of chivalry and family loyalty.*

'There are answers to all those concerns, my dear,' he said gently. 'Your father is perfectly safe here. He has enough money for his needs and, even if I were to die, I have altered the terms of my will slightly to ensure that he is secure. He will receive a pension in the event of my death and the use of a house on the estate.'

'You had already done that?' she whispered.

He nodded. 'That was how Simms knew where to find him. I sent my instructions to him. The necessary documents came in the same post. It's all done and on the way back to London.'

'I see.' He had made quite sure of her father's security. Her heart ached. Kind, loyal, he was everything a woman could want in a husband.

'I still can't go to London. I…I don't want to marry.' She would never be able to bring herself to marry anyone else, even if anyone offered, which was doubtful.

He disabused her of that misapprehension at once. 'With ten thousand pounds, even with a slight misunderstanding in your past, you are perfectly eligible. Not a prize for the fortune hunters, but dowered well enough to gain a respectable offer.'

She shuddered at the thought. Marriage was unthinkable now. She could not give herself to another, loving him as she did.

He went on in a low voice. 'Even if you feel repugnance towards marriage after…after what has happened, the money will serve to make you independent. As a governess, you would always be at risk.'

She snatched at the chance. 'Very well, then. I don't need to go to London. You haven't thought, my reputation—'

His voice turned molten. 'Believe me, Cressida, if Fairbridge dares to open his mouth about what he did, I'll shut it for him. Permanently.'

Horror washed through her in an icy black flood. He meant to challenge Fairbridge. And Fairbridge was a crack shot…

'Jack, no…you mustn't…' Fear choked her, images of Jack wounded, dying, dead. Dazedly she clutched the edge of the desk for support and met his implacable gaze.

'Don't waste too much sympathy on him, Cress,' he advised. 'He certainly wasted none on you or your father.'

He thought she was worried about *Fairbridge*?

'Please, Jack, I don't want you to call him out…' Her voice broke in anguish that he could think she was frightened for Fairbridge. Yet if she told him the truth…she could find herself sobbing out her love for him. There would be no escape then.

'I won't be able to if you come to London,' he said quietly. 'The last thing I want to do is stir up talk. Calling that…' he paused, took a deep breath '…calling Fairbridge out would be a last resort, if he talks. But he won't. He won't dare. I'll make quite sure he knows what he's risking if he does.'

'But—'

His voice cut across her harshly. 'You can't stay here, Cressida. It's impossible.'

Icy pain stabbed through her as his words went home. Knowing she had to leave, and knowing he wanted nothing more devoutly, were two entirely different sorts of hurt. 'I see.' She forced her voice to quiet indifference. 'Very well, then. When do you wish me to leave?' The words rang between them with merciless clarity.

Equally cold, he replied, 'Marc and Meg intend going home in a few days. They have suggested that you go with them and that they will take you up to town at the start of the Season in a couple of weeks, as Marc suggested on your birthday.'

As soon as possible.

A shiver knifed through her. He must really want to get rid of her quickly if he wouldn't even let her stay for another two weeks.

Unconsciously she clutched the edge of the desk, staring blindly at the bookshelves beyond him with their ranks of old estate books. The fire crackled mockingly, offering a warmth she could not feel. The cold striking through her came from deep within. She shivered again as the chill tightened its grip. Soon she would not feel the cold or the pain. She would be frozen.

'Go up to your chamber, Cressida.' Jack's harsh voice drew her momentarily from the ice of the abyss. 'I'll have a tray sent up to you there.'

'Thank you,' she said tonelessly. She wouldn't cry. She wouldn't. Tears were warm. And they hurt too much. They would thaw out the ice, leaving her exposed to hope. And more hurt.

Jack watched her leave, battling the urge to leap to his feet, grab her and kiss her into submission. Hell, she needed warming! She looked so cold and tired. As though all the life had been drained out of her. *Better a fire and dinner on a tray than you pressing an unwanted suit on her.*

Thank God she had agreed to go to London! Lord, he hadn't even been able to sit in the same room with her for five minutes without wanting to make love to her! Just as well he'd been seated at the desk the whole time. Otherwise she'd have known exactly what was on his mind.

He had spent the last two weeks trying to show her that he cared about her. She had spent the last two weeks trying to avoid him. Every time he entered a room she froze. If she could, she made a quiet excuse to remove herself. And if he touched her in any way, he could feel the tension coiling within her.

There was no point remembering the sweetness of her mouth under his, the feel of her curves fitting so perfectly against his body. If she had ever felt anything for him, if there had ever been the potential for her to care for him as he now cared for her, then he had destroyed it the night he accused her of being a thief and offered to take her as his mistress.

Morosely, he returned to his estate tallies. Usually it was a job he enjoyed, but now all he could think of was how much he would have liked to show Cressida how it was done. How much he would have enjoyed seeing the quick comprehension flood her vivid face. How much he would have enjoyed her laughter and questions as they shared the task. As they shared their lives. He'd thought he wanted a wife who would leave his life much as it had been. A smiling, undemanding presence on the edges of his world that he could care for. Fate had ignored him and sent him exactly what he needed. And he, damned fool that he was, had handed it straight back without even realising it.

Cressida wandered out into the garden and looked up at the house. Mellow golden stone smiled back at her. She blinked back tears. This might have been her home. It still could be if she went to Jack and accepted his offer. But he wanted her to go. He had offered when she had nothing to recommend her to anyone else. When his honour demanded it. Now she had a dowry, connections. She had suddenly become eligible. And Jack had arranged for her to leave.

She would be going to London for the Season and she might as well enjoy it as best she could. Never mind that she had no intention of accepting any offer of marriage. After the Season was over, she would find herself a small cottage in the country where Papa could visit her occasionally. She had ample money to live simply. And if she found somewhere near Lord Rutherford's principal seat, then she would have a friend close by.

She was a great deal better off than she had been when they left Cornwall. Papa had a safe and respected position, she had an independence and at least one dear friend. So why on earth were the budding flower borders disappearing in a haze of tears? She dragged a handkerchief out of her sleeve and blew her nose violently. Surely in time her pain would fade? Wouldn't it? She drew a deep breath. Whether it faded or not was immaterial. What she had to do now was behave as though it had done so already.

Chapter Twelve

'Are you quite sure about this neckline, Meg?' Cressida looked at the silk-clad vision in the modiste's mirror and blinked. Surely that could not possibly be her? Why, she actually looked elegant, pretty even. The shimmering blue-green silk did odd things to her eyes as well. But the unaccustomed exposure of her cleavage... 'It looks very low.'

Meg's sister-in-law, Lady Diana Carlton, chuckled.

Meg glared. 'Tell me, as an academic question—if you saw it on another woman, me for instance, would you think it scandalous?'

Caught by surprise, Cressida considered the matter dispassionately. Meg had worn a gown cut low across the breasts just the previous night. It had looked lovely. And there was no mistaking Lord Rutherford's opinion. His often rather cold grey eyes had flared as they rested on his wife gowned for a ball.

'Well?'

A reluctant smile tugged at her lips. 'No. I wouldn't. But you are a Countess...'

'Granted,' said Meg, 'that gown would not do for a girl of seventeen in her first Season, but you are one and twenty, possessed of a respectable fortune and Jack Hamilton's cousin to boot. Di agrees with me.' She turned to Lady Diana. 'Don't you, Di?'

Lady Diana nodded. 'Perfectly unexceptionable. Indeed, I can think of only one person who will be at all shocked by that neckline.'

The modiste added her mite. '*Ravissement, mademoiselle! Les gentilhommes* will be, 'ow do you put it? *Bouleversé?*'

'Bowled over?' suggested Meg.

'*Exactement!*' enthused the modiste. 'An' *moi*, I tell ze truth. It does my business no good if you wear the wrong dress! Now, consider if you please, ze pelisse…'

Cressida gave up. If Meg, Lady Diana Carlton and a fashionable modiste all thought the gown appropriate, who was she to argue? If they all said no one would be offended, then no one would be offended. Except, of course, for that mysterious someone alluded to by Lady Diana. Oh, well. One person couldn't matter all that much, surely.

Jack glared at the swirl of dancers in puritanical disapprobation. Why had he never before realised just how disgracefully low women's necklines had become. Brazen hussies! Lord, he wondered that they didn't all contract an inflammation of the lungs. While he, on the other hand, felt far too hot. Just thinking of that gown Cressida was almost wearing, as she pranced about Almack's Assembly Rooms with every gazetted rake in London, was more than enough to heat his blood. His cravat felt as if it would choke him! As did his satin kneebreeches, which, in deference to the immutable laws of Almack's almighty patronesses, he had donned with much cursing and reluctance.

Just what the hell had Meg been thinking of when they ordered that gown anyway? Chaperons were supposed to bait the trap and display the goods, so to speak. But damn it all! The bodice practically grazed Cressida's nipples! Which was precisely what he wanted to do. With his teeth.

He clenched one fist and glared a bit harder. Thank God no one had yet given Cressida permission to waltz here. The sight of her whirling in the embrace of one of his lecherous friends would probably consign him to Bedlam, worrying if she were about to fall out of her gown.

The music drew to a close and he watched possessively as Cressida came off the dance floor with Lord Parbury. He'd always considered Parbury a friend, but what the devil did the fellow think he was up to, flirting like that with the chit? There! She was laughing again. Practically giggling. Dash it all, he'd never found anything Parbury uttered worth laughing over.

But at least she was happy again. Somewhere, between Leicestershire and London, Meg had managed to dispose of the sad, dispirited girl who had left Wyckeham Manor. In her place was the outspoken, impertinent elf of old. Flirting with all the *ton*'s most eligible bachelors, with the notable exception of Mr Jack Hamilton.

To his utter horror he saw Lady Stanhope, with dear Alison in her wake, sailing in his direction. Good God! He could end up dancing with the wench! Panicked, he reacted instinctively and found to his immense surprise and annoyance, that he had automatically moved to intercept Cressida and Lord Parbury as they headed back towards Lady Rutherford.

'I'll escort Miss Bramley, Parbury. No doubt you have other fish to fry this evening.' He really couldn't help the growl in his voice. It just happened. Something about his stiff jaw, no doubt.

Parbury's answering grin didn't help in the least. 'But none so charming as your little cousin, Jack, old fellow. Permit me to congratulate you on acquiring such a lovely ward.'

'She's *not* my ward!'

'I'm *not* his ward!'

The hasty denials tumbled over each other in their vehemence.

Lord Parbury choked, an endeavour in which Jack felt seriously tempted to assist. In the nick of time he recalled the impropriety attached to strangling a peer of the realm within the sacred portals of the Marriage Mart.

'Of course not, old chap,' Parbury said soothingly. 'But you do such a sterling imitation! Have you been taking lessons from Rutherford? I note he's got the jealous-husband routine down to a fine art. Miss Bramley, if you will excuse me, I'll leave you to your cousin. I'm sure he will return you safely to Lady Rutherford. Perhaps you might care to drive with me one day in the Park?'

Cressida replied with what Jack considered to be quite unnecessary enthusiasm. 'I should like that very much, my lord.'

'I shall call, then,' he assured her as he bowed gracefully over her hand. 'Your servant, ma'am. Evening, Jack.' He strolled off and Jack's hackles subsided somewhat.

Only to rise again as Cressida asked resignedly, 'Very well, Mr Hamilton—what's wrong with him?'

'Damned rake and libertine!' growled Jack as he started walking. If they stayed still, Lady Stanhope would have every opportunity for a broadside.

'What? Another one? But Meg assured me he was a friend of yours!' She looked up at him challengingly. 'Don't you have *any* respectable friends?'

Jack wondered which he wanted to do more—throttle her or run his finger along beneath the edge of her bodice.

Dragging in a deep breath, he forced himself to accept that neither alternative would meet with society's approval. Then he found a use for the breath he had taken—enumerating to Cressida exactly which of society's single men he considered suitable dance partners for her. A detached and irritatingly astute part of his brain suggested that there could only be one motive for leaving out every unmarried man between the ages of twenty and sixty.

He only realised the danger his preoccupation had invited when it was breathing down his neck.

'At last! My dear Mr Hamilton, I vow it has been impossible to come at you. But I knew you would like to see dear Alison, so I have persevered!'

Lady Stanhope came up with the quarry in full cry, Alison close on her heels.

'Ah, Miss Bramley. How very singular. Do you know, I have just had the most interesting chat with my cousin.' Lady Stanhope paused and bestowed upon Cressida the full benefit of her long-nosed stare. 'My cousin who lives in Cornwall, I mean. The Dowager Lady Fairbridge. I understand you to be quite well, ah, known to her.' Her eyes glittered with malice.

Every nerve in Jack's body flared to full battle alert. The presumptuous *cow*! 'Yes, indeed, Lady Stanhope. Miss Bramley's father did mention the connection. Perhaps you might be good enough to convey to his lordship's mother my desire to further explore the issue with her son.'

Lady Stanhope discovered herself to be dangerously exposed to superior firepower and beat a hasty retreat.

'Jack! Please…' He felt Cressida's hand tighten convulsively on his sleeve. 'Can't I go home? She knows! They must have talked. I *knew* this would happen! Please, let me go.'

He looked down into her stricken face. 'Tell me, Cress. If it were not for the Fairbridges and Lady Stanhope, would you enjoy London?'

She stared as if she thought he had gone mad. Stupid question. What female would not enjoy the social whirl, the shops, the opera, the gossip? 'Well, of course I would. Only…only not all year.' Her eyes grew distant. 'Not even every year. Just imagine; never seeing the spring flowers, never seeing the woods go mad with bluebells and the trees bud. I suppose coming up to town for a week or so would be nice, but…isn't being at home better?'

His heart lurched violently, but his response died in his throat as another voice chipped in.

'Hello, hello! Jack, old man! Is this your little cousin? I heard she was charmin'. Quite charmin'. Lord Danville, Miss Bramley. Perhaps you might have a dance free for me?'

Meg, having watched Jack chase off Lord Parbury, with mingled amusement and consternation, turned to Lady Jersey in exasperation. 'What is wrong with him!'

The Countess of Jersey didn't reply for a moment, being fully occupied with Lady Stanhope's forlorn hope. Then she shrugged. 'Who knows? He's a man, my dear. Could it be that? Mind you, my love, he did see off Lady Stanhope in fine style. Much must be forgiven him for that effort. Such a tedious creature!'

Despite her annoyance, Meg laughed and then frowned as she watched Jack don full battle dress for the inoffensive Lord Danville.

'Goodness me,' breathed Lady Jersey as Jack saw off Lord Danville. 'I always thought Jack's eyes were grey! A delightfully stormy grey for the right woman, no doubt, but I do believe I detect the merest hint of green this evening! How splendid! And such utterly splendid sport to see dear Jack engaged on two fronts.'

Meg laughed again behind her elegant chickenskin fan and darted a glance sparkling with challenge at her friend. 'Sally, are you feeling suitably meddlesome this evening?'

The Queen of the *ton*, and its most inveterate gossip, didn't bat so much as an eyelash. 'But of course, my dear. Did you have something particular in mind, or just general nosiness?'

Meg smiled seraphically. 'Wouldn't you say that my protégée's behaviour is unexceptionable, Lady Jersey?

And you are a Patroness, after all. What use is power if one doesn't wield it?' She gazed pointedly at Jack. 'Isn't the next dance a waltz?'

Lady Jersey smothered a grin and said unsteadily, 'I believe so, Lady Rutherford. How deliciously convenient. After all, only a madman fights on three fronts at once.'

Their eyes met and saw that they were in agreement just as a deep voice behind them said, 'My dance, I believe, my lady. Hello, Sally.'

Meg swung around, struggling to quell her laughter and aware from the palpable suspicion on Marc's face that she had not succeeded in the least. His glance flickered from one laughing countess to the other.

'Hmm. Should I ask, or would ignorance be safer?' He possessed himself of Meg's hand and kissed it.

'Much safer, my lord,' she said, smiling at him. 'But if you watch Sally…'

His gaze followed Lady Jersey as she stalked her quarry through the crowd… 'Good God! She's not? Is she?'

'Dear Jack,' purred Lady Jersey, 'how splendid, simply splendid, to see you here! And Miss Bramley! I do hope you are enjoying yourself, my dear. You seem to have danced every single dance this evening. Lady Rutherford and all your well-wishers must be delighted at your success.'

Cressida blushed and stammered a disjointed response as Jack eyed the peeress warily. There was no escape. What the devil was Sally about now?

He found out.

'Miss Bramley, it would be such a pity to break your run, so to speak, but the next dance is a waltz, of course. So I just popped over to say how much pleasure it would give all of us to see you take part.' She smiled with what Jack considered to be wholly malicious intent as the orchestra struck up. 'Goodness me, how vexatious. There is no time to find you an eligible young man. But perhaps Mr Hamilton might care to oblige? Just this once, of course! When it is perceived that you have our approval, you will be swarmed under with eager gentlemen.'

She sailed off with a final wave, having completely out-flanked her opponent.

Even as he realised that he had won several battles, only to lose the war, Jack wondered which would be the greater trial—watching Cressida take the floor in a waltz with any other man in London, or dancing with her himself. Grimly he looked down at Cressida and discovered her biting her lip.

'There is absolutely no need for you to put yourself out, sir. I quite understand that you do not wish to dance with me. Perhaps you might escort me to Lady Rutherford.'

His heart clenched at the carefully indifferent tone. He'd hurt her. Again. Understandably, she saw only that he didn't wish to dance with her. And drew the obvious conclusion.

'It will be my great pleasure to escort you to Lady Rutherford,' he said huskily, and drew her into the dance.

Shocked green eyes flashed to his face. 'Jack? I mean—'

'Jack,' he said firmly. God, but she felt sweet in his arms, just as he remembered, so warm and silken, her waist so deliciously supple under his hand... He smiled down at her, consigning all his misgivings to hell. As he whirled by, he bestowed upon Lady Stanhope and dear Alison the most radiant of smiles and then returned his adoring gaze to Cressida. They could report *that* to the Fairbridges.

'But...but you said you would escort me to Meg,' she protested, her own gaze fully focused on the top button of his waistcoat.

The curve of his lips deepened as he answered. 'Meg, if you will but look about you...' he swung her around expertly '...is dancing with Marc. But don't imitate them,' he warned, observing that the Earl of Rutherford had, as usual, drawn his Countess scandalously close and was doubtless whispering sweet nothings in her ear, very much as he wished to do to Cressida. His whole body tingled at the thought of drawing her closer, feeling her thighs, not just the silken skirts, slide past his.

His arms tightened instinctively before he could check himself. To his utter horror he realised that he had encouraged her to do exactly what he had just warned her against. That his unthinking, possessive action had brought her dangerously close, that the dreamy, summery scent of rosewater was wreathing its enchantment, seducing his senses.

He stifled a groan and concentrated on dancing, trying to ignore the pounding of his blood. She looked so lovely this evening. The blue green silk Meg had helped her choose did something to her eyes. Or was that just his heart? And her hair looked so silky, so soft, he ached to stroke it, to feel the sensuous slide of it through his fingers.

Desperately he fought the urge to tighten his hand on her back, to bring her closer still. Music swirled around them, the rhythm sweeping them along. She felt like thistledown in his arms, moving with him so lightly and easily.

How could dancing with Jack be so totally different from practising with her dancing master? Or the Earl of Rutherford? Cressida pondered this dizzily as Jack whirled her around the room. After the initial shock of dancing in a man's arms, she had found dancing with Signor Ridolpho and Marc quite easy. Indeed, the Earl had been only too happy to help her practise the steps when he found her practising with Meg in the drawing room at Rutherford House.

Dancing with Jack was another matter entirely. Not a single shiver had feathered up and down her spine dancing with Signor Ridolpho. Not even the devastatingly handsome Earl of Rutherford had made her feel flustered. He'd teased and instructed her in the steps and her heart had remained unmoved in its place. Now it pounded so hard, she could not think rationally about Lady Stanhope's half-voiced threat.

Dimly she knew that between them Lady Stanhope and Lady Fairbridge could destroy her, but Jack's arms encircled her like steel and she felt safe. His body radiated heat and power and her wretched heart had bolted like a runaway horse. Her whole body tingled at the nearness of his. Her breasts felt most peculiar, flushed and aching, so that she longed to press against him to ease their torment. Or to increase it. And she felt safe. She had never been in more danger.

The room had become insufferably hot. She'd expected to freeze in this light gown with its scandalous neckline, despite Meg's insistence that she'd be quite warm enough. Meg had been right. Blushing like this would warm a marble statue. And the look on Jack's face didn't help in the least. Set in stone, his expression suggested that he had slammed the lid on something unwanted.

'Is something bothering you?'

Her question obviously caught him off guard. He tried to dissemble. 'How did you…? No! Why?' The flush of colour on his cheekbones, as well as the near slip, betrayed him.

Aware that he had slipped, Jack tried to relax slightly, to smile at her. But the hard tension sang in his body, pounded in his veins.

'Because you look as though you are in pain,' she said as he whirled her around. 'I thought perhaps your shoulder…'

As he shook his head, he caught Marc's amused, and not unsympathetic, glance. The Earl of Rutherford would have a very fair idea just which portion of Jack's anatomy was in most discomfort. And it certainly wasn't his shoulder.

'My shoulder is quite all right,' he said tightly. The rest of him might have tied itself in knots, but his shoulder had recovered nicely.

The end of the dance came eventually, leaving Jack uncertain as to whether it had been joy or torture. To his absolute horror he could see any number of eligible gentlemen with their eyes firmly on Cressida. Sally Jersey had given the chit permission to waltz. As far as the men were concerned, that was enough. Open season.

Seeing that he was about to be besieged by half the men in London, he turned Cressida towards the refreshment tables. 'A glass of lemonade, Cress.' He was tempted to down one himself if it had enough ice in it. Something had to cool him down. A languid voice stopped him in his tracks and made every muscle in his body leap to full battle alert.

'Miss Bramley, how charming to meet you here. Do you know, I couldn't quite believe it when my mama informed me that you had come up to town.'

Jack felt Cressida's hand freeze on his arm. He looked down sharply as she turned. Her face was quite composed, her voice utterly calm.

'Good evening, Lord Fairbridge.'

Somehow Jack contained his simmering rage as he looked the Viscount up and down. A mill at Almack's was out of the question, yet he could not control the instinctive clenching of his fists, or the note of contempt that crept into his voice.

'My cousin has mentioned her *acquaintance* with you, Fairbridge. You might wish to consider the fact that she is under *my* protection now. I do hope Lady Stanhope conveyed my message to you.'

The barely leashed menace in his voice brought Cressida's head around with a jerk. Never, even when he had been angriest with her, had she heard that particular note. And his eyes—they had gone hard, like stone, flint. Cold and dangerous. She had always thought of him as civilised, quiet, scholarly. A thorough-going gentleman. Evidently she had missed something.

So, apparently, had Lord Fairbridge. 'Your cousin, is she, Hamilton?' The Viscount did not seem to have noticed Jack's narrowed eyes and clenched fists. He was busily engaged in removing a speck of dust from his coat sleeve. 'Miss Bramley never mentioned that.' He favoured Cressida with his most charming smile. 'And how does your father go on, Miss Bramley? I trust he has recovered from his indisposition.'

She could barely bring herself to answer civilly. This was the man who had plotted to deprive her father of his living and then threatened to have him transported.

He could still do it if you offend him. Fear shivered through her. Jack and the Rutherfords might be able to salvage her reputation if Andrew gossiped, but if once he went to Bow Street, nothing would save her father. So she forced a smile to her lips and spoke lightly. 'My father is very well, my lord. I shall tell him you asked when next I write to him.' The lie nearly choked her.

'You're looking as fine as fivepence, Miss Bramley.' His eyes wandered and Cressida wished, not for the first time, that she had resisted Meg's ideas on necklines far more strenuously. His gaze seemed to creep over her with an almost tangible slither.

Never before had she been so conscious of the unyielding strength of Jack's arm as she was now, when her gloved hand lay on his sleeve. To the world it must look as though she had two eligible bachelors dangling on her string. She felt more like a lamb hiding behind a very large sheepdog to escape the jaws of a wolf.

'Miss Bramley, might I escort you to my mother?' suggested Lord Fairbridge. 'Mama said she would look forward to renewing the acquaintance.'

Dizzily, Cressida attempted to reconcile this assertion

with the matron who had stigmatised her as a scheming little slut at their last meeting. Perhaps she wanted to re-state her case.

'Then you might do me the honour of dancing with me,' he went on, his tone suggesting that he was the one be-stowing the honour.

Before she could even draw breath to respond, Jack saved her the trouble. 'Another time, Fairbridge,' said Jack. 'I have promised to return my cousin safely to her chaperon. And I believe Miss Bramley's card to be full this evening. No doubt Lady Rutherford will be happy to receive Lady Fairbridge should she wish to call in Gros-venor Square.'

Fairbridge looked startled. 'The Countess of Ruther-ford?'

For a moment Cressida thought the sheepdog had turned into a wolf. Only a fool would have thought Jack's smile friendly.

'Quite so, Fairbridge. I hope that clarifies the situation for you and Lady Fairbridge.'

She found that she was being led away inexorably. Re-lief sang through her. Perhaps seeing him would become easier as she gained confidence, but somehow she doubted it. Why ever had he come up to her? Did he intend to renew his *offer*? That didn't sound quite right, but she couldn't think what else to call it. Proposition? Proposal? No matter. The important thing now was to convince Jack that Fairbridge's presence didn't bother her in the least.

She could feel the anger surging out of him. His arm, under her white gloved hand, had turned to steel, and, when she glanced up, his jaw looked as though it had petrified. The fear that he might use the slimmest of pre-texts to challenge Fairbridge slammed back into her. Vi-sions of Jack, dead or maimed on her behalf, choked her. Forcing a deep breath into her lungs and offering up a mental apology for the lie she was about to utter, Cressida said, 'It's so nice to see a familiar face after so many strangers. How kind of him to speak to me. I wonder if Lady Fairbridge will call?'

How Jack managed to return a civil reply was more than he could understand. But he did. Wondering just how he could have been so stupid as to send Cressida up to London with a respectable dowry.

Much to Cressida's horror Lady Fairbridge did call. The very next day.

She had caught only fleeting glimpses of the Viscountess through the crowd at Almack's. The only dances she had free had been the waltzes and they were soon snapped up by eager gentlemen. But she had been conscious very often of a cold, considering gaze upon her.

She was sitting in the drawing room of Rutherford House alone, when the butler came to inform her that Lady Fairbridge had called.

He smiled kindly. 'Naturally I told her that her ladyship was not at home, but she said she would be happy to see you. I said that I would ask if you were at home.'

Cressida took a deep breath. Meg was upstairs, nursing Jon. What should she do? She could ask Delafield to deny her. The last thing she wanted was to confront Lady Fairbridge alone. On the other hand, it might be best to see her alone. No doubt she had observed her son last night and wished to make her opposition to any connection quite plain. A shiver took her. It would be better to see Lady Fairbridge alone. Then she could assure her that she had no interest in Lord Fairbridge. That she would prefer never to see him again.

There was no point in hiding.

'Please inform Lady Fairbridge that I am at home,' she said at last.

She did not have long to wait.

'Lady Fairbridge.' Delafield closed the door behind the dragon and Cressida rose to her feet, coming forward.

'How do you do, ma'am?' She might as well be polite. 'Will you not be seated?'

She was enveloped in a heavy cloud of ambergris and purple satin. 'My dear Miss Bramley! I am in tolerable health. So surprised we were to hear of your presence in town! How naughty of you not to write and let me know! But it's always so nice when old friends appear unexpectedly! And how is your dear papa? Recovered from his malady, I trust?'

Disbelief robbed Cressida of rational thought, let alone speech, as she emerged gasping.

'I…er…he's very well. I didn't think…that is…you were not…'

Her ladyship sailed on. 'Of course, Fairbridge was delighted to see you last night. I had no idea that Mr Hamilton was a connection. And how is his dear mama, Lady Anna? Such a charming creature, don't you think? Is she not in London?'

Lady Fairbridge disposed her amply cushioned behind on the sofa and patted the place beside it invitingly.

Cressida pretended not to see and moved to the bellpull. Stumbling over the words, she explained that Lady Anna Hamilton was staying with her daughter in Yorkshire, that she had never met either lady and would Lady Fairbridge care for some refreshment?

Lady Fairbridge indicated the place beside her again. Gingerly Cressida seated herself at the extreme end of the sofa. What had Jack done? He had assured her that Fairbridge would not dare to cause trouble. Could he possibly have issued enough threats to cause this *volte face*? Had he, in fact, informed Fairbridge that he owed Miss Cressida Bramley marriage?

Clinging to the conventions governing polite conversation, Cressida smiled and responded to her guest, searching.

for a clue that might explain the mystery. It came as she poured a cup of tea. 'Sugar, ma'am?' She held the tongs poised.

'Oh, just a teeny lump, my dear. Thank you.' Lady Fairbridge accepted the cup. 'What a happy circumstance for you, that little legacy! I heard all about it, you know. So handy for a girl!'

How had she heard? They had said nothing to anyone.

Lady Fairbridge gave a tinkling laugh. 'Now, my dear! You must not look so surprised. These things get about in the country. My cousin, Lady Stanhope, knew all about it!'

She rattled on, enumerating all the advantages of a girl with a respectable dowry. Shaking inwardly, Cressida saw the true significance of her dowry. It could turn the Vicar's daughter from a useful tool, no better than she should be, into an eligible débutante, courted by eligible bachelors and their mamas.

The delicate basaltware teacup she held rattled on its saucer. She took a deep breath to steady herself. Perhaps Lady Fairbridge had been misinformed. Could ten thousand pounds really be sufficient bait for a Vicar's scheming daughter to hook a whole, live Viscount? Or had rumour exaggerated her circumstances?

'Of course, it wasn't a terribly big legacy,' she said confidingly. 'Only ten thousand pounds, you know.'

Lady Fairbridge didn't bat so much as an eyelash. 'Of course not, my dear. But it still helps. Of course, I have a girl in my eye for Andrew.' She smiled conspiratorially. 'So important that he should settle down and secure the succession, you understand. A marriage of the right sort is so important.'

Listening to the clues dropped by Lady Fairbridge, Cressida came to the conclusion that the Dowager had an absolute paragon in mind for Andrew. Lady Fairbridge was understandably coy about stating exactly what she meant by a *respectable dowry*, but no doubt the girl had a dowry of land and enough liquid assets to make her own fortune seem paltry. She wished them joy of each other.

The advent of Lady Rutherford took the conversation into other channels. Meg apologised charmingly for not being present to greet her guest and said with a smile, 'But Miss Bramley is quite invaluable to me.'

Cressida continued to be amazed at this side of Meg—the glittering society hostess. Charming, delightful, but with a reserve that kept Lady Fairbridge at a distance. Skilfully she deflected all of Lady Fairbridge's questions and made it obvious at every turn that Cressida was a close friend.

Eventually Lady Fairbridge rose to take her leave.

Lady Rutherford rang the bell. 'Goodbye, ma'am. Shall we see you at Lady Verner's soirée this evening?'

Lady Fairbridge preened slightly. 'Oh, yes. Aurelia is always very select about whom she invites to her soirée. I have prevailed upon Fairbridge to escort me.' She cast an indulgent glance at Cressida. 'I dare say you and he will have a great deal to say to one another. I know he thought escorting his mama would be a dead bore. We shall look out for you.'

'How lovely. We shall look forward to it.' Meg's practised charm covered Cressida's very undignified gasp. Good God! Surely she didn't think…? *She* couldn't be Lady Fairbridge's well-dowered paragon…could she? With an Amazonian effort, Cressida managed to pull herself together to bid Lady Fairbridge farewell.

'So delightful to see you, dear Cressida. Perhaps you might escort me to my carriage? We shall not trouble Lady Rutherford to ring for her butler that way.'

Far too shocked to come up with a good excuse, Cressida acquiesced. Lady Fairbridge continued to expatiate on the elegance of Rutherford House until they reached the front door.

Then, 'Dear Cressida, I do hope you will feel inclined to pass over our little misunderstanding last winter. Dear Andrew...' she gave vent to a tinkling laugh '...I had no idea he was so constant! But he is of the same mind as ever, so I must withdraw my opposition and hope you will forgive him and...and...well, *you* know!'

Bile rose in Cressida's throat. Cold denials jostled on her lips, until she noticed the stolid-faced footman holding the front door open. If any hint of this got back to Jack, if he thought her unwilling to be pursued by Fairbridge... She shuddered. She would have to come up with some other way of putting Andrew off.

She summoned a smile and a few non-committal words and took herself back to the drawing room after seeing Lady Fairbridge into her landau.

Meg was on the sofa, fanning herself with the *Morning Post*. 'Phew! I do wish she'd wear less scent! Well, there you are. At least one mama with a hopeful son is courting you! What a pity it had to be her.'

'Do they really do that?' Despite her horror at the thought of being in Lady Fairbridge's matrimonial sights, Cressida found the idea intriguing. Besides, she wanted to head Meg away from the idea of Lady Fairbridge pursuing her.

Meg chuckled. 'Those with younger sons to dispose of do. They don't usually have to bother about the eldest sons. They might need a little prodding to get them out of the clubs and into the Marriage Mart, but their expectations will do the rest of the job for them. The younger sons, however, generally need to marry money. Or so Diana tells me.' She frowned. 'You can hint him away easily enough, I dare say. Or I can have Marc do so. Better not to ask Jack. His temper seems a little touchy at the moment.'

Cressida hesitated and then said, 'Meg, I think at the moment it might be best not to hint Lord Fairbridge away.' She wouldn't wager a groat on the likelihood of Marc not telling Jack and Jack wouldn't wait to be asked. He'd go and do his own hinting.

'Are you sure?' Meg sounded worried.

Cressida plastered a determined smile on her face. 'Oh, yes. There is no point in offending Lady Fairbridge. And I dare say that now I have a dowry, Andrew will look on me with greater respect. There cannot be anything to worry about!'

Just over a month later Jack sat in the reading room of Brook's, inwardly fuming. He would have liked to fume outwardly but Marc had not yet arrived to keep their appointment. He glared at the newspaper. Mindless drivel, all of it. He folded it and set it down with a snap.

What the devil was keeping…ah, there he was. No doubt he'd been tying his cravat for two hours.

'You took your time,' he growled.

'The gossip's getting worse, old man.' Marc ignored the snarl in Jack's voice as he sank into a chair. 'Apparently one or two hostesses have asked just how long Meg will be "obliged" to chaperon Miss Bramley.'

He leaned forward and poured himself a brandy while his best friend cursed fluently and at length, ending with, 'I swear I'll kill him!'

'Sssssshhhhhhhh!'

The indignant protest came from the opposite corner where a group of the commons were attempting to have a serious political discussion over a friendly game of hazard.

'You're interrupting play, old chap,' observed Marc laconically. 'Or the governance of the nation. But I dare say the former is of more consequence!'

Despite his rage, Jack laughed at this cynicism as he glanced at the group in the corner. 'Oh, they're all right. They just need something to keep their minds occupied while they talk politics.' Then he frowned. 'You're trying to head me off,' he accused.

'Mmm. I thought I'd succeeded,' answered Marc. 'If you must have it, while calling Fairbridge out might afford you satisfaction, it will not help Cressida in the least. You know how these affairs go: the moment someone reacts with a challenge, the rumour is confirmed. Besides, there's nothing to suggest that the talk started with him *per se*. Let's face it, little though you, or even I, might like it, to all appearances he's courting the girl.'

Frustration howled, but Jack forced himself to nod his head curtly. 'Very well. I'll have to think up some other pretext to put a ball into him. Any ideas?'

Marc spluttered over his brandy. 'Ah, not just off hand.'

'Damn it, Marc!' said Jack in savage undertones. 'You nearly took a horsewhip to Winterbourne in front of Sally Jersey when he tried to abduct Meg! Are you seriously telling me that I have to sit back and let that bastard Fairbridge ruin Cressida?'

Marc was silent for a moment. Then, very quietly, he said, 'Jack, it's quite possible that he really does mean marriage this time. The circumstances have changed. Cressida is no longer unprotected. Don't you think it's possible that Cressida's dowry was a big enough bait to land him?'

Jack felt sick. It had never occurred to him that Fairbridge would have the hide to renew his pursuit of Cressida. And while she didn't encourage him, neither had she discouraged him. She smiled at him, danced with him and strolled in the park as she did with a dozen others. But whereas the others paid attention to other young ladies, Fairbridge had singled out Miss Bramley exclusively.

Then the rumours had started. Nothing much. Just a suggestion that Miss Bramley was not quite up to the rig. That *poor Jack Hamilton and the Rutherfords have been sadly taken in*…nothing a man could get his hands on and choke to death.

The idea of any man possessing Cressida appalled him. The idea of Fairbridge possessing her sickened him. His whole being revolted at the thought. Parbury would be bad enough… He snorted inwardly at this idiocy. Parbury was a rattling good fellow. His objection to Parbury was plain jealousy. His reaction to Fairbridge was revulsion. Revulsion at the thought of a man who had offered a gently bred girl a slip on the shoulder and then offered marriage when she acquired a dowry.

He'd always loathed the *ton*'s prevailing attitude towards marriage, but this took hypocrisy to hitherto unplumbed depths.

He took an irreverent gulp of brandy and relaxed slightly as it burnt its way down. Fury at his helplessness ate at him. If only she'd married him! They'd be at home in Leicestershire right now, probably having a cosy evening in the library. Although he somehow doubted they'd be cataloguing many books. A practical study of Ovid would be far more to the point.

Then he groaned. What would be the point of marrying her if the stubborn, loyal little idiot was secretly eating her heart out for a blasted fortune hunter? His body might burn with desire every time he set eyes on her, or thought about her, but he wanted more than that. He wanted all of her. Body, mind, soul and heart. He wanted her love.

Marc signalled for a waiter. 'Another bottle of brandy, if you please. And an extra glass.'

'Thanks,' said Jack morosely. 'After all, if I can't do something, I may as well end up in my cups.'

Marc grinned. 'On a third of a bottle of brandy? I somehow doubt it.'

Jack stared at him. 'A third? What are you…? Oh, hello, Toby.' He forced a smile for the benefit of Marc's brother-in-law. 'I didn't realise you were in town.'

Sir Toby Carlton disposed himself in a chair with languid grace and sent a shuddering look at the far corner. 'Dear God. Aren't they a trifle over-enthusiastic? Gambling *and* politics.' He shook his head and then responded to Jack's remark. 'Came up this morning.'

Despite his gloom, Jack smiled. 'You found the energy to come to Brook's so soon, and you complain about others being overly lively? This is unheard of for you, Toby.'

Sir Toby looked pained and gestured at Marc. 'Blame him. He sent me a letter saying I had to come up immediately, and if I didn't, he'd fetch me himself. I came. And what does he do? Descends upon me the moment I arrive with instructions to go around to Boodle's and memorise the contents of the betting book for the last month!'

Jack blinked. '*Boodle*'s betting book?' He'd known Marc to do some odd things during the course of their friendship, but this had him fairly gapped. 'Why did you want Toby to look in Boodle's betting book?'

'Because he's a member and you and I aren't,' explained Marc. 'Wake up, Jack. I wanted to see if there was anything in the betting books that might refer to Cressida. There's nothing here, which was to be expected. No one would be corkbrained enough to put a bet like that in the book here, where you might see it. But there's nothing at White's either.'

'I'm a member there as well,' Jack pointed out.

'True,' said Marc, 'but you hardly ever go there, except with a friend for dinner. The likelihood of your poking your nose into the betting book there is remote.'

Jack nodded. It was true enough. He'd always preferred the slightly less aristocratic atmosphere of Brook's. 'But, why…' He broke off as his brain swung into action. 'Hold hard there…if there was gossip about Cressida, you think it would show in one of the betting books.'

Marc shrugged. 'You'd think so, but unless Toby found something…' He directed a querying gaze to his brother-in-law.

Toby shook his head. 'Not a thing.' He paused. 'Unless

you count a bet as to whether a certain Mr J. H. will take a bride with the initials C. B. this year.'

Jack's explosive *'WHAT?'* nearly drowned Marc's crack of laughter.

'Sssssshhhh!'

'Bloody impertinence!' growled Jack. For goodness' sake! In Boodle's of all places!

'Harmless, really,' said Toby, helping himself to brandy. 'No nasty innuendoes—ah, that's better—just the suggestion that the gentleman might take a bride, with those initials.'

Jack subsided. He frowned and racked his brains. 'Then, if the clubs and men aren't talking yet, it's unlikely that Fairbridge started the rumours, so who—?' Understanding crashed upon him with brutal force. 'Oh, my God! Lady Fairbridge!'

He groaned. This was worse. Much worse. While gossip in the clubs might be damaging to a woman's reputation, it could be killed. A few well-chosen threats in the right quarters would have dealt with it. If the society hostesses turned on Cressida, then she was ruined. No one would receive her. Doors would close in her face and her chances of marriage would be slim. And there was not a damned thing he could do to prevent it. He couldn't call Lady Fairbridge out... Or could he?

He might not be able to challenge her as he would a man, but he could certainly make things difficult for her socially. Especially since she had a daughter to establish. He clenched his fists. Damn the woman! Couldn't she see that Cress had no interest in Fairbridge? That she avoided him when possible and never granted him a waltz?

Lady Fairbridge had called on Cressida...been all sweetness and light according to Meg.

His brain tripped over that. Why would Lady Fairbridge call on Cressida if she disapproved of the connection and meant to ruin the chit?

'But…' He looked up from his brandy and found both his friends watching him.

'Can you make anything of it?' asked Marc. 'It has me foxed. Why would Lady Fairbridge gossip maliciously if she's still calling in Grosvenor Square behaving as though Cressida were an intimate friend of the family?'

Jack stiffened. Put like that… 'For a man who's puzzled, you certainly know how to sum up a situation,' he said. 'Conniving bitch! It's obvious, isn't it? Cressida Bramley, daughter of impoverished Vicar—totally unacceptable as a daughter-in-law. But Cressida Bramley, heiress to ten thousand pounds—there you have a potential bride for your son.'

Fury at the barefaced hypocrisy of Lady Fairbridge seared him. And the perfidy of Lord Fairbridge. He'd known that Cressida cared for him, trusted him. And he had used her mercilessly to ruin her father. Now, no doubt, he intended to stand back while his mother blackmailed the girl into marriage with him.

'There's something else you might consider, too, Jack,' said Marc.

Jack looked his question.

'Lady Stanhope is a cousin of Lady Fairbridge, remember. The pair of them are quite close.'

Jack swore as all the ramifications of that occurred to him.

'Stanhope?' Toby frowned. 'That neighbour of Jack's with the daughter? Interesting.'

Interesting didn't begin to describe Jack's opinion. Lady Stanhope would be only too happy to wreck Cressida's chances. Especially if she thought those chances involved Jack Hamilton.

'One-horse race,' said Toby, summing it up succinctly. 'If they blacken Miss Bramley's name enough, then the girl has no choice but to marry the only man to offer. Leaving Jack free for the Stanhope chit.'

Marc shook his head. 'It won't work. To my certain knowledge, Miss Bramley has already refused one more-than-eligible offer. At the time she might well have thought it was the only offer she'd ever receive and she didn't have a penny to her name. And unlike most girls her fortune is settled on her absolutely. She doesn't have to marry.'

Jack met his eyes reluctantly.

'Ah,' said Toby. 'But is Lady Fairbridge aware of this eccentricity on the part of Jack's ward?'

'She is *not* my ward,' snarled Jack rather more loudly than he intended.

'Sssssshhhhh!' The commons turned as one and glared.

Toby raised his brows. 'Oh? Dare say it's just as well. Always looks a bit off when a man marries his own ward. Anyway, we'd better go, or that lot over there will be issuing challenges. Besides, shouldn't be bandying a lady's name around in here. Come on, Jack.' His glance took in Jack's immaculate evening dress. 'Di told me to meet her at Lady Wragby's ball. And I understand Meg will be there with Miss Bramley.'

With a growl that both Marc and Toby took to be assent, Jack heaved himself out of his chair and stalked out.

'Di didn't exaggerate, did she?' murmured Sir Toby as he rose.

'About what,' asked Marc.

'About the peculiar effect love has had on our hitherto unflappable friend.'

Marc grinned as the door banged behind Jack to the indignation of everyone else in the room. 'Hmm. Just as well I didn't mention the bet in the book here on his likely marriage this year.'

Toby looked interested. 'Oh? Who placed that bet?'

'I did,' said Marc. 'Couldn't get a taker against, but Parbury was happy to wager a monkey against it happening within the next month!'

Chapter Thirteen

Not all the brilliance of Lady Wragby's ball, nor her ladyship's kindly greeting could make Cressida think the evening anything but a penance when she realised that Lord Fairbridge was in attendance. On her.

She managed to avoid waltzing with him, by dint of telling an outright lie, but was obliged to partner him for two country dances. After the second dance he commented on her heightened colour.

'I'll take you on to the terrace,' he said. 'No need to disturb Lady Rutherford. It's this way.'

Cressida baulked. 'Thank you, my lord, but I feel perfectly well and have absolutely no need of fresh air.'

Did he think she was all about in her head? Or that Meg and Di would not have warned her about going aside with any man on to the terrace? Not that she needed to be warned about Fairbridge.

She tried to pull her hand from Lord Fairbridge's arm, but he had his other hand clamped hard across hers.

The time had definitely come to hint Lord Fairbridge away, but he appeared to be impervious to hints. Grimly, Cressida considered more direct methods, only to dismiss them. Delivering a solid punch to Lord Fairbridge's nose would not only be impolitic in the middle of Lady

Wragby's ballroom, but also, for one of her height, down-right impossible. She might, just might, manage to hit his chin. If she kept on reminding herself of all this, it was even odds that her free hand would stay safely by her side.

If only he would take the hint and stop pestering her, then maybe the rumours would stop. They must be emanating from Lady Fairbridge. Didn't the horrid woman understand that she would as soon sign a marriage contract with the devil himself as with her ladyship's precious son! All that conciliating air of hers must have meant that she was still terrified that an action for breach of promise would be brought against Andrew.

She flicked a glance at her companion, furiously aware that people had noted them together and Andrew's proprietary hand over hers.

'My lord, have you considered the distress your pursuit of me must be causing Lady Fairbridge? She has made it quite plain that she disapproves of me. And I have no desire to distress her.'

'Mama?' Fairbridge's tone bordered on patronising. 'I fear it is you who misunderstands, my dear Cressida.'

His dear Cressida nearly tied her fingers in knots in the folds of her apple-green silk evening gown.

'Mama has absolutely no objection to my pursuit of you—in fact, it has her blessing.'

It did? Then why…could it, after all, be someone else who had started the whisper that Miss Bramley was not quite the thing? But who?

She knew Jack had heard something. He was going about with the blackest, most excoriating frown on his brow. And it was usually directed at her. Especially when he had arrived this evening with Marc and Sir Toby. She thrust the thought back where it belonged—in a dark corner of her mind. Thinking of Jack's anger and disappointment hurt too much. No doubt he had counted on being able to get her off his hands easily.

Unfortunately most of the gentleman who danced with her didn't seem to be interested in marriage, Not with her anyway. They liked her apparently. They sent her posies, bouquets and strolled with her in the park. They flirted outrageously, but none of them ever gave the least impression of wishing to make her an offer. Which didn't really matter because she didn't wish to marry. Not them, anyway.

Even if she had felt inclined to accept an offer, the only gentleman seriously pursuing her was Lord Fairbridge, and she had no hesitation in dismissing him as a contemptible maw worm. She had to get rid of him.

She turned her scornful gaze upon him and he said, 'After all, you have to marry someone. And no one else is coming up to scratch, are they?'

Under cover of his hand, Cressida administered a savage pinch to his arm. And smiled beatifically as he jerked his arm away, swearing.

With another beaming smile, she responded, 'I fear you are mistaken, sir. I have no need to marry.' She clasped her hands before her in an attitude of maidenly decorum.

He smiled unpleasantly. 'Are you so sure you have no need to marry, my dear? After all, you seem to enjoy London society. It would be such a shame if London decided once and for all that it didn't like you.'

Somehow Cressida's fingers got themselves untangled and turned into fists, clenched in fury.

'So when would you like to be married?' he asked.

Heaven preserve her from domineering males who took everything for granted. But at least he'd asked her something!

'Never,' she answered with a wholly false smile. 'I have given the whole business much thought and feel that while such dreadful rumours persist, I cannot, in all honour, accept an offer from any gentleman.' She might as well get what use she could out of the situation.

'What!' His lordship's eyes bulged and his jaw hung slack. 'But you can't…I mean…no one will think anything of it once you're married to me.'

She sighed mournfully.

He glared at her, suspicion flaring in his face. 'This is all a hum. You have no other choice, my dear.'

'Blessed singleness is still a choice,' she shot at him.

'Not for a woman who wishes to ensure her father's safety, it isn't.'

The silken indifference of his voice shivered through Cressida. *No, not that. They couldn't!*

Trying to quell the inward shaking, she said, 'My cousin…'

'Will have little influence at Bow Street. Think on it, Miss Bramley. Think on it.'

Utterly dazed, sick and shaking, Cressida didn't even realise that she was standing beside the glass doors opening on to the terrace until Fairbridge shouldered her through them.

Jack moved steadily through the crowded rooms, searching for Cressida. He hadn't seen her for at least ten minutes and it bothered him. He smiled and nodded automatically at Lady Jersey, who had waved to him from a chaise longue. *Silence* holding court, he thought. No doubt gossiping over the peculiar and entertaining behaviour of Mr Jack Hamilton. And his *ward*'s matrimonial chances.

He simply couldn't understand it. Night after night he watched Cressida cut a swathe through the ballrooms of the *ton*. Her dance card was always full. Charming and eligible gentlemen flocked to her side—well, Meg and Di described them as eligible and charming. *He* thought they were a pack of rakes and libertines—but apparently none of them had made any serious overtures. Of any sort.

He nodded and smiled at Lady Gwydyr. Not automatically. He always had to remind himself to greet that haughty dame.

Some of the ladies were a little stiff with Cressida, but the support of Lady Rutherford, Lady Jersey and Lady Diana Carlton had kept the damage to a minimum. The gentlemen had ignored the rumours completely. So why hadn't he or Marc been besieged with offers for Cressida's hand? As far as he could see, the only man seriously pursuing her was Fairbridge.

The idea of that was enough to turn his stomach. What was wrong with all the others? Were they blind? Or merely mad? Even Parbury—the damned rake!—would be a better choice than Fairbridge.

A jovial gentleman nearly emptied a glass of champagne over him and he dodged, waving away the fulsome apologies proffered. It all served to remind him just how much he disliked this sort of thing anyway. What the devil was he doing at a squeeze like this? It was so crowded you could barely breathe. The answer presented itself to him with irritating ease—he was trying to find Cressida so that he could see if she had a dance free for him.

He snorted. No doubt Parbury had snabbled the supper dance. His eyes narrowed. There was Parbury now, chatting with Petersham. Comparing snuff boxes, no doubt. Fribbles! Oh, hell and the devil! Petersham had seen him. He couldn't cut them. After Marc, Parbury was one of his closest friends. And Petersham was always entertaining with his everlasting tea and snuff. Besides, they might have seen Cressida. Setting his shoulders, he forged a path through to them.

'Hullo, Jack,' said Viscount Parbury. 'I saw your… er…ward a few minutes ago. Danced with her, actually. You're a lucky dog! Isn't he, Petersham?'

Lord Petersham nodded. 'Charming girl, quite charming.'

'She's not my ward!' growled Jack.

'No, no. Of course not!' soothed Parbury. 'Didn't mean to imply that things aren't just as they ought to be. Everyone knows you wouldn't take advantage of the chit's situation. Just drop a hint in your ear though, old chap. While most of us are pleased to see you happy and willing to deny ourselves the pleasure of stealing the filly from under your nose, young Fairbridge ain't so particular. Came up to walk with her, you know. Not much I could do about it, beyond scribbling your name against the only dance she had left, but he's not at all the thing, that lad. You might want to hurry up the official announcement, y'know. Not the sort of feller to take a hint, and lord knows I've given him a few.'

'Which official announcement would that be, Parbury?' Jack kept his voice very casual. Parbury couldn't, simply couldn't, mean what he *thought* he meant.

'Your betrothal, of course,' said Parbury. He frowned slightly. 'You really ought to hurry it up. Settle these damned rumours. Tell you something else, too. Young Fairbridge appears to be in a spot of bother. Got in over his head in a card game a few weeks ago, my brother tells me. Apparently his trustees are cutting up stiff about settling more gambling debts. And they've been paying off his brother's debts. Not but what I understand they've managed to settle some family living on him now.'

Jack swallowed a few choice expletives.

'Exactly,' said Parbury, just as if he'd spoken. 'Ten to one Lady Fairbridge would rather someone else paid his debts this time, and there ain't no denyin' it; ten thousand is a tidy little fortune. Especially when it's wrapped up in a cosy little package like Miss Cressida.'

Jack managed to respond to that. It wasn't intelligible—fortunately—but it was a response.

Petersham, delicately raising a pinch of snuff to one nostril, added his mite. 'Shouldn't let Fairbridge...' he inhaled the snuff and smiled beatifically '...steal a march on you with Miss Bramley. Sheer waste. Like offering you snuff.' He put his snuff box back in his pocket.

'Did you say that my cousin is strolling with Fairbridge?' asked Jack. Much better to ignore the rest and just concentrate on the bits he could deal with.

Parbury nodded. 'Sorry, old chap, but short of telling him to…well, you know, in front of a lady and all that. And she didn't give me any hint that she *wanted* me to tell him to—' He broke off and bowed to Lady Sefton.

Part of Jack's brain registered Maria Sefton. Just enough to realise that he'd given her the cut direct. He kept going, trusting to Parbury and Petersham to make his excuses.

Upon occasion Jack found his height a nuisance. It was practically impossible to hide in a ballroom. Any horse under seventeen hands was utterly useless to him and most females seemed to have utterly fascinating conversations with his chin, or worse, the top button of his waistcoat. Usually he cursed his height.

Right now he gave sincere and heartfelt thanks for it, especially when he spotted Fairbridge edging Cressida out on to the terrace.

She knew perfectly well that she was in trouble. No properly brought up young lady went out alone on to the terrace with a gentleman. Quite apart from that, she had no desire to be anywhere alone with Lord Fairbridge. The gentle silver glow of moonlight mocked her.

'I am *not* going to marry you, my lord.'

Cressida didn't wait for Lord Fairbridge to open negotiations, but stated her position as clearly as she knew how. She couldn't, she wouldn't believe that even Andrew could be base enough to actually threaten her father to force her consent. She wasn't sure just how much more forcefully she could refuse an offer, but judging by what she could see of Lord Fairbridge's face in the light streaming from the ballroom, she would have to think of something.

He shrugged.

'You will, my dear. You have no choice. Either you marry me or your precious father will face a magistrate and see the inside of Newgate. Besides, if I keep you out here for long enough, someone is bound to catch us. Then you won't have any choice at all. You were happy enough to think I wanted to marry you down in Cornwall. Nothing has changed after all.'

She thought she might actually be sick. The marble flags of the terrace heaved under her feet and the buzz of chatter interspersed with the violins suddenly came from a vast distance as the night swirled around her.

Hard fingers clasped her arm, dragging her further away from the light and chatter of the ballroom towards the steps leading down into the garden.

Understanding came to her. If he could compromise her…it would not make the least difference to her reply, but the disgrace would hurt Meg. She baulked, trying to wrench herself free, but he grabbed her wrists in one powerful hand and bore them down easily.

'Stop! I told you—'

Her protest was smothered as he trapped her against the balustrade and forced his mouth on hers. His free hand thrust into her coiffure, seizing a handful of hair and holding her helpless.

Before she could do anything a savage voice ripped through the night. 'What the devil do you think you're about, Fairbridge?'

Jack's furious voice brought Fairbridge's head up sharply and Cressida pulled herself away from him, shaking. Nausea shuddered through her and she breathed deeply, trying to steady herself. A few hairpins pattered to the flags.

Jack. With Meg and Lord Rutherford on his heels. And Lady Jersey.

'Sealing my betrothal, Hamilton.' All the air left her

body as though at a blow. 'Your, ah, ward has just accepted my hand in marriage. Perhaps you and your companions might like to be the first to congratulate me.' A few more avid faces peered around the doors on to the terrace. From the dropped jaws it was evident that they had heard this announcement, had taken in her dishevelled appearance.

Horrified, Cressida fought for the breath to deny the claim, only to hear Jack's cold voice seal the trap.

'I see. My congratulations, on your good fortune, my lord. I shall wish you happy of it.' He turned on his heel and strode back into the ballroom, the growing crowd parting before him, only to swirl back, staring and whispering.

Only the balustrade against her back held Cressida upright as she watched him walk away from her, saw him disappear into the crowd.

Meg hurried forward, forcing Fairbridge to step away from Cressida. 'How very interesting to be sure, Lord Fairbridge. No doubt you will call upon my lord or Mr Hamilton in the near future to discuss the matter in a *proper* setting.'

'Indeed, Fairbridge.' Lord Rutherford stepped forward in his Countess's wake. 'Hamilton and I will look forward to it.'

Between them they escorted Cressida back into the ballroom. Desperately she searched the eddying crowd, but the press of silk and superfine defeated her. He had gone, but she could tell which direction he had gone in.

Half the crowd was staring at her, eyebrows raised. Fairly licking their lips in speculation. The other half was staring towards the main entrance. Even as she watched a tall, immaculately clad figure ascended the stairs and left the ballroom. Something about the purpose in his stride and the set of the broad shoulders told Cressida that his exit was permanent.

'You can't leave.' Rutherford's low voice held both apology and understanding.

Her stomach flipped over. Stay? With every eye on her for the rest of the night? She couldn't! Shaking, she looked up at Marc, ready to contradict him flatly.

His eyes held a challenge. 'One melodramatic exit is quite enough titillation for them for one evening. Any more and they'll expect it every night. Put your chin up and smile. Think of what you are going to do to Jack next time you see him.'

Her spine stiffened at the thought. Without thinking, she said, 'He's too tall!'

Marc choked. 'Then, my dear, I suggest you stand on a chair.'

From her other side, Meg muttered, 'I'd suggest you hit him with the chair and be done with it!'

Marc raised an eyebrow in mute query as Meg joined him in his bedchamber.

'And how do we handle tonight's little disaster?'

'Murder Jack.'

Her tones startled Marc considerably. She sounded as though she'd like to skin Jack. Inch by inch. And then use his hide as a hearthrug.

He went to her and drew her into his arms. 'Sweetheart, that's not going to help if Fairbridge has offered for Cressida and she accepts him. And right now that's exactly what everyone is expecting.'

He pressed a gentle kiss on her hair as she nestled against him.

'I know,' she admitted. 'But there was something odd about that announcement of his. Cressida looked absolutely stunned. I thought for a second she was about to deny it, and then Jack opened his big mouth. Now she's clammed up and won't talk about what really happened.'

Marc felt the tension in her and began rubbing her shoulders.

'Idiot,' she muttered.

'Who? Me?'

She chuckled. 'Not this time. Jack. Everyone thinks of him as in charge of Cressida. By reacting like that, he's made it much harder for her to reject Fairbridge's offer without looking like a jilt.'

'Mmm.' Marc rubbed a bit harder. 'You don't seriously think that would stop her, do you?'

'What the devil's wrong with him?' she burst out. 'Can't he see how unhappy she is? She loves him, for goodness' sake, and he's making her miserable!'

'He did offer for her,' Marc pointed out, duty bound.

Meg snorted. 'She told me. Because he felt obliged to.'

Marc smiled. 'Amazing, the stupid things a man will say when he's confused. And love is very confusing at first.'

Meg's eyes widened. 'Are you saying Jack knows he's in love?'

Marc laughed deeply. 'Oh, yes. He's got that far at least. Now, forget Jack and his problems for the time being. It's after three and there isn't a single thing you can do about any of it. Come to bed instead.'

Cressida sat curled up in the window seat and listened to rain spatter against the glass as she stared unseeingly into the night. Lamplight gleamed back from the rain-washed cobbles, dancing and flickering wetly. Light blazed from many of the houses and the clop of hooves drifted up to her as people began returning to their houses after the evening's entertainment.

She shivered. Anyone who had attended Lady Wragby's ball would be agog, waiting for the newspapers over the next couple of days. Enough people had heard Andrew's announcement and Jack's cold congratulations for the news to be at every breakfast table by tomorrow. The clock on the chimneypiece chimed and Cressida winced. By later this morning.

Her brain felt leaden, but unless she thought of something fast she was going to find herself betrothed to Andrew Fairbridge. Her stomach clenched and she began to shake uncontrollably. She couldn't do it. She couldn't!

She might have to. Breathing deeply, she fought down her panic and forced her mind to work. The most important consideration was Papa. He had to be protected. But she baulked at the idea of turning Papa's money over to Fairbridge to squander on gaming and…and…debauchery. She'd heard enough of the Viscount's reputation since coming up to town to have not the least doubt that his notion of marital fidelity would have nothing to do with his own behaviour and everything to do with hers. Not that she cared much about that. She wanted as little to do with him as possible. She simply hated the thought of giving her father's legacy to a family who would destroy him without a moment's hesitation… How tightly was the money tied up? How tightly could it be tied up?

She caught herself up with a violent shudder. What was she thinking? Was she seriously considering marriage to Andrew? She could taste bile in her mouth as nausea flooded her. What choice did she have? If a report was made to Bow Street, nothing could save her father.

How tightly was the money tied up? Marc had explained it all to her, but apart from the fact that she couldn't touch the capital and would have an allowance paid to her quarterly until her marriage, she hadn't taken much in. At that point she hadn't intended to marry.

She frowned. Women had very few rights. Anything she owned at the time of her marriage or inherited later would become her husband's property. Unless it was tied up in a trust. Could she have it tied up in a trust? So that they had the income but not the capital? Or would she need her husband's consent? She passed a hand over her aching brow. Her eyes were sore, too, from crying. She had heard that sometimes money was tied up very tightly with the capital settled on the next generation.

The first thing was to find out what could be done. She would send a message to Messrs Chadwick and Simms tomorrow.

'Now, is all that quite clear, Miss Bramley?'

She nodded at the little man. 'I think so, Mr Simms. Let me see if I have understood. The capital is not available to me, or, if I marry, to my husband. Instead it is settled on my children, to become theirs after my death...' She frowned. 'But what if I don't marry, or, even if I do, don't have children?' Would Fairbridge inherit the money under those circumstances?

Mr Simms smiled. 'I don't think we need worry about you not marrying, my dear. But in any case, if you die without children, then your husband would have no further claim on it. The capital would revert to Mr Hamilton, of course. Or to his heirs.'

It would? She stared at him blankly. 'I beg your pardon? Why would it do that?'

Mr Simms looked puzzled. 'Well, it seemed the logical solution when I drew up the deed of transfer for Mr Hamilton. He was quite adamant that your husband should not have any interest in the money. He was most concerned that you might become a target for a fortune hunter.'

A shiver took her. That was exactly what had happened. But why would Jack have directed that Papa's money go to himself? And *how* could he have arranged it? Surely no reputable lawyer would have...surely the money should go back to Papa's heirs, his old college, or school... Maybe Papa had designated Jack his heir...that would explain it, but something still didn't quite fit.

She knotted her brow, trying to think. The lawyer's

words came back to her—*when I drew up the deed of transfer for Mr Hamilton*... The truth crashed over her with all the force of a physical blow. There was only one possible explanation.

'Sir, under whose instructions did you settle this money upon me? My father's or Mr Hamilton's?'

If Mr Simms had looked puzzled before, he now looked totally bewildered.

'Why, Mr Jack's, of course. He has sole control of his fortune.'

She was never quite sure how she got herself out of the lawyer's chambers and back into the waiting carriage with her maid. All the way back from Lincoln's Inn the knowledge pounded into her with the rattle of wheels and hooves over the cobbles.

Jack's money. Jack had provided her with a dowry out of his own fortune. Slow tears rolled down her cheeks. Why had he done such a thing? Her brain just wouldn't work. Every time she tried to think, Jack's image got in the way. Every argument they had ever had echoed through her. And the kisses.

The memory of his mouth and hands possessing her sent fire coursing down every vein to pool, hot and mysterious, between her thighs. Nothing made sense. He desired her, yes. She didn't doubt that any more than she could deny her own desire. But what else did he feel for her? Why would a man settle a dowry of ten thousand pounds on a woman he disliked for whom he had no responsibility? That went far beyond family duty.

He felt enough for you to offer marriage. No. That was honour. He said as much.

More tears trickled down her cheeks. Just because she had fallen in love and hidden it, was no reason to suppose that Jack had fallen in love. After all, there was nothing particularly lovable about her. He, on the other hand, was eminently lovable, the big, chivalrous idiot that he was!

Grimly she faced something else. She could not marry. Least of all Fairbridge. Even if he could never touch the principle, she could not stomach the thought of Jack's money, Jack's decency, benefiting a man of that ilk in any way whatsoever.

The carriage had halted. She sat there dazed, lost in despair. How could she protect her father if she had to refuse Fairbridge? If only she could get rid of the money, Fairbridge would cease to want her! But there was nothing she could do to return the money to Jack. What Mr Bell had said about the terms governing trusts had made that abundantly clear. She had no power to touch that money or bestow it on anyone, not even St Peter himself.

'Miss? Miss? Are you all right?'

The concerned voice penetrated the fog of misery. Vaguely she looked up and recognised one of the Rutherford footmen holding the carriage door open for her. By the look on his face, he had been doing so for some considerable time.

With a confused apology she got down. Only one thing mattered. She had to make sure Papa was safe. As far as she could see there was only one way to do it. She would have to send for Jack.

He came straight after breakfast the following morning.

Delafield announced him in tones positively stiff with disapproval. 'Mr Hamilton to see you, Miss Cressida.' He shut the door of the breakfast parlour behind the disgracefully early caller with what could only be described as a near bang.

Cressida set down her coffee cup carefully and faced her visitor. She might have summoned him, but she really hadn't expected to see him before afternoon. After all, very few young ladies were out of bed at this hour of the morn-

ing. Most would not arise until noon or so after attending
a ball, so what the devil did he think he was doing here
this early? For most social aspirants, nine o'clock in the
morning ranked as the middle of the night. Indeed, she felt
as though it was the middle of the night, but her internal
clock just couldn't get used to sleeping late.

'You wished to see me, Miss Bramley.'

She shivered slightly. A Gunter's ice would be a tropical
delight after his gelid tones.

'Y…yes, yes, I did.' Furiously, she bit the inside of her
cheek. Where had that despicable wobble come from? And
why did he have to look so disgustingly attractive, even if
his jaw did look as though it might break if he smiled?
And if there wasn't a law against gentlemen with legs like
that appearing in buckskin breeches before innocent maidens when they'd scarcely swallowed their breakfasts, then
there ought to be. Along with a law about the maximum
breadth of shoulder a gentleman was permitted to sport.

He strolled over to the chair opposite hers and raised
his brows in mute query.

Fiery heat scorched her cheeks. 'Please, will you sit
down, Mr Hamilton? Would you care for coffee?' She
thought he frowned. No doubt, since he was in breeches,
he had been riding and didn't wish to keep his horse standing.

He sank into the chair with his customary grace and
stretched the long legs out comfortably. 'Thank you. Coffee sounds excellent. Black.'

She knew that. She knew all his odd little habits. Black
coffee. The tiniest splash of milk in his tea. And he hated
sugar. Except in spice biscuits, of course. She reached for
the coffee pot, realising as she did so that she really ought
to have rehearsed what she was going to say. At the very
least she ought to have worked out if she was going to ask
him about the money or just tell him straight out that she
knew. Then, of course, she had the problem of explaining

why she wanted him to take it back. And she must not, under any circumstances, let him realise the pressure Fairbridge had brought to bear on her...

'I did not see you at Almack's last night.' His voice sounded utterly indifferent.

'I wasn't there.' She concentrated hard on pouring the coffee. If he could state the obvious, then so could she. There was no need to tell him that she had spent the evening with a blinding headache—a very natural consequence after spending the afternoon crying her eyes out. 'I can't accept your money,' she blurted out. The coffee cup rattled in its saucer as she handed it to him.

It didn't seem possible that his jaw could harden even more, but somehow it gave that impression. His whole body seemed to stiffen. 'I beg your pardon?'

Oh, lord. If she had this wrong, then she would look the most complete henwit. 'That supposed legacy,' she said. 'It's all a hum. There was no money—'

'There most certainly is!' he snapped. 'What do you mean, no—'

'I mean there was no legacy,' she interrupted, blinking to force back the tears pricking at her eyelids. 'There is money, yes. But no legacy. You invented that, didn't you? And then persuaded Papa to settle the money on me, when all the time it was your money. You knew I would never accept a dowry from you, so you tricked me!'

His first sip of coffee scalded even as her words burnt into him. How the hell had she found out? The question screamed in his brain. He closed his eyes in pain. The money had served its purpose. Caught her a husband. Bile rose in his throat at the thought of the sort of pond scum ten thousand pounds could lure to the surface.

He forced his voice to normal. 'Cress, how did you know about the money?'

She told him in a voice that ached with tiredness, finally saying, 'When I found out the money came from you, I realised that I couldn't marry him, no matter what happened. You'll have to take the money back.'

He didn't quite follow that. 'Cress, the money is yours. Signed over. Even you can't give that money to anyone except in marriage. No matter how much I dislike your choice, I have no power to take the money back, or…or stop your marriage.' Except, of course, by standing up in the middle of the marriage ceremony and claiming her as his. Or, preferably, strangling Fairbridge.

She shook her head. 'No, Jack. Even tied up as it is, I can't marry Andrew and let him benefit from your kindness. I won't do it. I…I can't marry anyone. Least of all him. Not after he threatened—'

It seemed to Jack that she caught herself up with a gasp. Something was not quite right here, but he couldn't put his finger on it. And he didn't dare believe what his senses were screaming at him—that she didn't want to marry Fairbridge. He had to be wrong. She would have said something the other night. Wouldn't she? 'Cressida…if you want to marry Fairbridge…'

'*I don't!*'

He could only stare, his jaw dropped. 'You don't? Then why the hell didn't you tell him so the other night?' Anger surged through him. 'Good God, what a muddle! He called on me yesterday, trying to get my consent to a notice in the papers!'

'I did tell him.' The quiet despair in her voice stopped him dead.

'You refused him? Then why…?'

A shiver went through her and he watched in horror as she rubbed at her arms, hugging herself as if to keep warm or to protect herself.

My job, he thought savagely. *Both of them.*

'Andrew isn't used to taking no for an answer,' she said wearily. 'I said *no* and he grabbed me. You and the others came out on to the terrace and he announced our betrothal. You know the rest.'

'But you didn't say anything!'

'Haven't you ever found yourself in the situation where you are so stunned at what is going on that you can't say anything?' she asked angrily. 'And even if you could, you don't know what to say?' Her control broke. 'I had just refused him. Point blank. The last thing I expected was that he would announce our betrothal!' A tear spilt over and she dashed it away with a shaking hand. 'Or that you would congratulate him! What could I say after that? I was too busy trying not to be sick!'

A tangle of emotions battered at his self-control. Horror flooded him at the realisation that in his hurt fury he'd helped Fairbridge tighten the noose around her neck. And then he'd walked out on her. Because he hadn't trusted himself not to tear Fairbridge's throat out and then toss her over his shoulder in front of everyone.

He knew, because Marc and Parbury had told him, that she had got through the rest of the evening with her chin up and her smile gay. When no doubt all she longed for was a quiet corner in which to hide. And weep.

The need to take her in his arms and comfort her nearly overwhelmed him. He mustn't. He didn't dare. Not with the need to take her and show her incontrovertibly that she was his, and his alone, still pounding in his blood. She didn't want to marry Fairbridge. She had meant to refuse him. Even before she found out the truth about her dowry. That didn't mean she wanted to marry *him*. Did it?

'Will I be ruined when I don't accept him?'

That jerked him back to reality. 'No,' he grated.

Her next question rocked him. 'What if he…he may be very angry. Could he do anything to Papa? If he talked…'

'You and your father are perfectly safe.' He tried to control his fury, but his eyes narrowed. 'Fairbridge, however, isn't.' Scurvy bastard! If he tried to have a charge brought against Dr Bramley!

'Jack, please don't call him out. Please...'

She was on her feet, her eyes dilated with fear. His jaw tightened at the terror in her voice. Loyal, stubborn little idiot! Even after all this she could still care enough for the brute to worry about him...

'Jack!' His heart clenched as she came to him in a tumble of muslin skirts and gripped his arm. 'You must promise me! I couldn't bear it if you were hurt...please! You mustn't!'

She was worried about him? Slowly he covered her small hand with his large one. Did she care just a little bit? Could that little bit of caring be fanned to a blaze to match the need consuming him? He lifted her hand from his arm and raised it to his lips. So soft. Her hand trembled as his lips brushed over her fingers. Oh, hell. He'd have to try again. Surely he could convince her that he loved her. Couldn't he? After all, the rest of London had had no trouble in coming to that conclusion. Why couldn't the one person who mattered see it?

Drawing a deep breath, he plunged in. 'Cressida, do you remember that I once asked you to marry me?'

Chapter Fourteen

Pain lanced through her as she turned away, tugging her hand free of his. Remember? The memory quivered in her heart every time she thought of him. Unable to force a response past the choking lump in her throat, she nodded.

'Would you reconsider your answer and marry me?'

She shut her eyes against the pain of having to refuse him. But the constrained note in his voice pierced her. And he'd stiffened up again, as he always did when he touched her or danced with her. As though he could not bear to be near her, let alone touch her. Perhaps even his desire for her had died, leaving him with only guilt.

And now she felt guilty. He had cared enough to try to protect her, even to the extent of providing her with a dowry. She would give it back if she could, but she couldn't. There was absolutely no way she could hand that money over to anyone. Except by marriage, and that was out of the… Her churning thoughts faltered, tripping over the bitter logic of the trap fate had set for her.

Marriage wasn't out of the question. It was the only way in which she could repay him. She could marry Jack and repay her dowry that way. And it might even be the best way to ensure her father's safety. No. She shouldn't do it. He didn't love her.

A wave of cold chills washed through her. Why couldn't she do it? As far as the men of his world were concerned, marriages were generally made for very logical reasons—money, power, status, and an heir. If one was lucky, affection might develop.

But she wanted love. From him, anyway. She didn't deceive herself. If she had never met Jack, she might well have been content to settle for logic and affection. But she had met him and she could give him nothing except a tarnished name. And his own money. No doubt he didn't want love. Did it really matter if she did? She would not be lying when she took her vows. Merely terrified of betraying herself when she consummated them.

'I have nothing that you want, Jack,' she said painfully. 'No money, no connections. Only a dubious reputation and my...' Her fingers twisted together as she choked back the word *love*.

'You do have money, Cressida,' he pointed out. 'Not that it's an—'

She drew a breath so ragged it tore at her soul. 'Yes,' she said carefully. 'Your money. So, on that basis, I have no choice but to accept your offer.' She kept her eyes on the carpet, determined he should not see the tears burning her eyelids, threatening to become a flood of despairing grief.

Jack felt as though he had taken a full body blow from Gentleman Jackson himself. His plan to protect Cressida had backfired. Instead he had trapped her. She wouldn't even look at him. What he could see of her face was wreathed in shadows.

Fighting to keep his voice steady, he asked, 'Is honour the only reason for our marriage, Cressida?'

He thought she shuddered.

'What else could there be?' The bleakness in her voice struck through him.

Her next words shamed him.

'You desired me. That's all. You said yourself that was not enough for marriage. You even suggested that I should be your mistress—'

'That was because I thought you were teasing me on purpose and I was trying to teach you a lesson about the dangers of flirting!' he growled.

'Then you offered for me because you felt you had to,' she went on as if she hadn't heard him.

'I offered because I wanted to protect you!' he snapped, 'and because—'

She interrupted. 'I...I know you feel responsible—'

'Responsible be damned!' His voice was tight as he reached for her. 'What I felt was desire and—'

'No!' She panicked, jerking back from him. If he touched her now she'd betray herself. Her treacherous heart and body ached with the longing to yield to him. If he touched her, she'd break. Breathing hard, she fought for control. 'Andrew desired me. It wasn't enough. It wasn't enough for you either. Money made the difference for him. Honour has made the difference for you. And for me. I have no choice.'

He stopped dead and she watched him through a bright blur. His hand was still stretched out to her.

'My dear, you're wrong, I do care for you...very much. I...I love you, Cressida.' His careful, restrained tone of voice sent splinters of pain bursting through her. It was as if he had to force himself to say it. Maybe he even had to exert will power to keep his hand held out. If only he would let it drop, before the temptation to place hers in it and leave it there forever overwhelmed her resolve.

'You told me you wanted to marry me because your honour demanded it,' she reminded him. 'I can't think of any particular reason why you should love me, and you've never given me the least reason to believe that you do. But my honour demands that I accept your offer. It is the only way I can return your money.' The splinters lodged a little deeper as his mouth tightened and his hand sank back to his side. She should be glad he was no longer reaching for her.

Her eyes burning with tears, she stood up and said, 'Perhaps you will excuse me, Jack. I must write an answer to Lord Fairbridge.'

'You refused him, didn't you?'

She shivered at the hard note in his voice. 'Y…yes.'

'Then there is no need for either of us to give him any further response. The announcement of our betrothal will be response enough.'

A nod. That was all she could manage. Her throat ached with unshed tears. She had to reach the door somehow, before any of them fell. And then her room. Which meant she had to get past Jack, standing like a mountain before her, his eyes like gunmetal, hard and blank. His entire body looked as though it had turned to stone.

One step. She could take one step. She took it. Then another. One step at a time, because she dared think no further than the next step, Cressida walked past Jack. Slowly. The bright Persian rug on the floor swirled in misty reds and blues. He might reach out to stop her, sweep her into his arms and tell her what a little fool she was, that he really did love her, that their marriage would be based on love… If only he would kiss her, love her…

One step at a time she made her way to the door. He was there before her. Her heart shuddered to a stop, hope blazing up, unbidden, unwanted.

He opened the door for her.

One more step and she was through. The hallway was cold after the warmth of the breakfast parlour. She clenched her teeth against a sob of pain at knowing she'd been right. He was letting her go.

'I will arrange for the announcement in the papers the day after Meg's ball. We will make the announcement at supper.'

It was all he could say. His throat felt tight. His entire body screamed with the need to sweep her into his arms and kiss her. And then drag her back into the parlour, lock the door and show her how much he loved her. It wouldn't work. She'd think it was nothing more than lust. He would not lower himself to the level of Fairbridge by attempting to overcome her resistance by force.

Somehow he managed to shut the door on Cressida and on his own need. He stared blankly at the closed door and wondered just exactly where he'd gone wrong first. He'd misjudged her initially of course. He'd been quite pig-headed about that, as though he was determined to think the worst of her. Why? He wasn't usually that stupid, was he? His undeniable case of lust hadn't helped. He had to admit that. He'd scarcely been able to focus his mind enough to eat since he'd met her. But why hadn't he real-ised sooner that he loved her?

Because she's not the sort of girl you expected to love. With a dazed shake of his head, he thought about his imag-inary, ideal bride. Quiet, gentle, submissive. Someone who wouldn't turn his world upside down. Lord, a marriage like that would have bored him to death.

A long scratch on one of the door panels caught his attention. What had caused that? And what was he doing, staring at the door? He really ought to go. Dear God. What was he to do now? He'd wanted her to accept his offer. Never had he imagined that she might accept it to return his money! He cursed fluently. As if he needed money! That was the final, cutting irony. That she should marry him to return a miserable ten thousand that he wouldn't have noticed missing anyway.

Disgustedly he wandered over to the breakfast table, sat down and sipped his now tepid coffee. At least they were betrothed. And if she had accepted on the promptings of honour, then she was unlikely to try and back out of it. It was grim comfort.

The door opened and he turned his head.

Meg gazed back and said blandly, 'Congratulations.'

He groaned. 'Don't, Meg. What the hell am I going to do? Did she tell you why she accepted?'

Taking the chair Cressida had vacated, Meg nodded.

'I never meant to trap her like that.' He felt sick at the thought. 'She doesn't love me.' Automatically he poured coffee for Meg and handed it to her.

She sipped and asked, 'Did she actually tell you, in as many words, that she doesn't love you?'

He ran his hands through his hair distractedly. 'She didn't have to! What the deuce am I supposed to think when the girl accepts me because she feels honour bound to return a paltry ten thousand pounds?'

Meg's coffee cup rattled in its saucer and a choke of laughter escaped her. 'Paltry? Ten thousand pounds, paltry?'

Jack had the grace to blush.

Sobering, Meg went on. 'Jack, all I could get out of Cressida was that you had renewed your offer and that she had accepted because of the money. Then she burst into tears. Apparently you told her that you love her and she doesn't believe you?'

The faintly questioning note got to him. 'Damn it, Meg! Of course I love her! The problem is her not lov—'

'Fudge!' said Meg roundly. 'Why would she be so upset about *you* not loving *her* unless *she* was head over ears in love with *you*?'

Jack left Rutherford House twenty minutes later with his wits in total disarray. She loved him? All he had to do was convince her that her love was returned?

Meg had been full of advice on how to achieve that end. Most of it was so obvious, that he blushed to think of it. Instead of growling at her all the time he could send her flowers, take her to Hatchard's and to Gunter's afterwards for an ice, drive her in the park, dance all the supper waltzes with her and utterly monopolise her company. In short, he could woo her properly and make a complete and utter spectacle of himself.

The prospect was enough to make him shudder. Sally Jersey would be in alt.

Gazing into the silken, glittering mob at Lady Harwood's ball that evening, Cressida wished with all her heart that it had not been necessary to attend, but Meg had explained how vital it was not to give the gossips the least idea that she was avoiding Andrew. Was he here already, or would he appear later? Would he approach her?

She had discussed with Meg exactly how she should handle him. They'd even practised it, with Meg borrowing one of Marc's coats and pretending to be Lord Fairbridge. The session had ended in laughter, which, oddly enough, had buoyed Cressida's confidence.

'Jack's in the far corner,' Meg told her. 'Talking to…good lord! That's Lady Anna! I had no idea she was in town.'

'Who is Lady Anna?'

'Who…oh, his mother, of course. Lady Anna Hamilton. Jack wrote to her. She's been staying in Yorkshire with Jack's sister, but—'

'*Jack*'s mother is here? *That* Lady Anna?' Jack had said nothing to her about writing to his mother. Had she come to town to rescue her son from his disastrous entanglement? She took a deep, if careful, breath. Despite Meg's assurances, she was never quite sure that something wouldn't fall out of her bodice one evening and this green silk gown made her very nervous.

'Yes, oh…he's seen us. They're coming over. Why don't we just wait here for them?'

An excellent idea, thought Cressida hollowly. Get it over and done with. No doubt Lady Anna would have any number of arguments that would persuade her son to withdraw his offer. Although she couldn't help hoping that the fashionable crowd would slow down Jack's progress towards them.

Lord Parbury came up. 'Evening, Lady Rutherford, Miss Bramley. Shocking squeeze, ain't it? Marc here this evening?' He chatted on and Cressida relaxed slightly, letting the conversation wash over her. No doubt Jack and his mama had been waylaid by other acquaintances. Lady Anna might have already convinced him of the foolishness of pursuing such an unequal match. Nothing had been made public. She could release him without anyone being the wiser. The thought did absolutely nothing to raise her spirits.

'Perhaps you might do me the honour of standing up for a dance, Miss Cressida?'

She forced herself to smile at Lord Parbury. 'Whichever you like, my lord.'

'Except the first waltz and the supper waltz,' came a deep voice. 'They're mine. Just bear that in mind, my lord.'

Outraged, Cressida turned to glare at Jack. And encountered a smile that would have melted a statue.

'Yours?' she challenged, despite the pounding of her heart and the breathless little voice that said he was welcome to the dances and anything else he liked to claim.

'Mine,' he affirmed with an absolutely wicked grin as he caught the dance card at her wrist. Her immediate reaction was to jerk it out of his hand, but the light caress of his fingers sent a wave of dizziness through her, even through her long kid gloves. She dragged in a deep breath as her heart raced and caught his mother's glance.

Familiar dark grey eyes twinkled at her out of a woman's face and an amused voice said, 'I apologise, my dear. I did my best, but as you've probably noticed, he's dreadfully stubborn.'

Cressida stared. Heavens! How alike they were! And realised that Jack had managed to write his name down on her dance card. Twice.

Lady Anna Hamilton continued. 'Since we have a little time before Jack claims you for the first waltz, perhaps you might like to walk with me a little. Your papa was used to visit a great deal years ago. We were sorry to lose contact with him after he moved to Cornwall. I'm so glad you came to Jack.'

She was?

By the time Jack claimed her for the first waltz her convictions had taken a severe battering. Lady Anna betrayed no sign that she disapproved of her future daughter-in-law. And it was obvious she knew. *You'll make Jack so happy. Thank you, my dear. He needed something to shake him up a bit.*

How could she possibly make Jack happy? And whatever did Lady Anna mean about shaking him up? She knew she drove him insane at times, but for the life of her, she couldn't see how that would make him happy.

She shivered as he swung her into the waltz. Judging by the impersonal way he was holding her, he probably didn't even desire her any more... *He doesn't love you. You know that. He's kind, chivalrous and protective, but he doesn't love you.*

She caught sight of Meg and Marcus in the whirling throng. They were dancing with eyes only for each other, close enough to have every tongue in the room wagging if they hadn't been married. She would love to dance like that with Jack, close enough to...

He whirled her through a turn and drew her closer to avoid another couple, close enough to feel the heat of his body, to smell the cologne he used and the faint, musky odour of himself beneath it. Close enough to feel his thighs brush against hers, melting every bone in her body. Close enough that he filled her entire vision as well as her heart.

'Jack…' Her voice came out as a sort of squeak. 'Do you think we're close enough?' Irony was not going to work with her voice wobbling everywhere. 'I mean, shouldn't you—?'

'Not nearly close enough,' he said softly. 'But I can't do anything about it now. If I kiss you, all hell will break loose.'

If he… 'What did you just say?'

There was no sort-of-squeak about her voice this time. It was unquestionable squeak.

'I can't kiss you here,' he said obligingly. 'You'll have to wait until later.'

Her mind whirled even faster than the violins. 'I…I don't want you to kiss me,' she lied.

He grinned. 'Do you know what a terrible liar you are?'

There was no answer to that.

Lord Parbury claimed her for the next dance. He confused her even more.

'About time,' he said without preamble. 'Lord, if I ever knew Jack to be such a slowtop! I'm sure you'll be very happy, m'dear. Lady Anna looks to be in alt, too.'

But…

None of it made sense. She found that Jack was constantly at her side between dances, but he no longer growled at her admirers, rather he chatted easily with men who were obviously his friends. And kept her hand anchored safely on his arm the entire time until he had to relinquish it for her to dance with someone.

Eventually, when he swept her on to the floor for the supper waltz, she asked, 'Why are you doing this?'

This time he didn't bother to wait for the excuse of a near collision to draw her closer. He simply did it and smiled that heartshaking smile. 'I'm showing you,' he said.

'Showing me?'

'You didn't believe me yesterday, so I'm showing you.'

His hand at her waist drifted scandalously low, sending

waves of heat through her. What hadn't she believed yesterday? Her brain had melted along with the rest of her. No wonder Meg always looked and sounded distracted after she'd danced with Marc.

What hadn't she believed yesterday? *That he loves you.* But… She stared up at him and found another smile on his face, even more heartstopping than the other one. Her jaw dropped.

'That's right, sweetheart.' He swung her around effortlessly and said, 'From now on the first waltz and the supper waltz are mine. Even if I'm not there to claim them at the start of the evening.'

A quiver of delight ran through her. That was the exact arrangement Marc had with Meg. No one ever solicited Lady Rutherford for either of those two dances.

'But—'

'No buts,' he growled softly. 'They're mine.' The possessive tone in his voice suggested that he'd like to claim a few other things as his while he was at it.

Marc and Meg joined them at the end of the dance and they made up a party for supper, gathering Parbury, Petersham and Lady Anna.

Cressida watched, entranced, as Jack attended to his mother, making sure she had everything she required. He did it all without seeming to realise, as though caring for his mother was second nature to him, something that was so deeply engrained it was a part of him. She thought back to all the times he had grabbed for her, despite his injured shoulder. And the writing table. Helping people was normal for Jack. Caring for people was normal. He did it without thinking.

And she could no longer doubt that he cared for her in much the same way. Her heart ached with unspoken love, even as she wondered if he would ever care just that little bit more. That little bit that included so much more than the promptings of honour and chivalry.

* * *

Over the next week Cressida's certainty about Jack's chivalrous intent wavered. He said not one word of love, but if she'd had a pocket, he would have been living in it.

As it was he made do with attending her everywhere, monopolising her company, taking her to Hatchard's bookshop—and Gunter's afterwards. He made good his threat to dance every supper waltz with her and no longer bothered to wait for an excuse to drag her scandalously close. He just did it. Right at the start of the dance.

And he seemed happy to be with her. Content. Proud. He teased her, laughed at her, told her scandalous stories about all society's most starched-up pillars. He strolled with her in the park every day at the fashionable hour. In short, he made a complete and utter spectacle of himself in front of all society.

By the end of the week Cressida suspected that the raised eyebrows of London's gossipmongers were going to result in some permanent wrinkles. Yet apparently not a word was said in disparagement. Even the other gossip died away.

Meg remarked on that. 'They wouldn't dare, of course.'

Cressida blinked. 'They wouldn't? Why not?'

It was Meg's turn to blink. 'With Jack involved? He's made his intentions quite plain. No one would dare cross him!'

Cressida tried in vain to reconcile a Jack that no one would dare cross with the big, chivalrous mere Mister she was betrothed to.

'But he's not titled, or in Parliament…or…or anything like that,' she said. 'I mean, I know the family's very old and he's wonderful and kind, but…' Words failed her.

Meg grinned. 'And so disgustingly wealthy that he referred to your wretched dowry as a *paltry ten thousand*. Quite apart from which, everybody likes him, from the patronesses of Almack's down. So with Sally Jersey and all the others beaming upon the whole situation, no one else will say a word.'

Cressida shook her head at the unfathomable ways of society. Apparently a mere Mister could wield a great deal of subtle power. Oddly enough, although she had seen Andrew and his mama on several occasions, neither had made the least push to approach her. And that worried her. Somehow she could not quite credit that the Fairbridge arrogance would be deterred by anything less than a public announcement of her betrothal.

She banished the thought. After all, she had never been happier. Only one thing niggled at the edges of her dream: Jack never kissed her, never touched her in any way that could be construed as lover-like. Unless you counted the way he waltzed with her. And even that had her puzzled. He seemed to be a mass of tension during and immediately after those dances.

Did he really want her? Or was it all a façade?

'Meg, I'm really not convinced about that…um, that nightgown. It's rather…well, you know!' Apart from anything else, she'd freeze in it!

Cressida was still fighting a valiant rearguard action as she followed Meg over the threshold of Rutherford House after a morning's shopping. The ball was the next day and Meg had commandeered her from Jack, announcing that there were several important items to be purchased for her protégée. Cressida had a sinking feeling that the contested nightgown had been the focal point of the expedition and that she had been cozened by an expert.

The Countess of Rutherford very properly ignored her protégée's craven attitude, as indeed she had done all the way from Regent Street, and smiled cheerfully at the footman holding the door for them.

'Good morning, Thomas. There are a few parcels in the

carriage. Could you please carry them up to Miss Cressida's chamber?'

Miss Cressida could only blink at this staggering understatement. The shopping spree Meg had dragged her on when she came up to London had left her breathless. This one beggared the imagination, leaving very little room in the carriage for passengers.

'Meg!' cried Cressida. 'That nightgown…'

Meg turned with an absolutely wicked grin on her face. 'Will be simply perfect.'

For what? wondered Cressida. Her appearance in a seraglio?

Meg answered the unspoken question. 'For your wedding night.' With a smile she called out to the footman, staggering up the steps under a pile of dress boxes. 'Thomas…is his lordship home?'

Thomas peered around the teetering pile. 'Yes, m'lady. His lordship is in the ballroom, fencing with Mr Hamilton.'

'Fencing!' Cressida forgot all about Meg's perfidious behaviour. 'In the ballroom?' It seemed an incongruous setting to say the least.

'Better than the library,' commented Meg. 'That's where they used to practise because Marc keeps the foils and *épées* in the cupboards under the bookcases.'

'Oh,' said Cressida weakly. Jack and Marc?

'Come and watch, if you like,' said Meg cheerfully. 'We can stand at the top of the steps just inside the doorway. They won't mind as long as we don't make any noise. Although I dare say they're only using foils with the buttons on. Quite harmless.'

Bemused, Cressida followed her to the ballroom. The doors stood slightly open and as they approached Cressida could hear the swift hiss and clash of steel, the thud of feet.

Meg frowned slightly. 'Funny. They usually talk while they practise.' She led the way into the ballroom and stopped short. Cressida peered around her shoulder and stifled a gasp.

She had never seen any swordplay before, but her heart nearly stopped at the fire and pace of the match. And the blades looked far heavier than she had imagined. More deadly. Swallowing hard, she clenched her fists. Dear God, if she didn't know that the two men below were the best of friends, she'd swear they were intending to kill each other.

She had experienced Jack's strength before, but never had she been confronted with his sheer athleticism. She had never realised that for all his height and powerful physique, he could still move with the speed and grace of a striking cat.

Plainly they had been at it for some time. Jack's shirt was soaked with sweat and clung to his body as he fought. Cressida's mouth went dry as she watched.

It seemed to her that he was attacking the whole time, constantly thrusting, only to be met with a parry each time and forced back by Marc's blade. The blades hissed and sang, clashing again and again until at last she felt Meg's hand on her wrist.

Reluctantly she turned her head and saw Meg gesture towards the door.

Once outside she gave voice to her question. 'Meg, were those foils? They look much heavier than I'd thought. And I couldn't see any buttons.'

The Countess of Rutherford shook her head. 'There weren't any buttons,' she said, sounding rather preoccupied. 'And those weren't foils. They were using Marc's *épées*.'

Épées? Duelling swords? Every drop of blood thickened in fear.

'Meg…' she began.

'Cressida, they fence all the time!' Meg assured her. 'I dare say they just got the *épées* out for a change of weight, or pace…or…or something.' She slipped her arm around Cressida's shoulders. 'No one duels with swords anymore. They all use pistols. If Jack were planning to challenge Fairbridge, he and Marc would be down at Manton's, culping wafers.' She grinned. 'At least I hope so. I'd have a bit to say if he practised for a pistol duel in our ballroom!'

Cressida refused to be diverted. 'But, Meg! What if he does challenge Fairbridge?'

Frowning, Meg said, 'He wouldn't be so idiotish.' But she didn't sound at all convinced. Then she brightened. 'Besides, if he did, it would be Fairbridge's choice of weapons, you know. And he'd choose pistols. So stop worrying. Jack and Marc like fencing because it's good exercise.'

Jack lowered his blade.

'Enough?' asked Marc calmly. He sounded very slightly winded.

Jack nodded. 'For now. We might have another session tomorrow.' He dragged a handkerchief out of his pocket and mopped his face. His shoulder ached liked the very devil, but a few more bouts with a fencer of Marc's calibre would take care of that.

'How does your shoulder feel?' asked Marc, glancing at him shrewdly.

Jack rolled it around and shrugged. 'Tired, but I don't think it slowed me too badly.'

His lordship snorted. 'Hardly! And there I was, counting on it to give me an advantage.'

'Did you need one?' Jack pulled on his boots. 'Did you notice Cressida and Meg? They came in part way through and left again.'

'Mmm. I saw them.' He picked up his coat from the balustrade. 'You'd better come upstairs and borrow a clean shirt,' he continued. 'You can't put your coat on over that one. Go on up and ring for my man. I'll put the blades away.'

'Do you think Cressida noticed we were using the *épées*?' asked Jack.

'I've no idea,' returned Marc. 'Any more than I've the least notion why you want to practise your swordsmanship. I feel it encumbent upon me, as your likely second at the impending bloodbath, to point out that in the face of a challenge from you, Fairbridge will opt for pistols. And so would I,' he added feelingly, shaking out his sword arm. 'No one in their right mind would accept a challenge from you in your current mood and then plump for swords!'

'It won't be my challenge,' said Jack quietly.

Marc stared. 'It won't?' His eyes narrowed as he thought about it. 'No,' he said slowly. 'Of course it won't. Hmm. I dare say it's better this way. Too easy to kill with pistols, and if you kill the bastard there'll be the devil of a kick-up. You'd be spending a very protracted honeymoon abroad.'

Jack smiled very slowly. 'That's not the point at all, Marc.'

Marc swore. 'Curse it, Jack! You're meant to be the level-headed one! Mr Jack Never-Seen-Him-Ruffled Hamilton. You can't be meaning to kill Fairbridge! You'd have to leave the country!'

Seeing Marc's genuine concern beneath his expostulations, Jack relented. 'I've no intention of killing him. But I've every intention of carving a few strips out of his hide. Slowly.'

He grinned at Marc's disbelieving stare.

The Earl looked at him narrowly. 'Let me be quite sure I understand what I'm getting myself into: you intend to provoke Fairbridge into challenging you, so that you can choose weapons, time and place. Would you mind very much letting me know the time and place so that I can make a note of it in my diary?'

Jack straightened up from pulling on his boots. He met Marc's eyes and stated, 'The next time he attempts to force Cressida to accept his suit. Then and there.'

'Any use my pointing out that one of the first duties of a second is to attempt a reconciliation?' asked Marc drily.

'You probably have more useful things to do with your breath. I certainly won't be wasting mine on apologies.'

'Hmm.' Marc appeared to consider this. He shrugged. 'Ah, well. At least I am spared the indignity of thinking up a convincing lie to explain to Meg just why I'm leaving our bed so early. Dawn appointments are always so inconvenient.' He appeared to consider something further. 'Er, Jack, have you entertained the possibility of Fairbridge trying to force Cressida's hand at our ball?'

Only a fool would have described Jack Hamilton's smile as pleasant. 'I'm counting on it.'

The Earl of Rutherford groaned. He didn't need second sight to foresee that the Countess of Rutherford's first ball was fated to go down in history as one of the Season's most talked-about entertainments. He could only hope that Jack Hamilton's legendary self-control would be sufficient to prevent him from actually killing Lord Fairbridge. Right now, Jack's assurances to the contrary would not have inspired him to wager any considerable sum on the chance.

Chapter Fifteen

Her hand anchored firmly on Jack's arm, Cressida came off the dance floor with him after the first waltz of the Rutherford House ball. Perhaps if she stood still for a moment her head might stop revolving. She refused to believe that her heart would ever stop spinning.

'The notice will be in the papers tomorrow.'

Her heart did more than spin. Then his voice registered. He sounded odd. Grim almost. Her heart plummeted.

She met his eyes. 'Jack…' She couldn't go on. Why did he look so strained? What was bothering him? He'd seemed happy enough at the start of the dance. But, as always, by the end of the dance he'd turned into a statue. Heavens, he looked as if a smile would break his jaw.

He smiled down at her. She'd never realised that it was possible to smile with a locked jaw, but he did it. What had she done wrong? Or was it just that he couldn't keep up the façade any longer?

Lord Petersham came up to claim her for the next dance and Jack watched her go, practically breathing a sigh of relief. Surely if he couldn't see her, or feel her, he would be able to control his urge to bundle her out of the ballroom and into a quiet unused parlour where he could give rein to the urgent need building inside him.

The past week had been hell. His control was in tatters, smoking around the edges. He hadn't dared to touch her in any way beyond keeping her hand on his arm except during their waltzes. And the temptation to kiss her senseless in the Rutherfords' carriage after an evening party had been appalling. He'd resisted, knowing exactly where that would have ended. And she deserved better than a carriage seat for her first experience of lovemaking. She deserved a bed and a wedding ring.

He drew a tentative breath. Oh, God. The light scent of rosewater hung about his clothes, clinging, seducing. And her face, turned up to his, worried and uncertain, haunted him. Something was bothering her. Had she realised just how much he desired her? Did that frighten her? He wouldn't blame her if it did. It frightened the hell out of him. One thing was certain. Their betrothal was going to be one of the shortest on record.

'Miss Bramley, my dear! How delightfully you look this evening! Have you seen Andrew yet? I believe him to be looking for you everywhere!'

Cressida stiffened as Lady Fairbridge enveloped her in a waft of scent. She drew breath to respond, but found herself sneezing instead.

Lady Fairbridge sailed on regardless. 'Good evening, Petersham. Perhaps you might leave me to speak privately with Miss Bramley.'

Thinking fast, Cressida smiled up at Lord Petersham. 'Thank you so much for a lovely dance, my lord. I shall look forward to our next.'

'So shall I, my dear,' he assured her, bowing deeply over her hand. 'Servant, Lady Fairbridge.' He favoured Cressida with a friendly smile and Lady Fairbridge with a brief nod and strolled off.

Reminding herself to breathe deeply and keep a tight

rein on her temper, Cressida manufactured a polite smile for Lady Fairbridge.

The Dowager's opening remarks nearly wiped it off her face. 'I saw you dancing with Mr Hamilton, my dear. Petersham is harmless enough, but you would do well to be a little careful with Mr Hamilton. I have noted that he always engages you for the first waltz and the supper waltz. A little too particular, my love, if you don't mind my saying so. Of course, I do understand that he is your cousin, but—'

'As a matter of fact, I do mind. Very much.' Cressida spoke as quietly as she could, but anger bubbled over. Firmly, she pinned the smile back in place.

Lady Fairbridge favoured her with an indulgent smile. 'Now, now, my dear! I quite understand that you and Andrew have had a little difference of opinion, but you must not tease him by encouraging the attentions of other men! That would be sadly unkind in you!' She lowered her voice to a conspiratorial whisper. 'He tells me that he has renewed his offer and I wish you to know the match now has my full support. You need feel no scruples in—'

'Refusing his suit,' finished Cressida. She hung on to her temper desperately. Words blazed on the tip of her tongue, but she quenched her rage and forced them back. She utterly refused to tell Lady Fairbridge that she and Jack were betrothed. The announcement would be made at supper. Then she would know. And Andrew would have to give up his pursuit of her.

Her eyes bulging, Lady Fairbridge stammered, 'You c…can't be serious! Refuse *Fairbridge*?' Her voice rose a couple of octaves, carrying even over the roar of conversation, so that several people turned in eager curiosity.

Cressida flinched. Good Lord! Did people have nothing better to do with their lives that they needs must take such a suffocating interest in one's personal affairs? Plainly she had made a serious mistake. This was not the right venue for this particular discussion.

Lady Fairbridge voiced exactly what she was thinking. 'My dear Miss Bramley, perhaps you would do me the favour of withdrawing to somewhere a little more private where you may explain yourself.'

Reflecting that it would all be much simpler if either Lord Fairbridge or his mother had ever learned to take *no* for an answer, Cressida agreed.

'Certainly, Lady Fairbridge, I will be only too happy to explain my decision to you.'

'Excellent,' purred Lady Fairbridge. 'I'm sure I can give your thoughts a happier direction. The library perhaps?'

Cressida hesitated. Meg had not intended the library to be used this evening. On the other hand, it would probably be empty and, since she had every intention of telling Lady Fairbridge very plainly exactly what she thought of Andrew's offer, that would be a distinct advantage.

'The library,' she agreed.

Jack saw her go and breathed a sigh of relief. Far better if she told Lady Fairbridge that she had refused the Viscount's offer. He couldn't bear to think of her so much as being in the same room as Fairbridge, let alone speaking to him. Her ladyship could convey the fell tidings to her precious son. While it would have afforded him immense satisfaction to carve a few chunks out of Fairbridge, the course of wisdom was to avoid scandal, not cause it.

Gloomily he turned and snaffled a glass of champagne from a passing footman. He'd never realised how boring wisdom could be.

Someone had lit the fire in the library and left one small lamp burning. Despite her simmering anger, Cressida had to suppress a smile as she saw Marc's *épées* lying on a console table. Jack had come around for some more fencing in the morning and Delafield had chased his noble master out of the ballroom when the housemaids and foot-men complained. Obviously they had forgotten to put the blades away.

Turning to face Lady Fairbridge, Cressida stated baldly, 'I have refused Lord Fairbridge's offer. You cannot pos-sibly believe that, after what has passed between us, his offer would be acceptable to either myself or my father?'

Her ladyship swelled with indignation. 'Your *father*? Do you tell me that he has the temerity to forbid the match? When *I* approve it? Do you imagine that you can attract a better offer? Think carefully, girl. I can ruin you!'

'You've already tried, haven't you?' flared Cressida. 'All those whispers! The suggestions that I was fast! They came from you!' It all made sense now. To someone like Lady Fairbridge, any husband would be better than none. So she had tried to make sure her son was the only one to offer.

Lady Fairbridge snorted. 'D'you think I'm stupid, girl? My cousin, Kate Stanhope, did all the talking! Lord! The ninnyhammer was convinced Hamilton was about to offer for you instead of Alison.' She laughed scornfully. 'The idea! Jack Hamilton to offer marriage to a little provincial nobody with a soiled reputation! He don't need to marry money! Unfortunately, not everyone can afford to be so choosy.'

Nausea left Cressida cold and shaking.

Lady Fairbridge was still talking. 'So you'll marry An-drew, my girl, or I'll ruin you. And your father will end up where he belongs. Hamilton can't call me out, and no one will support him if he calls my son out to account for my actions!'

Rage lashed Cressida, burning away the fear and nausea. 'Lady Fairbridge, you and your precious son may go to the devil!' she blazed.

The door opened and she spun around.

'Ah, Mama. I did tell you she was stubborn, didn't I?'

Lord Fairbridge sauntered into the room. 'I'll deal with it now, ma'am.' He bowed to his mother. 'Thank you for getting her here.'

Lady Fairbridge headed for the door, saying, 'You've got about ten minutes, Andrew.' She stalked out and shut the door firmly behind her.

Ten minutes? What in God's name did she mean by that? The question hammered in Cressida's brain along with the realisation that she had been trapped. Her every nerve focused on Andrew as he started towards her. Instinctively she backed up, circling until she had the sofa between them. It stood directly opposite the fire and she allowed herself a swift, desperate glance at the hearth. The fire irons were missing. She dragged in a deep breath. Only one thing would recall Fairbridge to his senses—she would have to tell him she was betrothed to Jack.

Lord Fairbridge laughed softly. 'I'm not a fool, my dear. I moved them earlier. Give up now. They will find us soon and you will have no choice but to accept my offer.'

Fury swept her, banishing all rational thought. 'When snow lies in hell!' she spat. 'You must be mad! What do you think my cousin will say to this?'

He shrugged. 'Why should I care? If he is fool enough to issue a challenge, I am a good enough shot to account for him. Anyway, why should he bother? I'm offering marriage. It's the best offer you'll get once my mother opens her budget.'

He smirked. 'And believe me, she can do so very convincingly. Bemoaning my *infatuation*, that your dowry was the final straw. She's a very fine actress. At this moment she is busily fainting in the ballroom and wondering feebly where I might be. And my cousin, Alison Stanhope, will conveniently remember that she saw me go in this direction. Any moment now, someone, probably several some-ones, will come in and find us.'

'Not much of a discovery,' she mocked. 'You on one side of the sofa and me on the other.'

His smile sent chills down her spine. 'If necessary, they will find you with your skirts around your waist and me on top of you.'

She jerked backwards, her knees shaking. He was much taller than she was. If he caught her... She shuddered, remembering his strength. All her senses at the stretch, she waited as he began to circle the sofa slowly. She edged away. If she could get to the other side, she would have a clear run to the door...

He vaulted over in an effortless move.

She had a split second's warning to whirl and run, but, hampered by her skirts, she had scarcely taken three strides before he was on her, spinning her against him and clamping a hand over her mouth. Struggling wildly, she was borne back towards the sofa.

'For God's sake, you little spitfire!' he hissed viciously as she kicked him on the knee. He forced her on. She fought the more furiously. If once he got her to the sofa...his very weight would subdue her.

She heard a tearing sound as her bodice ripped in the struggle and bit down savagely on his hand. Swearing, he loosened his grip and she managed to turn towards him, getting in one blow to his nose and spitting in his face.

She was free and leapt back.

He still stood between her and the door. The slow smile as he wiped his face said that he knew it.

Cressida fought to steady her breathing. Fear lashed her. She must not get caught in a compromising position. She couldn't bear for Jack to marry her under those circumstances. Somehow she had to stay out of Fairbridge's hands. Literally. If only she could get to the door, she knew the house and would be able to escape.

She couldn't get past him. If once she made a break for the door, he would be on her.

'That torn bodice will pretty well do the job for me when they find us,' said Fairbridge.

Cressida resisted the temptation to shrug. 'I'll tell the truth, that you—'

He interrupted. 'Became carried away by passion when I begged you to marry me.'

She smiled. 'And were so dreadfully disappointed when I told you I had accepted my cousin's offer instead.'

He froze. Then, 'You're lying. What would Hamilton want with a soiled little dove? *He* doesn't need your dowry.'

He came towards her, steadily, inexorably, but Cressida had seen what she needed. There would be only one chance. Abandoning caution, she darted for the door and, as Fairbridge charged after her, swung around, rushing at him.

He checked, startled. And swore as Cressida flung herself down in his path and rolled under his feet bringing him down heavily. Gasping for the breath he had kicked out of her, she surged to her feet in a flurry of silken skirts, coming up against the console table with a crash that nearly shook it loose from the wall.

Grabbing an *épée*, she whirled around to face him.

Every rib felt battered, but she said coolly, 'Checkmate, my lord.'

He came to his feet slowly and his eyes narrowed. 'If you say so, my dear.'

'I do,' she said. 'You are running out of time, my lord. If anyone comes in now... How many men, making an *honourable* offer to a woman, are held off with a sword?' She fought down the knowledge that being caught like this would spell ruin as surely as if Fairbridge had succeeded.

He did not answer, but waited. And waited.

The minutes stretched out until Cressida's arm began to ache with the strain of holding the sword up. At first it had felt light enough, but holding it up, and keeping it steady...

She could feel the fine trembling in her arm. She did not dare set her other hand to it. It would be too awkward. And too revealing. If Fairbridge did not already know that the sword was too heavy for her, Cressida had no intention of telling him.

All her nerves alight, she considered her situation. It was not really checkmate. He could still move freely. More like check. He could not approach her, but if she tried to move for the door, he would be able to take the second sword and disarm her. She could see the clock on the chimney-piece out of the corner of her eye and shivered. She had defeated Fairbridge and time would defeat her. Could she take both swords? Impossible. One sword was heavy and unwieldy enough.

As she watched him, he took off his coat. He was going to try and catch the blade through it.

Then she heard it. A hubbub of conversation from the hall. Numbness gripped her. This, then, was the end of her brief dream of happiness. Not even to return the dowry could she marry Jack in the aftermath of a scandal like this.

The door opened. 'Maybe he's in here…this is the libr— Oh! I say! Er…sorry to interrupt and all that, but, ah, Lady Fairbridge has…' Young Mr Guilfoyle's voice trailed off as his startled gaze landed on Cressida.

'Conveniently fainted in the ballroom,' suggested Cressida, hitching up her torn bodice.

'Oh…well, um…yes,' he said, eyes goggling. He seemed to recollect himself. 'Well, it wasn't convenient exactly, but…'

'I'll come at once,' said Fairbridge smoothly. 'My betrothed will excuse me if I don't give her any more fencing tips tonight.'

She would have consigned him to hell, along with all the people crowding avidly in the doorway, but she never got the chance.

'*Your* betrothed, did I hear you say, Fairbridge?' came a deep voice, pouring cold water on the excited simmer of incipient scandal. '*Your* betrothed?' Jack forced his way through the door with little or no regard for those in his way.

Cressida's heart lurched. She was vaguely aware that Marc stalked close behind him, but her eyes fixed on his face. Terror rushed through her. His face was locked in lines of savage fury. He was going to call Fairbridge out.

Only iron control kept Jack from launching himself at the Viscount's throat as he came through the door. There must be no misunderstanding about the situation. He had to make quite sure everyone understood what they had interrupted.

Swiftly he searched for Cressida. And felt his jaw nearly dislocate itself as he saw her, gripping one of the *épées*. By God, she had held the bastard off. With a sword. His little Cressida. Gallant to the last.

Marc's urbane voice came from just behind him. 'Hmm. What a redoubtable girl. And you're going to marry her. Good luck.'

Jack ignored that. 'I can think of three reasons why it is impossible for you to be betrothed to Miss Bramley,' he informed Lord Fairbridge. 'She has accepted *my* offer of marriage and the announcement of our betrothal will appear in the papers tomorrow. With her consent.'

A shocked hush fell over the curious crowd seeping into the library.

Jack stood and waited, cold patience holding him in check.

'Er, that's only two reasons at most, Jack, old fellow,' pointed out Lord Parbury, politely edging his way past Mr Guilfoyle. 'What's the third?'

'The third?' asked Jack, trying not to sing with triumph. 'The third is that Fairbridge has shown himself to be such a contemptible cur, that no woman of even moderate breeding and intelligence would choose to sully herself by such an alliance.'

This time the hush was deathly, but Jack didn't have long to wait.

'Why, you arrogant bastard! You'll answer for that! Name your seconds!'

Jack saw the choking fury in Fairbridge's face with savage satisfaction. 'Certainly, my lord,' he said promptly. 'Rutherford and Sir Toby Carlton will act for me. Choose yours quickly, Fairbridge. I have no intention of missing supper over this affair.'

'What the hell do you mean?' snarled Fairbridge. 'My seconds will call on yours! Or aren't you familiar with the rules governing an affair of honour?'

Jack permitted his lips to curve in satisfaction. 'Oh, I'm perfectly familiar with them, my lord. You, on the other hand, seem to be a little out of touch with the niceties of honourable conduct. Your challenge, Fairbridge. My choice of time and place.' He paused. 'And weapons, of course.' His glance roved around the library. 'Right here, right now. And no doubt Rutherford will be happy to lend us his swords. I repeat: name your seconds, coward!'

'Oh, I say, Hamilton! That's coming it a trifle strong!' protested Mr Guilfoyle.

'Is it, Mr Guilfoyle?' asked Jack. 'Let me ask you: what name would you give a man who courted a gently reared girl with promises of marriage and then told her his mother would never countenance the match and asked her to be his mistress instead? What name would you give him when, in the face of her refusal, he attempted to force himself on her? What name would you give him when it transpired that his whole intent was to ruin the girl and thus force her father out of his living? What name would you give him when he ensured the girl's name and reputation were destroyed?'

Mr Guilfoyle blanched.

Jack paused and turned slowly to Fairbridge. 'There are several names for the man who did all that and then attempted to force the girl into marriage when she acquired a generous dowry that would cover his gaming debts. Since there are ladies present I shall have to content myself with calling him: coward.'

'By God, I'll teach you a lesson, Hamilton!' exploded Fairbridge. 'Would you question the word of a gentleman over this little trollop?'

Jack shook off Marc's restraining hand. 'Yes,' he grated. 'I would. But the question doesn't arise, since you fail to qualify as a gentleman. But that will not deter me from teaching you a lesson for insulting Miss Bramley. Your seconds! Quickly. Or have you thought the better of your challenge? I'm sure we would all understand if that were the case.'

For a moment it seemed all too possible that Fairbridge would deprive Jack of satisfaction by dying of apoplexy. He turned purple and literally shook with rage. He looked around wildly. No one stepped forward.

'I'll act for myself!' he snarled. 'If I might examine the blades?'

'I'll act for Fairbridge,' said Mr Guilfoyle suddenly. 'Awkward affair. Rutherford's a second in his own house. His blades, too. Dashed irregular anyway. Not that I'm implying anything dishonourable, my lord,' he added hastily as Rutherford raised his eyebrows. 'But it's best to have everything all snug.'

'Oh, very well,' sighed Lord Petersham, edging past Lady Jersey. 'Excuse me, Sally. I must say this goes against the grain, but Guilfoyle has the right of it. I'll act with him. Just to oblige you, Jack!'

'My thanks, gentlemen,' Fairbridge sneered. 'How very gallant of you! Rutherford, Carlton! You may deal with Mr Guilfoyle and Lord Petersham.'

Marc nodded and went to Cressida.

She looked at him, dazed. When her elegant, easy-going host been replaced with this cold, grim aristocrat? He met her glance and the chilly eyes softened slightly.

His quiet words reached only her. 'Don't worry, Cressida. Nothing will happen to him.' Then, a little louder, 'I do apologise that you were subjected to such unpleasantness under my roof, Miss Bramley. If I might have both swords, please?'

Automatically she moved so that he could reach the sword on the console table. She flinched slightly as his fingers touched hers. Puzzled, she looked down and discovered that she still held her sword, clenched tightly.

Jack was going to fight a duel. He had insulted Fairbridge publicly, openly questioning his honour. Fairbridge would be ready to kill. It was all her stupid fault. And even if Jack won…what if he killed Fairbridge? He'd have to flee the country, ruin his life just because she had made an unholy mess of everything. Shivering she looked at Jack. The expression on his face said very clearly that no arguments would alter his decision.

'Cressida, let go. You are safe now. Come, you must give me the sword.'

Again she looked down and discovered that Marc was uncurling her fingers from the hilt, one by one. She jerked back from him, still gripping the sword. Her voice came out queerly detached. 'I'll give it to him.'

Keeping the blade lowered, she walked steadily towards Jack. Fairbridge stood in her way, his blue eyes scornful. Coldness spread and firmed inside her, sheathing her resolve in bitter ice. Reaching Fairbridge, she stopped.

'You'll never live the gossip down,' he mocked. 'You know that, don't you?'

She nodded. 'I might have been naïve, my lord, but I'm not stupid.' She smiled at him gently. 'Of course, in that situation I have nothing to lose. They might as well have something worth gossiping over.' So saying, she lifted the sword in one swift motion and lunged.

Jack's roar of protest nearly drowned out the Viscount's scream of shocked pain as he staggered back, clutching his right arm just above the elbow. His forearm hung useless and a slow trickle of blood squeezed from between his fingers.

'Bloody hell!'

Rutherford strode past her, his dropped jaw radiating disbelief. Lord Petersham, Sir Toby and Mr Guilfoyle all converged on the disabled duellist.

Still dumbfounded, Rutherford turned back to Cressida. Then the corner of his mouth twitched. 'I thought you meant to give the damn thing to Jack.'

The guilty flush burnt her cheeks. 'I…I know you did. I'm awfully sorry, my lord. I thought if you knew what I intended…you'd stop me.'

The twitch became an outright grin. 'Don't waste your apologies on me, my dear. Unless I'm much mistaken, Jack is about to peel one out of your hide, since you've saved Fairbridge from him.' He looked at her with an approving smile and added very softly, 'And a damn good thing, too. Well done. I'm sure you'll both be happier in Leicestershire than on the continent.'

Jack's voice sliced through the confused babble at the door. 'Perhaps if everyone would like to remove themselves,' he said, 'I might be permitted to discuss the situation with *my* betrothed.'

They were alone and Cressida finally faced Jack's blistering anger.

'What the devil did you do that for?' he demanded.

Whatever had surged through her blood, giving her the strength to face down Fairbridge and defy him, whatever had kept her chin up while the others remained in the room, Cressida had no idea. All she knew was that it had deserted her, leaving her drained and exhausted.

'I...I...' Cold, she was so cold. And she couldn't stop shaking. Shudders racked her until she could barely stand. She rubbed clumsily at her arms, but her hands felt cold, clammy. The room swung about her in sickening swoops.

If I don't sit down... She took a step and staggered as a wave of blackness hit her. Somehow she had made it to the sofa and he was there, enfolding her in his arms, pressing her head to lie against his shoulder.

'Sshh. You're safe now,' he murmured. 'Take a deep breath, relax. He won't touch you again.' His heat poured through her, but she continued to shake, wondering if she were about to laugh or cry. Nothing made sense. She was safe. Jack was safe.

And she had to release him from their betrothal. 'I...I'm releasing you...' she whispered. She felt every muscle surrounding her tense and his hand stilled on her hair. The breath he took shivered through her.

'Sweetheart, in case you hadn't noticed, *I'm* holding *you*. And I have no intention of releasing you. Ever. Under any circumstances.'

Oh, God. He's being chivalrous again! And after I made him look a complete fool in front of the entire ton! She struggled to free herself and sit up. 'But you must! It's quite all right, Jack. I know that I can't marry you after tonight. We...we don't need to say anything. Even if the notice is in the papers tomorrow...'

'It will be,' he interpolated.

She hurried on. 'No one will say anything. At the end of the Season I can go away and...and everything will be just as it was. People will forget and...and...' She would spend the rest of her life crying herself to sleep.

'That's your idea of *all right*, is it?' Jack asked in a very neutral voice.

Shakily she nodded.

'Well, it's not mine,' he said bluntly. 'You're forgetting something,' he went on. 'You've still got something of mine.'

Wildly she tried to imagine what. She had nothing of his, except…

'You want the necklace back.' Try as she might, she could not disguise the wobble in her voice. It might have little value, but to her it was all the riches of the Orient.

'I don't want anything back,' he said quietly. 'Not even my heart. I'll settle for yours instead.' He gave Cressida no further warning of his intentions. He moved with all the speed of a striking cat, and had her locked in his arms. Anything she might have said was lost as his mouth came down on hers in fierce possession.

His control fractured as she gave herself completely into his embrace. There was nothing gentle about his kiss, or about the arms that locked around her. Nothing gentle and everything possessive. Nothing mattered except convincing her once and for all of his love. He could feel sobs racking her and released her mouth to whisper kisses over her brow and cheeks.

'I thought he might kill you,' she whispered. 'If you had died…' Her fingers shook as she stroked his cheek, drew his mouth back to hers again.

He kissed her gently, his mouth drifting over hers as he murmured soothingly. Sobs still shuddered through her and he tasted tears on her lips, her cheeks. With clumsy, shaking hands he framed her face and wiped the tears away with his thumbs.

'Oh, Cress, you little idiot. If you think I'll let you go now…' His arms tightened around her and he sought her mouth again. She gave it unhesitatingly with a sweet generosity that seared him, her lips parting in wordless invitation. He took instant advantage, plundering the vulnerable softness in fierce possession. His hands roved, claiming every feminine curve until his control threatened to break completely.

'You have to marry me, sweetheart.' He felt her stiffen and he held her closer. 'I know. You thought I offered for you because I think you need protecting. It's partially true, because I can't help myself. Damn it, Cressida, I've been in love with you for weeks.' He corrected himself. 'No. I think I've been in love with you from the moment we met, but I was too curst stubborn to see it.'

'You love me? Really love me?' The aching hope in her voice turned like a knife in his soul. 'You don't just feel obliged to protect me?'

He shook his head against her hair, a soft auburn cloud, teasing his senses. 'No. I need to protect you. And I need you. Like I need to breathe.' He floundered, lost for words to tell her how he felt. 'I can't help it, Cress. Any more than you could help trying to protect your father, or worrying about me challenging Fairbridge.' His jaw clenched. 'You're mine. And I'm not going to let you wriggle out of our betrothal.' He waited, conscious that he hadn't said it all. That he didn't know how. All he felt for her seemed to have frozen his wits and tongue.

The quiet stretched between them as Cressida stared at him, trying to see his face in the fire lit shadows. She couldn't think, her heart still raced, her blood still burned in the aftermath of his kisses. He had said he loved her. He had said he needed her. That she was his. She couldn't doubt him. Only one emotion could possibly blaze with that sort of protectiveness and possessiveness. Her heart sang with the sincerity of his declaration, but still she hesitated. Was she doing the right thing in accepting him? Would he come to regret it one day? What would his mother and sister think of such a connection?

Before she could speak again, he slipped a hand into his coat pocket and brought out something that glittered, and flashed fire in the flickering light. Reaching for her left hand, he slipped the delicate marquise ring on to her third finger.

'It belonged to my great-grandmother.' Cressida could hear the smile in his voice and her fingers trembled in his gentle hold. 'She of the spice biscuits. My great-grandfather gave it to her on their fiftieth wedding anniversary.' He cleared his throat. 'I never saw her without it. She left a note saying I was to have it when Mama was ready to give it to me. I never understood why until she gave it to me tonight.'

He lifted her hand to his lips and kissed it. 'I'm yours, Cress. Will you be mine?'

She couldn't speak. The words, whatever they were, had stuck somewhere in her throat, clogged with tears of joy. But she did manage to nod and stroke his jaw with shaking fingers before he drew her back into his arms and kissed the tears away. His lips feathered over her eyes and cheeks, burning in their tenderness. 'Mine.' It was a low, possessive growl.

Her response breathed from her very soul. 'Always.'

Their kiss left him shaking with urgency. Desire hammered in his blood as he locked every muscle against the need to sweep her up into his arms and carry her to the sofa. Dazed, he reached for the easy self-control he had used with every other woman he had ever had. It wasn't there.

Even as he grappled with the knowledge and strove for something, anything to rein himself in, a small hand reached up and stroked his cheek. A butterfly's caress over his jaw, gentle and yearning. That did it. Scooping her up into his arms, he stood up and headed for the door.

'Jack? Why are we in my bedchamber?'

He drew a deep breath. 'Because I'm making love to you and the library is a trifle public.' Even as he spoke, his hands skimmed over her waist, tracing the sweet curve down and over her hip to flex gently.

'M…making love to me? Why?'

'Because I want you.' He kissed her gently on the lips. 'Because I can't help myself.' This time he traced her lips with his tongue, tasting and biting until she opened her mouth for him. Groaning, he took what she offered, sliding his tongue deeply and rhythmically into the honeyed warmth. He shuddered in delight as he felt her answer, felt her body melt against his.

With an effort he drew back and said raggedly, 'Because I love you, Cressida. You're mine. Do you understand?'

All the breath left Cressida's body as the reality of his words finally hit her and the truth of what he had said blazed in his eyes. Storm-dark grey, they held nothing as soft as pity or chivalry. Only a hard-edged need, which should have terrified her in its intensity.

'You…you want me that much?' she stammered. 'You can't.'

'Oh, yes, I can,' he whispered against her mouth. 'And I'm about to demonstrate.'

She gasped and shuddered as she felt him draw her lower lip into his mouth and bite down gently. Heat streamed through her, welling up endlessly as his mouth plundered hers, tenderly, mercilessly. Eagerly she kissed him back, sliding her own tongue against his, pressing herself closer and closer to his shockingly hard, hot body. Her fingers sank into the surging muscles of his shoulders under the fine linen of his shirt. Heat poured out in waves, melting, intoxicating.

When he finally broke the kiss she whimpered in protest, wildly aware that her lips were swollen and tingling from the pressure of his mouth.

'Cress.'

She could scarcely recognise his voice. It sounded hoarse and strained.

'I'm telling you now; I need you to be mine. In bed.' He dragged in a deep breath. 'If you want me to wait until our wedding night, you'll have to kick me out and lock the door. Not very chivalrous of me, but it's the best I can do.'

She looked up in disbelief. 'You want me so much that you'd…you'd…take me n…now.'

He nodded, a rueful smile on his face. 'Right now,' he affirmed softly. 'As long as you swear you'll make an honest man of me as soon as we can get back to Leicestershire for your father to marry us.'

She trembled as she felt his powerful hands flex on her hips. Fire shot through her until she could scarcely think. His eyes, stormy with desire, didn't help her confusion in the least. Jack Hamilton, renowned for his chivalry, kindness and honourable behaviour under all circumstances, had actually begged her to go to bed with him before they were married. And the closest he could get to chivalrous behaviour was warning her to kick him out if she didn't want him to take her. He plainly had no intention of kicking himself out. She could see the tension in his body, the locking of every muscle. Except those hands, which didn't seem able to help themselves.

Why? What had driven him to this state?

He answered her unspoken question. 'Sweetheart, I can't explain. I don't understand it myself. I've never been like this with a woman. Unable to control myself. I thought I'd go mad when I realised what was happening…' He shuddered. 'And I thought I'd kill Fairbridge when I found you.' His jaw clenched.

'You'd have been angry no matter who the woman was, though,' she pointed out quietly.

He nodded. 'Yes. Angry, disgusted. And you're quite right. I would have helped any woman in trouble.' Shaking, he pulled her against his body again. 'But I wouldn't be in her bedchamber now trying to seduce her.' He kissed her gently. 'Chivalry didn't have very much to do with it, Cressida. Possessiveness, protectiveness; they were driving me. If you're expecting chivalry, we have a problem. I've none where you're concerned. Only love.'

Her mouth went dry and she had to force words past the tears clogging her throat. 'That...that will do to be going on with. Are you going to take me to bed now?'

His voice shook with raw need. 'Are you sure, Cress?' Even as he spoke his mouth sought hers.

'Yes,' she whispered against his seeking lips. 'I don't want chivalry. Only you. Now.'

His mouth answered her, taking hers in a kiss that both possessed and cherished. Without breaking the kiss, he lifted her into his arms effortlessly. Swirling streamers of heat writhed through her, coiling tighter and tighter as she again realised his power; and his passion, hovering on the brink of frenzy. She twined her arms about his neck, straining to get closer as he carried her to the bed and lowered her to it. Then nervousness assailed her.

Swallowing hard, she watched as he removed his shoes and stockings. Shyly she reached out and traced the shifting muscles in his shoulder, felt them flicker in response. Then he turned to her and took her hands, placed them at the top button of his shirt. Her eyes widened as shock lanced through her at the realisation that he wanted her to undress him.

Jack watched enthralled as understanding dawned in her eyes. He reined in the urge to tumble her back on the pillows and ravish her, as trembling, uncertain fingers fumbled with the buttons of his shirt. He set his jaw and endured, as light accidental caresses scorched his burning skin.

He had to touch her or die. Slowly he reached for the laces of her torn gown and felt her fingers still on the last button. Huge, questioning pools of green stared at him. One by one he loosened the laces. He shifted his hands to her shoulders and pushed it down to her waist. His blood thundered as he saw the chemise it had concealed. God alone knew what Meg had been thinking of when she recommended that little wisp of silken temptation. Sheer ivory silk, he doubted that it was warming Cressida, but it was certainly causing his already heated blood to boil over. Taut pink buds thrust pleadingly against the diaphanous material.

With a groan he tore his shirt off over his head and pulled Cressida back where she belonged, into his arms. Heat burned through him as his hands shifted over her, shaping and learning every delicate curve under the silk. Her mouth under his, yielding and passionate as he possessed it deeply, rhythmically. Small hands on his shoulders, stroking, exploring, a sweet fire on his body.

Cressida was far beyond thought. A sob of delight escaped her lips as he pressed her back into the pillows and followed her down. A strong hand beneath her hips lifted her slightly and swept the ruined gown away leaving her in just the chemise and a petticoat. Then the petticoat and chemise were gone and his hands roamed unhindered on her burning flesh.

Large, strong hands that wielded a tender power over her senses, beguiling, adoring. Instinctively she responded in the same way, stroking and exploring the curved muscles of his shoulders, his broad back. His groans and the shudders that racked him had heat pooling in her belly and lower. Never had she imagined that desire was like this, a burning, shimmering fire in her soul.

She cried out as she felt his teasing fingers slide lower, into her soft curls, pressing intimately into the melting heat between her thighs. Shivers coursed through her as she felt his hand stroke her inner thigh, lightly, possessively. His mouth came to hers again, licking and biting tenderly at her lips. 'Open for me, little one.' The velvet-dark voice caressed her heart as surely and intimately as his hands and mouth caressed her body.

Frantic with need, she opened her mouth, wanting to feel him inside her, filling her mouth, ravishing her with his kiss. He continued to tantalise with light, teasing caresses. She had to have more. Her entire body sang with longing. Distantly she could hear someone sobbing, begging, 'Please…oh, please…'

Her own voice, torn from her throat. Her body, arching against his in sensuous pleading as her thighs parted in surrender.

He gave her more. His fingers teased with such shattering intimacy that she cried out, scarcely able to comprehend what he was doing. Heat coiled in her. She arched again and felt his other arm slip beneath her, holding her as his mouth blazed fire over her throat to one breast.

He thought he might die. He'd never known anything like this in his life. Not this hot, sweet wanting that burned in his blood and soul. Never had he needed to take a woman like this. Never before had he known, to the depths of his soul, that he couldn't stop, short of death. That he needed her like he needed breath.

He needed to feel her all around him, all that soft, wet heat holding him safely. Now. He groaned. Not yet. He circled her swollen breast hotly, lifting her into the savage heat of his mouth, drawing the sweet flesh deep, moulding the taut peak with his tongue, scoring with his teeth in fierce restraint. He felt her body's response as urgent heat welled up between her thighs, spilling helplessly over his fingers. Burning in passion's grip, he pressed gently at her entrance with one finger, felt her still in sensual shock.

Words were beyond him, but he had to make sure she understood. Releasing her breast he took her mouth again, deeply, intimately, his tongue penetrating and retreating in rhythmic surges. And felt her response, felt her kiss him back, draw him deeper. Locking every muscle in his body against the savage need to open his breeches and sink himself to the hilt in her sweetness, he continued to play, sought out the secrets between her thighs even as he plundered her mouth and drank her cries of pleasure.

She couldn't think, only feel as he taught her the secrets of her own body. And want. She wanted him inside her. Now. Empty, aching, she wanted to feel him deep within. Desperately she lifted against him, fire raging through every vein as she fought to get closer. Through his breeches she could feel the hard male flesh riding against her hip as he lay half over her. Instinctively she reached for it, sliding her hand over the front of his breeches, between their bodies. His whole body jerked, tightened and she felt one probing, wicked finger slide within as his thumb found a place that laced her body with jagged lightning.

Shock held her motionless, her hand still on the throbbing front of his breeches, dazed at the intimacy of his touch, at the pleasure rippling out from her very centre. He stroked gently, deeply and she felt his flesh stir under her hand.

'Am I hurting you?' The words were harsh, ragged, spoken against her mouth. As if he could barely force them out. She couldn't even answer. She could only cling tightly and move against him as her response pulsed hotly between them.

He needed no further answer. Jack clenched his jaw, his entire body, against the need to take her. Now. At once. Five minutes ago. She felt so soft and hot, her body tightening sweetly around him. He ravished her mouth instead as talons of desire raked him mercilessly.

Trembling fingers continued to stroke over the front of his breeches. He shuddered at the pleasure and tried not to think about how it would feel without a layer of satin muting her curiosity. Releasing her mouth, he rested his brow on hers and whispered, 'Are you trying to kill me?'

At once she stopped and took her hand away. 'Jack? Am I hurting you?'

'No,' he groaned. 'You're killing me. There's a difference.'

Her innocence burnt at his control. It was time. Gently he withdrew his hand from the lush sweetness between her thighs, savouring her sob of protest. He kissed it tenderly from her lips and sat up.

Her eyes were dazed, so dilated that all he could see of the green was a smouldering rim around the black. Cat's eyes, burning in the night, and like a cat she arched her body towards him in need.

Slowly his fingers went to the front of his breeches, where he held her suddenly focused gaze as he unbuttoned them. Her breath caught somewhere in her throat as she watched the breeches slide off, revealing the tip of that arrow of black hair, which pointed to...

He reached for her.

'Jack...' It had never occurred to her that her lack of height and small frame would be such a problem, but as she gazed, stunned, at his body, she realised that it was. Heat pulsed between her thighs as she remembered his finger teasing and probing, sliding deep...her entire body quivered in sensual need...but it had to be impossible.

His hands slid over her shoulders, drawing her up against him. He knelt in front of her and pulled her into his arms, his lips feathering over her face, gentle hands roving over heated skin so that fire flickered and spread, melting through her veins. His mouth settled ravenously over hers, devouring, seducing. The hot penetration of his tongue brought her pressing urgently against him, feeling the rasp of his hair roughened chest on her swollen, aching nipples.

She felt the buried groan, deep inside him as he shifted against her sensuously. A gasp escaped her as his hands stroked and cupped her bottom, and brought her gently

against his loins. And he rocked. Back and forth, his hard
length pressing into her soft belly. She clung to him, stroking his shoulders, his back, feeling the taut muscles flicker
and tighten under her hands.

'Touch me.' The husky whisper seared through her.

Her hands stilled. 'There?' Heat flooded her at the
thought of touching him so intimately.

'Yes. There.' He caught her hand and brought it between
their bodies, curving her fingers around him. So hot, so
silky smooth. And hard. The heat at her core redoubled in
a melting surge.

Then his hand slid away, between her trembling thighs,
searching and finding. A sob of anticipation escaped her,
but his fingers, traced, circled, teased. No more. And she
needed him. Needed to feel him inside her. Urgently she
shifted, trying to move his fingers to the right spot.

'Are you still scared?'

Had she been scared? She looked up into the burning
grey eyes and whispered, 'No.'

He took her mouth and brought her to him, pulling her
across his thighs so that she straddled him, his hands resting possessively on her hips.

'Jack?'

'It's all right,' he murmured, taking tiny biting kisses
on her lips, as one hand slid between her thighs. 'Like
this.' And he pressed her down, opening her hot, swollen
flesh with gentle fingers as he did so. Her eyes flew open
as she felt him, hard and blunt at her entrance, pushing
inside.

She tensed in shock and felt his body turn to iron as he
stopped. His mouth drifted down her throat, licking, suck-
ing at the wildly beating pulse. His hand between her
thighs moved and a lightning bolt struck through her as he
pressed knowingly. And his mouth found her breast, drew
the burning peak deep into the heat of his mouth. Every
nerve in her body exploded with a fiery need.

Jack felt the change at once. Every muscle locked against the urge to thrust deep into the melting heat that spilled over him, he rocked her body against his. Teasing her, torturing himself. And felt her press down further, enveloping more of him in silken heat. Tight, so tight. He shuddered and took her mouth fiercely, needing to be inside her, caressing her mouth with the intimate penetration of his tongue.

He drank the little cries of pleasure from her lips and rocked gently, encouragingly, his hand on the sleek curve of her hip urging her lower. All at once he felt it, a constriction, barring him from her most intimate depths.

He could barely breathe as he gripped her hips and lifted her. Carefully, with exquisite slowness, he lowered her again, his gaze on her face. This time she felt it, too. He could see it in the ripple of awareness as her eyes opened, hear it in the sharp intake of breath, felt it in her fingers digging into his shoulders.

Cressida had gone beyond frantic. Nothing existed beyond his hands burning on her body and his hard male flesh stretching, tantalising her. She wanted more, much more, but he had stopped, was holding rigidly still, his face harsh with restraint. And it felt as though he could come no further.

'Jack...' Her voice broke on a gasp as he shifted inside her, increasing the pressure.

'Stay still,' he ground out. 'It's all right. Just...stay... still.'

He moved again and fire splintered deeply, melting beneath her heated skin.

'Please...oh...please.' She clung to him, her hands sliding over his shoulders, her mouth capturing his in desperate entreaty, shredding at his control. She felt his grip on her hips flex, then harden as he lifted her. A broken cry of pleasure rippled from her and she tightened instinctively around him.

Fiery need scorched through the simmering remnants of Jack's control. With a groan of ecstasy he caught her lips and plundered as he brought her body down to meet his thrust. His mouth took her shocked cry as she shuddered against him. He set his jaw, fought the urge to tip her back on the pillows and ravish her. Every muscle and nerve turned to steel as he cradled her protectively and soothed her with kisses and tender murmurs, waiting for her body to ease in acceptance.

He slipped his hand between them to fondle her breast. Felt her pleasure—hot, liquid silk spilling between them. She shifted slightly and he felt it again, searing his shuddering flesh. He brushed his mouth over hers and closed his eyes on a groan as her whole body softened against him, around him.

He heard his name, whispered against his mouth on a sob of pleasure and held her tightly to him as he withdrew a short way and pressed in again slowly, finding only hot, yielding sweetness that held him in loving intimacy.

'Mine,' he whispered. 'Every hot, soft inch of you. Always. I'll never let you go.' Supporting her every inch of the way, he tipped her back into the pillows and came down over her, bracing himself on his elbows, still fully sheathed within her. She lay beneath him, eyes dilated with passion, her soft lips swollen and quivering. One small hand came up and traced his cheek, his jaw and the corner of his mouth.

The butterfly caress drew an aching groan from deep within him. He turned his head slightly to capture her finger with his lips and draw it into his mouth. Gently he bit down and groaned again as he felt the shudder of her response ripple through her.

Cressida cried out wildly as he moved deeply within her body in the oldest dance of all. Instinctively she caught the rhythm and matched it, lifting to meet his thrusts, knowing that she was both possessor and possessed. Lover and beloved.

The knowledge bloomed within her, even as her body flamed to incandescence beneath him, the tension coiling and spiralling, tighter and higher with every thrust and with the fierce mating of their mouths.

The tension wound tighter in the sweetest anguish, threatening, promising to break, to tear her apart. So close. She sobbed in her need and felt his hand slip under her hips, long fingers caressing and squeezing. Then his hand flexed, tilting her into his thrusts, holding her there helpless in the storm of his possession.

She broke, fire exploding through her with a shuddering cry that he stole from her lips even as he had taken her body and soul. Ecstasy held her stretched on the quivering rack of fire, burning her to her soul.

The shuddering pulses of her release stripped the last of Jack's control. White hot with raw, aching need, he took her again and again, in thrall to her passion, his own consummation breaking over him in an endless wave.

Stunned, he collapsed on top of her, every muscle relaxed and heavy. Joy sang through every vein. His. All his. Every soft, sweet, stubborn inch of her. Forever.

Jack lay steeped in contentment, as dawn stole into the bedchamber. He ought to leave, before one of the maids came in, but he couldn't. Cressida lay, a warm, trusting weight, in his arms. Her cheek rested on his shoulder, one rounded arm reached across his chest and a silken thigh lay trapped between his. If he left he'd disturb her. And she hadn't had a great deal of sleep.

Chivalry, it appeared, was dead. Only need and passion remained. No chivalrous man behaved as he had done, sneaking into his betrothed's bedchamber and then pre-empting the wedding night. Several times. He certainly didn't lie there in the pearly light of dawn pretending the only reason he hadn't left was fear of waking her. Not when he was, in fact, waiting for her to waken of her own accord so that he could have her again. And make quite sure she was convinced that he loved her, of course.

She stirred against him with a sleepy, questioning murmur that heated his blood even further. He rolled and settled her beneath him, taking her mouth even as her eyes fluttered open.

When he finally broke the kiss she smiled up at him and wriggled helpfully.

'Did I tell you I love you?' he whispered, brushing his mouth over hers again.

'Yes.' She twined her arms around his neck and drew him down to her.

He held back, resisting her sweet temptations. 'Did I convince you?' His loins shifted against her.

'Oh, *yes*.' She arched under him.

He lowered his mouth to hers. 'Good. Because I'm going to convince you again.'

Ten days later Cressida stood beside Jack facing her father before the altar. The bright crisp morning was dimmed to a gentle glow in the old church at Ratby. Very few people had been asked to come from town, but, none the less, the pews were full enough for Cressida. All the people she cared for were there. And the one she cared for most stood right beside her.

The words of the marriage service flowed over and through them in loving benediction. The only difficulty about the swiftness of the wedding had been Dr Bramley's uncertainty as to whether he should perform the ceremony or give his daughter away.

'Who giveth this woman to be married to this man?'

'I do.' The Earl of Rutherford's deep voice was a blessing in itself.

Her eyes full of tears, Cressida smiled up at Jack, as

Marcus placed her hand in his. Jack had solved even this problem. He had told her father that since his home would hence forth be the dower house at Wyckeham, he was not really giving his daughter away. And that there was no one he'd liefer be married by.

He smiled back at her as he repeated his vows steadily. The formal measured words only confirmed what his eyes told her. *Mine. Always.*

*   *   *   *   *

Four sisters.
A family legacy.
And someone is out to destroy it.

A captivating new limited continuity, launching June 2006

The most beautiful hotel in New Orleans,
and someone is out to destroy it. But mystery,
danger and some surprising family revelations
and discoveries won't stop the Marchand sisters
from protecting their birthright…
and finding love along the way.

HOTEL MARCHAND

This riveting new saga begins with

In the Dark

by national bestselling author

JUDITH ARNOLD

The party at Hotel Marchand is in full swing when the lights suddenly go out. What does head of security Mac Jensen do first? He's torn between two jobs—protecting the guests at the hotel and keeping the woman he loves safe.

A woman to protect. A hotel to secure. And no idea who's determined to harm them.

On Sale June 2006

**Hidden in the secrets of antiquity,
lies the unimagined truth...**

Introducing

a brand-new line filled with mystery
and suspense, action and adventure,
and a fascinating look into history.

And it all begins with DESTINY.

In a sealed crypt in
France, where the
terrifying legend of
the beast of Gevaudan
begins to unravel,
Annja Creed discovers
a stunning artifact
that will seal her destiny.

*Available every other
month starting
July 2006, wherever
you buy books.*

GRA1

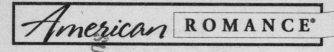

HARLEQUIN®

American | ROMANCE®

IS PROUD TO PRESENT A GUEST APPEARANCE BY

QUILL
BOOK
AWARD
WINNING
AUTHOR

NEW YORK TIMES bestselling author

DEBBIE MACOMBER
The Wyoming Kid

The story of an ex–rodeo cowboy, a schoolteacher
and their journey to the altar.

"Best-selling Macomber, with more than
100 romances and women's fiction titles
to her credit, sure has a way of pleasing readers."
—*Booklist* on *Between Friends*

The Wyoming Kid
is available from
Harlequin American Romance
in July 2006.